ERRANT STORY

VOLUME ONE

STORY & ART BY
MICHAEL POE

ERRANT STORY VOL. 1

Published by Keenspot Entertainment
P.O. Box 110, Cresbard, SD 57435
Phone: (605) 324-3332 FAX: (605) 324-3333
E-Mail: keenspot@keenspot.com
Web: www.keenspot.com

Co-CEO/Editor Chris Crosby
Co-CEO Darren "Gav" Bleuel
CFO Teri Crosby
CTO Nate Stone

ORDER KEENSPOT PRODUCTS BY PHONE
DIAL TOLL-FREE **1-888-KEENSPOT**

ISBN 1-932775-07-2 (Softcover Edition)
ISBN 1-932775-32-3 (Hardcover Limited Edition)

First Printing, June 2004
10 9 8 7 6 5 4 3 2 1
Printed in Canada

Dedicated to Nathan, Ashley, Bruce, Shaun, Mike, Jen, Sam, Josh, Nate, Chris, Travis, Mack (or what ever name he happens to be going by at the moment) and everyone else who has ever suffered my presence for any decent length of time without eventually trying to kill me...

...or at least not trying very hard to...

Oh yes... and special thanks go out to Ben Riley (www.themidlands.net) for coloring every single damn Errant Story page since I started this bloody thing.

I met a traveler from an antique land
Who said: Two vast and trunkless legs of stone
Stand in the desert. Near them, on the sand,
Hald sunk, a shattered visage lies, whose frown,
And wrinkled lip, and sneer of cold command,
Tell that its sculptor well those passions read
Which yet survive, stamped on these lifeless things,
The hand that mocked them, and the heart that fed:
And on the pedestal these words appear:
"My name is Ozymandias, king of kings:
Look on my works, ye Mighty, and despair!"
Nothing beside remains. Round the decay
Of that colossal wreck, boundless and bare
The lone and level sands stretch far away.

-Percy Bysshe Shelley
'Ozymandias'

Before this universe there was another one...
a happy universe filled with bunnies. But that
one got destroyed in a great cataclysm brought
about by a major plot point. Pay attention,
there will be a test later.

-Some Random Idiot In A Chat Room

ERRANT STORY

'I used to believe...'

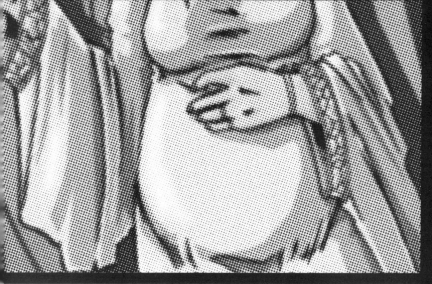

PROLOGUE

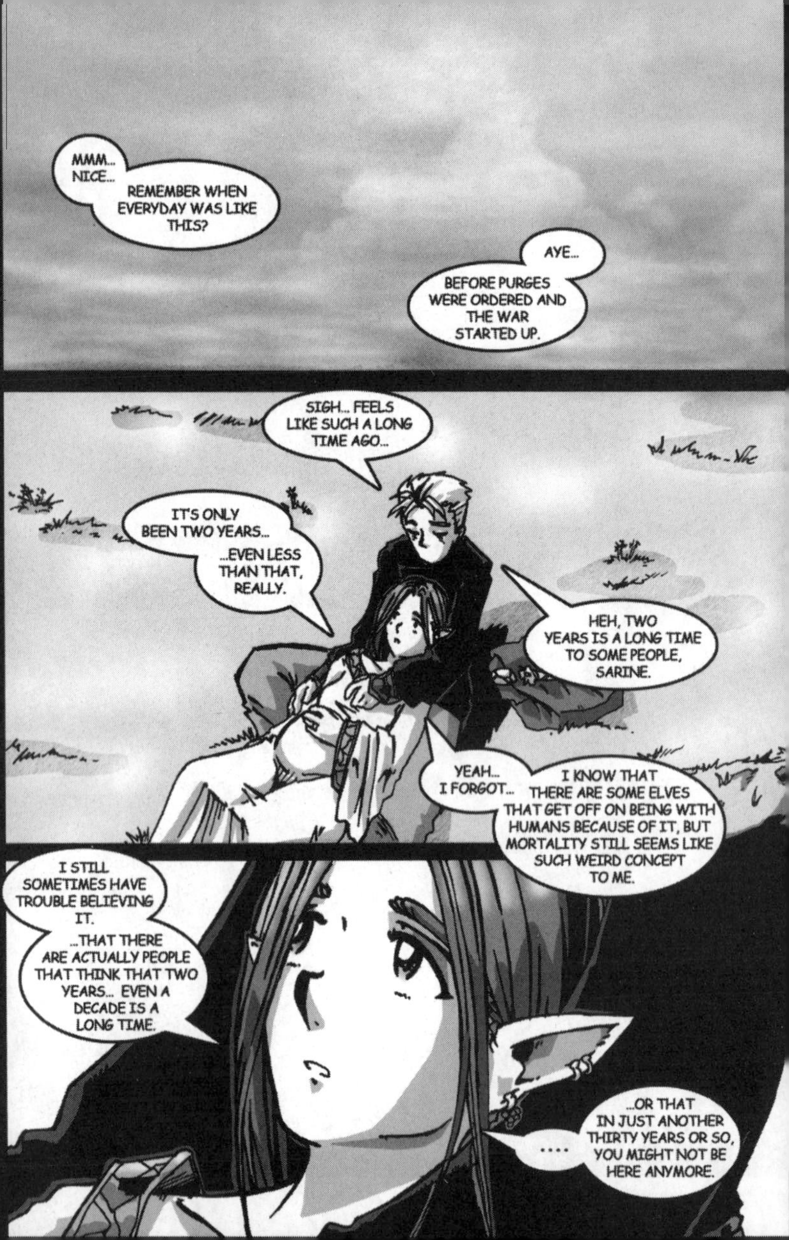
MMM... NICE...
REMEMBER WHEN EVERYDAY WAS LIKE THIS?
AYE...
BEFORE PURGES WERE ORDERED AND THE WAR STARTED UP.
SIGH... FEELS LIKE SUCH A LONG TIME AGO...
IT'S ONLY BEEN TWO YEARS...
...EVEN LESS THAN THAT, REALLY.
HEH, TWO YEARS IS A LONG TIME TO SOME PEOPLE, SARINE.
YEAH... I FORGOT...
I KNOW THAT THERE ARE SOME ELVES THAT GET OFF ON BEING WITH HUMANS BECAUSE OF IT, BUT MORTALITY STILL SEEMS LIKE SUCH WEIRD CONCEPT TO ME.
I STILL SOMETIMES HAVE TROUBLE BELIEVING IT.
...THAT THERE ARE ACTUALLY PEOPLE THAT THINK THAT TWO YEARS... EVEN A DECADE IS A LONG TIME.
....
...OR THAT IN JUST ANOTHER THIRTY YEARS OR SO, YOU MIGHT NOT BE HERE ANYMORE.

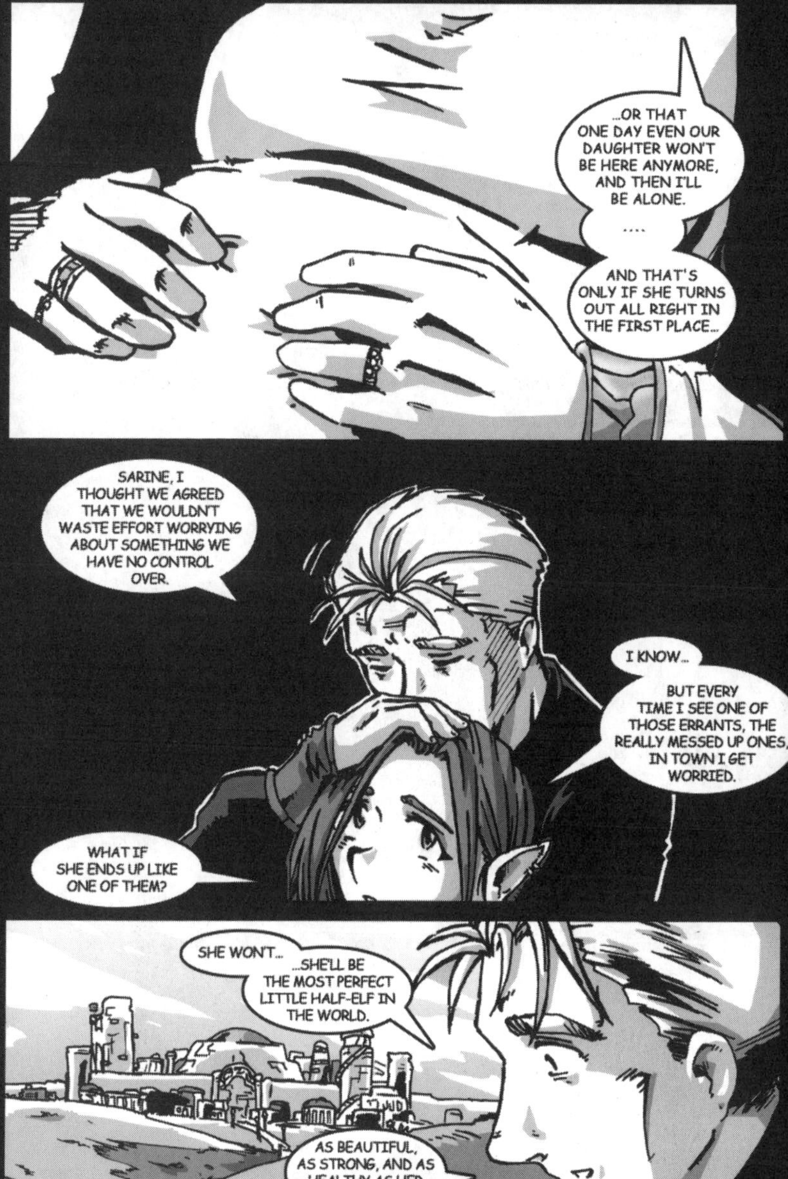
...OR THAT ONE DAY EVEN OUR DAUGHTER WON'T BE HERE ANYMORE, AND THEN I'LL BE ALONE.
....
AND THAT'S ONLY IF SHE TURNS OUT ALL RIGHT IN THE FIRST PLACE...
SARINE, I THOUGHT WE AGREED THAT WE WOULDN'T WASTE EFFORT WORRYING ABOUT SOMETHING WE HAVE NO CONTROL OVER.
I KNOW...
BUT EVERY TIME I SEE ONE OF THOSE ERRANTS, THE REALLY MESSED UP ONES, IN TOWN I GET WORRIED.
WHAT IF SHE ENDS UP LIKE ONE OF THEM?
SHE WON'T...
...SHE'LL BE THE MOST PERFECT LITTLE HALF-ELF IN THE WORLD.
AS BEAUTIFUL, AS STRONG, AND AS HEALTHY AS HER MOTHER...

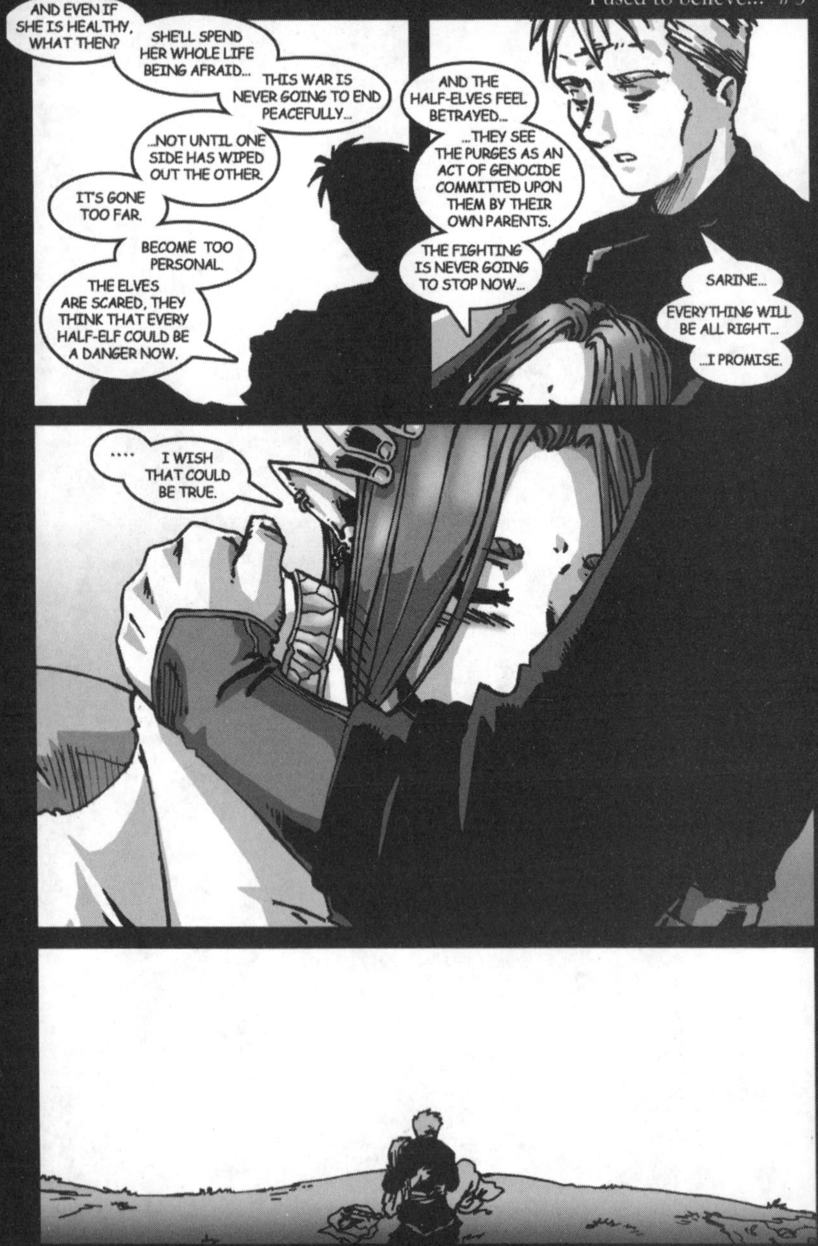
AND EVEN IF SHE IS HEALTHY, WHAT THEN?
SHE'LL SPEND HER WHOLE LIFE BEING AFRAID...
THIS WAR IS NEVER GOING TO END PEACEFULLY...
...NOT UNTIL ONE SIDE HAS WIPED OUT THE OTHER.
IT'S GONE TOO FAR.
BECOME TOO PERSONAL.
THE ELVES ARE SCARED, THEY THINK THAT EVERY HALF-ELF COULD BE A DANGER NOW.
AND THE HALF-ELVES FEEL BETRAYED...
...THEY SEE THE PURGES AS AN ACT OF GENOCIDE COMMITTED UPON THEM BY THEIR OWN PARENTS.
THE FIGHTING IS NEVER GOING TO STOP NOW...
SARINE...
EVERYTHING WILL BE ALL RIGHT...
...I PROMISE.
.... I WISH THAT COULD BE TRUE.

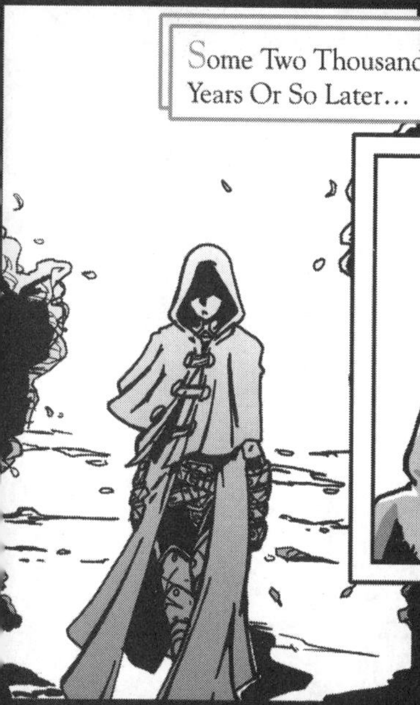
Some Two Thousand Years Or So Later…

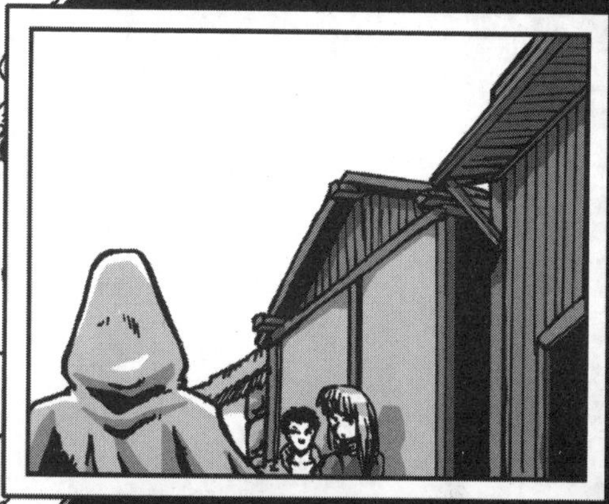

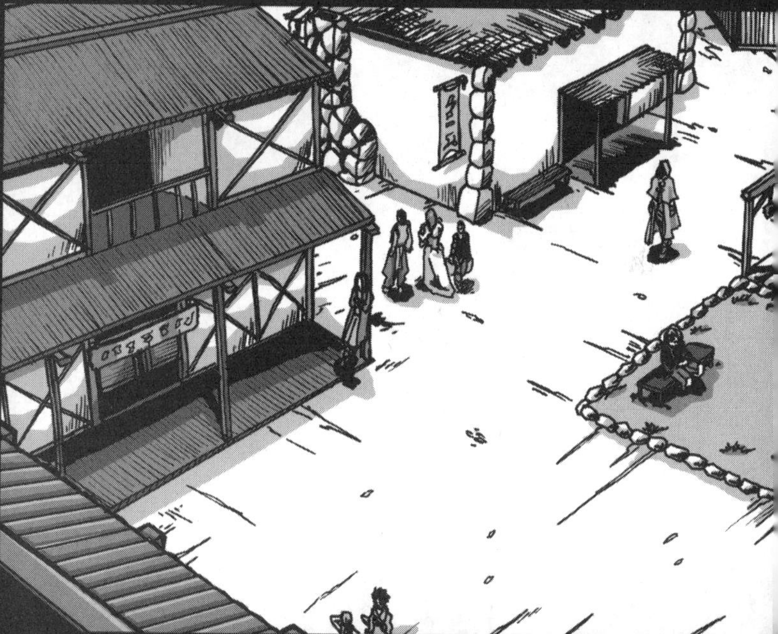

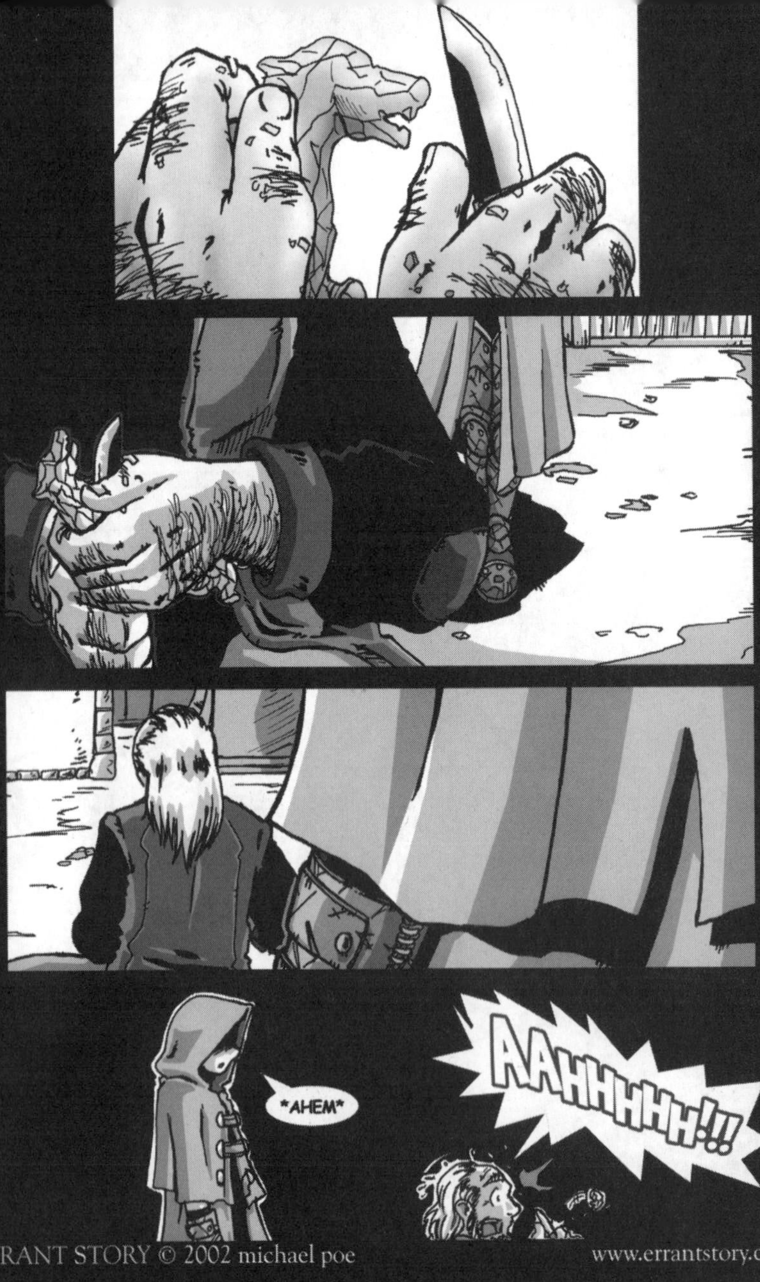
AHEM
AAHHHHH!!!

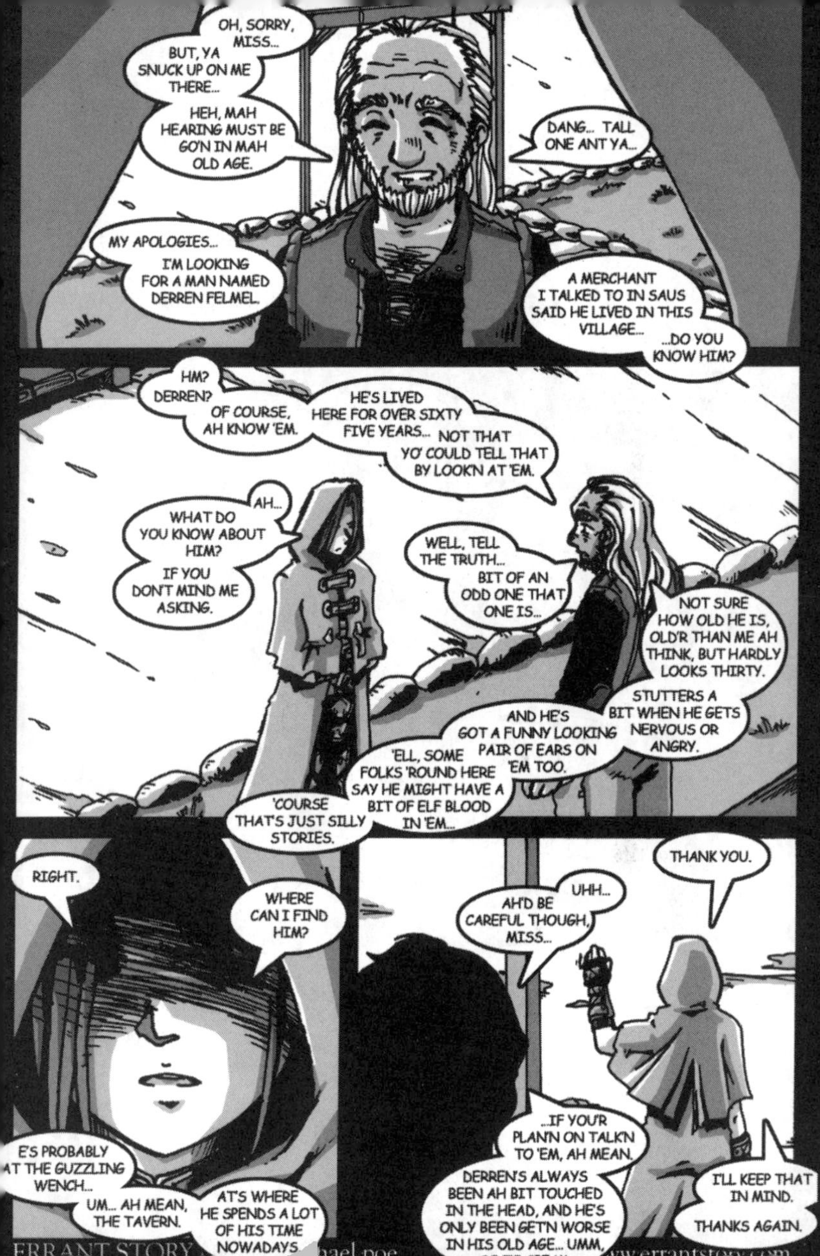
OH, SORRY, MISS...
BUT, YA SNUCK UP ON ME THERE...
HEH, MAH HEARING MUST BE GO'N IN MAH OLD AGE.
DANG... TALL ONE ANT YA...
MY APOLOGIES...
I'M LOOKING FOR A MAN NAMED DERREN FELMEL.
A MERCHANT I TALKED TO IN SAUS SAID HE LIVED IN THIS VILLAGE...
...DO YOU KNOW HIM?
HM? DERREN?
OF COURSE, AH KNOW 'EM.
HE'S LIVED HERE FOR OVER SIXTY FIVE YEARS...
NOT THAT YO' COULD TELL THAT BY LOOK'N AT 'EM.
AH...
WHAT DO YOU KNOW ABOUT HIM?
IF YOU DON'T MIND ME ASKING.
WELL, TELL THE TRUTH...
BIT OF AN ODD ONE THAT ONE IS...
NOT SURE HOW OLD HE IS, OLD'R THAN ME AH THINK, BUT HARDLY LOOKS THIRTY.
STUTTERS A BIT WHEN HE GETS NERVOUS OR ANGRY.
AND HE'S GOT A FUNNY LOOKING PAIR OF EARS ON 'EM TOO.
'ELL, SOME FOLKS 'ROUND HERE SAY HE MIGHT HAVE A BIT OF ELF BLOOD IN 'EM...
'COURSE THAT'S JUST SILLY STORIES.
RIGHT.
WHERE CAN I FIND HIM?
E'S PROBABLY AT THE GUZZLING WENCH...
UM... AH MEAN, THE TAVERN.
AT'S WHERE HE SPENDS A LOT OF HIS TIME NOWADAYS.
THANK YOU.
UHH...
AH'D BE CAREFUL THOUGH, MISS...
...IF YOU'R PLAN'N ON TALK'N TO 'EM, AH MEAN.
DERREN'S ALWAYS BEEN AH BIT TOUCHED IN THE HEAD, AND HE'S ONLY BEEN GET'N WORSE IN HIS OLD AGE... UMM,
I'LL KEEP THAT IN MIND.
THANKS AGAIN.

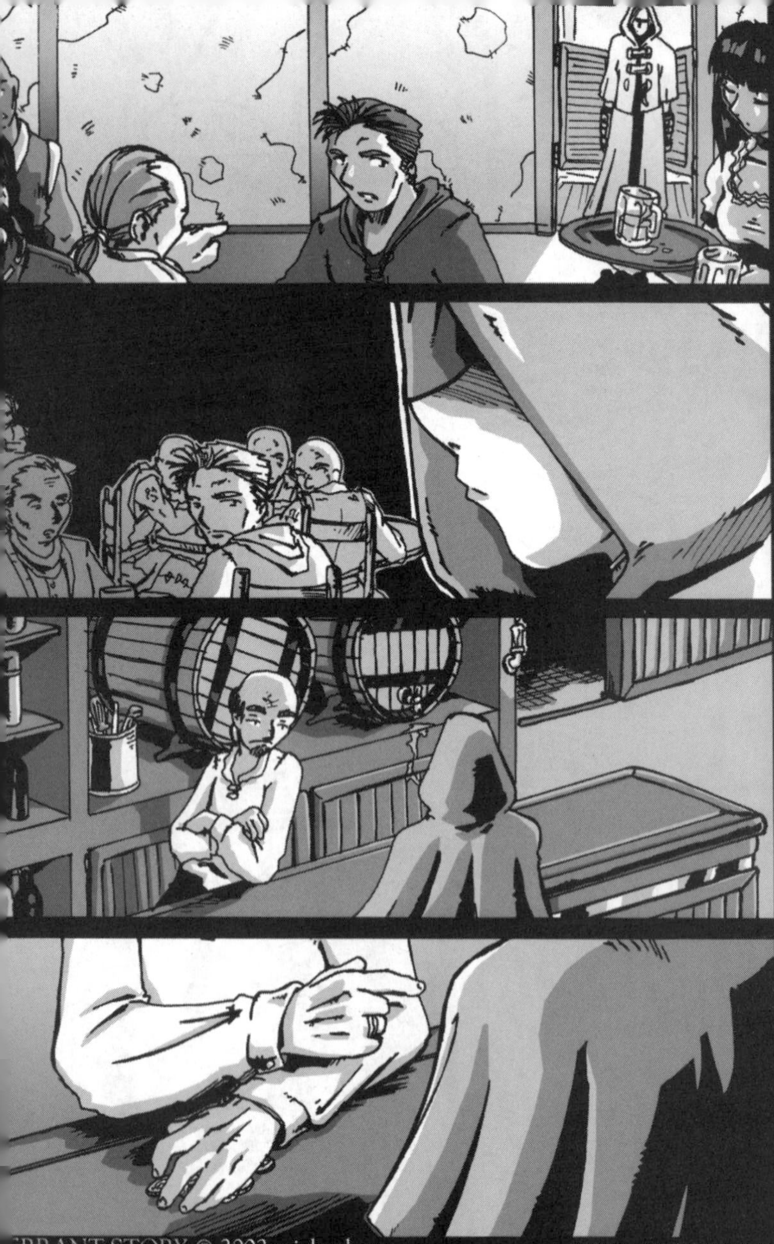

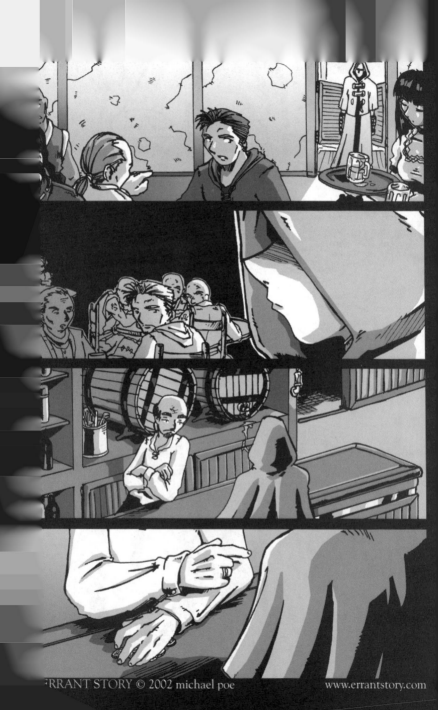

I used to believe... #8

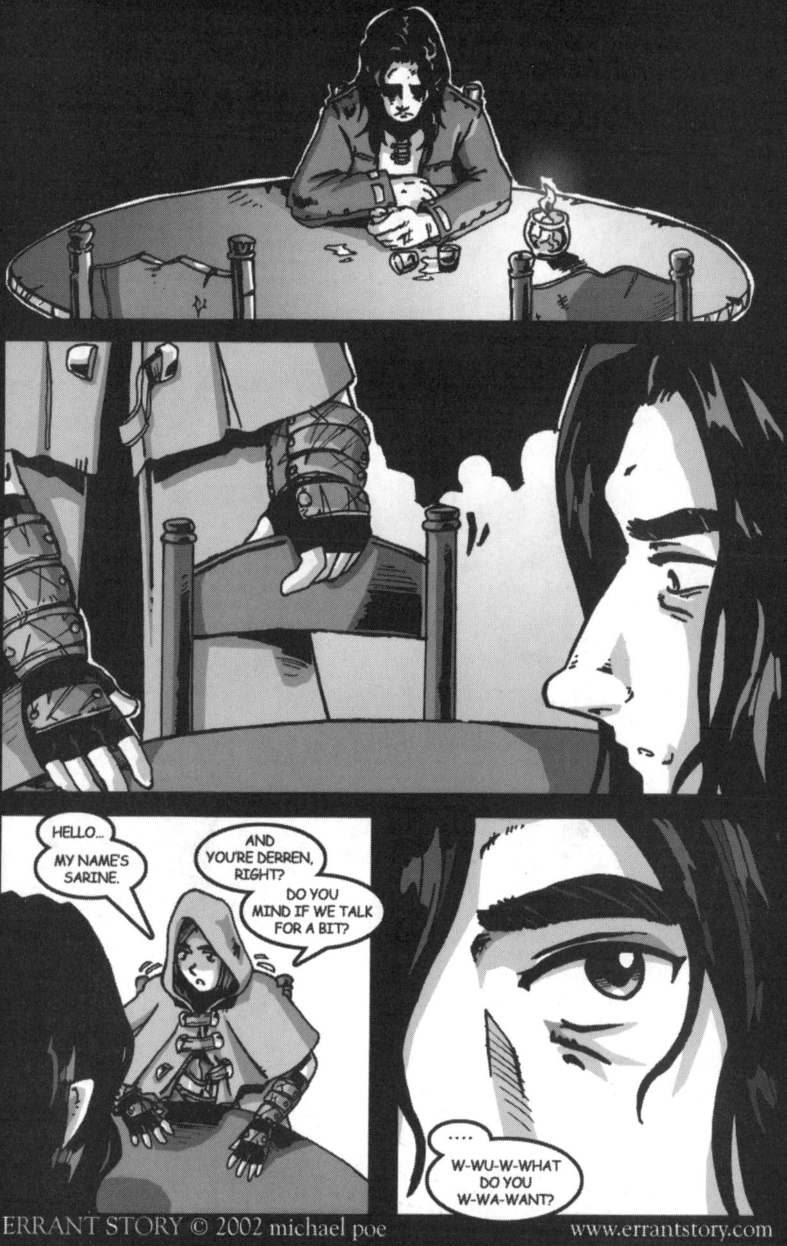
HELLO...
MY NAME'S SARINE.
AND YOU'RE DERREN, RIGHT?
DO YOU MIND IF WE TALK FOR A BIT?
....
W-WU-W-WHAT DO YOU W-WA-WANT?

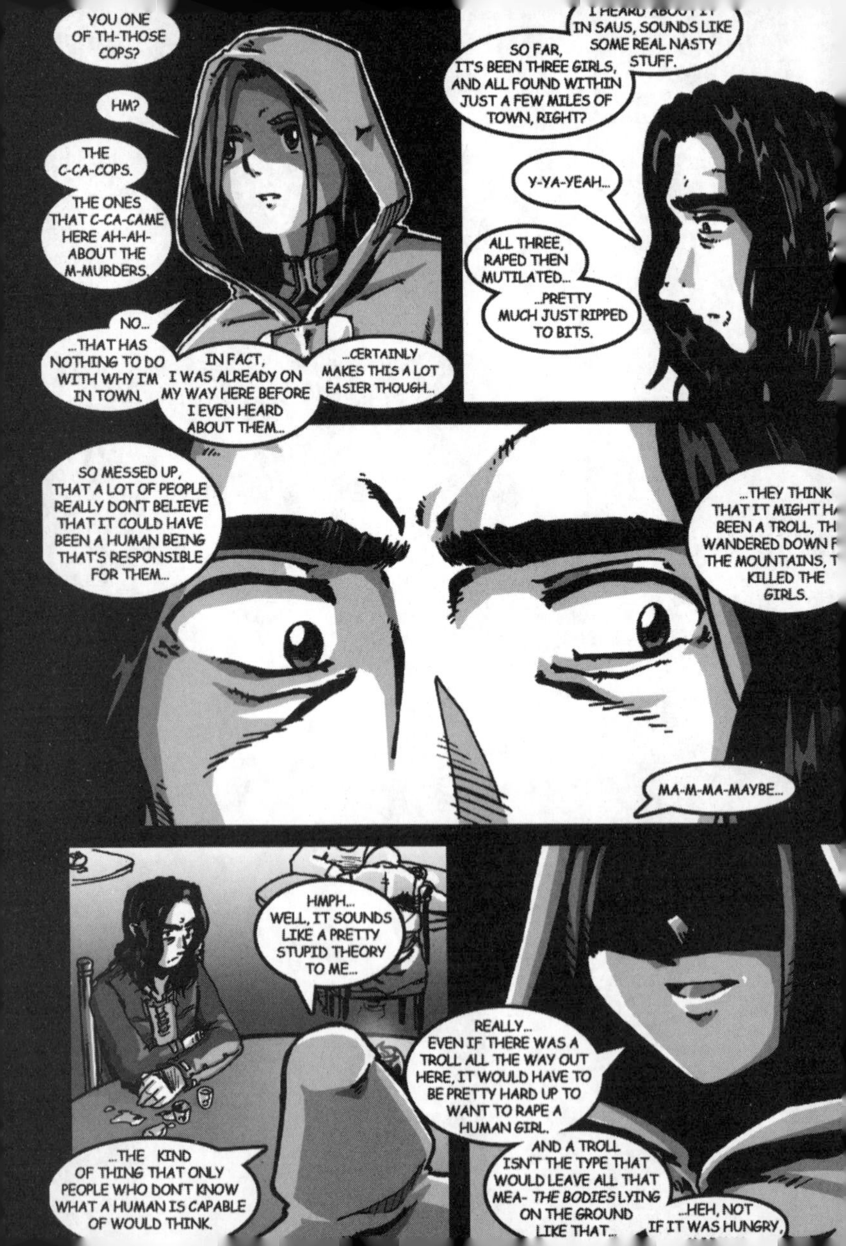
YOU ONE OF TH-THOSE COPS?
HM?
THE C-CA-COPS.
THE ONES THAT C-CA-CAME HERE AH-AH-ABOUT THE M-MURDERS.
NO... ...THAT HAS NOTHING TO DO WITH WHY I'M IN TOWN.
IN FACT, I WAS ALREADY ON MY WAY HERE BEFORE I EVEN HEARD ABOUT THEM...
...CERTAINLY MAKES THIS A LOT EASIER THOUGH...
IN SAUS, SOUNDS LIKE SOME REAL NASTY STUFF.
SO FAR, IT'S BEEN THREE GIRLS, AND ALL FOUND WITHIN JUST A FEW MILES OF TOWN, RIGHT?
Y-YA-YEAH...
ALL THREE, RAPED THEN MUTILATED...
...PRETTY MUCH JUST RIPPED TO BITS.
SO MESSED UP, THAT A LOT OF PEOPLE REALLY DON'T BELIEVE THAT IT COULD HAVE BEEN A HUMAN BEING THAT'S RESPONSIBLE FOR THEM...
...THEY THINK THAT IT MIGHT
BEEN A TROLL, TH
WANDERED DOWN
THE MOUNTAINS,
KILLED THE GIRLS.
MA-M-MA-MAYBE...
HMPH... WELL, IT SOUNDS LIKE A PRETTY STUPID THEORY TO ME...
...THE KIND OF THING THAT ONLY PEOPLE WHO DON'T KNOW WHAT A HUMAN IS CAPABLE OF WOULD THINK.
REALLY... EVEN IF THERE WAS A TROLL ALL THE WAY OUT HERE, IT WOULD HAVE TO BE PRETTY HARD UP TO WANT TO RAPE A HUMAN GIRL.
AND A TROLL ISN'T THE TYPE THAT WOULD LEAVE ALL THAT MEA- *THE BODIES* LYING ON THE GROUND LIKE THAT...
...HEH, NOT IF IT WAS HUNGRY,

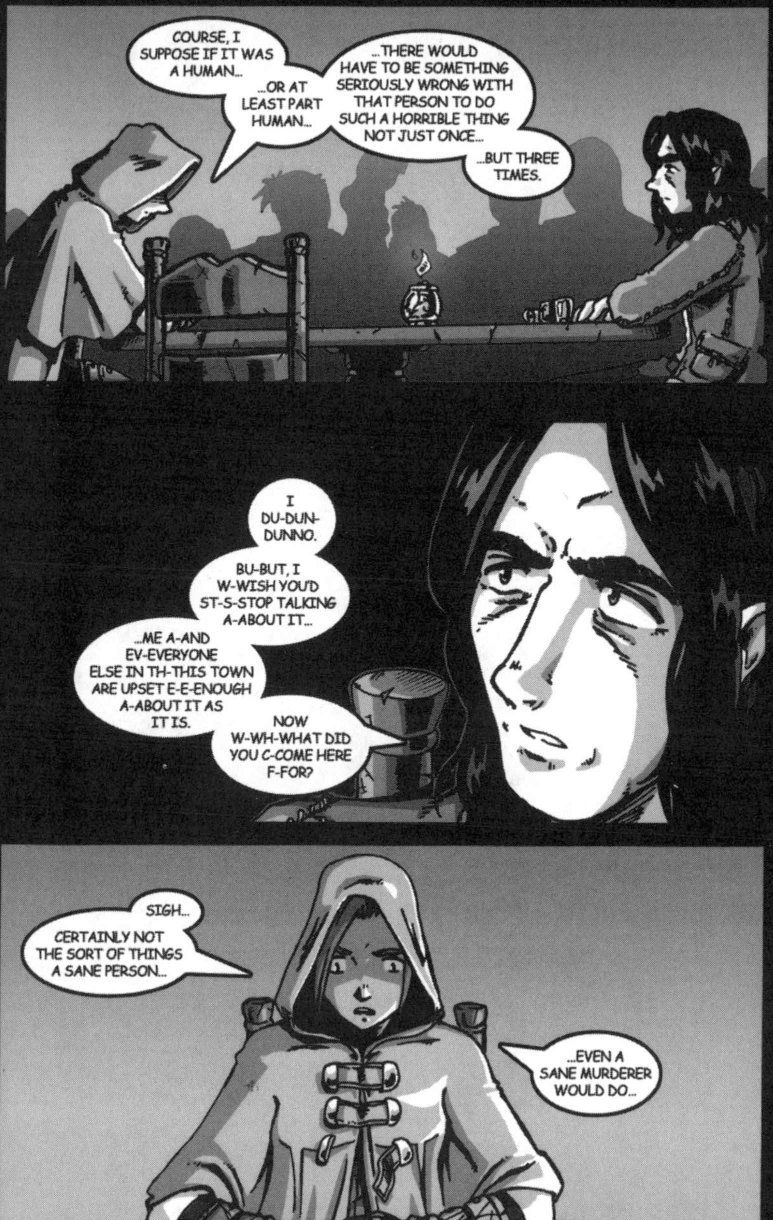
COURSE, I SUPPOSE IF IT WAS A HUMAN...
...OR AT LEAST PART HUMAN...
...THERE WOULD HAVE TO BE SOMETHING SERIOUSLY WRONG WITH THAT PERSON TO DO SUCH A HORRIBLE THING NOT JUST ONCE...
...BUT THREE TIMES.
I DU-DUN-DUNNO.
BU-BUT, I W-WISH YOU'D ST-S-STOP TALKING A-ABOUT IT...
...ME A-AND EV-EVERYONE ELSE IN TH-THIS TOWN ARE UPSET E-E-ENOUGH A-ABOUT IT AS IT IS.
NOW W-WH-WHAT DID YOU C-COME HERE F-FOR?
SIGH...
CERTAINLY NOT THE SORT OF THINGS A SANE PERSON...
...EVEN A SANE MURDERER WOULD DO...

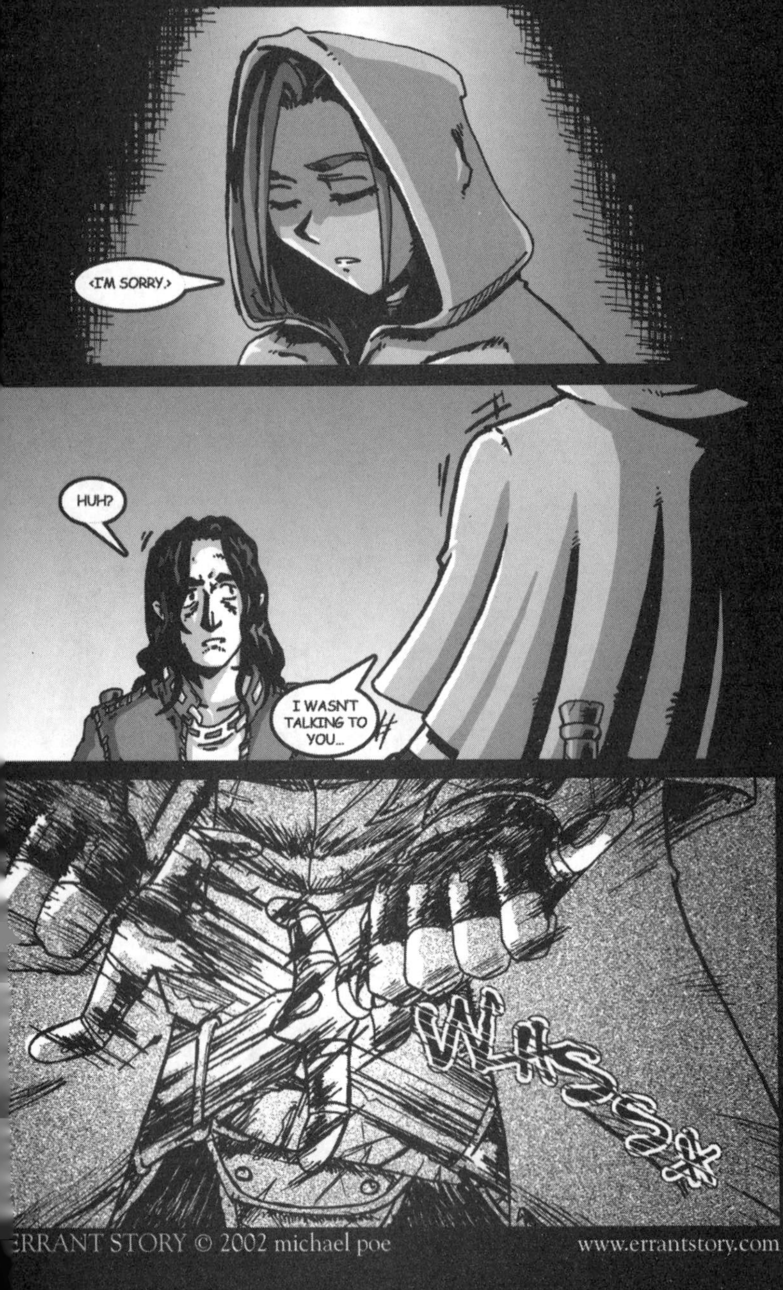
<I'M SORRY.>
HUH?
I WASN'T TALKING TO YOU...

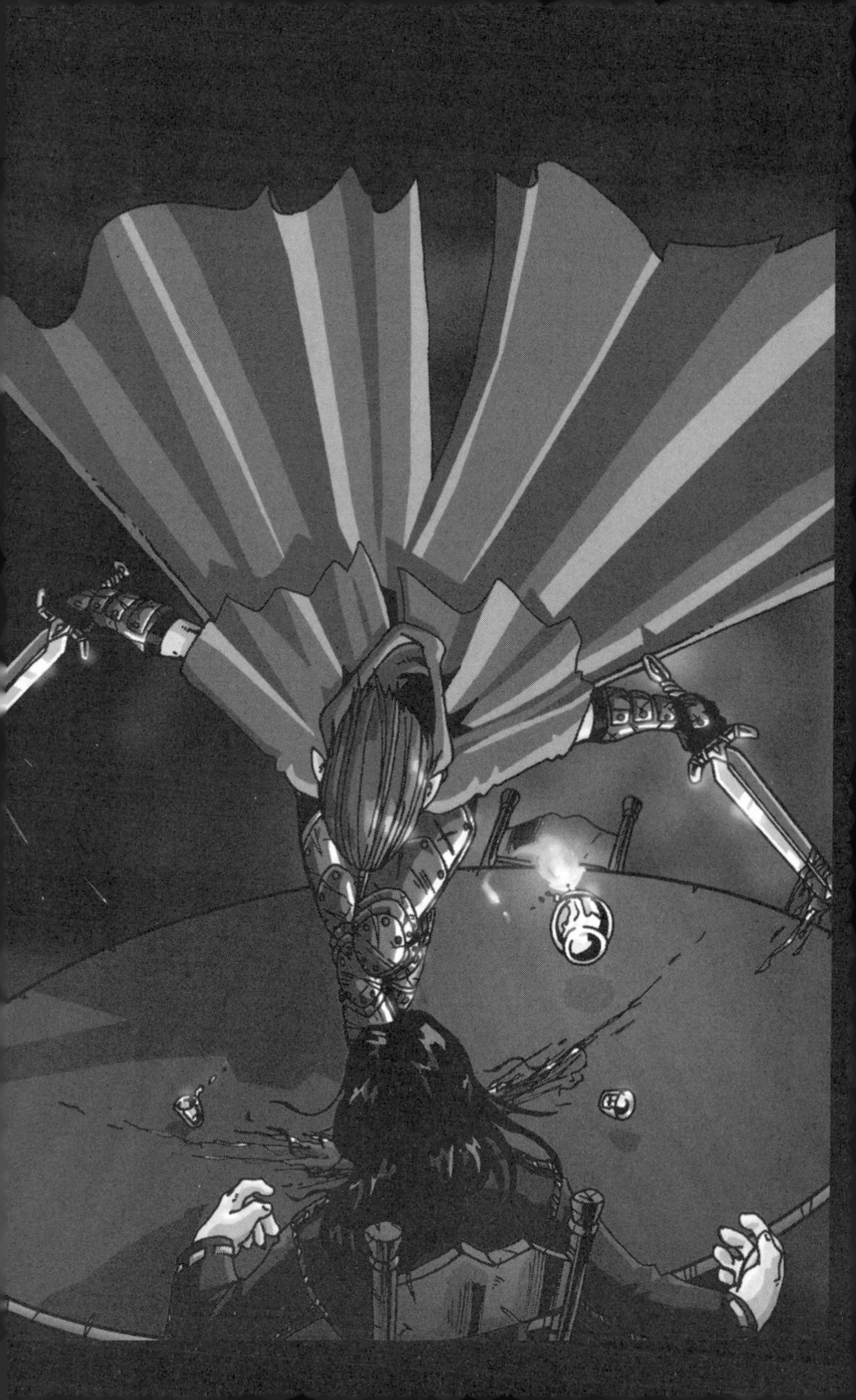

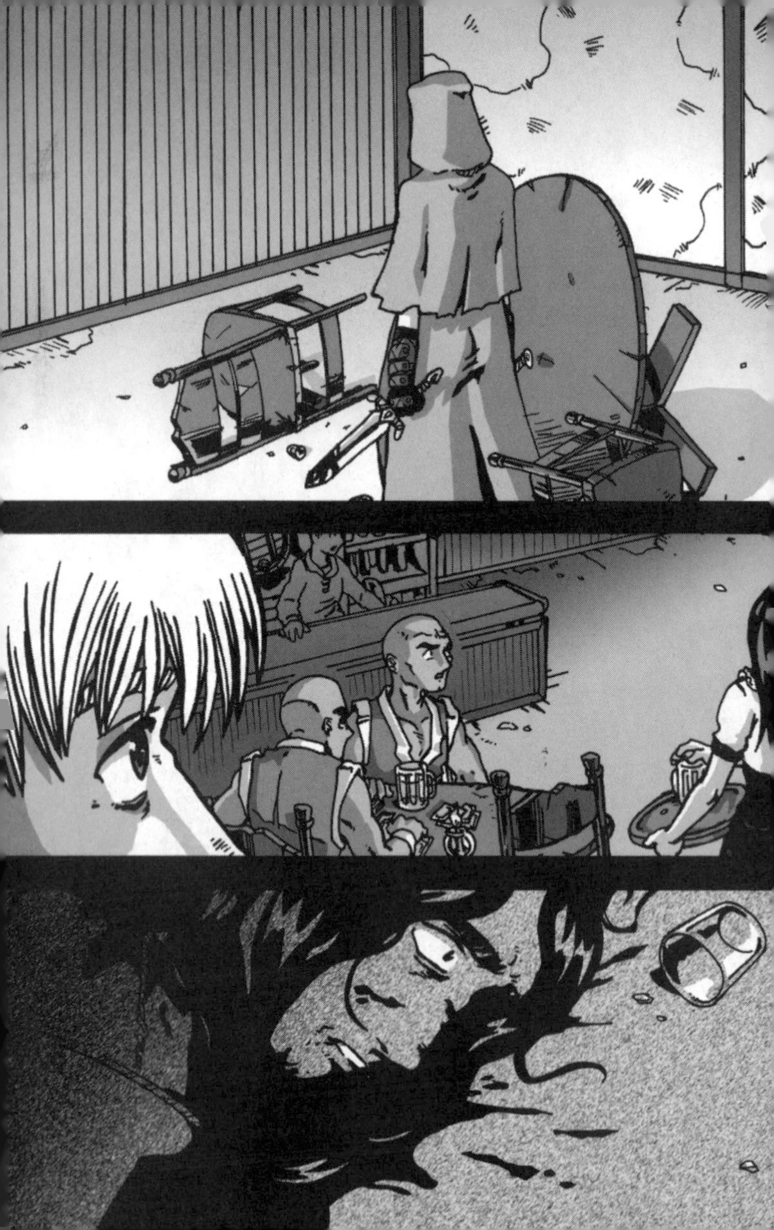

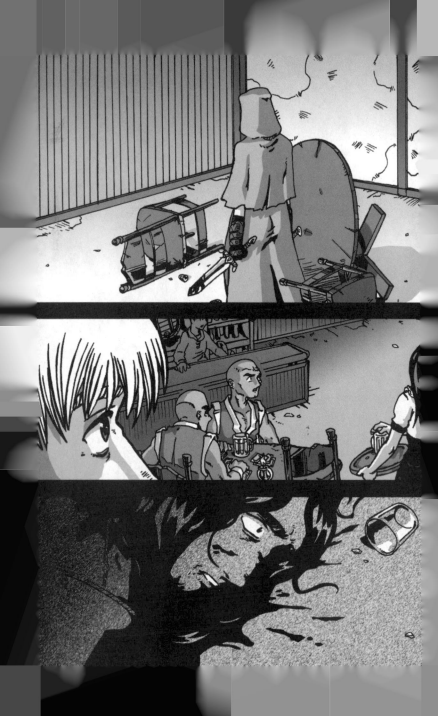

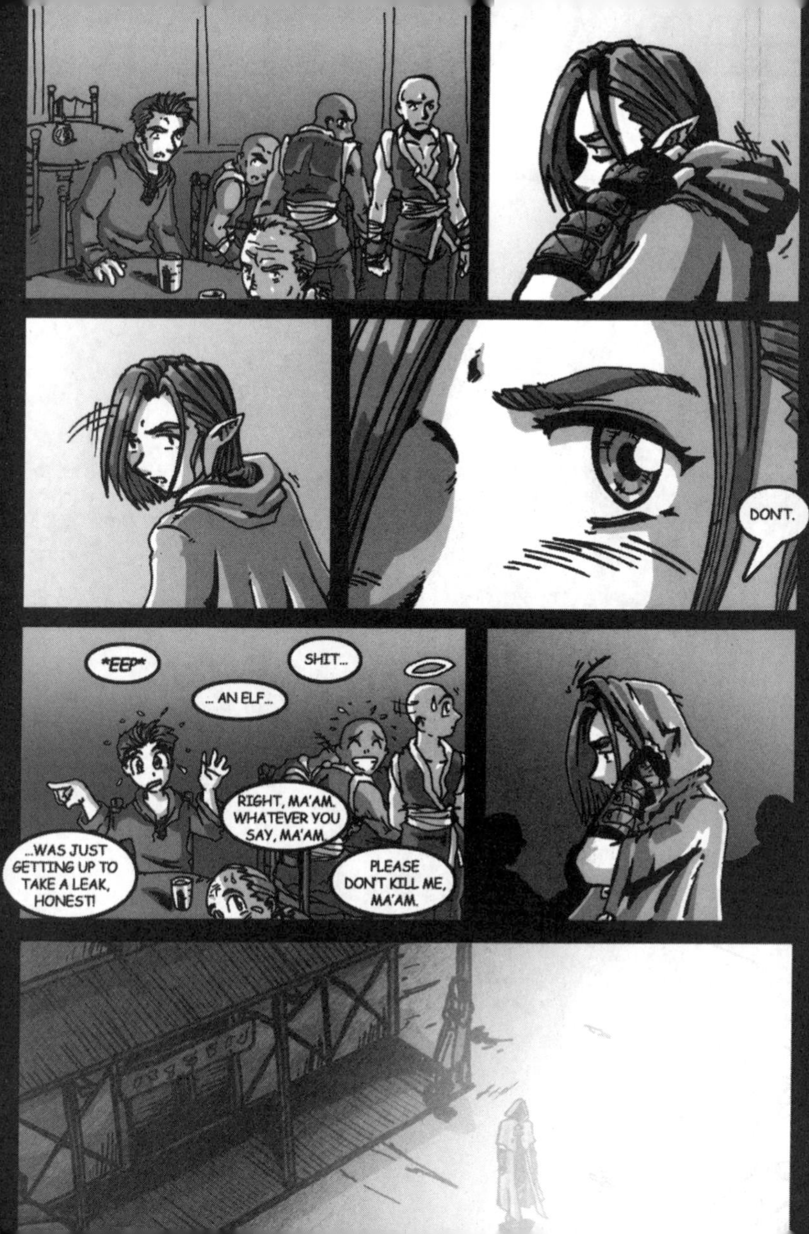
DON'T.
EEP
... AN ELF...
SHIT...
...WAS JUST GETTING UP TO TAKE A LEAK, HONEST!
RIGHT, MA'AM. WHATEVER YOU SAY, MA'AM.
PLEASE DON'T KILL ME, MA'AM.

ERRANT STORY CHAPTER ONE

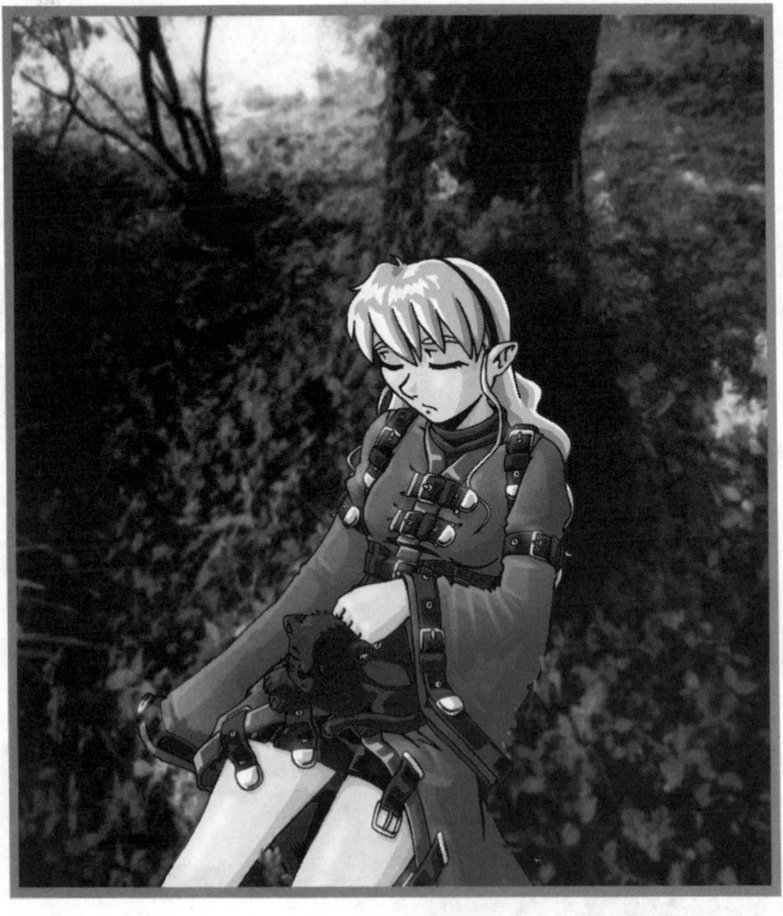

"Psychotic Mage Chick"

www.errantstory.com

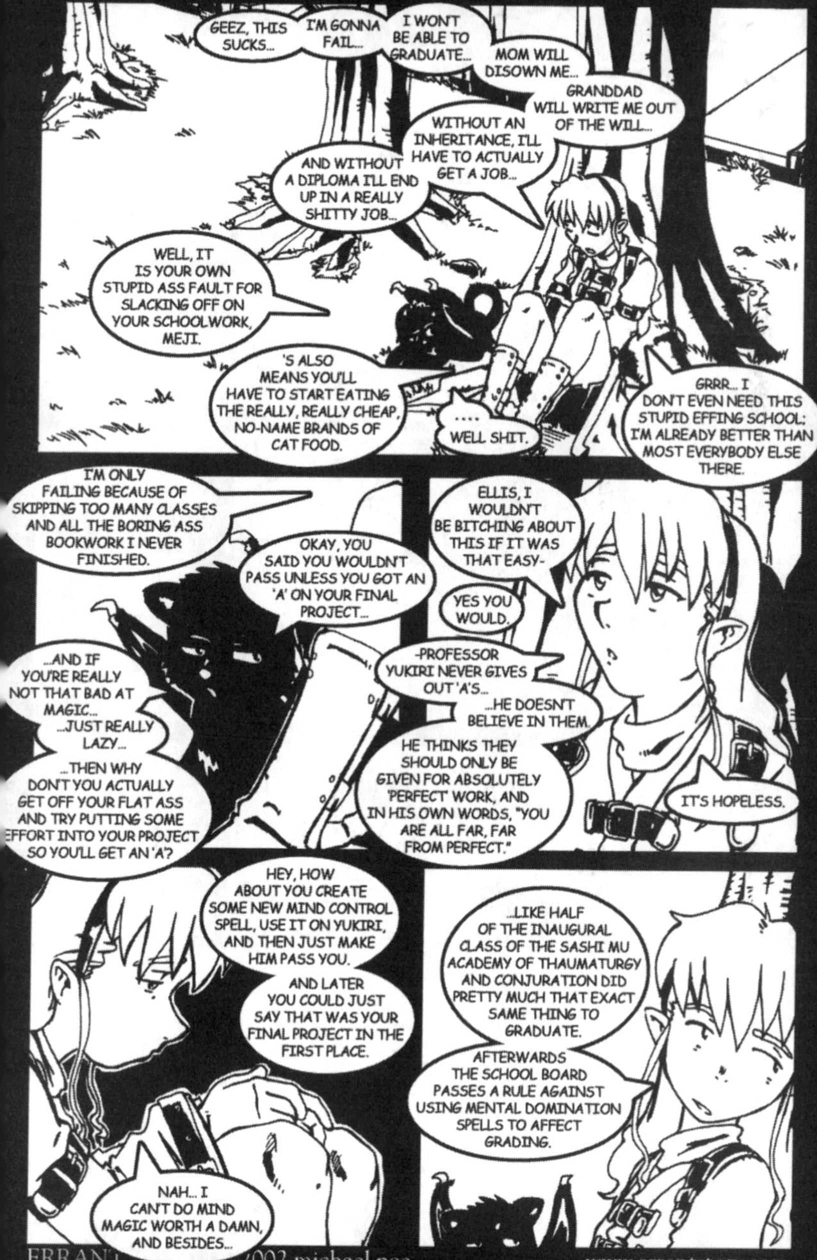
GEEZ, THIS SUCKS...
I'M GONNA FAIL...
I WON'T BE ABLE TO GRADUATE...
MOM WILL DISOWN ME...
GRANDDAD WILL WRITE ME OUT OF THE WILL...
WITHOUT AN INHERITANCE, I'LL HAVE TO ACTUALLY GET A JOB...
AND WITHOUT A DIPLOMA I'LL END UP IN A REALLY SHITTY JOB...
WELL, IT IS YOUR OWN STUPID ASS FAULT FOR SLACKING OFF ON YOUR SCHOOLWORK, MEJI.
'S ALSO MEANS YOU'LL HAVE TO START EATING THE REALLY, REALLY CHEAP, NO-NAME BRANDS OF CAT FOOD.
.... WELL SHIT.
GRRR... I DON'T EVEN NEED THIS STUPID EFFING SCHOOL; I'M ALREADY BETTER THAN MOST EVERYBODY ELSE THERE.
I'M ONLY FAILING BECAUSE OF SKIPPING TOO MANY CLASSES AND ALL THE BORING ASS BOOKWORK I NEVER FINISHED.
OKAY, YOU SAID YOU WOULDN'T PASS UNLESS YOU GOT AN 'A' ON YOUR FINAL PROJECT...
...AND IF YOU'RE REALLY NOT THAT BAD AT MAGIC...
...JUST REALLY LAZY...
...THEN WHY DON'T YOU ACTUALLY GET OFF YOUR FLAT ASS AND TRY PUTTING SOME EFFORT INTO YOUR PROJECT SO YOU'LL GET AN 'A'?
ELLIS, I WOULDN'T BE BITCHING ABOUT THIS IF IT WAS THAT EASY-
YES YOU WOULD.
-PROFESSOR YUKIRI NEVER GIVES OUT 'A'S...
...HE DOESN'T BELIEVE IN THEM.
HE THINKS THEY SHOULD ONLY BE GIVEN FOR ABSOLUTELY 'PERFECT' WORK, AND IN HIS OWN WORDS, "YOU ARE ALL FAR, FAR FROM PERFECT."
IT'S HOPELESS.
HEY, HOW ABOUT YOU CREATE SOME NEW MIND CONTROL SPELL, USE IT ON YUKIRI, AND THEN JUST MAKE HIM PASS YOU.
AND LATER YOU COULD JUST SAY THAT WAS YOUR FINAL PROJECT IN THE FIRST PLACE.
NAH... I CAN'T DO MIND MAGIC WORTH A DAMN, AND BESIDES...
...LIKE HALF OF THE INAUGURAL CLASS OF THE SASHI MU ACADEMY OF THAUMATURGY AND CONJURATION DID PRETTY MUCH THAT EXACT SAME THING TO GRADUATE.
AFTERWARDS THE SCHOOL BOARD PASSES A RULE AGAINST USING MENTAL DOMINATION SPELLS TO AFFECT GRADING.

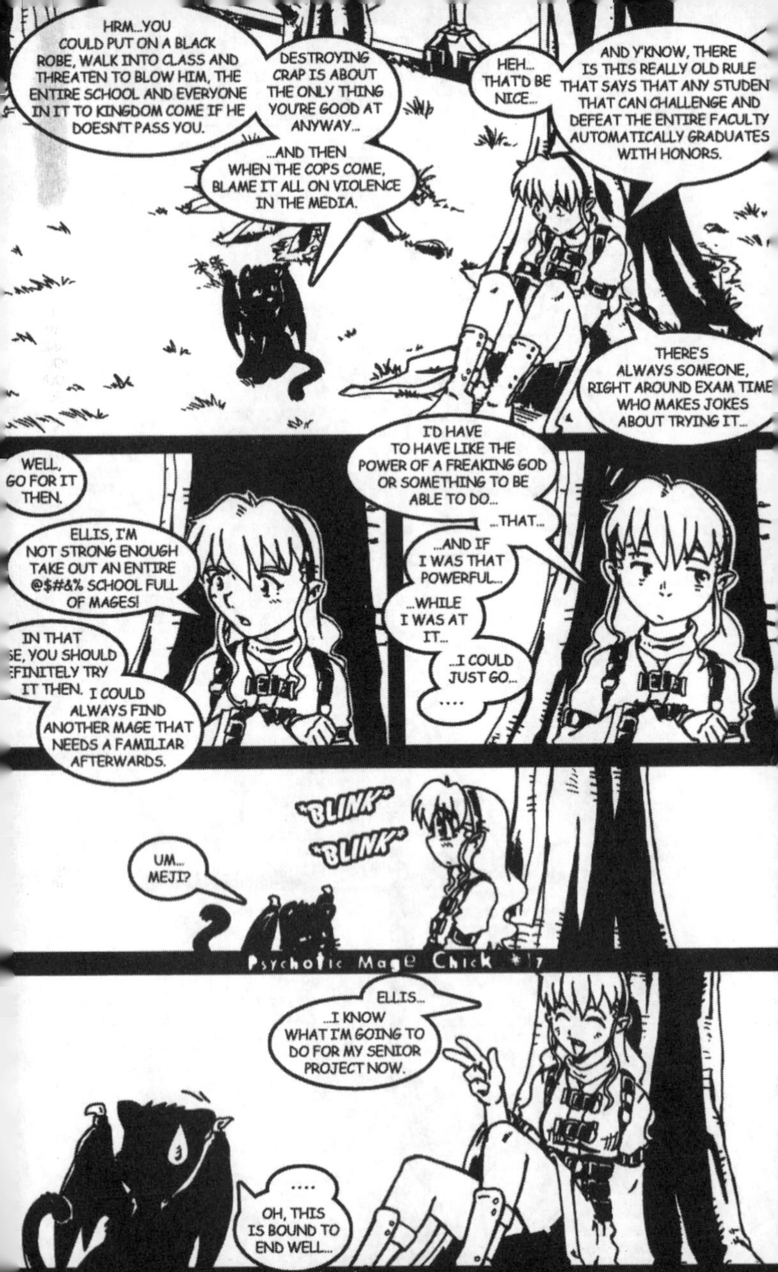
HRM...YOU COULD PUT ON A BLACK ROBE, WALK INTO CLASS AND THREATEN TO BLOW HIM, THE ENTIRE SCHOOL AND EVERYONE IN IT TO KINGDOM COME IF HE DOESN'T PASS YOU.
DESTROYING CRAP IS ABOUT THE ONLY THING YOU'RE GOOD AT ANYWAY...
...AND THEN WHEN THE COPS COME, BLAME IT ALL ON VIOLENCE IN THE MEDIA.
HEH... THAT'D BE NICE...
AND Y'KNOW, THERE IS THIS REALLY OLD RULE THAT SAYS THAT ANY STUDEN THAT CAN CHALLENGE AND DEFEAT THE ENTIRE FACULTY AUTOMATICALLY GRADUATES WITH HONORS.
THERE'S ALWAYS SOMEONE, RIGHT AROUND EXAM TIME WHO MAKES JOKES ABOUT TRYING IT...
WELL, GO FOR IT THEN.
ELLIS, I'M NOT STRONG ENOUGH TAKE OUT AN ENTIRE @$#&% SCHOOL FULL OF MAGES!
IN THAT SE, YOU SHOULD EFINITELY TRY IT THEN.
I COULD ALWAYS FIND ANOTHER MAGE THAT NEEDS A FAMILIAR AFTERWARDS.
I'D HAVE TO HAVE LIKE THE POWER OF A FREAKING GOD OR SOMETHING TO BE ABLE TO DO...
...THAT...
...AND IF I WAS THAT POWERFUL...
...WHILE I WAS AT IT...
...I COULD JUST GO...
....
BLINK
BLINK
UM... MEJI?
Psychotic Mage Chick #17
ELLIS...
...I KNOW WHAT I'M GOING TO DO FOR MY SENIOR PROJECT NOW.
....
OH, THIS IS BOUND TO END WELL...

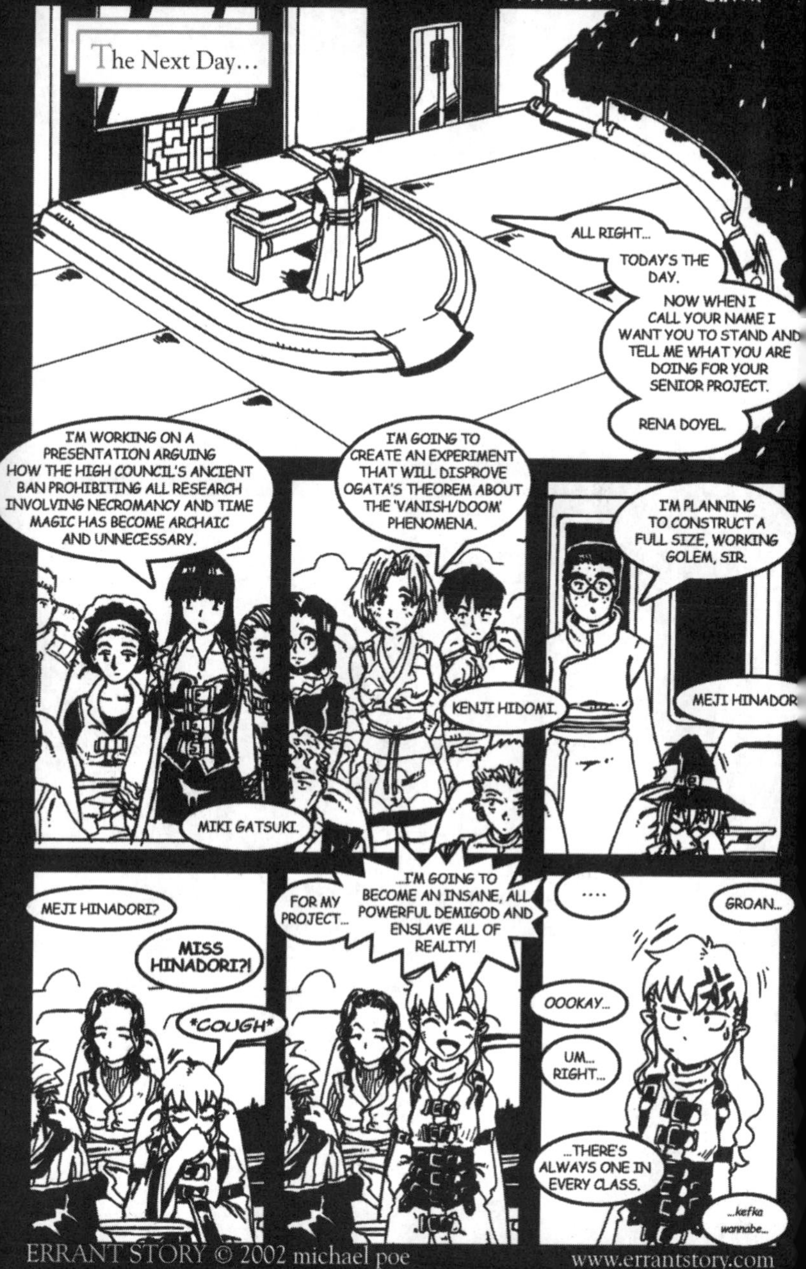
The Next Day...
ALL RIGHT...
TODAY'S THE DAY.
NOW WHEN I CALL YOUR NAME I WANT YOU TO STAND AND TELL ME WHAT YOU ARE DOING FOR YOUR SENIOR PROJECT.
RENA DOYEL.
I'M WORKING ON A PRESENTATION ARGUING HOW THE HIGH COUNCIL'S ANCIENT BAN PROHIBITING ALL RESEARCH INVOLVING NECROMANCY AND TIME MAGIC HAS BECOME ARCHAIC AND UNNECESSARY.
MIKI GATSUKI.
I'M GOING TO CREATE AN EXPERIMENT THAT WILL DISPROVE OGATA'S THEOREM ABOUT THE 'VANISH/DOOM' PHENOMENA.
KENJI HIDOMI.
I'M PLANNING TO CONSTRUCT A FULL SIZE, WORKING GOLEM, SIR.
MEJI HINADORI
MEJI HINADORI?
MISS HINADORI?!
COUGH
FOR MY PROJECT...
...I'M GOING TO BECOME AN INSANE, ALL POWERFUL DEMIGOD AND ENSLAVE ALL OF REALITY!
....
GROAN...
OOOKAY...
UM... RIGHT...
...THERE'S ALWAYS ONE IN EVERY CLASS.
...kefka wannabe...

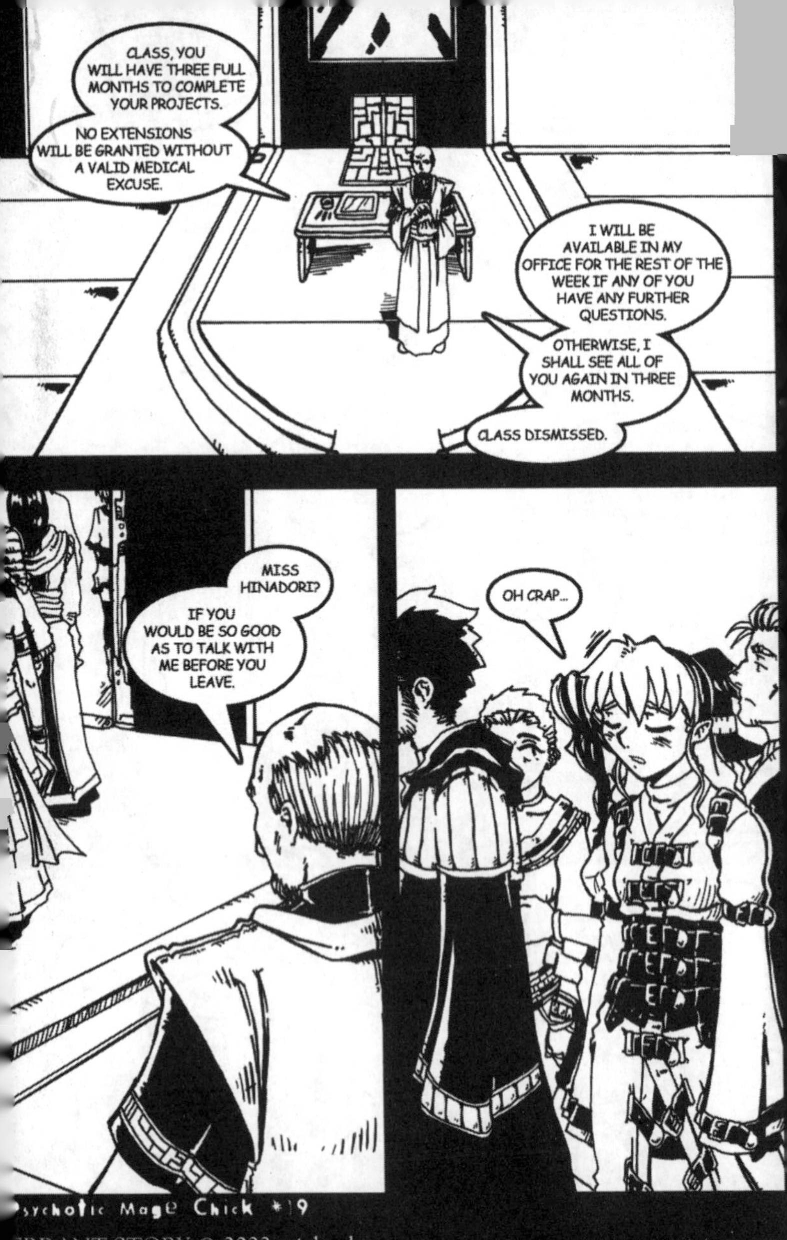
CLASS, YOU WILL HAVE THREE FULL MONTHS TO COMPLETE YOUR PROJECTS.
NO EXTENSIONS WILL BE GRANTED WITHOUT A VALID MEDICAL EXCUSE.
I WILL BE AVAILABLE IN MY OFFICE FOR THE REST OF THE WEEK IF ANY OF YOU HAVE ANY FURTHER QUESTIONS.
OTHERWISE, I SHALL SEE ALL OF YOU AGAIN IN THREE MONTHS.
CLASS DISMISSED.
MISS HINADORI?
IF YOU WOULD BE SO GOOD AS TO TALK WITH ME BEFORE YOU LEAVE.
OH CRAP...

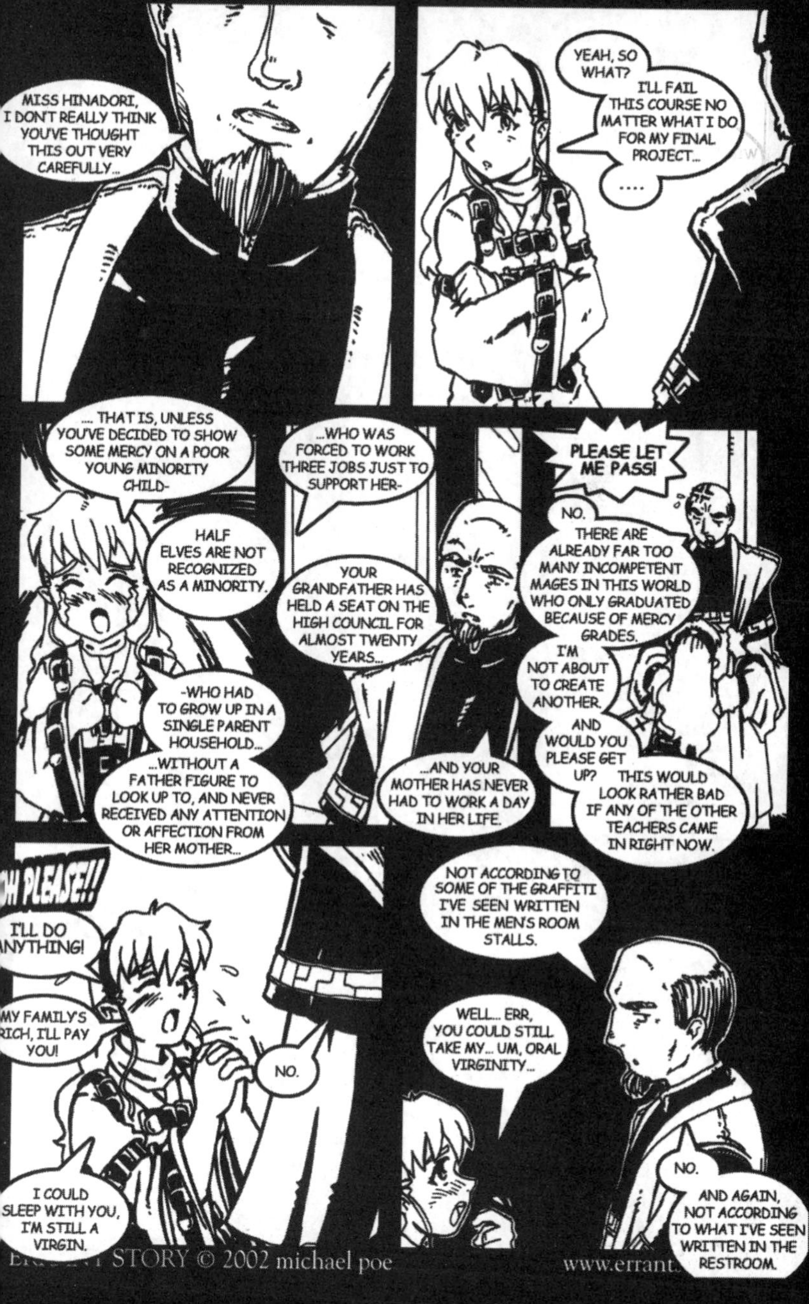
MISS HINADORI, I DON'T REALLY THINK YOU'VE THOUGHT THIS OUT VERY CAREFULLY...
YEAH, SO WHAT?
I'LL FAIL THIS COURSE NO MATTER WHAT I DO FOR MY FINAL PROJECT...
....
.... THAT IS, UNLESS YOU'VE DECIDED TO SHOW SOME MERCY ON A POOR YOUNG MINORITY CHILD-
HALF ELVES ARE NOT RECOGNIZED AS A MINORITY.
-WHO HAD TO GROW UP IN A SINGLE PARENT HOUSEHOLD...
...WITHOUT A FATHER FIGURE TO LOOK UP TO, AND NEVER RECEIVED ANY ATTENTION OR AFFECTION FROM HER MOTHER...
...WHO WAS FORCED TO WORK THREE JOBS JUST TO SUPPORT HER-
YOUR GRANDFATHER HAS HELD A SEAT ON THE HIGH COUNCIL FOR ALMOST TWENTY YEARS...
...AND YOUR MOTHER HAS NEVER HAD TO WORK A DAY IN HER LIFE.
PLEASE LET ME PASS!
NO.
THERE ARE ALREADY FAR TOO MANY INCOMPETENT MAGES IN THIS WORLD WHO ONLY GRADUATED BECAUSE OF MERCY GRADES.
I'M NOT ABOUT TO CREATE ANOTHER.
AND WOULD YOU PLEASE GET UP?
THIS WOULD LOOK RATHER BAD IF ANY OF THE OTHER TEACHERS CAME IN RIGHT NOW.
H PLEASE!!
I'LL DO NYTHING!
MY FAMILY'S ICH, I'LL PAY YOU!
NO.
I COULD SLEEP WITH YOU, I'M STILL A VIRGIN.
NOT ACCORDING TO SOME OF THE GRAFFITI I'VE SEEN WRITTEN IN THE MEN'S ROOM STALLS.
WELL... ERR, YOU COULD STILL TAKE MY... UM, ORAL VIRGINITY...
NO.
AND AGAIN, NOT ACCORDING TO WHAT I'VE SEEN WRITTEN IN THE RESTROOM.

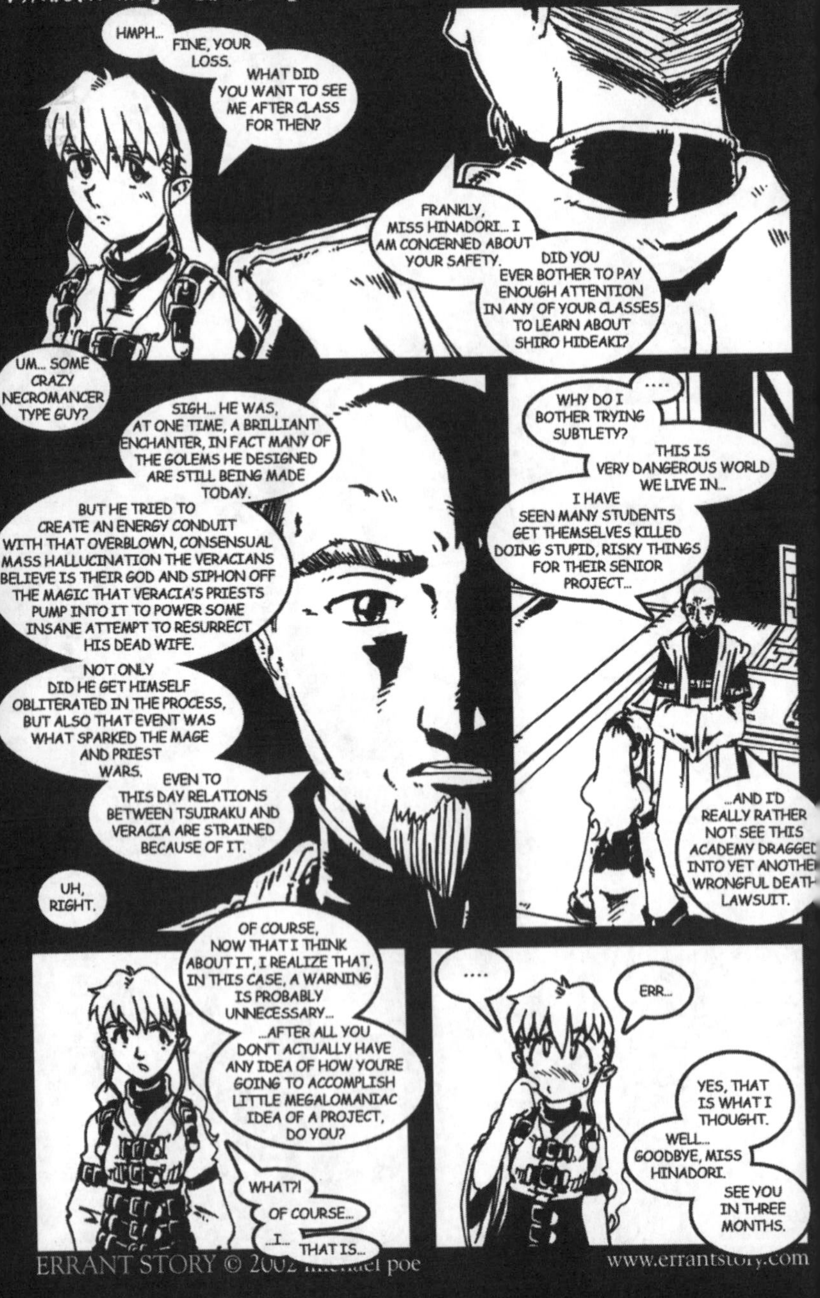
HMPH...
FINE, YOUR LOSS.
WHAT DID YOU WANT TO SEE ME AFTER CLASS FOR THEN?
FRANKLY, MISS HINADORI... I AM CONCERNED ABOUT YOUR SAFETY.
DID YOU EVER BOTHER TO PAY ENOUGH ATTENTION IN ANY OF YOUR CLASSES TO LEARN ABOUT SHIRO HIDEAKI?
UM... SOME CRAZY NECROMANCER TYPE GUY?
SIGH... HE WAS, AT ONE TIME, A BRILLIANT ENCHANTER, IN FACT MANY OF THE GOLEMS HE DESIGNED ARE STILL BEING MADE TODAY.
BUT HE TRIED TO CREATE AN ENERGY CONDUIT WITH THAT OVERBLOWN, CONSENSUAL MASS HALLUCINATION THE VERACIANS BELIEVE IS THEIR GOD AND SIPHON OFF THE MAGIC THAT VERACIA'S PRIESTS PUMP INTO IT TO POWER SOME INSANE ATTEMPT TO RESURRECT HIS DEAD WIFE.
NOT ONLY DID HE GET HIMSELF OBLITERATED IN THE PROCESS, BUT ALSO THAT EVENT WAS WHAT SPARKED THE MAGE AND PRIEST WARS.
EVEN TO THIS DAY RELATIONS BETWEEN TSUIRAKU AND VERACIA ARE STRAINED BECAUSE OF IT.
UH, RIGHT.
....
WHY DO I BOTHER TRYING SUBTLETY?
THIS IS VERY DANGEROUS WORLD WE LIVE IN...
I HAVE SEEN MANY STUDENTS GET THEMSELVES KILLED DOING STUPID, RISKY THINGS FOR THEIR SENIOR PROJECT...
...AND I'D REALLY RATHER NOT SEE THIS ACADEMY DRAGGED INTO YET ANOTHER WRONGFUL DEATH LAWSUIT.
OF COURSE, NOW THAT I THINK ABOUT IT, I REALIZE THAT, IN THIS CASE, A WARNING IS PROBABLY UNNECESSARY...
...AFTER ALL YOU DON'T ACTUALLY HAVE ANY IDEA OF HOW YOU'RE GOING TO ACCOMPLISH LITTLE MEGALOMANIAC IDEA OF A PROJECT, DO YOU?
WHAT?!
OF COURSE...
...I...
THAT IS...
....
ERR...
YES, THAT IS WHAT I THOUGHT.
WELL... GOODBYE, MISS HINADORI.
SEE YOU IN THREE MONTHS.

GRRR... THAT &#$#%$! BASTARD!! I'LL SHOW HIM!

CAREFUL, YOU'RE DRIFTING INTO THE CLICHÉD EVIL WIZARD DIALOG AGAIN, MEJI...

THIS LIBRARY IS ONE OF THE LARGEST COLLECTIONS OF OCCULT TEXTS AND ARCANE LORE IN EXISTENCE... ...THERE'S GOTTA BE SOMETHING HERE THAT I COULD USE.

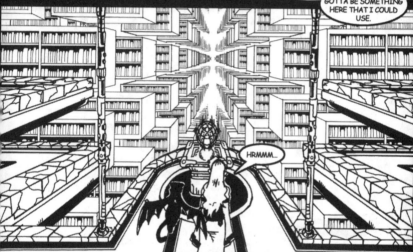

HRMMM...

YES, EMPHASIS ON THE WORD "LARGEST"... ...GOOD LUCK WITH FINDING ANYTHING.

NO... NO, FOR THIS, I HAVE A PLAN.

ERRANT STORY © 2002 michael poe

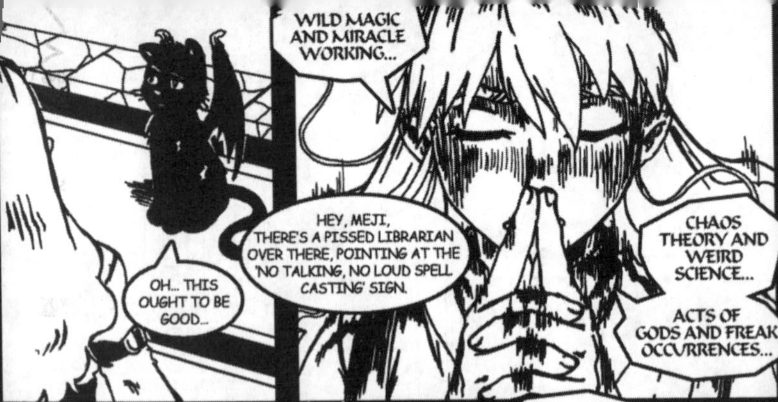
HEY, MEJI, THERE'S A PISSED LIBRARIAN OVER THERE, POINTING AT THE 'NO TALKING, NO LOUD SPELL CASTING' SIGN.
OH... THIS OUGHT TO BE GOOD...
WILD MAGIC AND MIRACLE WORKING...
CHAOS THEORY AND WEIRD SCIENCE...
ACTS OF GODS AND FREAK OCCURRENCES...

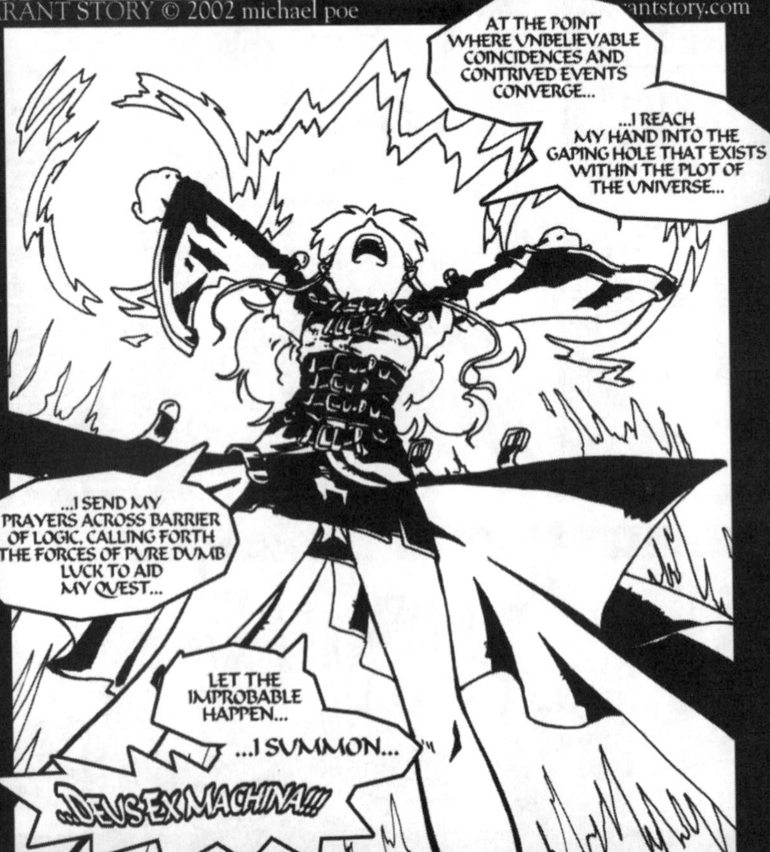
AT THE POINT WHERE UNBELIEVABLE COINCIDENCES AND CONTRIVED EVENTS CONVERGE...
...I REACH MY HAND INTO THE GAPING HOLE THAT EXISTS WITHIN THE PLOT OF THE UNIVERSE...
...I SEND MY PRAYERS ACROSS BARRIER OF LOGIC, CALLING FORTH THE FORCES OF PURE DUMB LUCK TO AID MY QUEST...
LET THE IMPROBABLE HAPPEN...
...I SUMMON...
..DEUS EX MACHINA!!!

.....
HUH?
HEY, WHAT THE @#$% GIVES?!
NOTHING EFFING HAPPEN!
HEEHEEHEE...
TOLD YOU THAT RIDICULOUS PROBABILITY SPELL WOULDN'T WORK.
I MEAN, WHAT DID YOU EXPECT TO HAPPEN?
A GIANT HAND COMING OUT OF THE SKY, POINTING AT SOMETHING THAT MIGHT HEL-
KAPOW
RROAW!
CRASH
OOF!

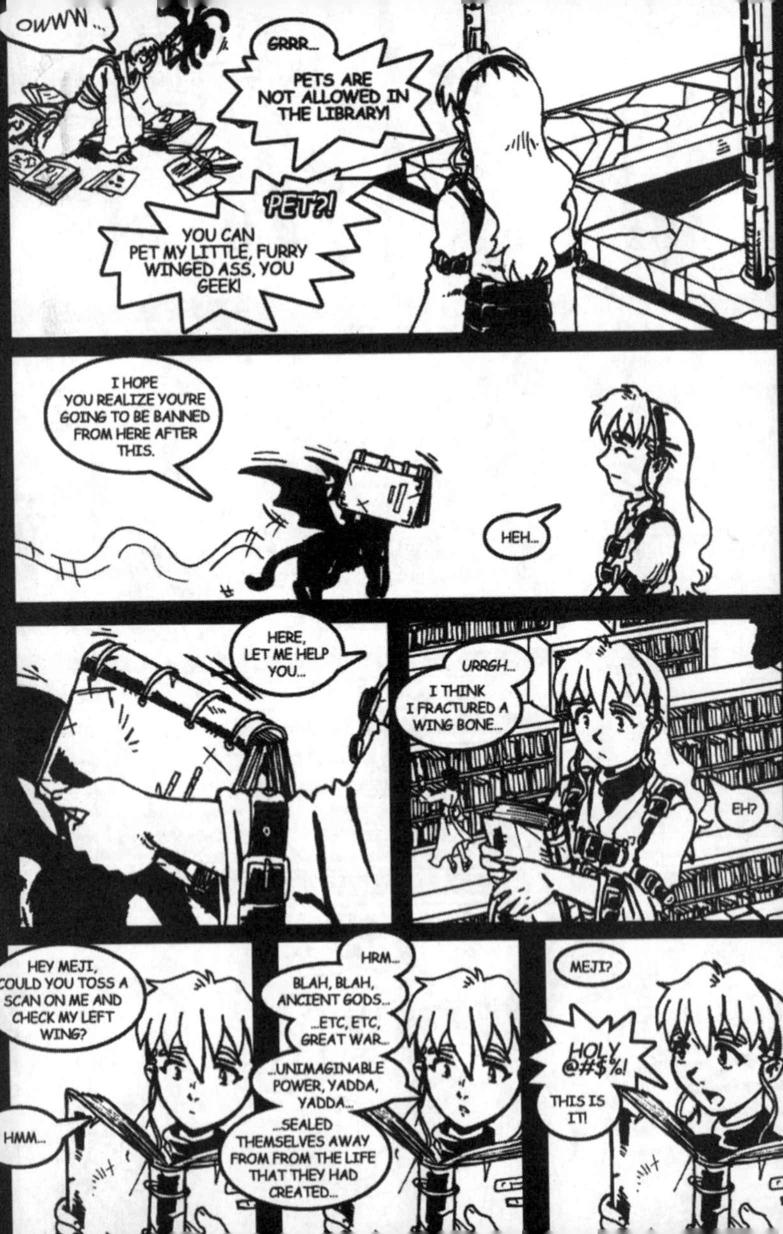
OWWW...
GRRR...
PETS ARE NOT ALLOWED IN THE LIBRARY!
PET?!
YOU CAN PET MY LITTLE, FURRY WINGED ASS, YOU GEEK!
I HOPE YOU REALIZE YOU'RE GOING TO BE BANNED FROM HERE AFTER THIS.
HEH...
HERE, LET ME HELP YOU...
URRGH...
I THINK I FRACTURED A WING BONE...
EH?
HEY MEJI, COULD YOU TOSS A SCAN ON ME AND CHECK MY LEFT WING?
HMM...
HRM...
BLAH, BLAH, ANCIENT GODS...
...ETC, ETC, GREAT WAR...
...UNIMAGINABLE POWER, YADDA, YADDA...
...SEALED THEMSELVES AWAY FROM FROM THE LIFE THAT THEY HAD CREATED...
MEJI?
HOLY @#$%!
THIS IS IT!

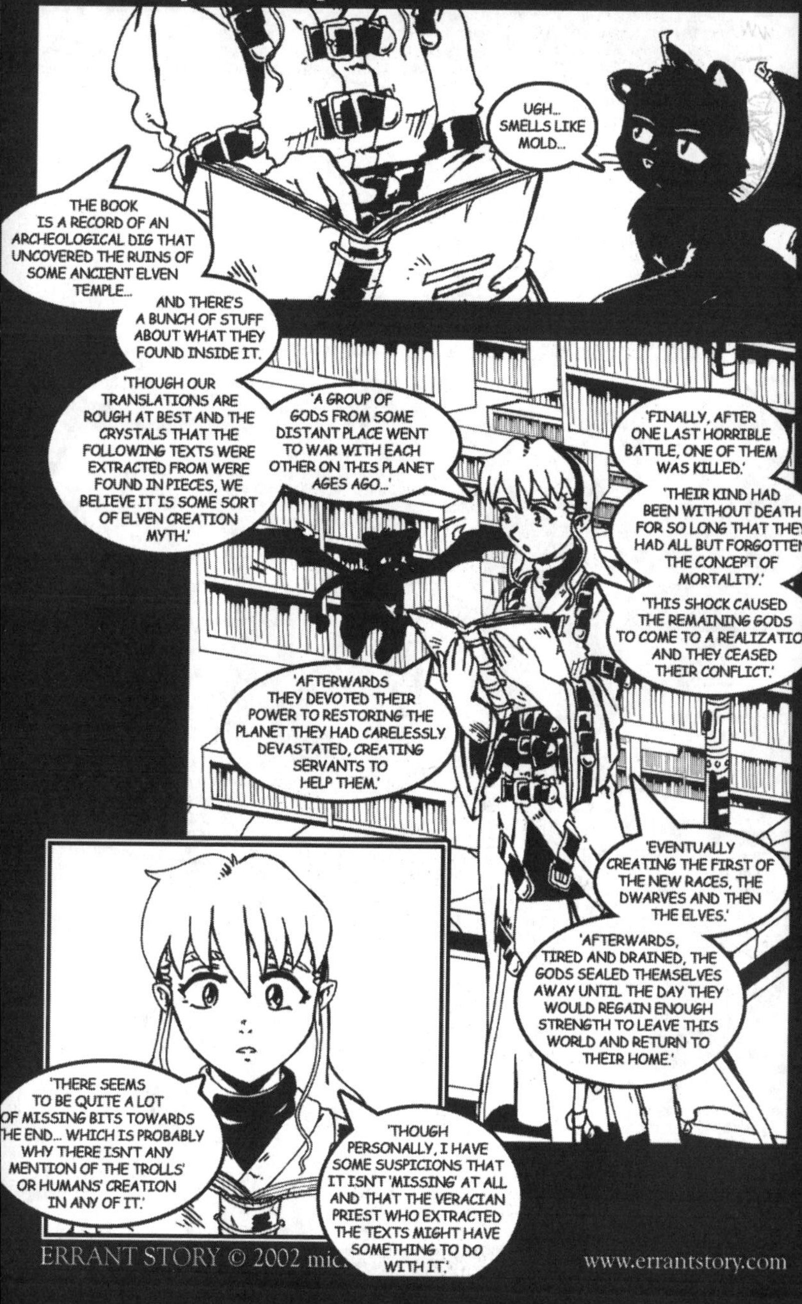
UGH... SMELLS LIKE MOLD...
THE BOOK IS A RECORD OF AN ARCHEOLOGICAL DIG THAT UNCOVERED THE RUINS OF SOME ANCIENT ELVEN TEMPLE...
AND THERE'S A BUNCH OF STUFF ABOUT WHAT THEY FOUND INSIDE IT.
'THOUGH OUR TRANSLATIONS ARE ROUGH AT BEST AND THE CRYSTALS THAT THE FOLLOWING TEXTS WERE EXTRACTED FROM WERE FOUND IN PIECES, WE BELIEVE IT IS SOME SORT OF ELVEN CREATION MYTH.'
'A GROUP OF GODS FROM SOME DISTANT PLACE WENT TO WAR WITH EACH OTHER ON THIS PLANET AGES AGO...'
'FINALLY, AFTER ONE LAST HORRIBLE BATTLE, ONE OF THEM WAS KILLED.'
'THEIR KIND HAD BEEN WITHOUT DEATH FOR SO LONG THAT THEY HAD ALL BUT FORGOTTEN THE CONCEPT OF MORTALITY.'
'THIS SHOCK CAUSED THE REMAINING GODS TO COME TO A REALIZATION AND THEY CEASED THEIR CONFLICT.'
'AFTERWARDS THEY DEVOTED THEIR POWER TO RESTORING THE PLANET THEY HAD CARELESSLY DEVASTATED, CREATING SERVANTS TO HELP THEM.'
'EVENTUALLY CREATING THE FIRST OF THE NEW RACES, THE DWARVES AND THEN THE ELVES.'
'AFTERWARDS, TIRED AND DRAINED, THE GODS SEALED THEMSELVES AWAY UNTIL THE DAY THEY WOULD REGAIN ENOUGH STRENGTH TO LEAVE THIS WORLD AND RETURN TO THEIR HOME.'
'THERE SEEMS TO BE QUITE A LOT OF MISSING BITS TOWARDS HE END... WHICH IS PROBABLY WHY THERE ISN'T ANY MENTION OF THE TROLLS' OR HUMANS' CREATION IN ANY OF IT.'
'THOUGH PERSONALLY, I HAVE SOME SUSPICIONS THAT IT ISN'T 'MISSING' AT ALL AND THAT THE VERACIAN PRIEST WHO EXTRACTED THE TEXTS MIGHT HAVE SOMETHING TO DO WITH IT.'

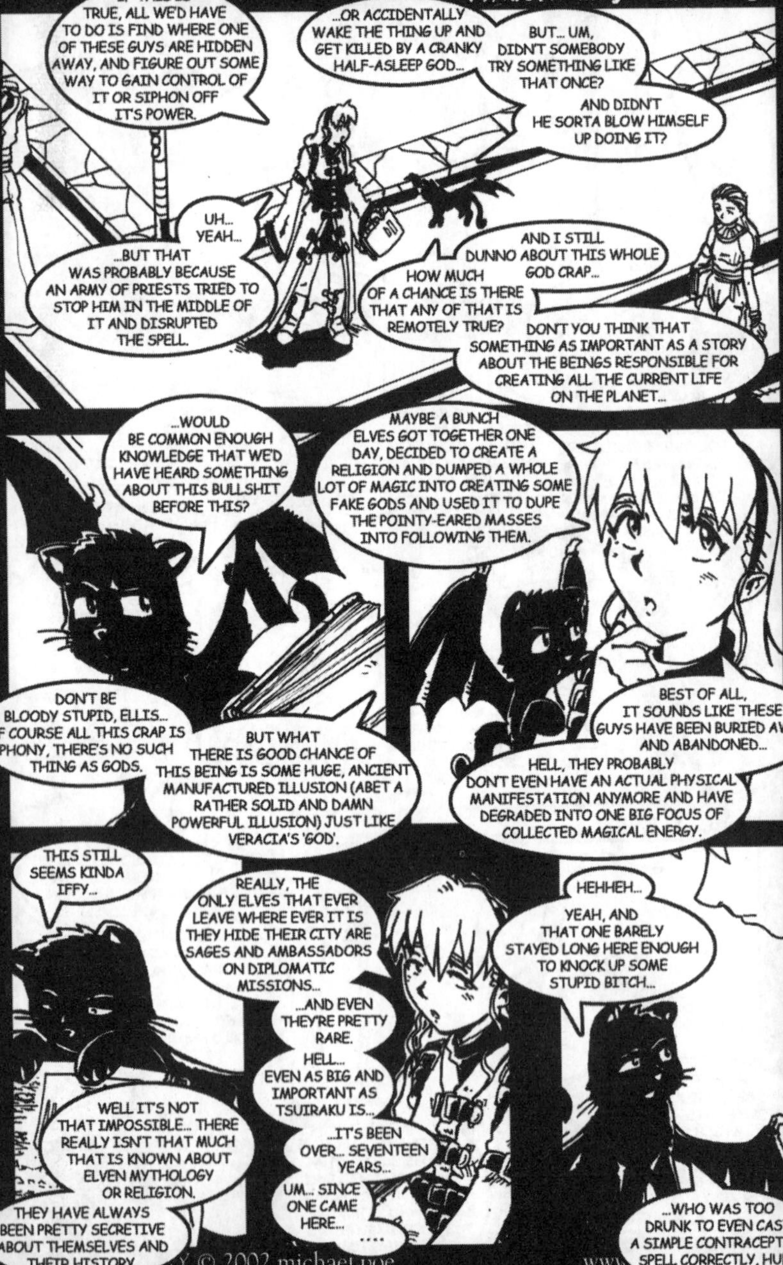
IF THIS IS TRUE, ALL WE'D HAVE TO DO IS FIND WHERE ONE OF THESE GUYS ARE HIDDEN AWAY, AND FIGURE OUT SOME WAY TO GAIN CONTROL OF IT OR SIPHON OFF IT'S POWER.
...OR ACCIDENTALLY WAKE THE THING UP AND GET KILLED BY A CRANKY HALF-ASLEEP GOD...
BUT... UM, DIDN'T SOMEBODY TRY SOMETHING LIKE THAT ONCE?
AND DIDN'T HE SORTA BLOW HIMSELF UP DOING IT?
UH... YEAH...
...BUT THAT WAS PROBABLY BECAUSE AN ARMY OF PRIESTS TRIED TO STOP HIM IN THE MIDDLE OF IT AND DISRUPTED THE SPELL.
AND I STILL DUNNO ABOUT THIS WHOLE GOD CRAP...
HOW MUCH OF A CHANCE IS THERE THAT ANY OF THAT IS REMOTELY TRUE?
DON'T YOU THINK THAT SOMETHING AS IMPORTANT AS A STORY ABOUT THE BEINGS RESPONSIBLE FOR CREATING ALL THE CURRENT LIFE ON THE PLANET...
...WOULD BE COMMON ENOUGH KNOWLEDGE THAT WE'D HAVE HEARD SOMETHING ABOUT THIS BULLSHIT BEFORE THIS?
DON'T BE BLOODY STUPID, ELLIS... OF COURSE ALL THIS CRAP IS PHONY, THERE'S NO SUCH THING AS GODS.
BUT WHAT THERE IS GOOD CHANCE OF THIS BEING IS SOME HUGE, ANCIENT MANUFACTURED ILLUSION (ABET A RATHER SOLID AND DAMN POWERFUL ILLUSION) JUST LIKE VERACIA'S 'GOD'.
MAYBE A BUNCH ELVES GOT TOGETHER ONE DAY, DECIDED TO CREATE A RELIGION AND DUMPED A WHOLE LOT OF MAGIC INTO CREATING SOME FAKE GODS AND USED IT TO DUPE THE POINTY-EARED MASSES INTO FOLLOWING THEM.
BEST OF ALL, IT SOUNDS LIKE THESE GUYS HAVE BEEN BURIED AWAY AND ABANDONED...
HELL, THEY PROBABLY DON'T EVEN HAVE AN ACTUAL PHYSICAL MANIFESTATION ANYMORE AND HAVE DEGRADED INTO ONE BIG FOCUS OF COLLECTED MAGICAL ENERGY.
THIS STILL SEEMS KINDA IFFY...
WELL IT'S NOT THAT IMPOSSIBLE... THERE REALLY ISN'T THAT MUCH THAT IS KNOWN ABOUT ELVEN MYTHOLOGY OR RELIGION.
THEY HAVE ALWAYS BEEN PRETTY SECRETIVE ABOUT THEMSELVES AND THEIR HISTORY.
REALLY, THE ONLY ELVES THAT EVER LEAVE WHERE EVER IT IS THEY HIDE THEIR CITY ARE SAGES AND AMBASSADORS ON DIPLOMATIC MISSIONS...
...AND EVEN THEY'RE PRETTY RARE.
HELL... EVEN AS BIG AND IMPORTANT AS TSUIRAKU IS...
...IT'S BEEN OVER... SEVENTEEN YEARS...
UM... SINCE ONE CAME HERE...
....
HEHHEH...
YEAH, AND THAT ONE BARELY STAYED LONG HERE ENOUGH TO KNOCK UP SOME STUPID BITCH...
...WHO WAS TOO DRUNK TO EVEN CAST A SIMPLE CONTRACEPTIVE SPELL CORRECTLY, HUH?

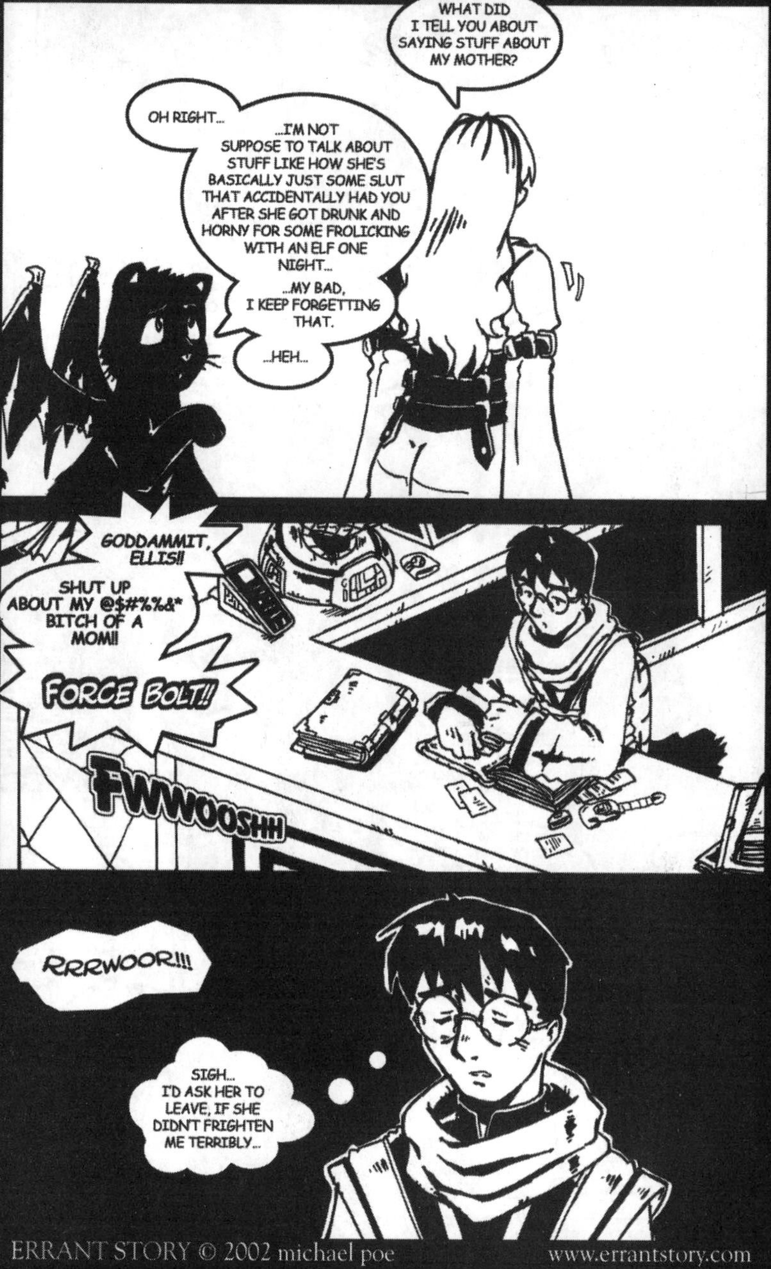
WHAT DID I TELL YOU ABOUT SAYING STUFF ABOUT MY MOTHER?
OH RIGHT...
...I'M NOT SUPPOSE TO TALK ABOUT STUFF LIKE HOW SHE'S BASICALLY JUST SOME SLUT THAT ACCIDENTALLY HAD YOU AFTER SHE GOT DRUNK AND HORNY FOR SOME FROLICKING WITH AN ELF ONE NIGHT...
...MY BAD, I KEEP FORGETTING THAT.
...HEH...
GODDAMMIT, ELLIS!!
SHUT UP ABOUT MY @$#%%&* BITCH OF A MOM!!
FORCE BOLT!!
FWWOOSHH
RRRWOOR!!!
SIGH... I'D ASK HER TO LEAVE, IF SHE DIDN'T FRIGHTEN ME TERRIBLY...

Psychotic Mage Chick #29

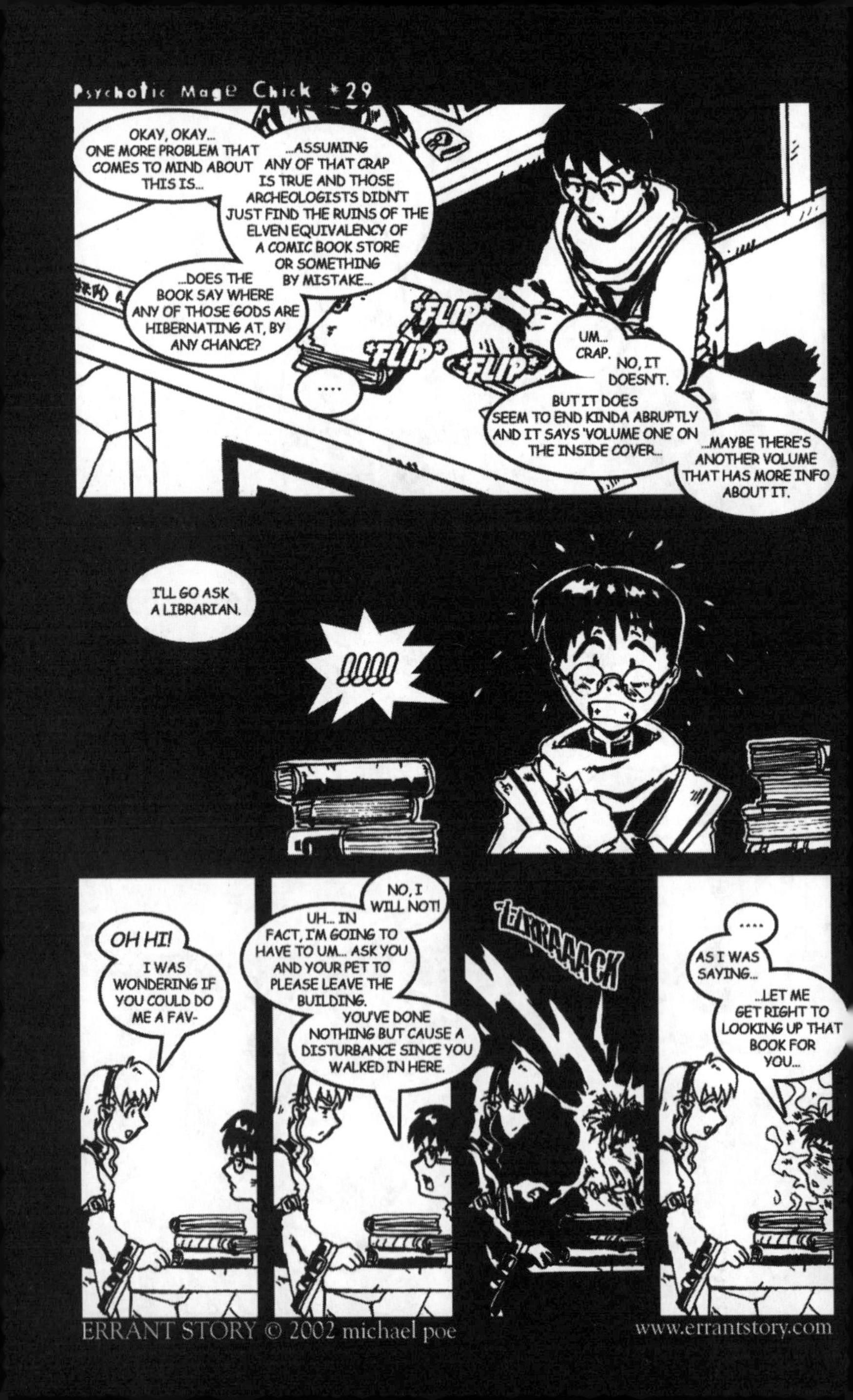
OKAY, OKAY... ONE MORE PROBLEM THAT COMES TO MIND ABOUT THIS IS...
...ASSUMING ANY OF THAT CRAP IS TRUE AND THOSE ARCHEOLOGISTS DIDN'T JUST FIND THE RUINS OF THE ELVEN EQUIVALENCY OF A COMIC BOOK STORE OR SOMETHING BY MISTAKE...
...DOES THE BOOK SAY WHERE ANY OF THOSE GODS ARE HIBERNATING AT, BY ANY CHANCE?
FLIP
FLIP
FLIP
....
UM... CRAP.
NO, IT DOESN'T.
BUT IT DOES SEEM TO END KINDA ABRUPTLY AND IT SAYS 'VOLUME ONE' ON THE INSIDE COVER...
...MAYBE THERE'S ANOTHER VOLUME THAT HAS MORE INFO ABOUT IT.
I'LL GO ASK A LIBRARIAN.
!!!!!
OH HI!
I WAS WONDERING IF YOU COULD DO ME A FAV-
NO, I WILL NOT!
UH... IN FACT, I'M GOING TO HAVE TO UM... ASK YOU AND YOUR PET TO PLEASE LEAVE THE BUILDING.
YOU'VE DONE NOTHING BUT CAUSE A DISTURBANCE SINCE YOU WALKED IN HERE.
ZZRRAAACK
....
AS I WAS SAYING...
...LET ME GET RIGHT TO LOOKING UP THAT BOOK FOR YOU...

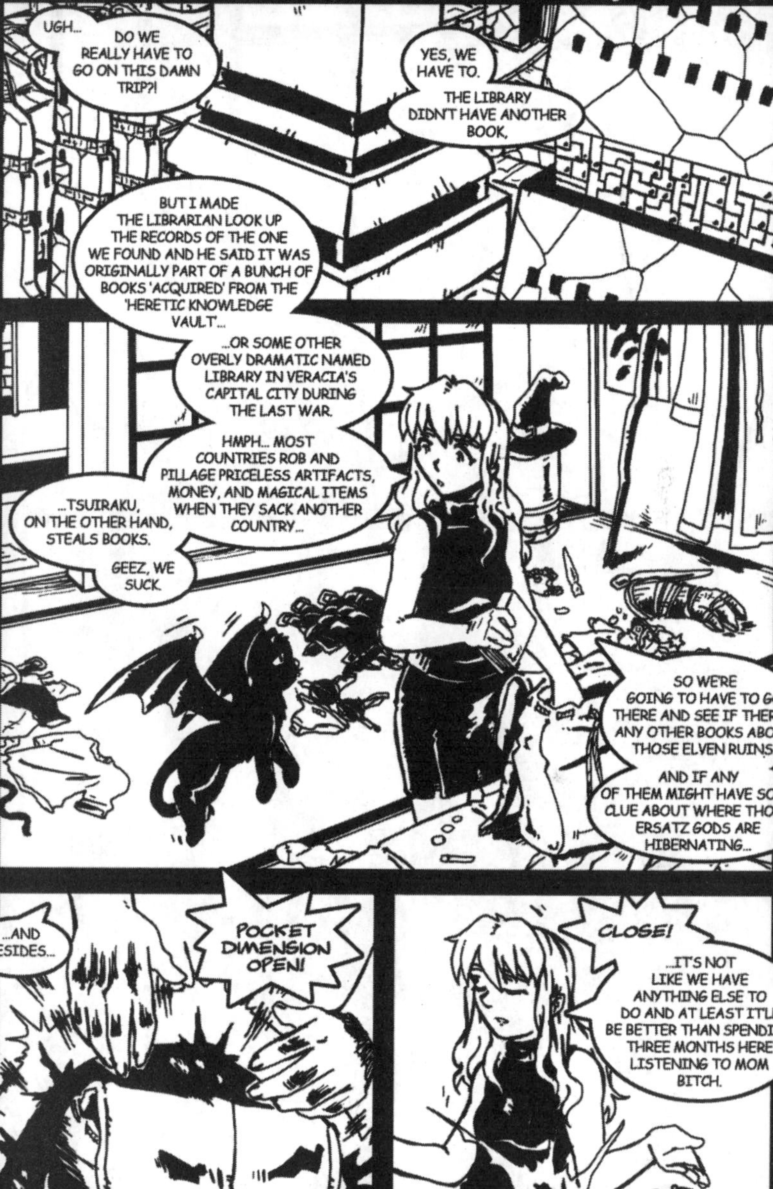
UGH...
DO WE REALLY HAVE TO GO ON THIS DAMN TRIP?!
YES, WE HAVE TO.
THE LIBRARY DIDN'T HAVE ANOTHER BOOK.
BUT I MADE THE LIBRARIAN LOOK UP THE RECORDS OF THE ONE WE FOUND AND HE SAID IT WAS ORIGINALLY PART OF A BUNCH OF BOOKS 'ACQUIRED' FROM THE 'HERETIC KNOWLEDGE VAULT'...
...OR SOME OTHER OVERLY DRAMATIC NAMED LIBRARY IN VERACIA'S CAPITAL CITY DURING THE LAST WAR.
HMPH... MOST COUNTRIES ROB AND PILLAGE PRICELESS ARTIFACTS, MONEY, AND MAGICAL ITEMS WHEN THEY SACK ANOTHER COUNTRY...
...TSUIRAKU, ON THE OTHER HAND, STEALS BOOKS.
GEEZ, WE SUCK.
SO WE'RE GOING TO HAVE TO GO THERE AND SEE IF THERE'S ANY OTHER BOOKS ABOUT THOSE ELVEN RUINS,
AND IF ANY OF THEM MIGHT HAVE SOME CLUE ABOUT WHERE THOSE ERSATZ GODS ARE HIBERNATING...
...AND BESIDES...
POCKET DIMENSION OPEN!
CLOSE!
...IT'S NOT LIKE WE HAVE ANYTHING ELSE TO DO AND AT LEAST IT'LL BE BETTER THAN SPENDING THREE MONTHS HERE LISTENING TO MOM BITCH.
POP

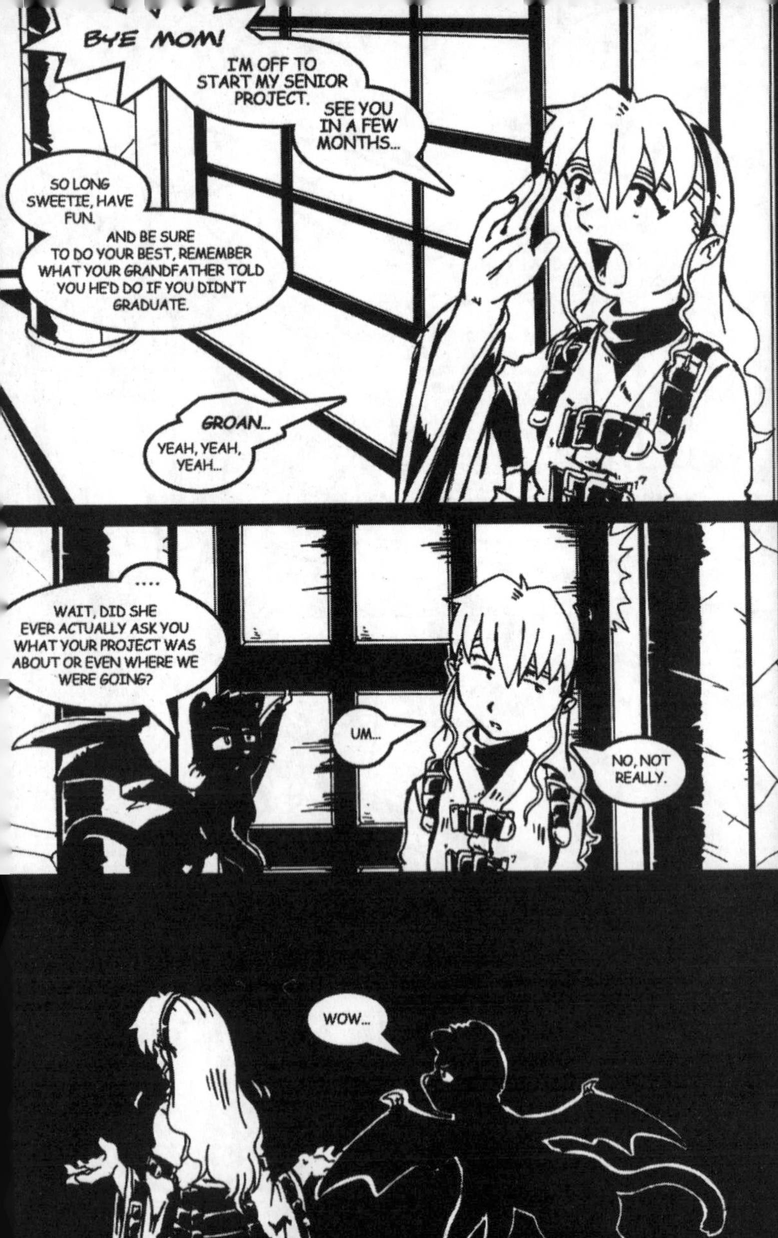
BYE MOM!
I'M OFF TO START MY SENIOR PROJECT.
SEE YOU IN A FEW MONTHS...
SO LONG SWEETIE, HAVE FUN.
AND BE SURE TO DO YOUR BEST, REMEMBER WHAT YOUR GRANDFATHER TOLD YOU HE'D DO IF YOU DIDN'T GRADUATE.
GROAN...
YEAH, YEAH, YEAH...
....
WAIT, DID SHE EVER ACTUALLY ASK YOU WHAT YOUR PROJECT WAS ABOUT OR EVEN WHERE WE WERE GOING?
UM...
NO, NOT REALLY.
WOW...

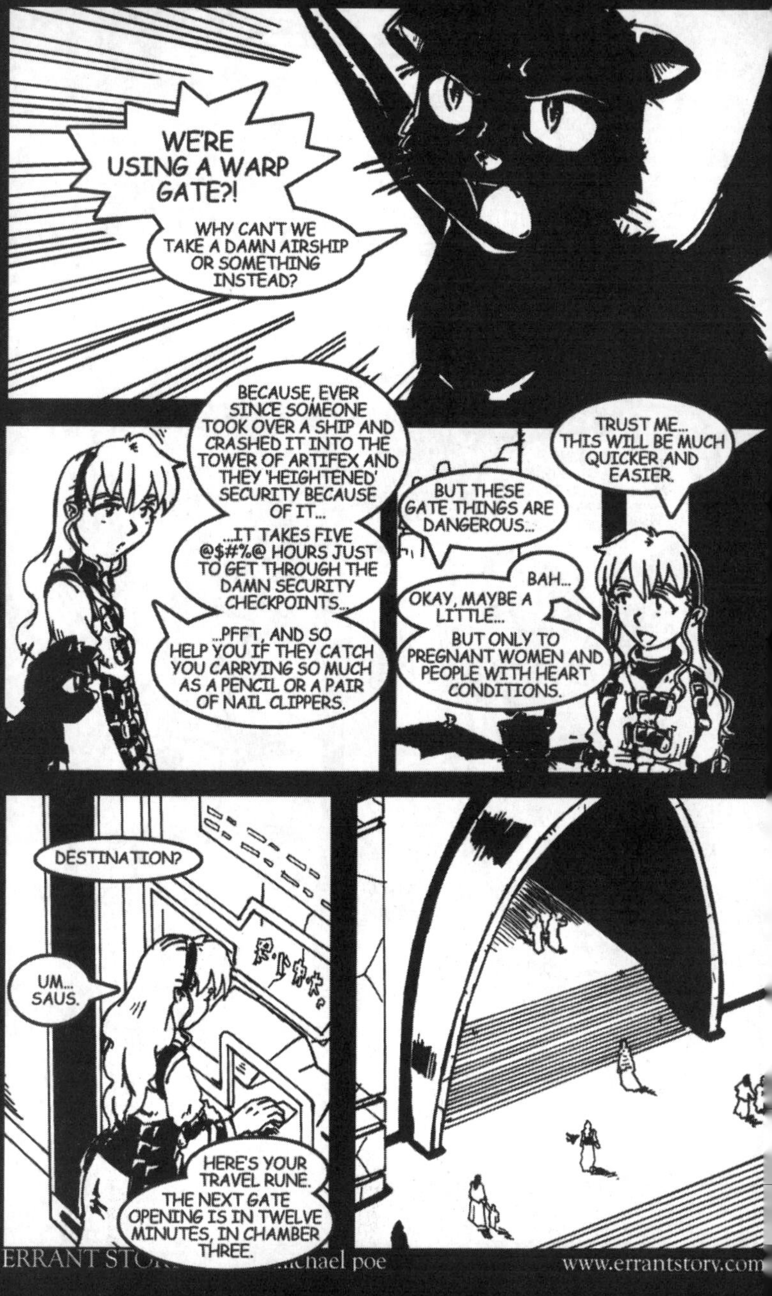
WE'RE USING A WARP GATE?!
WHY CAN'T WE TAKE A DAMN AIRSHIP OR SOMETHING INSTEAD?
BECAUSE, EVER SINCE SOMEONE TOOK OVER A SHIP AND CRASHED IT INTO THE TOWER OF ARTIFEX AND THEY 'HEIGHTENED' SECURITY BECAUSE OF IT...
...IT TAKES FIVE @$#%@ HOURS JUST TO GET THROUGH THE DAMN SECURITY CHECKPOINTS...
...PFFT, AND SO HELP YOU IF THEY CATCH YOU CARRYING SO MUCH AS A PENCIL OR A PAIR OF NAIL CLIPPERS.
TRUST ME... THIS WILL BE MUCH QUICKER AND EASIER.
BUT THESE GATE THINGS ARE DANGEROUS...
BAH...
OKAY, MAYBE A LITTLE...
BUT ONLY TO PREGNANT WOMEN AND PEOPLE WITH HEART CONDITIONS.
DESTINATION?
UM... SAUS.
HERE'S YOUR TRAVEL RUNE. THE NEXT GATE OPENING IS IN TWELVE MINUTES, IN CHAMBER THREE.

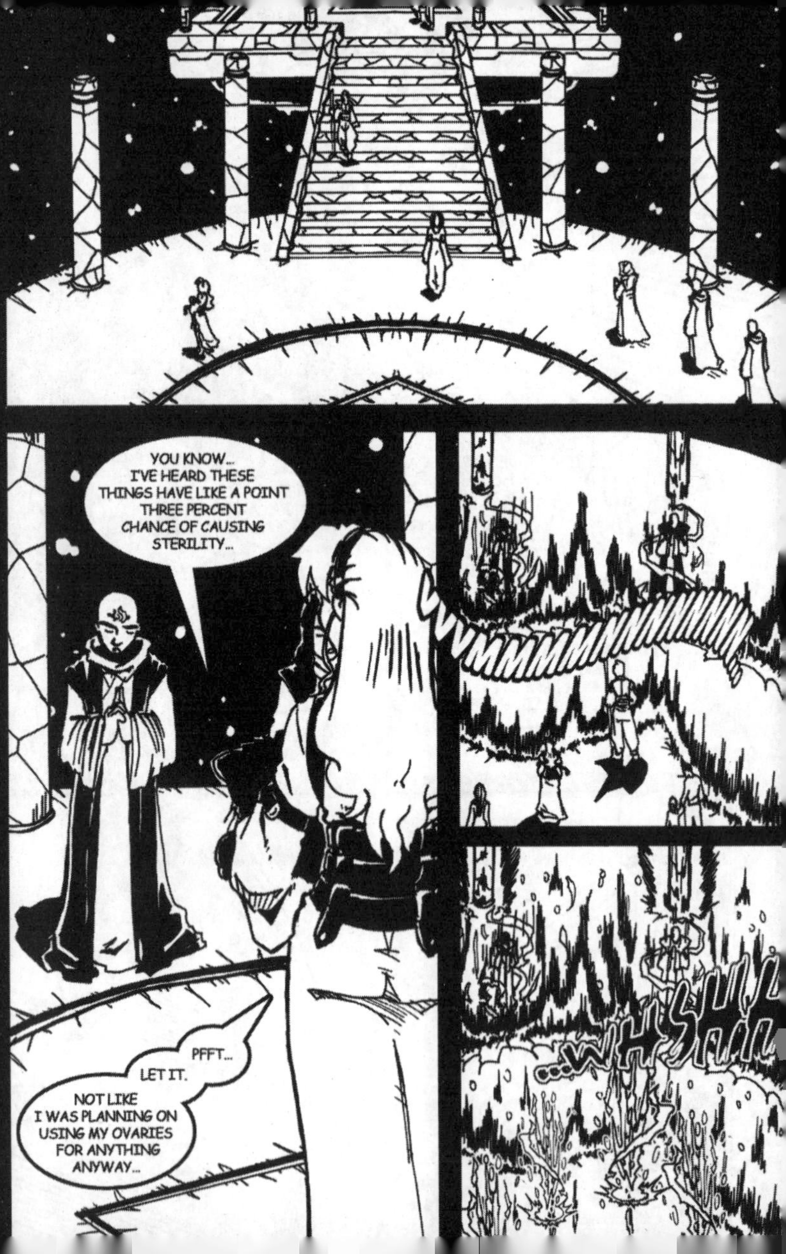
YOU KNOW... I'VE HEARD THESE THINGS HAVE LIKE A POINT THREE PERCENT CHANCE OF CAUSING STERILITY...
PFFT...
LET IT.
NOT LIKE I WAS PLANNING ON USING MY OVARIES FOR ANYTHING ANYWAY...

ERRANT STORY CHAPTER TWO

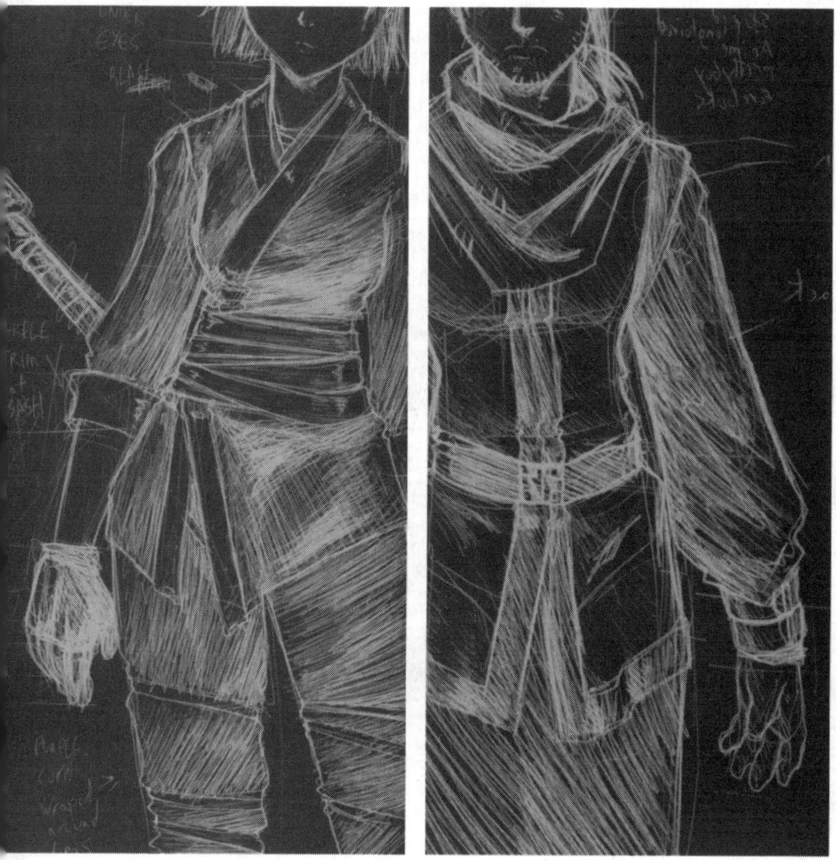

dead leaves

www.errantstory.com

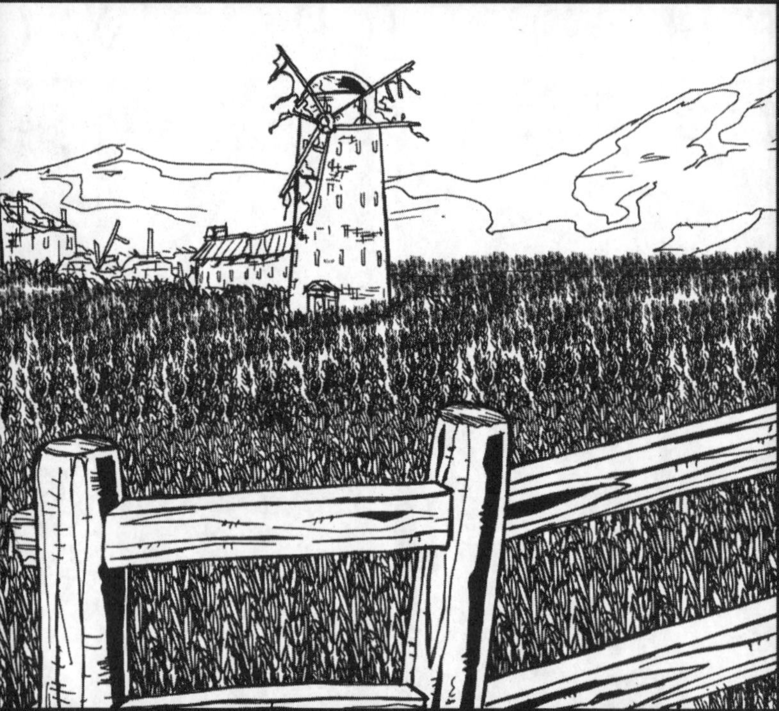

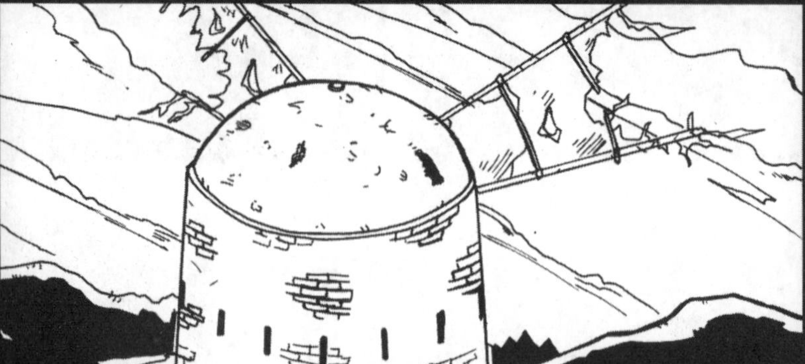

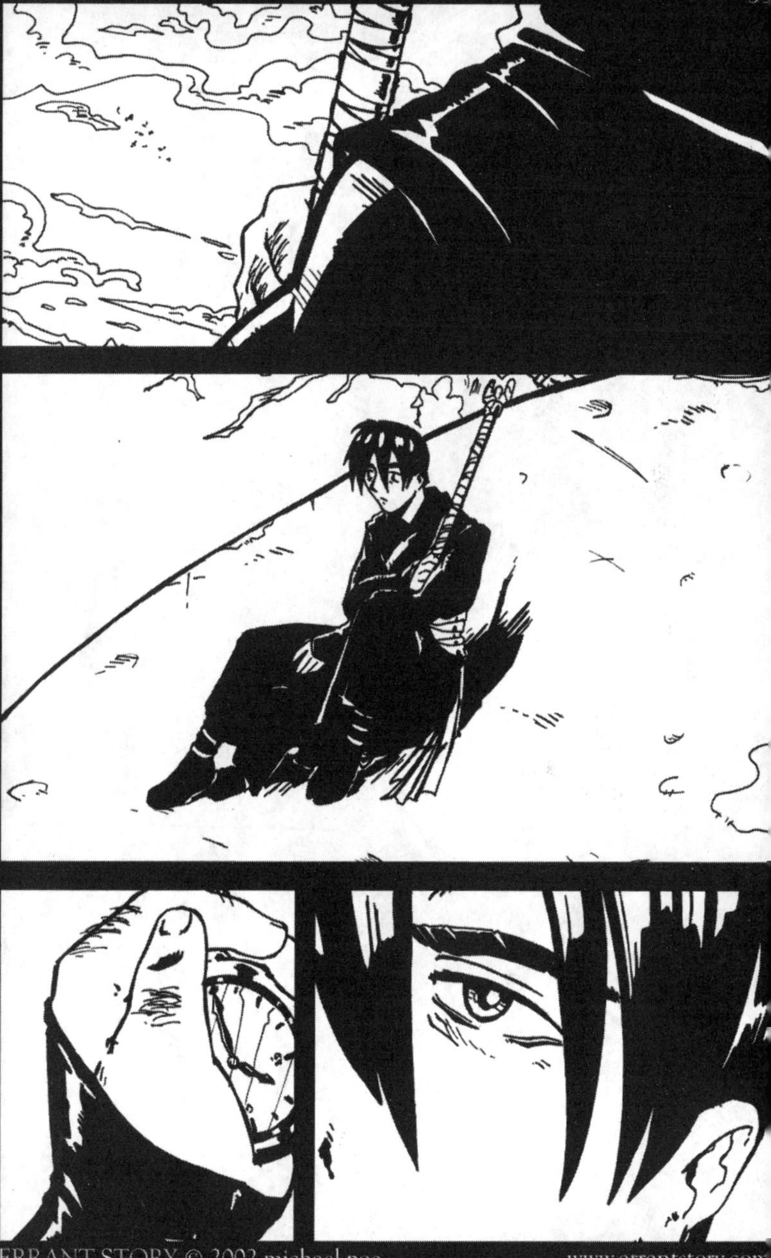

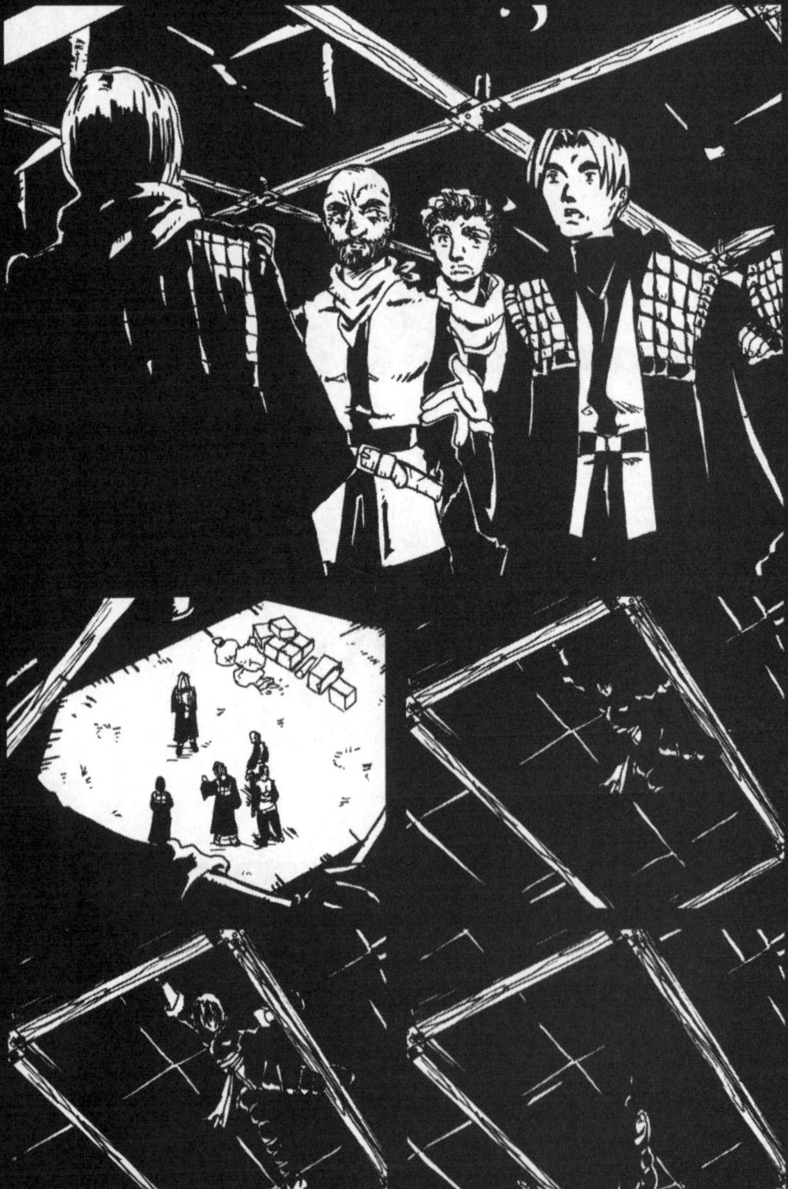

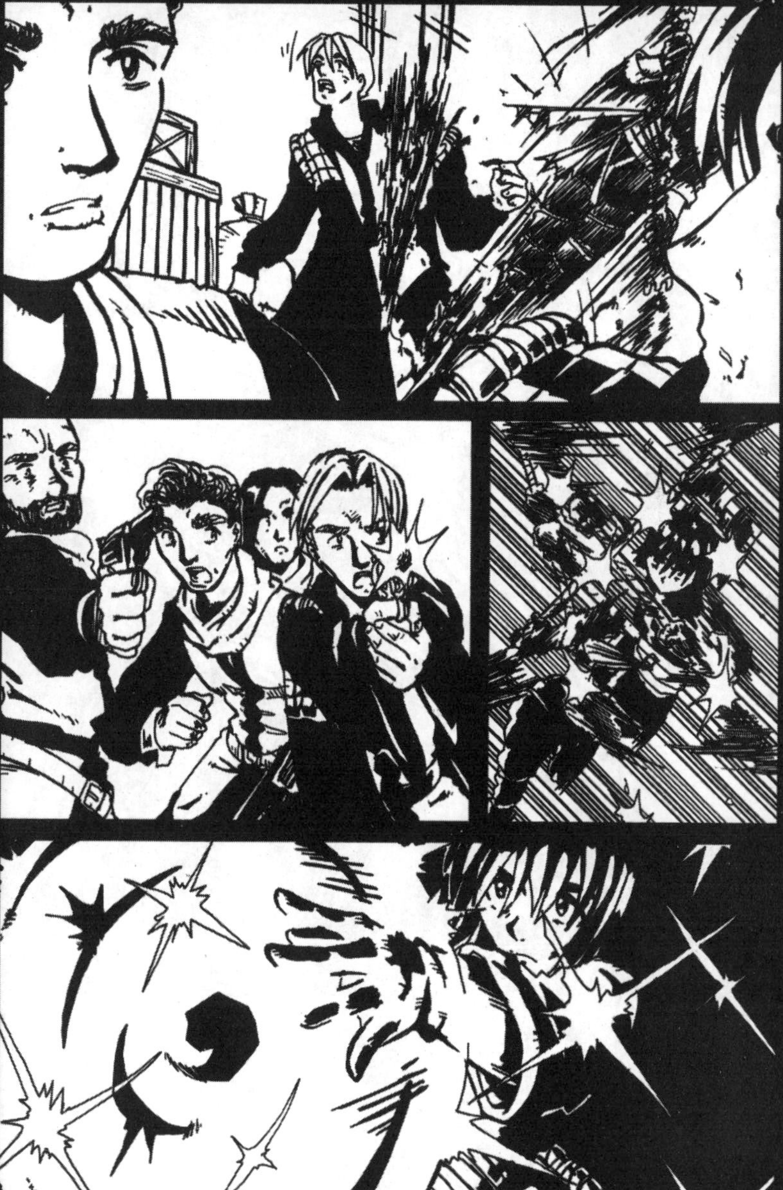

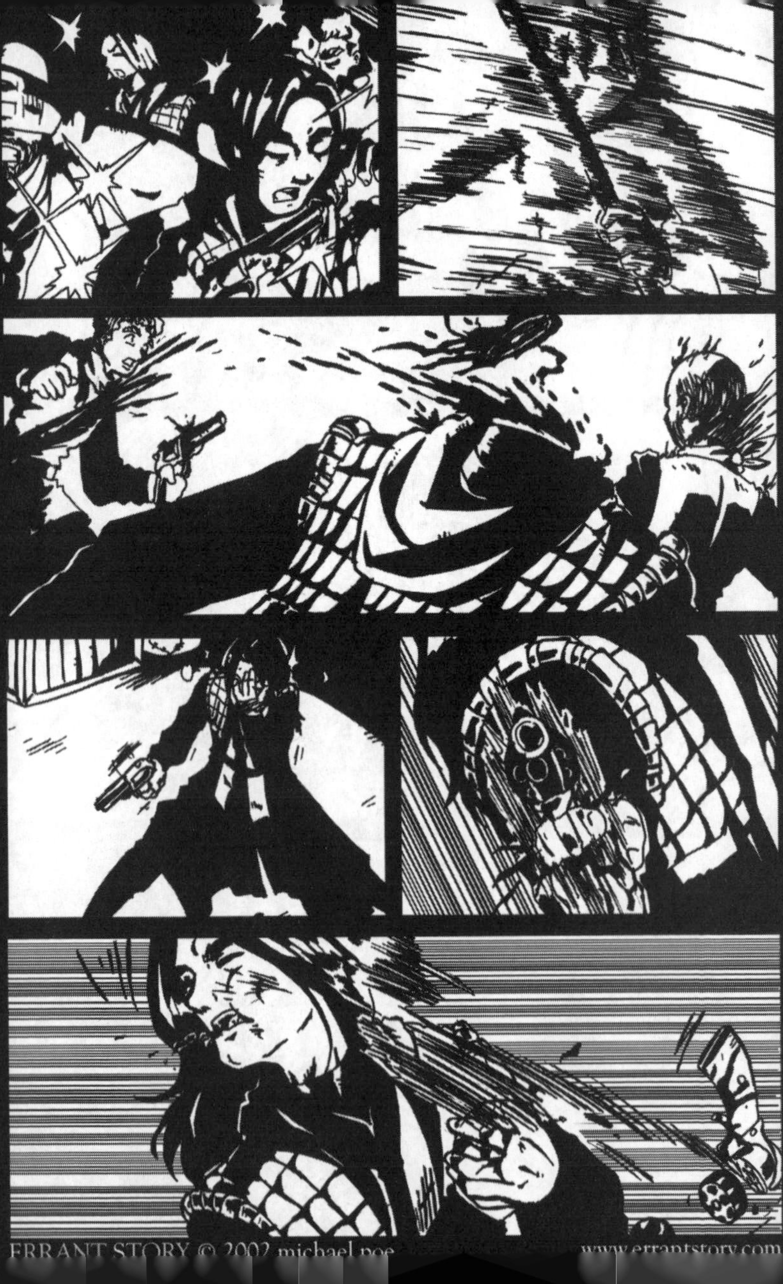

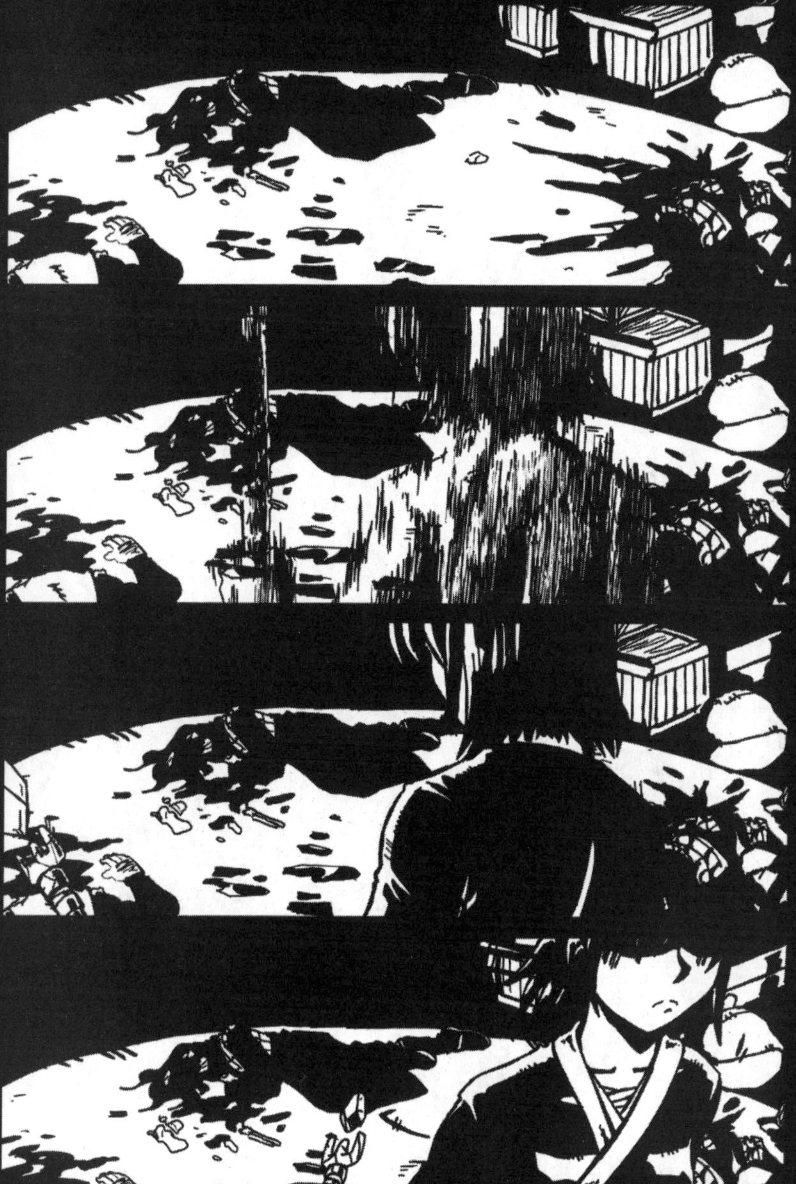

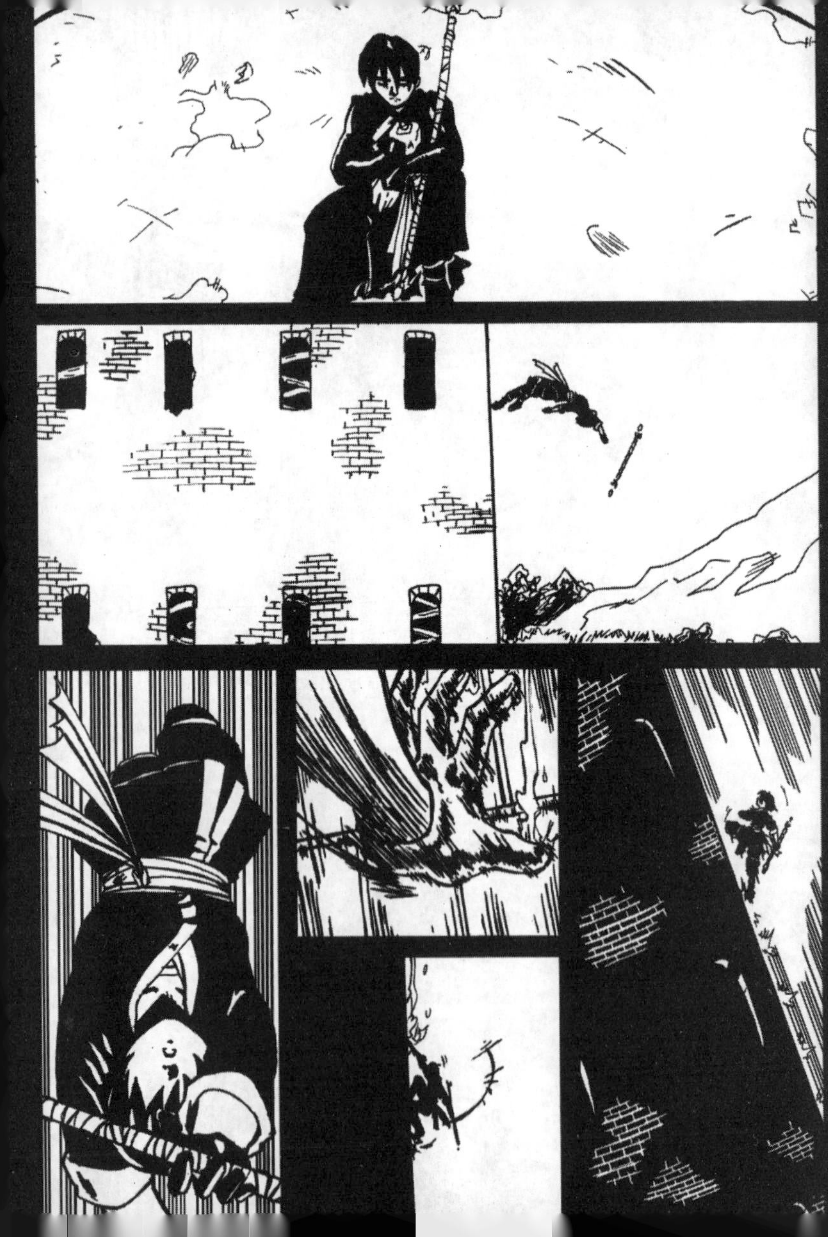

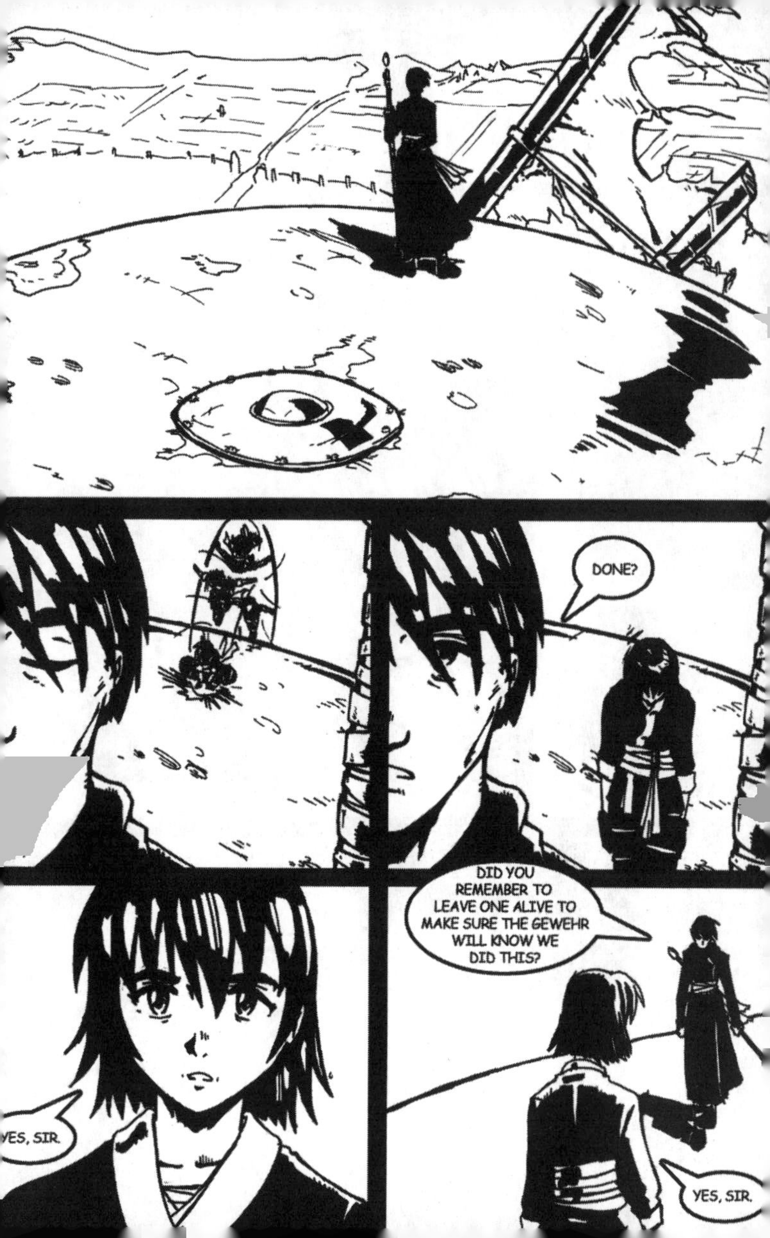
DONE?
YES, SIR.
DID YOU REMEMBER TO LEAVE ONE ALIVE TO MAKE SURE THE GEWEHR WILL KNOW WE DID THIS?
YES, SIR.

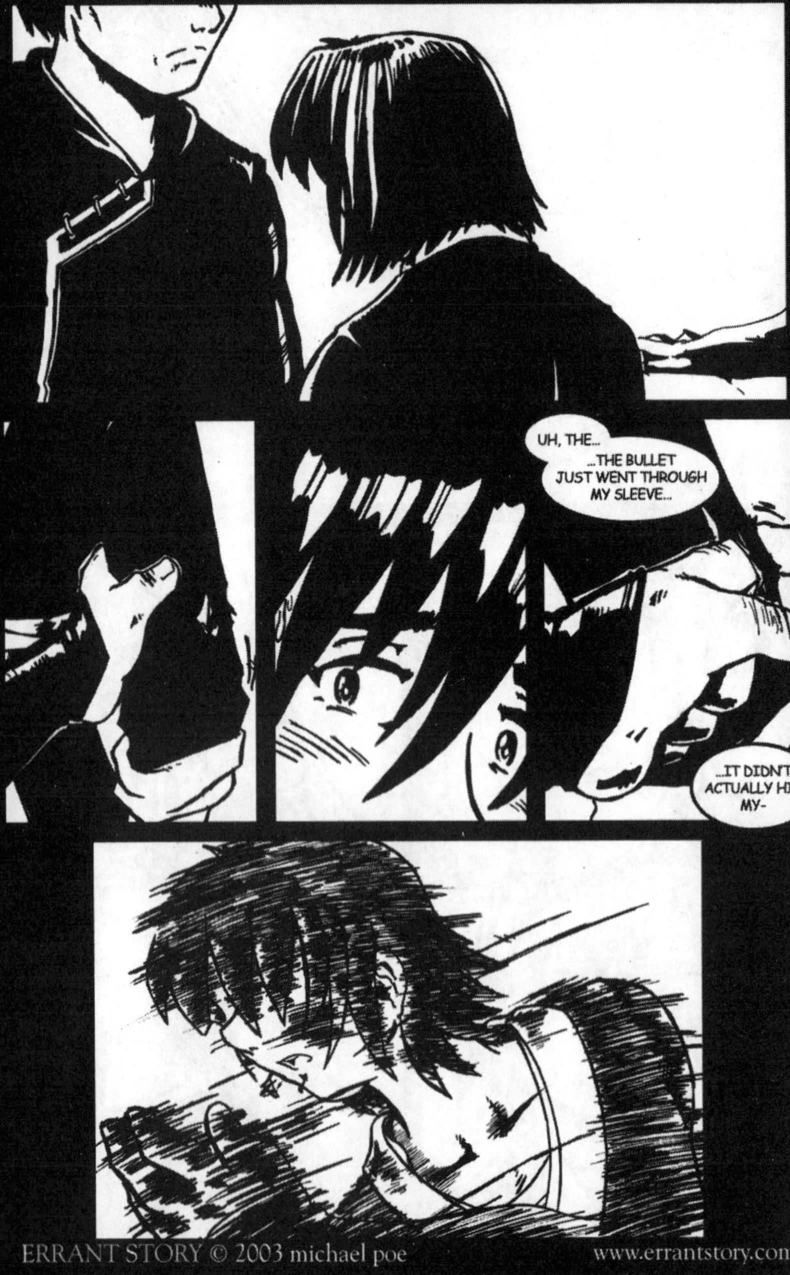
UH, THE...
...THE BULLET JUST WENT THROUGH MY SLEEVE...
...IT DIDN'T ACTUALLY HIT MY-

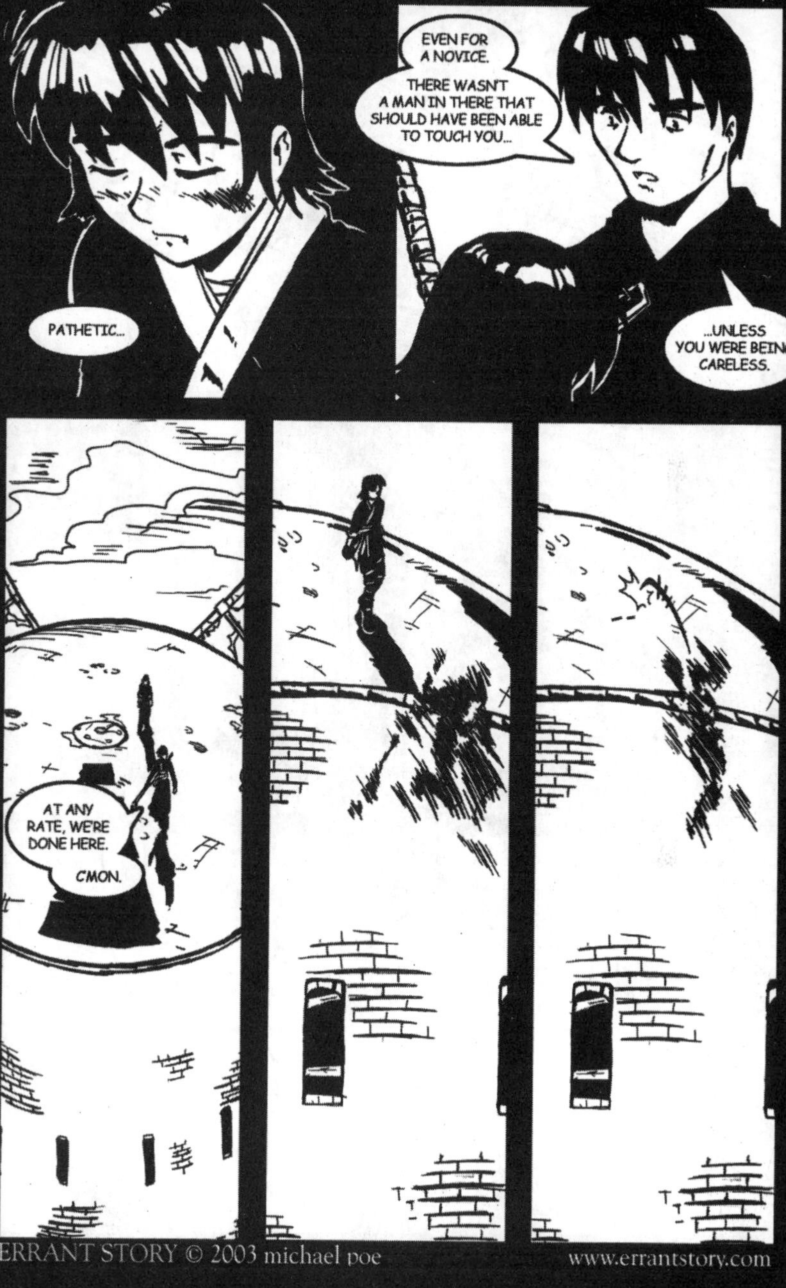
PATHETIC...
EVEN FOR A NOVICE.
THERE WASN'T A MAN IN THERE THAT SHOULD HAVE BEEN ABLE TO TOUCH YOU...
...UNLESS YOU WERE BEING CARELESS.
AT ANY RATE, WE'RE DONE HERE.
C'MON.

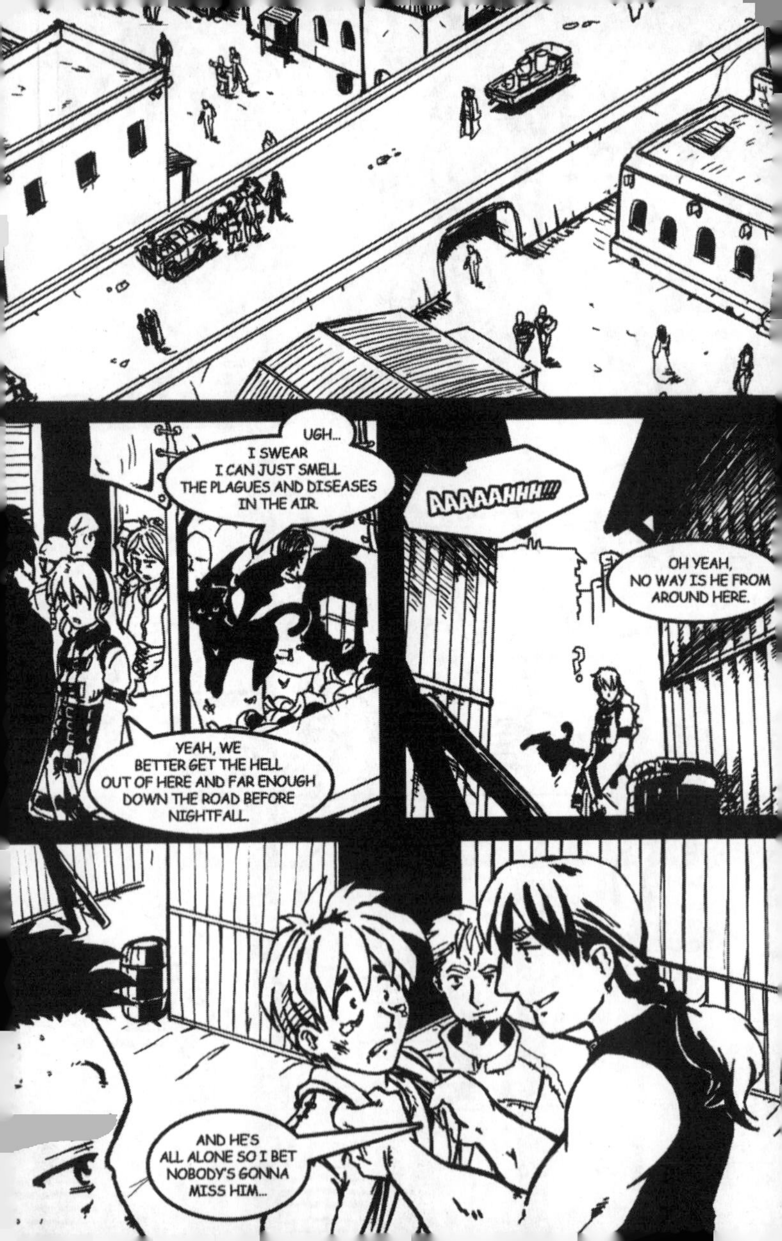
UGH... I SWEAR I CAN JUST SMELL THE PLAGUES AND DISEASES IN THE AIR.
YEAH, WE BETTER GET THE HELL OUT OF HERE AND FAR ENOUGH DOWN THE ROAD BEFORE NIGHTFALL.
AAAAAHHH!!!
OH YEAH, NO WAY IS HE FROM AROUND HERE.
?
AND HE'S ALL ALONE SO I BET NOBODY'S GONNA MISS HIM...

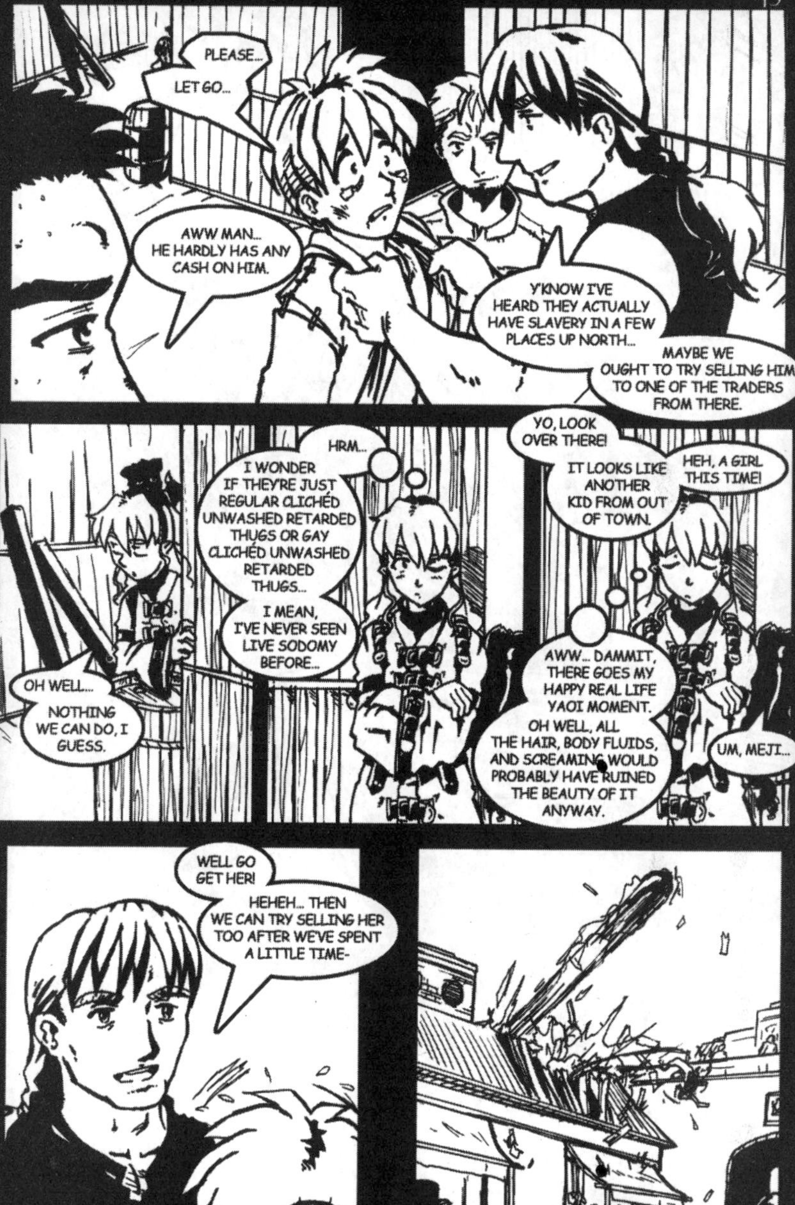
PLEASE...
LET GO...
AWW MAN... HE HARDLY HAS ANY CASH ON HIM.
Y'KNOW I'VE HEARD THEY ACTUALLY HAVE SLAVERY IN A FEW PLACES UP NORTH...
MAYBE WE OUGHT TO TRY SELLING HIM TO ONE OF THE TRADERS FROM THERE.
OH WELL...
NOTHING WE CAN DO, I GUESS.
HRM...
I WONDER IF THEY'RE JUST REGULAR CLICHÉD UNWASHED RETARDED THUGS OR GAY CLICHÉD UNWASHED RETARDED THUGS...
I MEAN, I'VE NEVER SEEN LIVE SODOMY BEFORE...
YO, LOOK OVER THERE!
IT LOOKS LIKE ANOTHER KID FROM OUT OF TOWN.
HEH, A GIRL THIS TIME!
AWW... DAMMIT, THERE GOES MY HAPPY REAL LIFE YAOI MOMENT.
OH WELL, ALL THE HAIR, BODY FLUIDS, AND SCREAMING WOULD PROBABLY HAVE RUINED THE BEAUTY OF IT ANYWAY.
UM, MEJI...
WELL GO GET HER!
HEHEH... THEN WE CAN TRY SELLING HER TOO AFTER WE'VE SPENT A LITTLE TIME-

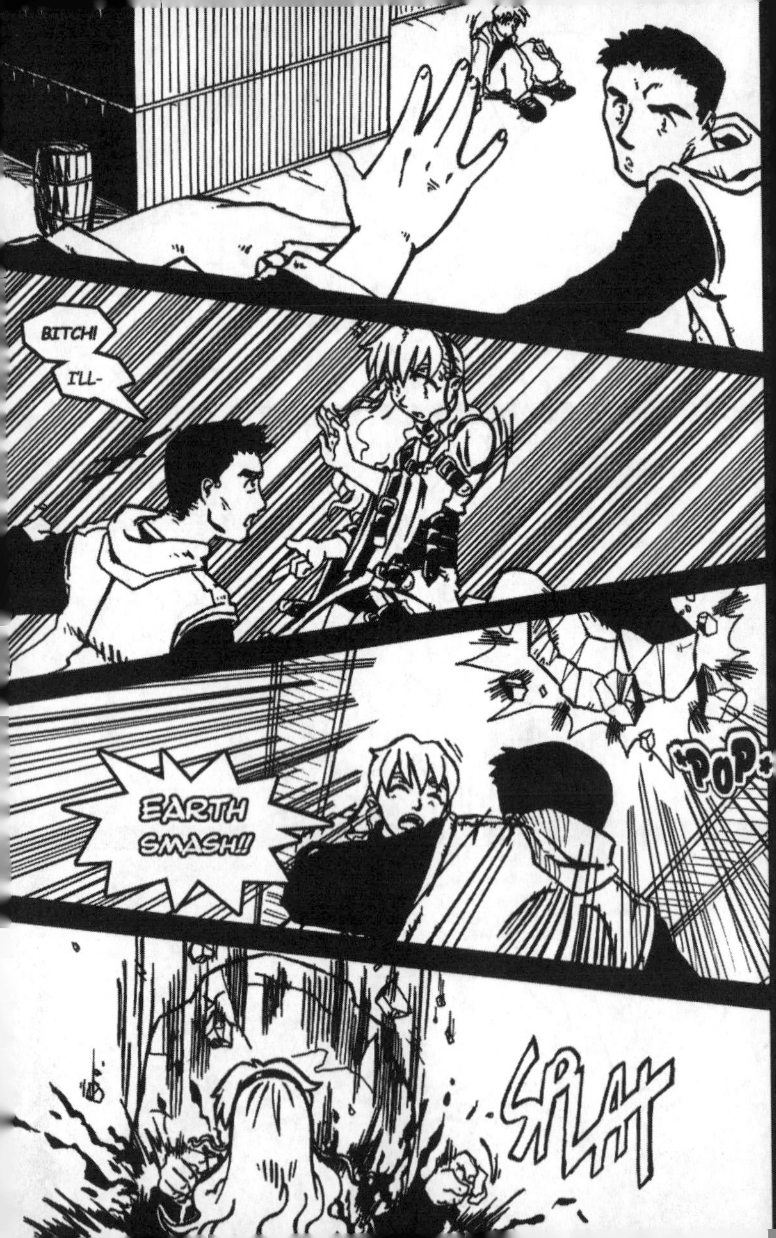
BITCH!
I'LL-
EARTH SMASH!!
POP
SPLAT

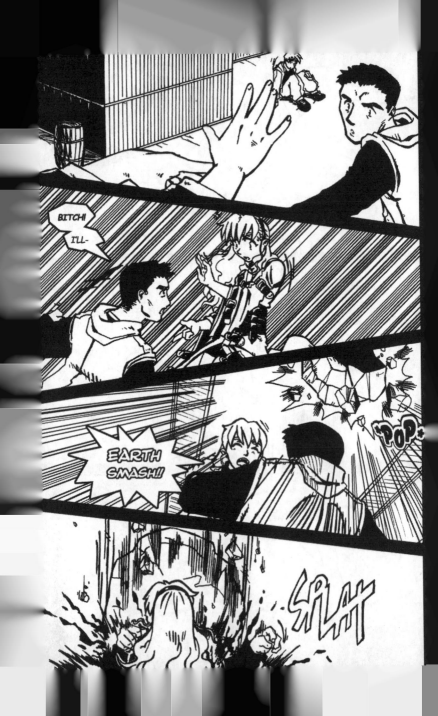

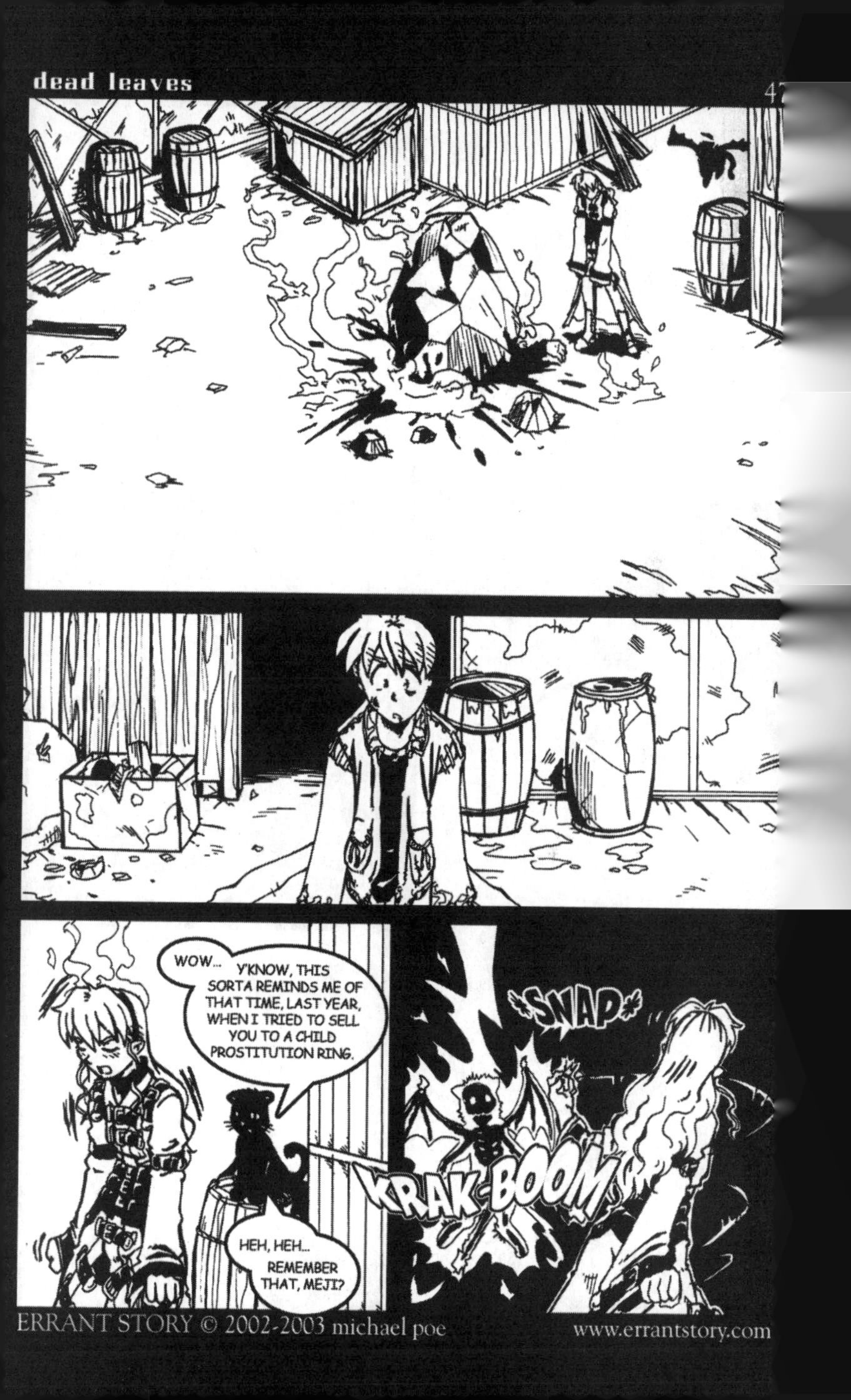
WOW...
Y'KNOW, THIS SORTA REMINDS ME OF THAT TIME, LAST YEAR, WHEN I TRIED TO SELL YOU TO A CHILD PROSTITUTION RING.
HEH, HEH... REMEMBER THAT, MEJI?
SNAP
KRAK-BOOM

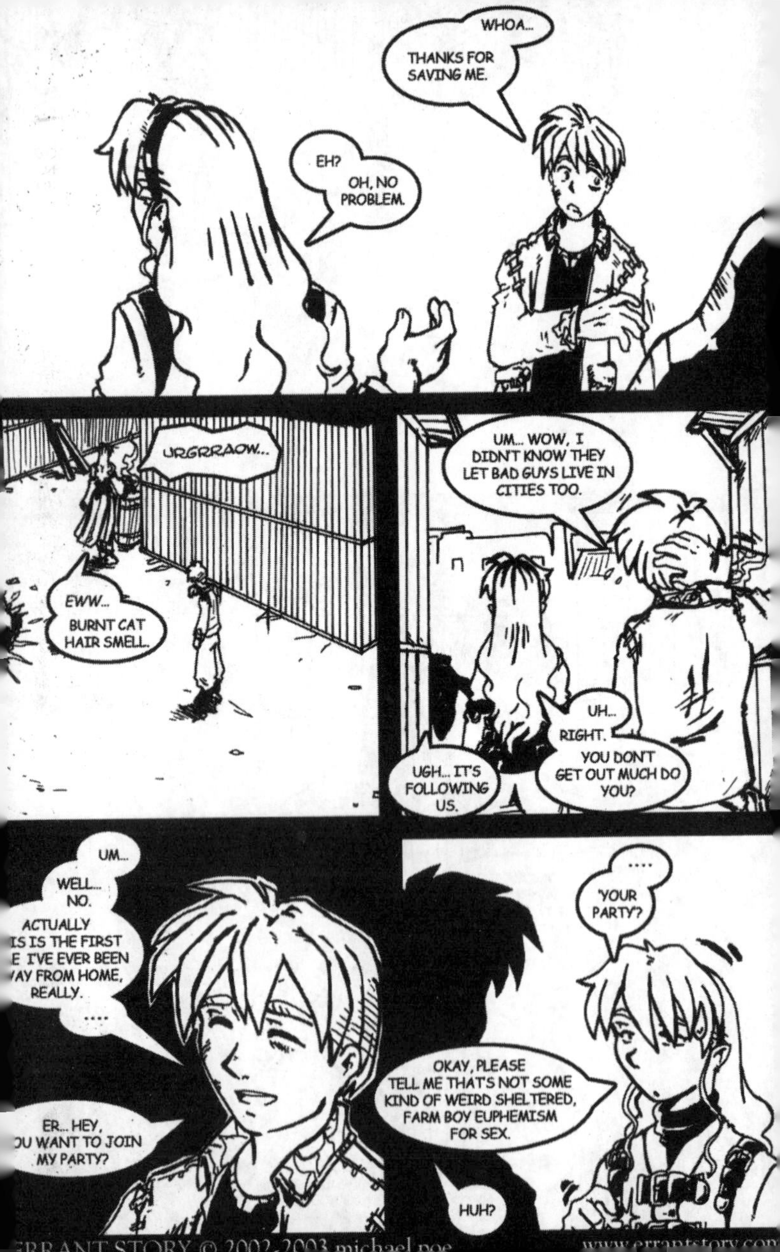
WHOA...
THANKS FOR SAVING ME.
EH?
OH, NO PROBLEM.
URGRRAOW...
EWW...
BURNT CAT HAIR SMELL.
UM... WOW, I DIDN'T KNOW THEY LET BAD GUYS LIVE IN CITIES TOO.
UH...
RIGHT.
YOU DON'T GET OUT MUCH DO YOU?
UGH... IT'S FOLLOWING US.
UM...
WELL...
NO.
ACTUALLY
IS IS THE FIRST
E I'VE EVER BEEN
AY FROM HOME,
REALLY.
....
ER... HEY,
OU WANT TO JOIN
MY PARTY?
....
'YOUR PARTY'?
OKAY, PLEASE TELL ME THAT'S NOT SOME KIND OF WEIRD SHELTERED, FARM BOY EUPHEMISM FOR SEX.
HUH?

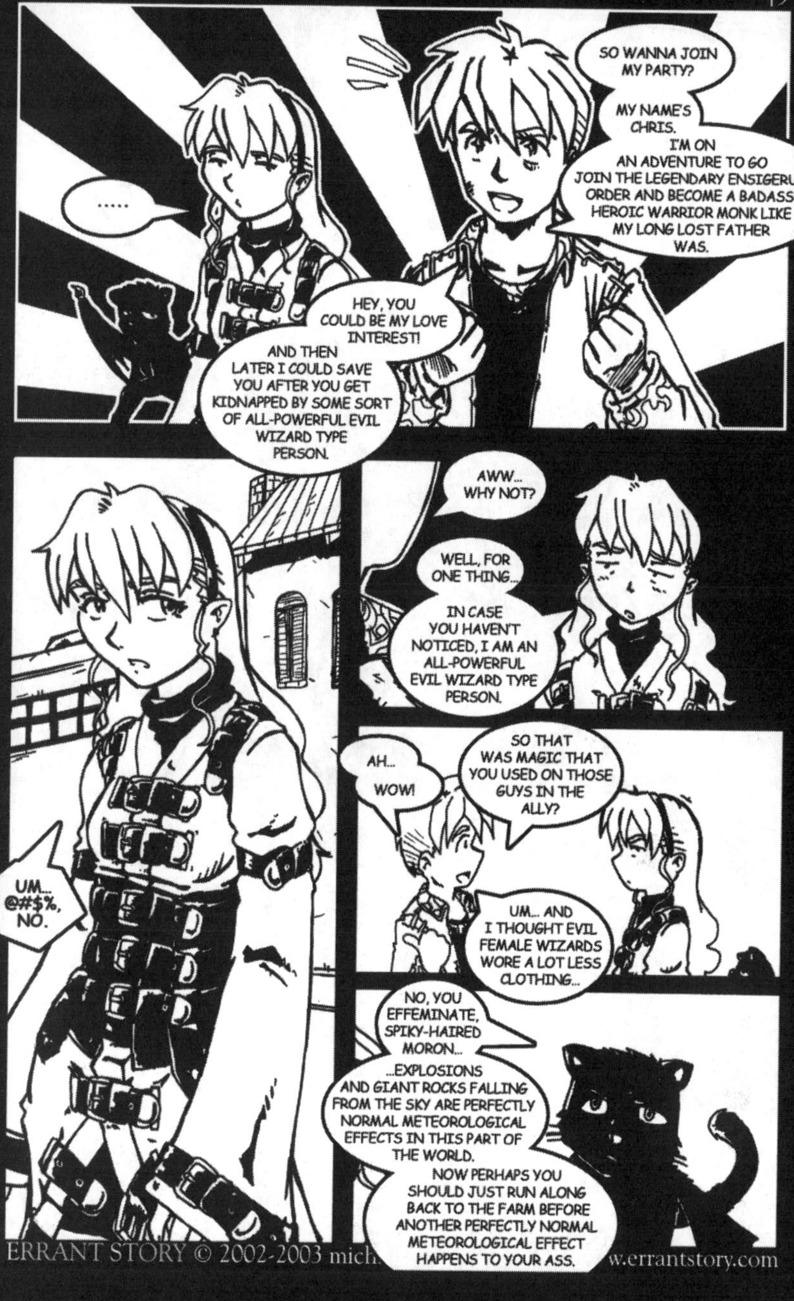
SO WANNA JOIN MY PARTY?
MY NAME'S CHRIS.
I'M ON AN ADVENTURE TO GO JOIN THE LEGENDARY ENSIGERUM ORDER AND BECOME A BADASS, HEROIC WARRIOR MONK LIKE MY LONG LOST FATHER WAS.
.....
HEY, YOU COULD BE MY LOVE INTEREST!
AND THEN LATER I COULD SAVE YOU AFTER YOU GET KIDNAPPED BY SOME SORT OF ALL-POWERFUL EVIL WIZARD TYPE PERSON.
UM... @#$%, NO.
AWW... WHY NOT?
WELL, FOR ONE THING...
IN CASE YOU HAVEN'T NOTICED, I AM AN ALL-POWERFUL EVIL WIZARD TYPE PERSON.
AH...
WOW!
SO THAT WAS MAGIC THAT YOU USED ON THOSE GUYS IN THE ALLY?
UM... AND I THOUGHT EVIL FEMALE WIZARDS WORE A LOT LESS CLOTHING...
NO, YOU EFFEMINATE, SPIKY-HAIRED MORON...
...EXPLOSIONS AND GIANT ROCKS FALLING FROM THE SKY ARE PERFECTLY NORMAL METEOROLOGICAL EFFECTS IN THIS PART OF THE WORLD.
NOW PERHAPS YOU SHOULD JUST RUN ALONG BACK TO THE FARM BEFORE ANOTHER PERFECTLY NORMAL METEOROLOGICAL EFFECT HAPPENS TO YOUR ASS.

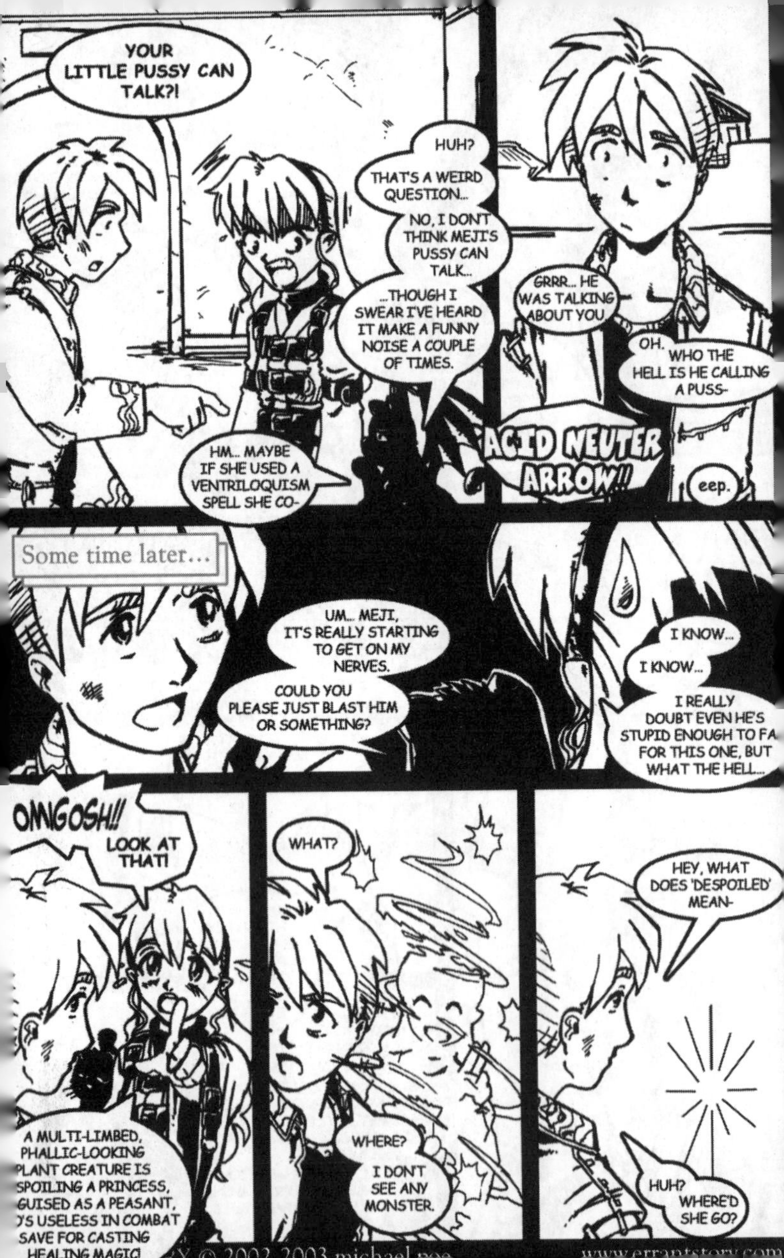
YOUR LITTLE PUSSY CAN TALK?!
HUH?
THAT'S A WEIRD QUESTION...
NO, I DON'T THINK MEJI'S PUSSY CAN TALK...
...THOUGH I SWEAR I'VE HEARD IT MAKE A FUNNY NOISE A COUPLE OF TIMES.
HM... MAYBE IF SHE USED A VENTRILOQUISM SPELL SHE CO-
GRRR... HE WAS TALKING ABOUT YOU.
OH.
WHO THE HELL IS HE CALLING A PUSS-
ACID NEUTER ARROW!!
eep.
Some time later...
UM... MEJI, IT'S REALLY STARTING TO GET ON MY NERVES.
COULD YOU PLEASE JUST BLAST HIM OR SOMETHING?
I KNOW...
I KNOW...
I REALLY DOUBT EVEN HE'S STUPID ENOUGH TO FA FOR THIS ONE, BUT WHAT THE HELL...
OMIGOSH!!
LOOK AT THAT!
A MULTI-LIMBED, PHALLIC-LOOKING PLANT CREATURE IS SPOILING A PRINCESS, GUISED AS A PEASANT, 'S USELESS IN COMBAT SAVE FOR CASTING HEALING MAGIC!
WHAT?
WHERE?
I DON'T SEE ANY MONSTER.
HEY, WHAT DOES 'DESPOILED' MEAN-
HUH? WHERE'D SHE GO?

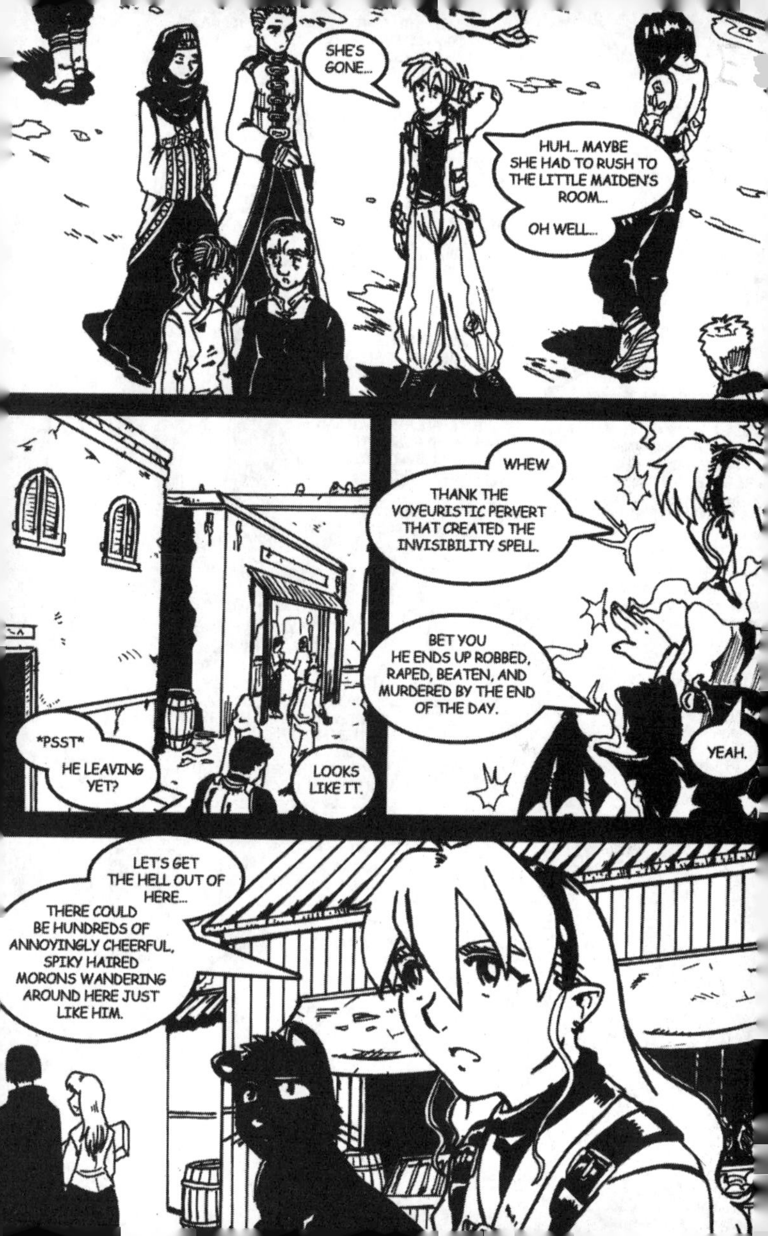
SHE'S GONE...
HUH... MAYBE SHE HAD TO RUSH TO THE LITTLE MAIDEN'S ROOM...
OH WELL...
PSST HE LEAVING YET?
LOOKS LIKE IT.
WHEW
THANK THE VOYEURISTIC PERVERT THAT CREATED THE INVISIBILITY SPELL.
BET YOU HE ENDS UP ROBBED, RAPED, BEATEN, AND MURDERED BY THE END OF THE DAY.
YEAH.
LET'S GET THE HELL OUT OF HERE...
THERE COULD BE HUNDREDS OF ANNOYINGLY CHEERFUL, SPIKY HAIRED MORONS WANDERING AROUND HERE JUST LIKE HIM.

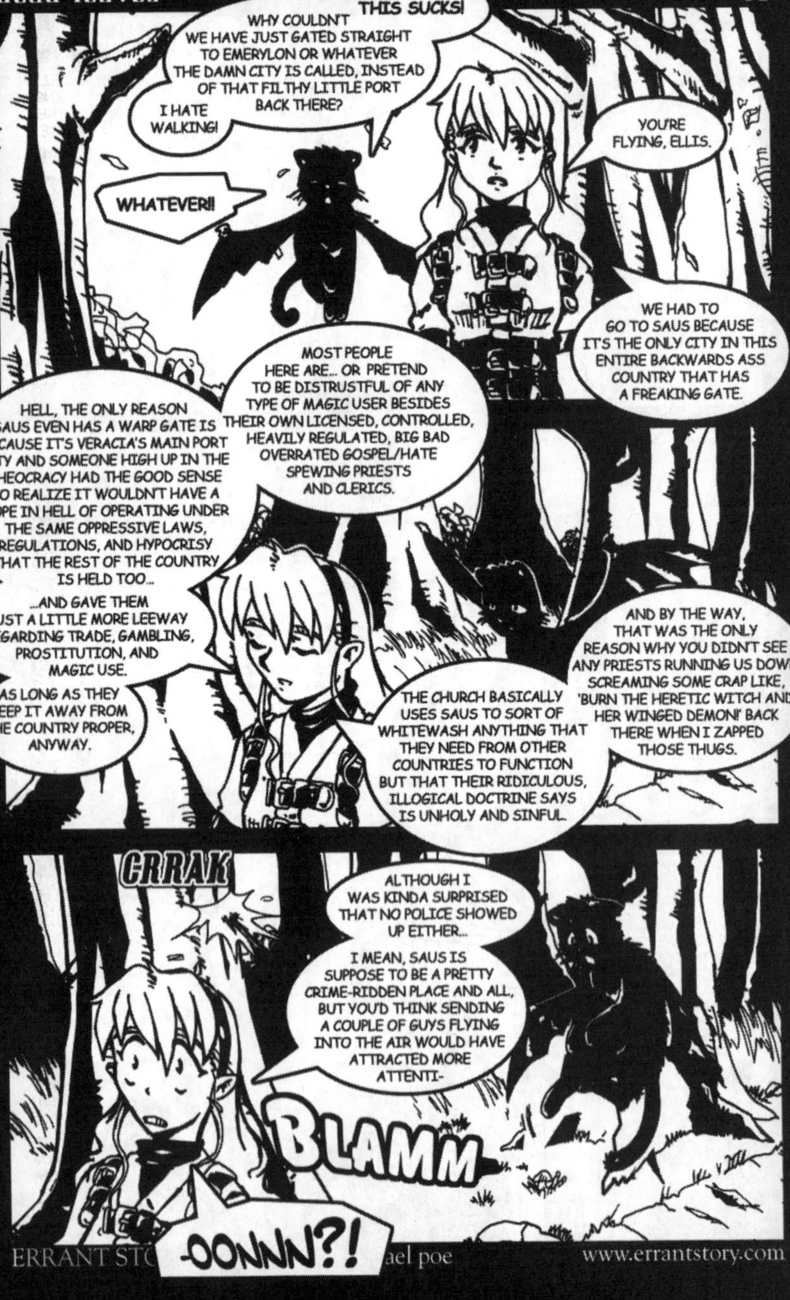
THIS SUCKS!
WHY COULDN'T WE HAVE JUST GATED STRAIGHT TO EMERYLON OR WHATEVER THE DAMN CITY IS CALLED, INSTEAD OF THAT FILTHY LITTLE PORT BACK THERE?
I HATE WALKING!
YOU'RE FLYING, ELLIS.
WHATEVER!!
WE HAD TO GO TO SAUS BECAUSE IT'S THE ONLY CITY IN THIS ENTIRE BACKWARDS ASS COUNTRY THAT HAS A FREAKING GATE.
MOST PEOPLE HERE ARE... OR PRETEND TO BE DISTRUSTFUL OF ANY TYPE OF MAGIC USER BESIDES THEIR OWN LICENSED, CONTROLLED, HEAVILY REGULATED, BIG BAD OVERRATED GOSPEL/HATE SPEWING PRIESTS AND CLERICS.
HELL, THE ONLY REASON SAUS EVEN HAS A WARP GATE IS BECAUSE IT'S VERACIA'S MAIN PORT CITY AND SOMEONE HIGH UP IN THE THEOCRACY HAD THE GOOD SENSE TO REALIZE IT WOULDN'T HAVE A HOPE IN HELL OF OPERATING UNDER THE SAME OPPRESSIVE LAWS, REGULATIONS, AND HYPOCRISY THAT THE REST OF THE COUNTRY IS HELD TOO...
...AND GAVE THEM JUST A LITTLE MORE LEEWAY REGARDING TRADE, GAMBLING, PROSTITUTION, AND MAGIC USE.
AS LONG AS THEY KEEP IT AWAY FROM THE COUNTRY PROPER, ANYWAY.
THE CHURCH BASICALLY USES SAUS TO SORT OF WHITEWASH ANYTHING THAT THEY NEED FROM OTHER COUNTRIES TO FUNCTION BUT THAT THEIR RIDICULOUS, ILLOGICAL DOCTRINE SAYS IS UNHOLY AND SINFUL.
AND BY THE WAY, THAT WAS THE ONLY REASON WHY YOU DIDN'T SEE ANY PRIESTS RUNNING US DOW SCREAMING SOME CRAP LIKE, 'BURN THE HERETIC WITCH AND HER WINGED DEMON!' BACK THERE WHEN I ZAPPED THOSE THUGS.
CRRAK
ALTHOUGH I WAS KINDA SURPRISED THAT NO POLICE SHOWED UP EITHER...
I MEAN, SAUS IS SUPPOSE TO BE A PRETTY CRIME-RIDDEN PLACE AND ALL, BUT YOU'D THINK SENDING A COUPLE OF GUYS FLYING INTO THE AIR WOULD HAVE ATTRACTED MORE ATTENTI-
BLAMM
-OONNN?!

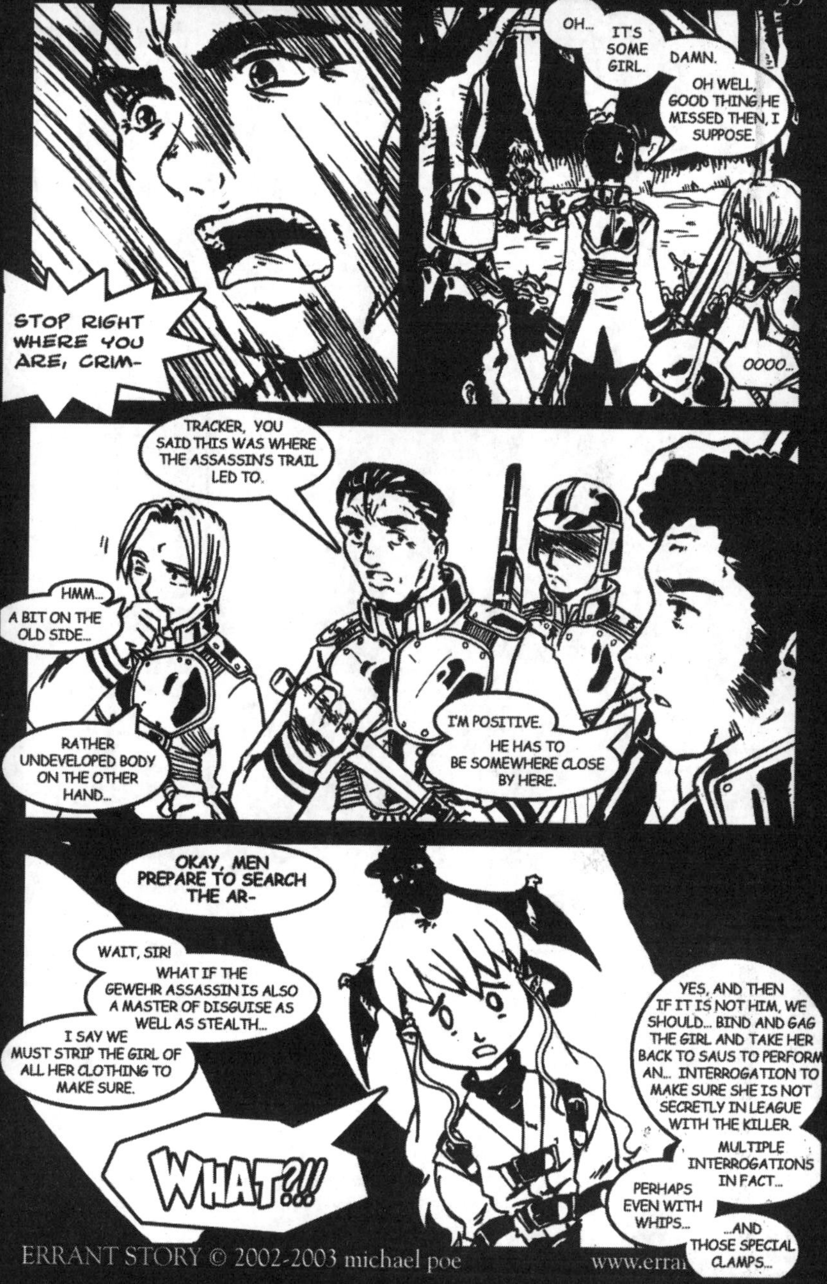
STOP RIGHT WHERE YOU ARE, CRIM-
OH...
IT'S SOME GIRL.
DAMN.
OH WELL, GOOD THING HE MISSED THEN, I SUPPOSE.
OOOO...
TRACKER, YOU SAID THIS WAS WHERE THE ASSASSIN'S TRAIL LED TO.
HMM... A BIT ON THE OLD SIDE...
RATHER UNDEVELOPED BODY ON THE OTHER HAND...
I'M POSITIVE.
HE HAS TO BE SOMEWHERE CLOSE BY HERE.
OKAY, MEN PREPARE TO SEARCH THE AR-
WAIT, SIR!
WHAT IF THE GEWEHR ASSASSIN IS ALSO A MASTER OF DISGUISE AS WELL AS STEALTH...
I SAY WE MUST STRIP THE GIRL OF ALL HER CLOTHING TO MAKE SURE.
WHAT?!!
YES, AND THEN IF IT IS NOT HIM, WE SHOULD... BIND AND GAG THE GIRL AND TAKE HER BACK TO SAUS TO PERFORM AN... INTERROGATION TO MAKE SURE SHE IS NOT SECRETLY IN LEAGUE WITH THE KILLER.
MULTIPLE INTERROGATIONS IN FACT...
PERHAPS EVEN WITH WHIPS...
...AND THOSE SPECIAL CLAMPS...

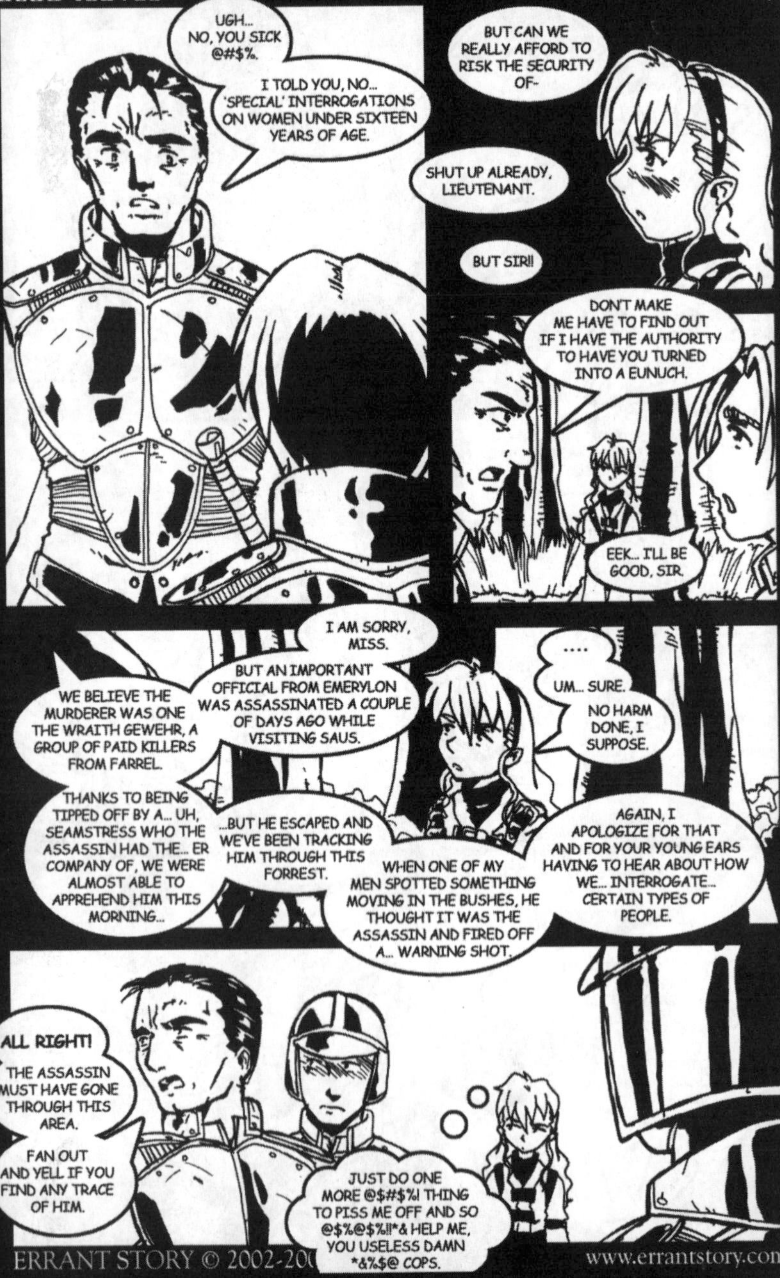
UGH... NO, YOU SICK @#$%.
I TOLD YOU, NO... 'SPECIAL' INTERROGATIONS ON WOMEN UNDER SIXTEEN YEARS OF AGE.
BUT CAN WE REALLY AFFORD TO RISK THE SECURITY OF-
SHUT UP ALREADY, LIEUTENANT.
BUT SIR!!
DON'T MAKE ME HAVE TO FIND OUT IF I HAVE THE AUTHORITY TO HAVE YOU TURNED INTO A EUNUCH.
EEK... I'LL BE GOOD, SIR.
I AM SORRY, MISS.
BUT AN IMPORTANT OFFICIAL FROM EMERYLON WAS ASSASSINATED A COUPLE OF DAYS AGO WHILE VISITING SAUS.
WE BELIEVE THE MURDERER WAS ONE THE WRAITH GEWEHR, A GROUP OF PAID KILLERS FROM FARREL.
THANKS TO BEING TIPPED OFF BY A... UH, SEAMSTRESS WHO THE ASSASSIN HAD THE... ER COMPANY OF, WE WERE ALMOST ABLE TO APPREHEND HIM THIS MORNING...
...BUT HE ESCAPED AND WE'VE BEEN TRACKING HIM THROUGH THIS FORREST.
WHEN ONE OF MY MEN SPOTTED SOMETHING MOVING IN THE BUSHES, HE THOUGHT IT WAS THE ASSASSIN AND FIRED OFF A... WARNING SHOT.
AGAIN, I APOLOGIZE FOR THAT AND FOR YOUR YOUNG EARS HAVING TO HEAR ABOUT HOW WE... INTERROGATE... CERTAIN TYPES OF PEOPLE.
....
UM... SURE.
NO HARM DONE, I SUPPOSE.
ALL RIGHT!
THE ASSASSIN MUST HAVE GONE THROUGH THIS AREA.
FAN OUT AND YELL IF YOU FIND ANY TRACE OF HIM.
JUST DO ONE MORE @$#$%! THING TO PISS ME OFF AND SO @$%@$%!!*& HELP ME, YOU USELESS DAMN *&%$@ COPS.

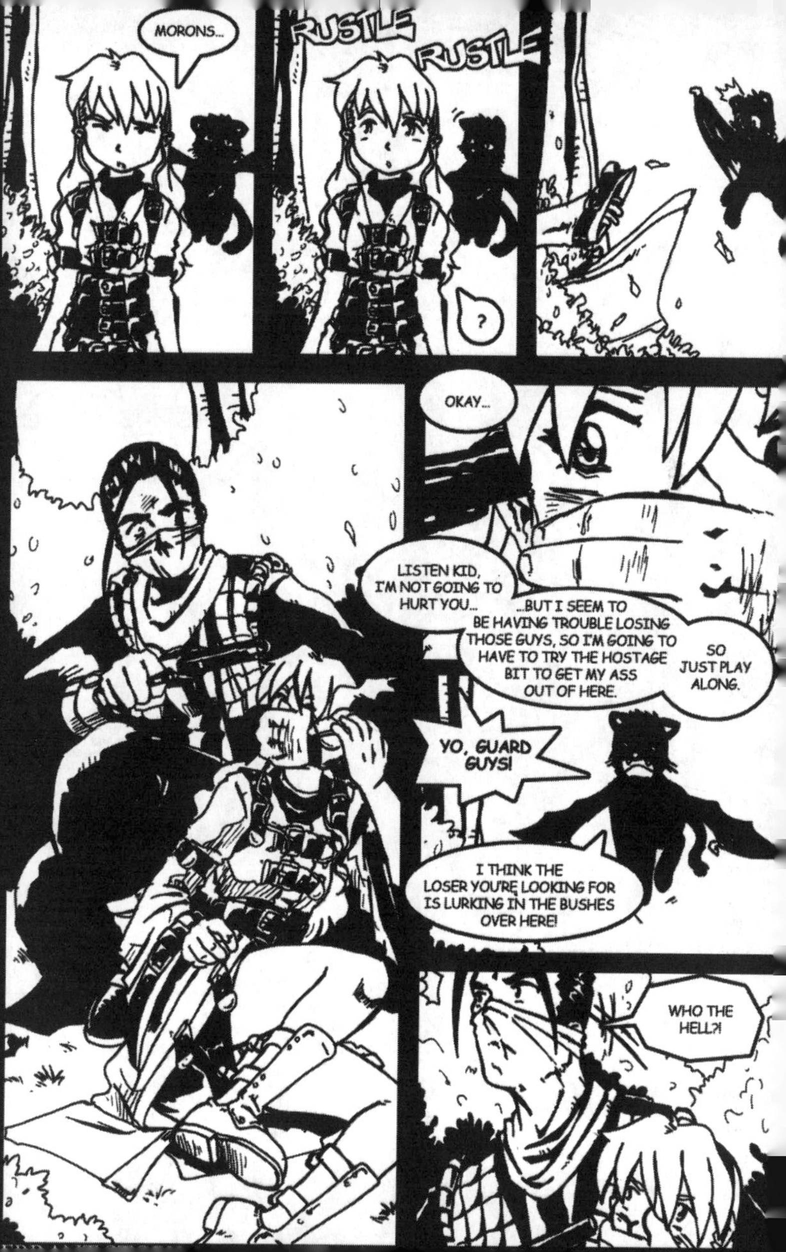

MORONS...
RUSTLE RUSTLE
?
OKAY...
LISTEN KID, I'M NOT GOING TO HURT YOU...
...BUT I SEEM TO BE HAVING TROUBLE LOSING THOSE GUYS, SO I'M GOING TO HAVE TO TRY THE HOSTAGE BIT TO GET MY ASS OUT OF HERE.
SO JUST PLAY ALONG.
YO, GUARD GUYS!
I THINK THE LOSER YOU'RE LOOKING FOR IS LURKING IN THE BUSHES OVER HERE!
WHO THE HELL?!

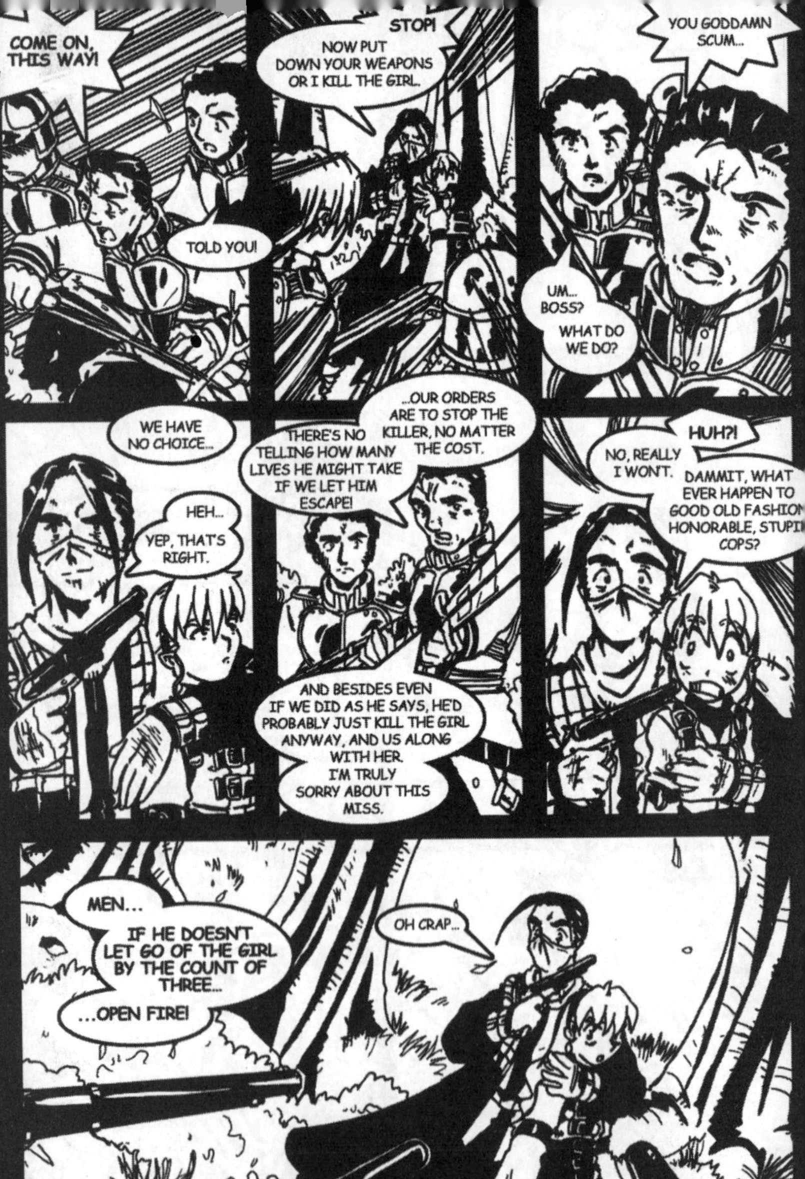
COME ON, THIS WAY!
TOLD YOU!
STOP!
NOW PUT DOWN YOUR WEAPONS OR I KILL THE GIRL.
YOU GODDAMN SCUM...
UM... BOSS?
WHAT DO WE DO?
WE HAVE NO CHOICE...
HEH... YEP, THAT'S RIGHT.
...OUR ORDERS ARE TO STOP THE KILLER, NO MATTER THE COST.
THERE'S NO TELLING HOW MANY LIVES HE MIGHT TAKE IF WE LET HIM ESCAPE!
AND BESIDES EVEN IF WE DID AS HE SAYS, HE'D PROBABLY JUST KILL THE GIRL ANYWAY, AND US ALONG WITH HER.
I'M TRULY SORRY ABOUT THIS MISS.
HUH?!
NO, REALLY I WON'T.
DAMMIT, WHAT EVER HAPPEN TO GOOD OLD FASHIO HONORABLE, STUPI COPS?
MEN...
IF HE DOESN'T LET GO OF THE GIRL BY THE COUNT OF THREE...
...OPEN FIRE!
OH CRAP...

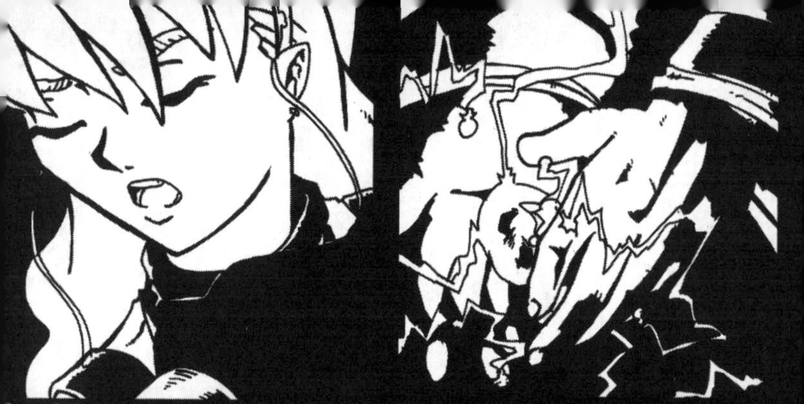

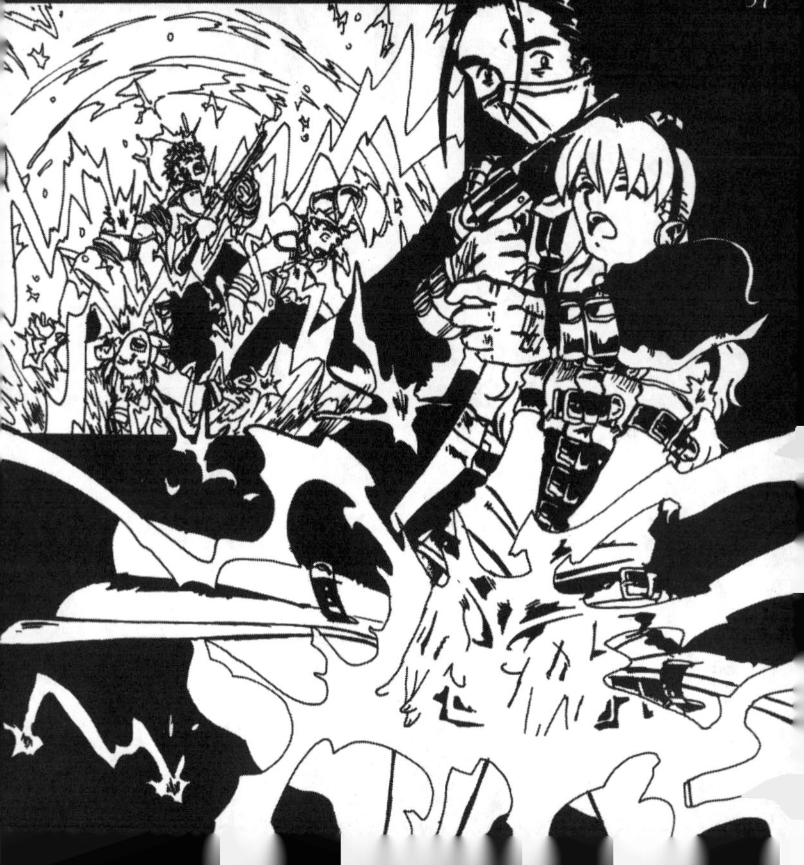

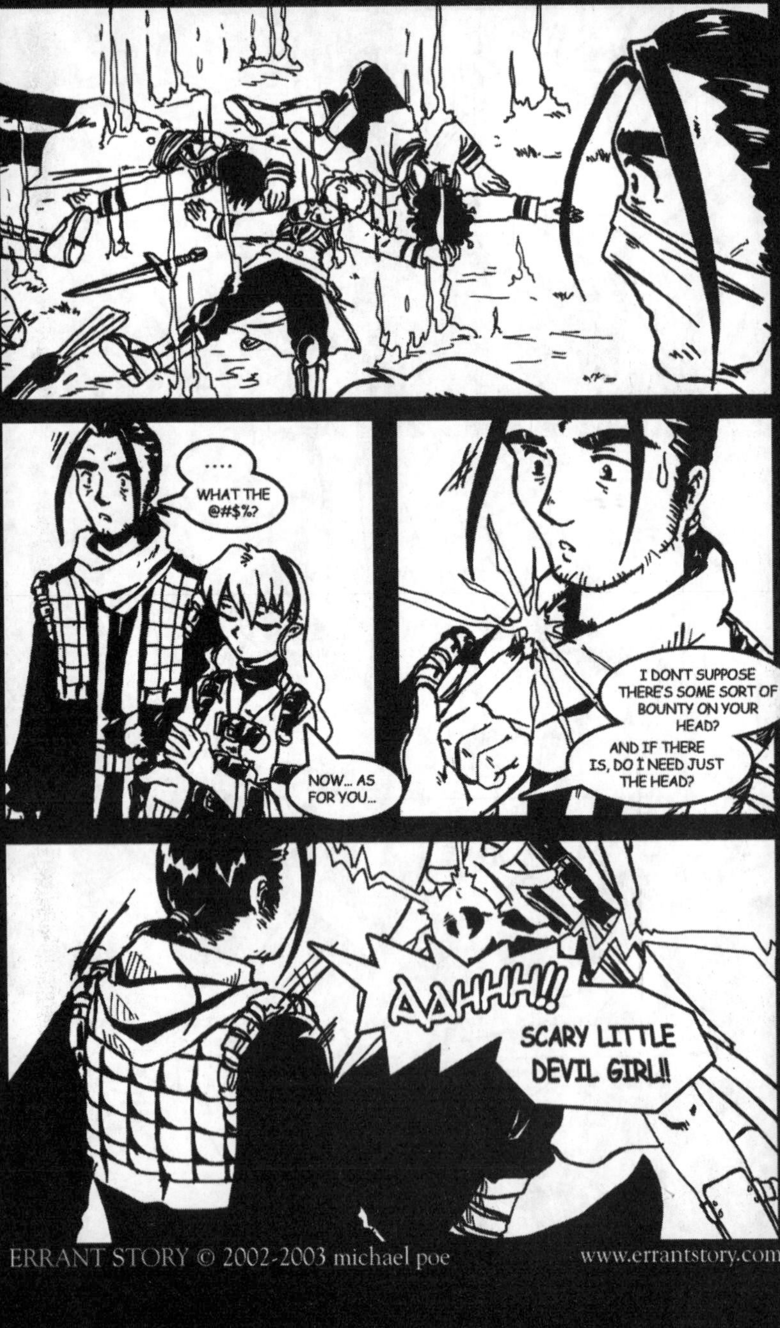
....
WHAT THE @#$%?
NOW... AS FOR YOU...
I DON'T SUPPOSE THERE'S SOME SORT OF BOUNTY ON YOUR HEAD?
AND IF THERE IS, DO I NEED JUST THE HEAD?
AAHHH!!
SCARY LITTLE DEVIL GIRL!!

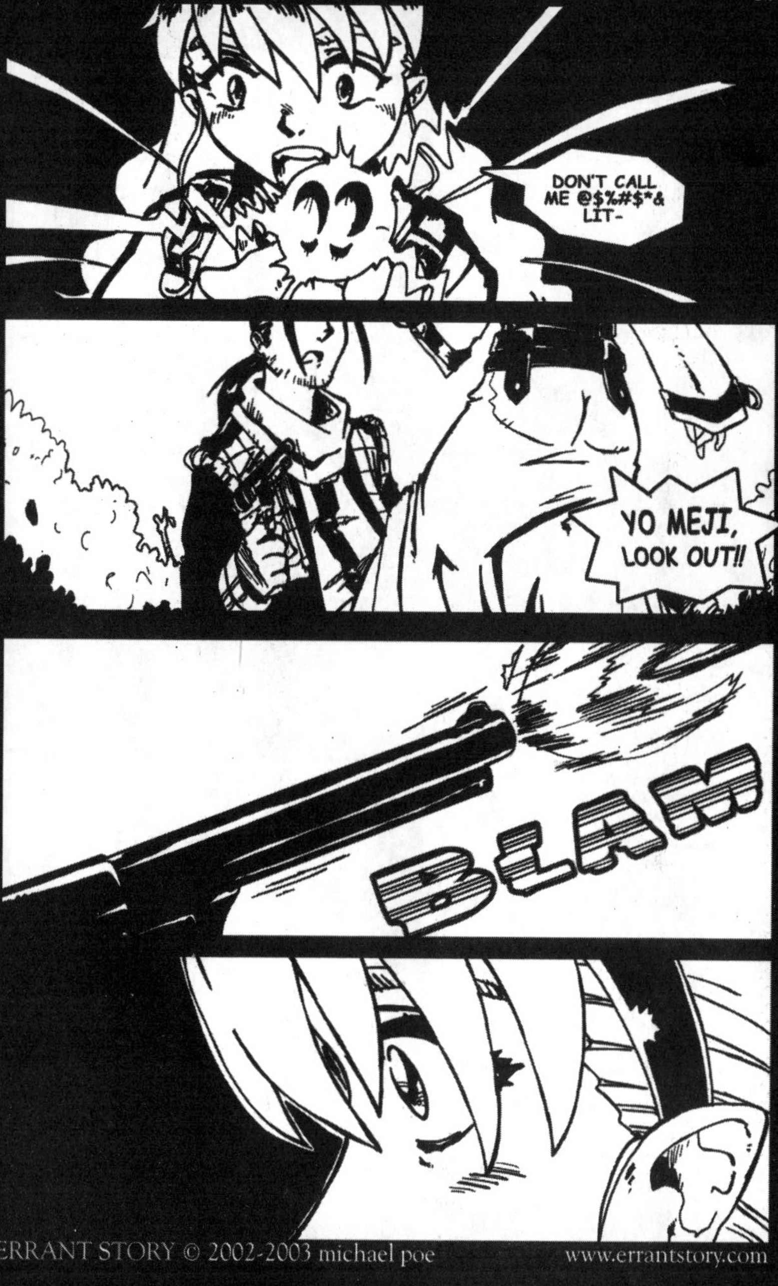
DON'T CALL ME @$%#$*& LIT-
YO MEJI, LOOK OUT!!
BLAM

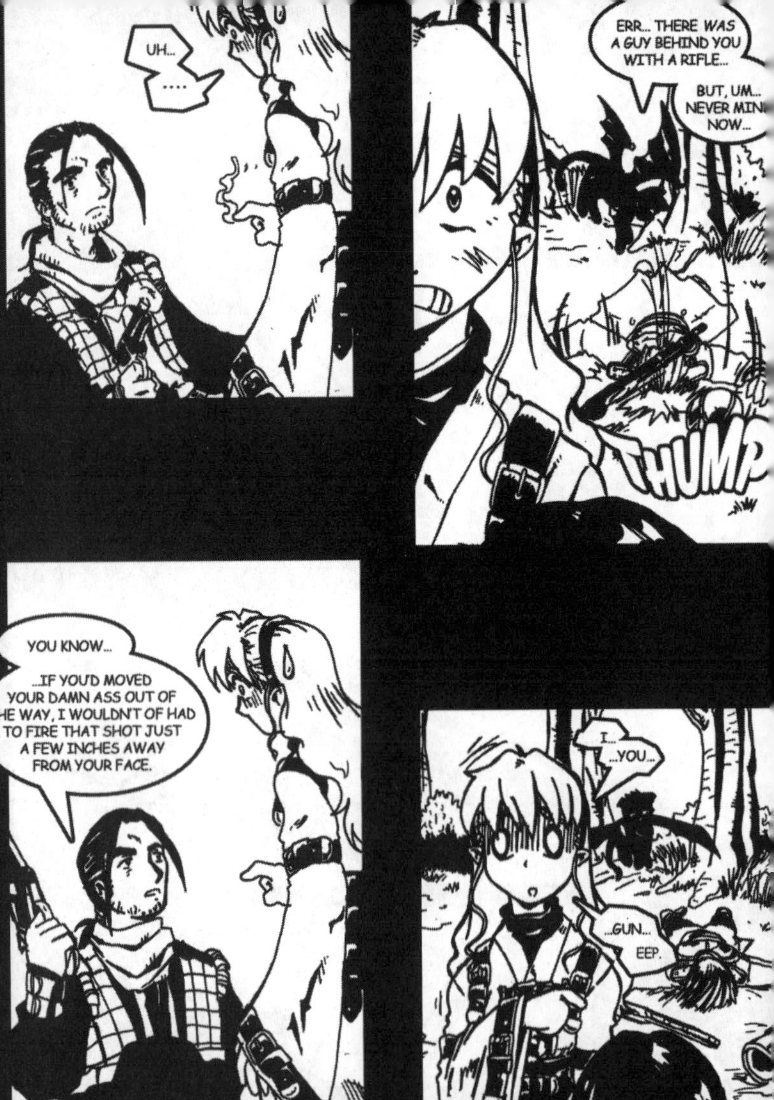
UH...
....
ERR... THERE WAS A GUY BEHIND YOU WITH A RIFLE...
BUT, UM... NEVER MIN NOW...
HUMP
YOU KNOW...
...IF YOU'D MOVED YOUR DAMN ASS OUT OF THE WAY, I WOULDN'T OF HAD TO FIRE THAT SHOT JUST A FEW INCHES AWAY FROM YOUR FACE.
I... ...YOU...
...GUN... EEP.

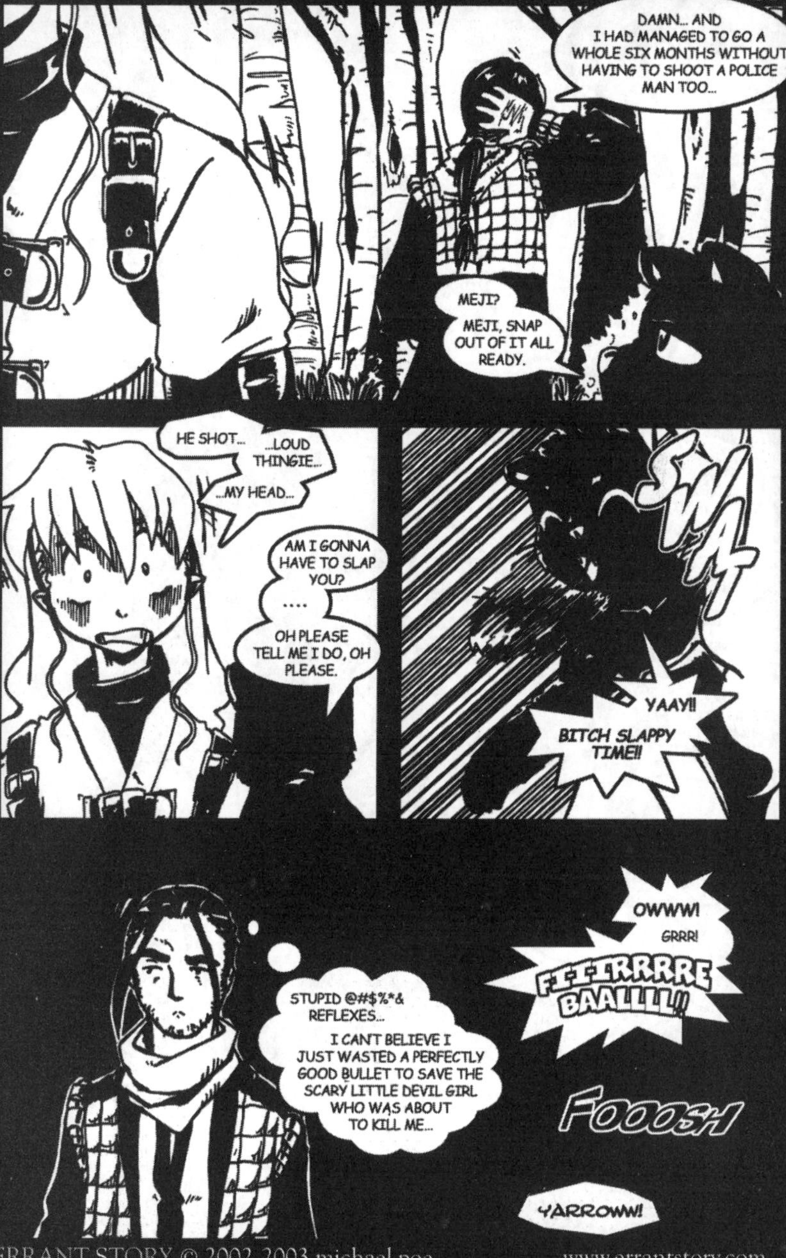
DAMN... AND I HAD MANAGED TO GO A WHOLE SIX MONTHS WITHOUT HAVING TO SHOOT A POLICE MAN TOO...
MEJI?
MEJI, SNAP OUT OF IT ALL READY.
HE SHOT...
...LOUD THINGIE...
...MY HEAD...
AM I GONNA HAVE TO SLAP YOU?
....
OH PLEASE TELL ME I DO, OH PLEASE.
SWAT
YAAY!!
BITCH SLAPPY TIME!!
STUPID @#$%*& REFLEXES...
I CAN'T BELIEVE I JUST WASTED A PERFECTLY GOOD BULLET TO SAVE THE SCARY LITTLE DEVIL GIRL WHO WAS ABOUT TO KILL ME...
OWWW!
GRRR!
FIIIRRRRE BAALLLL!!
FOOOSH
YARROWW!

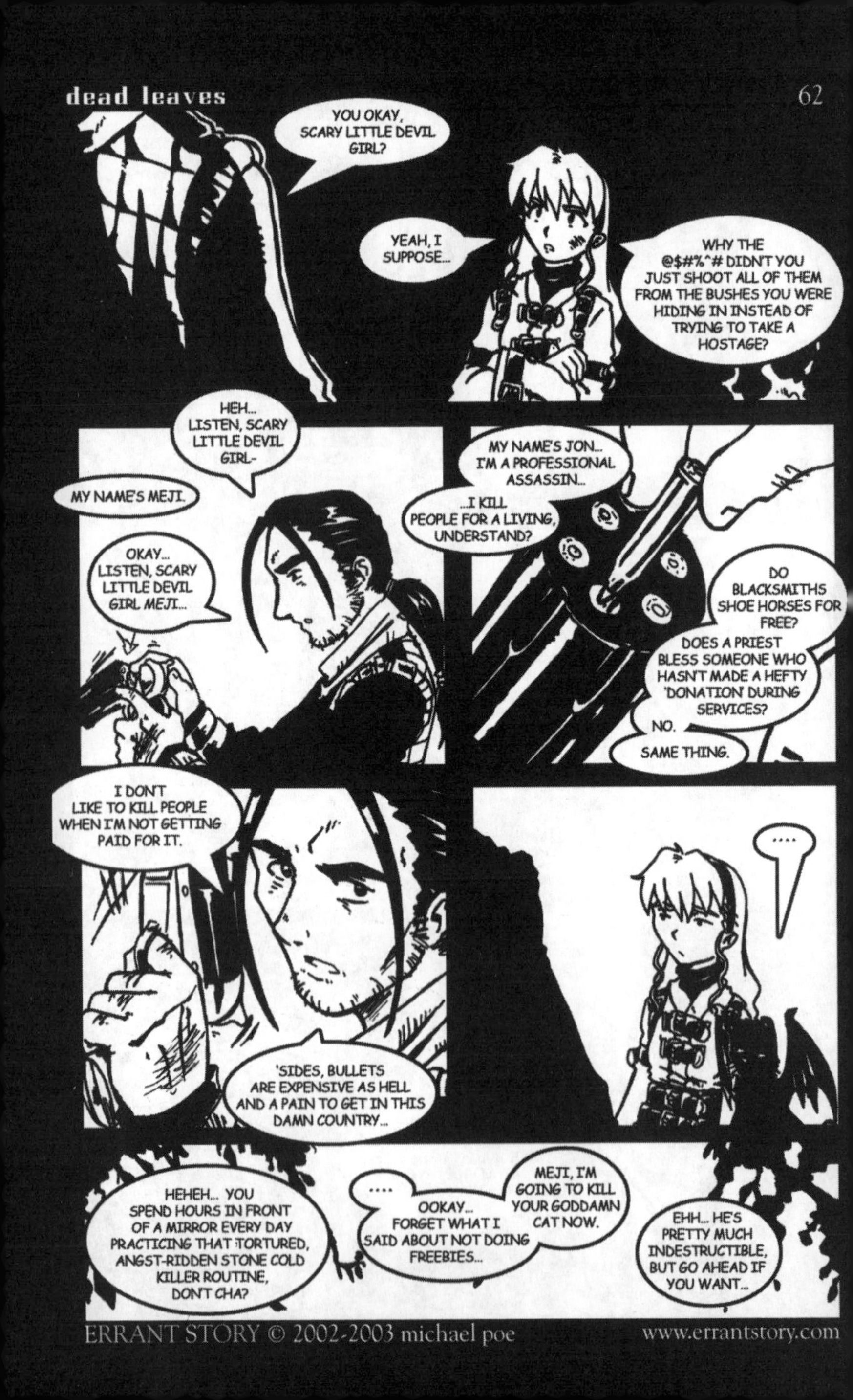
YOU OKAY, SCARY LITTLE DEVIL GIRL?
YEAH, I SUPPOSE...
WHY THE @$#%^# DIDN'T YOU JUST SHOOT ALL OF THEM FROM THE BUSHES YOU WERE HIDING IN INSTEAD OF TRYING TO TAKE A HOSTAGE?
HEH... LISTEN, SCARY LITTLE DEVIL GIRL-
MY NAME'S MEJI.
OKAY... LISTEN, SCARY LITTLE DEVIL GIRL MEJI...
MY NAME'S JON... I'M A PROFESSIONAL ASSASSIN...
...I KILL PEOPLE FOR A LIVING, UNDERSTAND?
DO BLACKSMITHS SHOE HORSES FOR FREE?
DOES A PRIEST BLESS SOMEONE WHO HASN'T MADE A HEFTY 'DONATION' DURING SERVICES?
NO.
SAME THING.
I DON'T LIKE TO KILL PEOPLE WHEN I'M NOT GETTING PAID FOR IT.
'SIDES, BULLETS ARE EXPENSIVE AS HELL AND A PAIN TO GET IN THIS DAMN COUNTRY...
....
HEHEH... YOU SPEND HOURS IN FRONT OF A MIRROR EVERY DAY PRACTICING THAT TORTURED, ANGST-RIDDEN STONE COLD KILLER ROUTINE, DON'T CHA?
....
OOKAY... FORGET WHAT I SAID ABOUT NOT DOING FREEBIES...
MEJI, I'M GOING TO KILL YOUR GODDAMN CAT NOW.
EHH... HE'S PRETTY MUCH INDESTRUCTIBLE, BUT GO AHEAD IF YOU WANT...

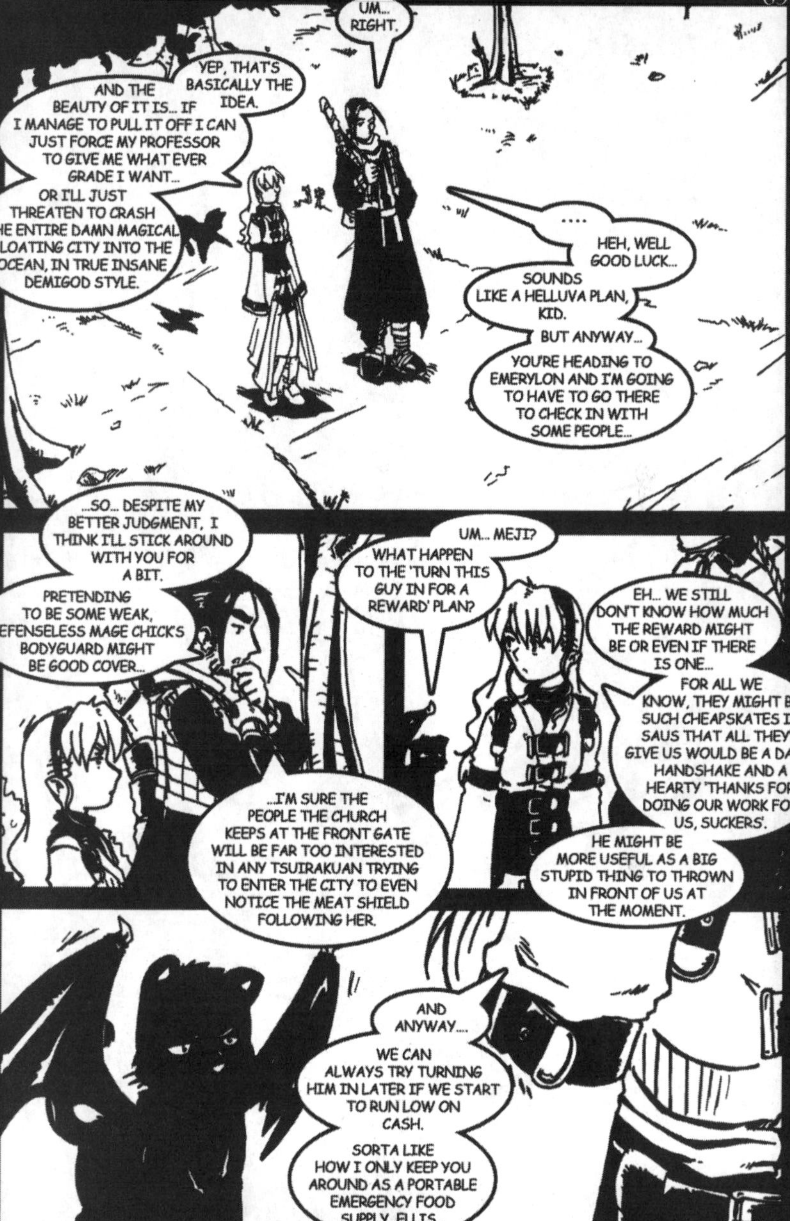
AND THE BEAUTY OF IT IS... IF I MANAGE TO PULL IT OFF I CAN JUST FORCE MY PROFESSOR TO GIVE ME WHAT EVER GRADE I WANT...
OR I'LL JUST THREATEN TO CRASH THE ENTIRE DAMN MAGICAL FLOATING CITY INTO THE OCEAN, IN TRUE INSANE DEMIGOD STYLE.
YEP, THAT'S BASICALLY THE IDEA.
UM... RIGHT.
....
HEH, WELL GOOD LUCK...
SOUNDS LIKE A HELLUVA PLAN, KID.
BUT ANYWAY...
YOU'RE HEADING TO EMERYLON AND I'M GOING TO HAVE TO GO THERE TO CHECK IN WITH SOME PEOPLE...
...SO... DESPITE MY BETTER JUDGMENT, I THINK I'LL STICK AROUND WITH YOU FOR A BIT.
PRETENDING TO BE SOME WEAK, DEFENSELESS MAGE CHICK'S BODYGUARD MIGHT BE GOOD COVER...
...I'M SURE THE PEOPLE THE CHURCH KEEPS AT THE FRONT GATE WILL BE FAR TOO INTERESTED IN ANY TSUIRAKUAN TRYING TO ENTER THE CITY TO EVEN NOTICE THE MEAT SHIELD FOLLOWING HER.
UM... MEJI?
WHAT HAPPEN TO THE 'TURN THIS GUY IN FOR A REWARD' PLAN?
EH... WE STILL DON'T KNOW HOW MUCH THE REWARD MIGHT BE OR EVEN IF THERE IS ONE...
FOR ALL WE KNOW, THEY MIGHT BE SUCH CHEAPSKATES IN SAUS THAT ALL THEY'D GIVE US WOULD BE A DAM HANDSHAKE AND A HEARTY 'THANKS FOR DOING OUR WORK FOR US, SUCKERS'.
HE MIGHT BE MORE USEFUL AS A BIG STUPID THING TO THROWN IN FRONT OF US AT THE MOMENT.
AND ANYWAY....
WE CAN ALWAYS TRY TURNING HIM IN LATER IF WE START TO RUN LOW ON CASH.
SORTA LIKE HOW I ONLY KEEP YOU AROUND AS A PORTABLE EMERGENCY FOOD SUPPLY, ELLIS...

AND BEFORE YOU GET ANY FUNNY IDEAS...
...YOU SHOULD KNOW THAT I'M A VERY, VERY LIGHT SLEEPER.
AND ELLIS HAS BEEN TRAINED TO GO FOR THE CROTCH OF ANYBODY WHO TRIES TO MOLEST ME.
LIKE HELL I WOULD!!
I'M NOT TOUCHING SOME GUY'S PACKAGE JUST TO SAVE YOUR BONY ASS!
UM... WHATEVER, SCARY LITTLE DEVIL GIRL.

ERRANT STORY

The Best of Intentions

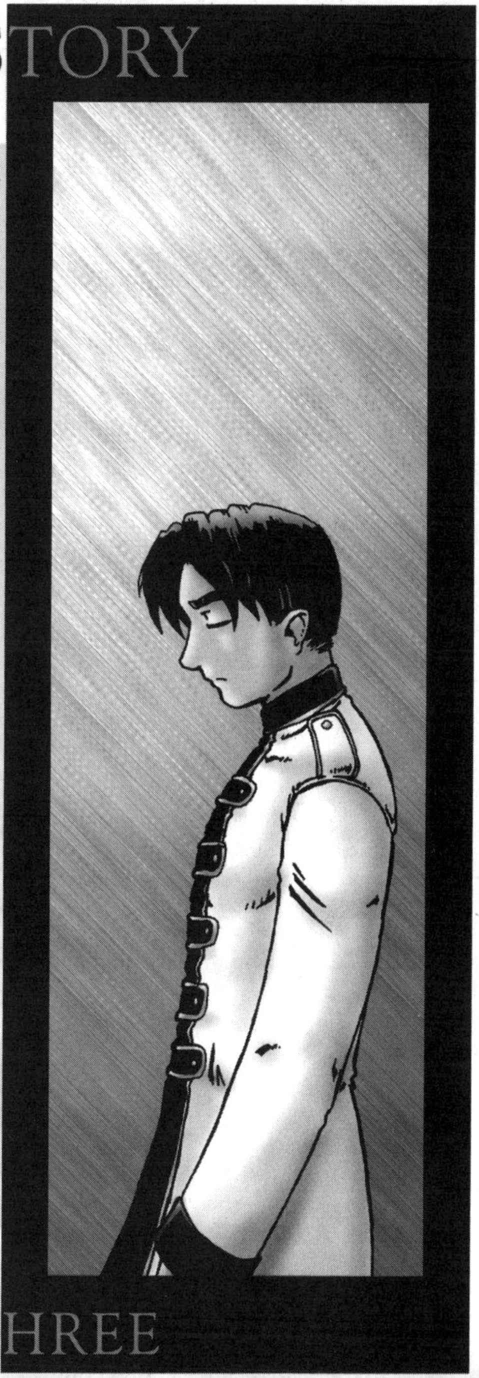

CHAPTER THREE

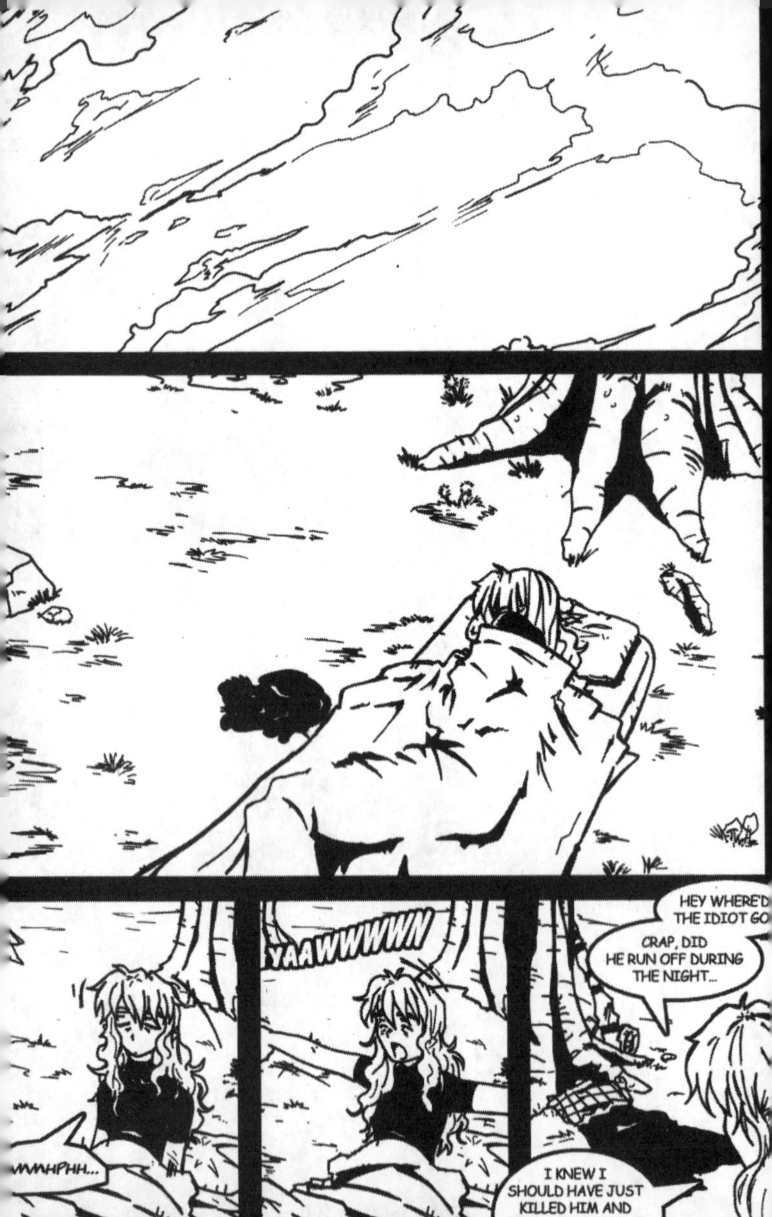
MMHPHH...
YAAWWWWN
HEY WHERE'D THE IDIOT GO
CRAP, DID HE RUN OFF DURING THE NIGHT...
I KNEW I SHOULD HAVE JUST KILLED HIM AND TRIED TO TURN THE CORPSE IN FOR A REWARD...

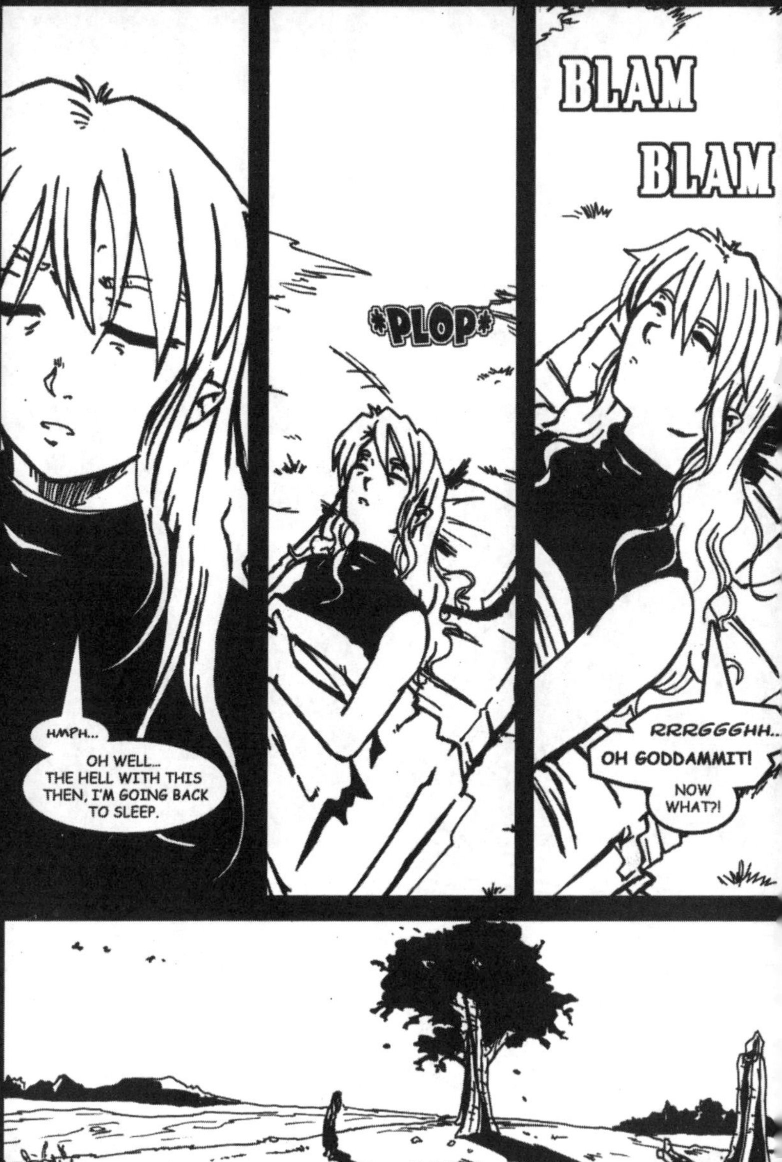
HMPH...
OH WELL... THE HELL WITH THIS THEN, I'M GOING BACK TO SLEEP.
PLOP
BLAM
BLAM
RRRGGGHH...
OH GODDAMMIT!
NOW WHAT?!

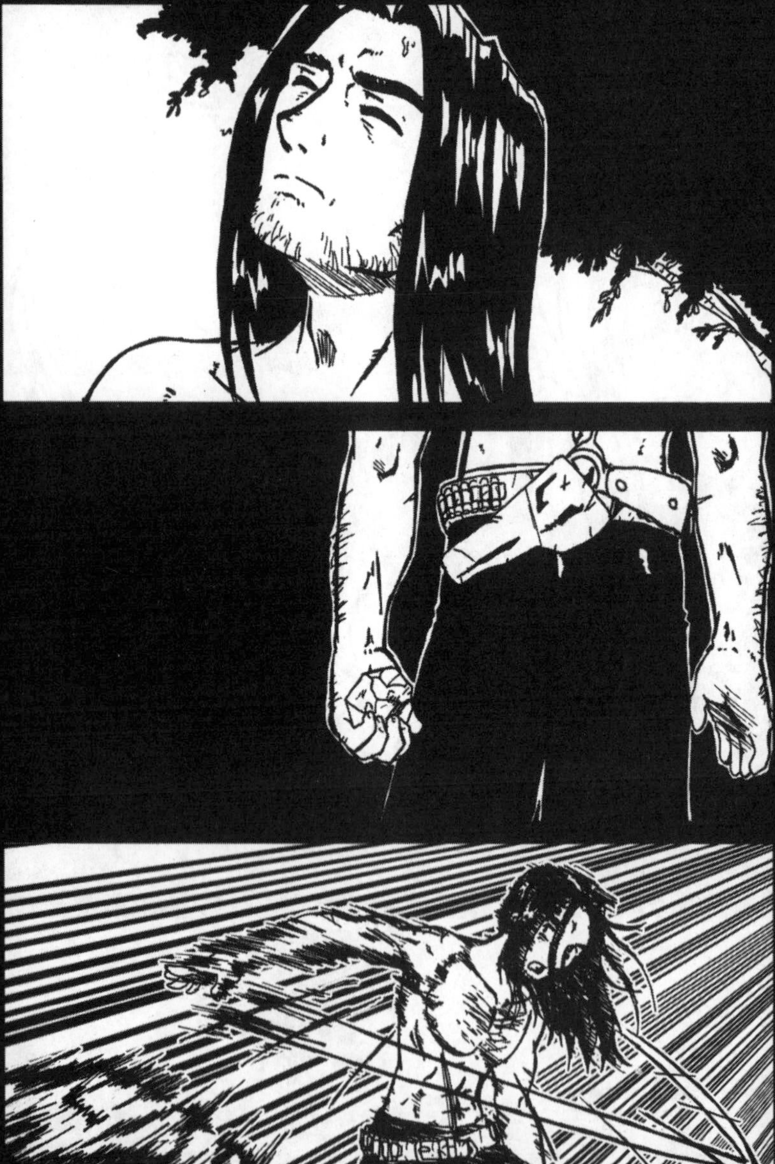

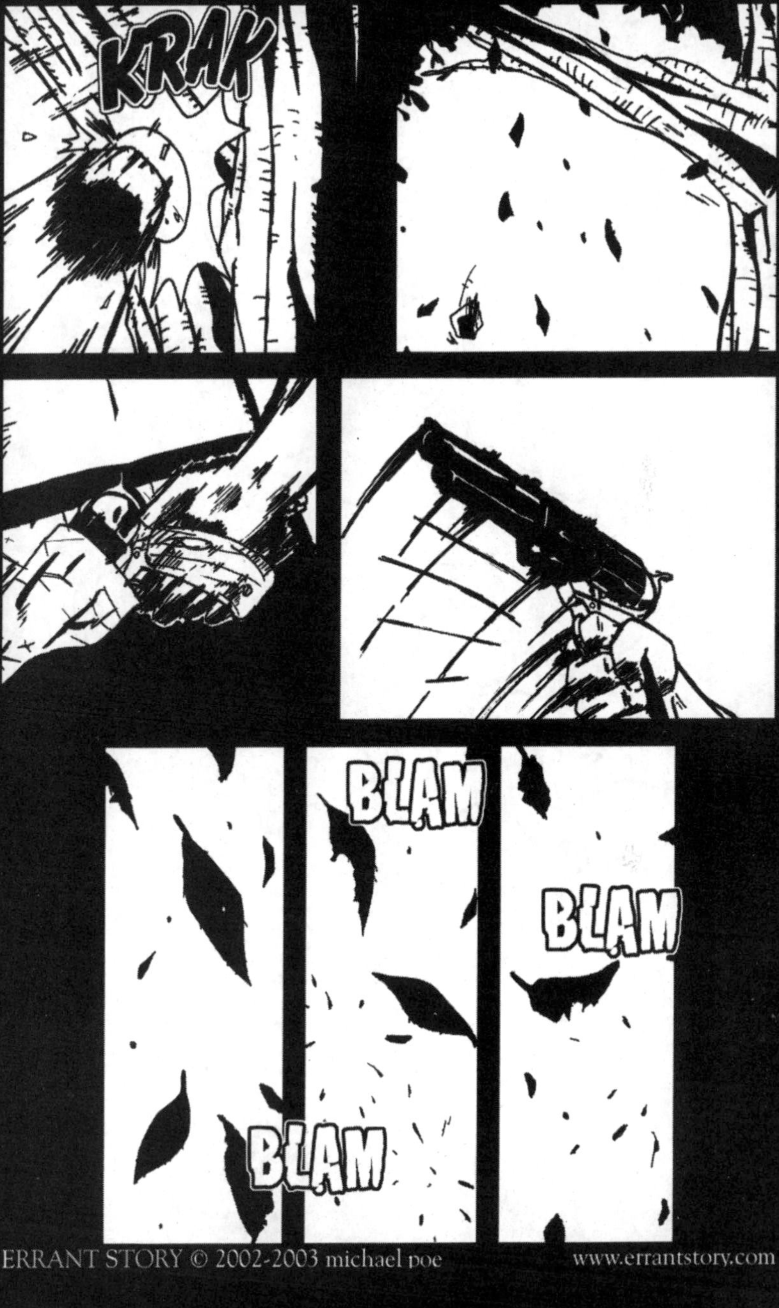
KRAK
BLAM
BLAM
BLAM

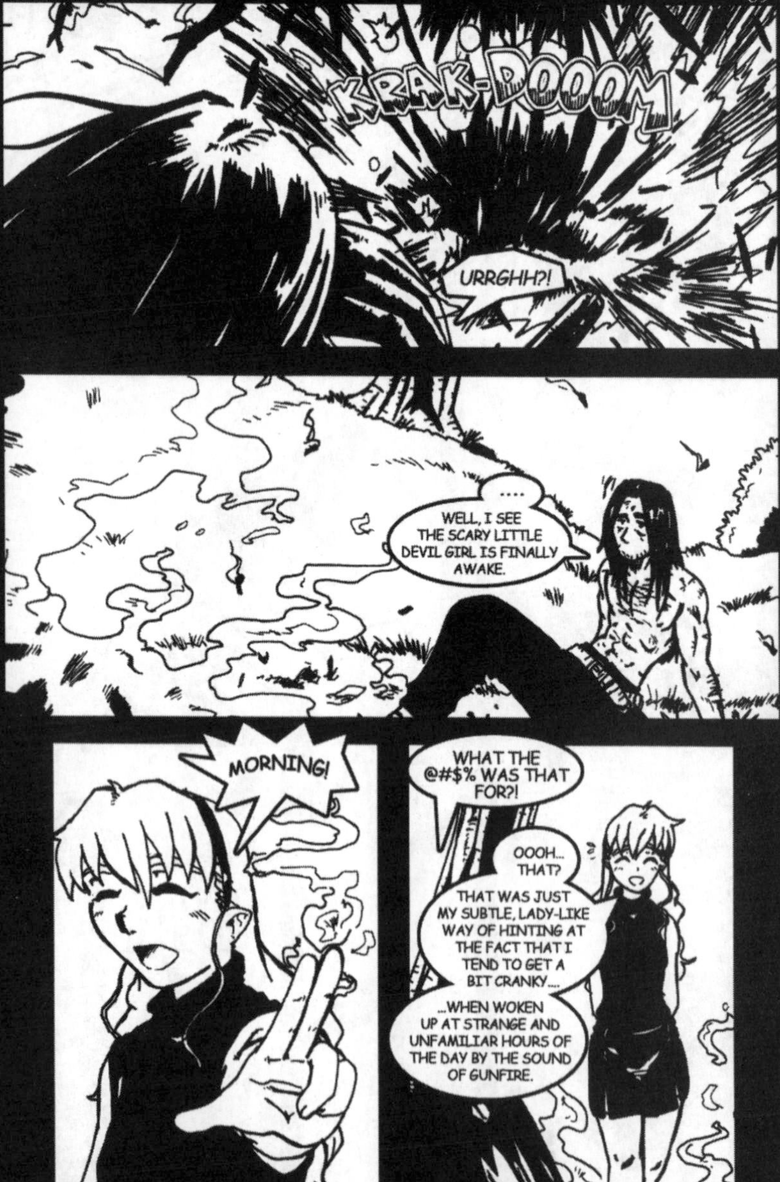
KRAK-DOOOM
URRGHH?!
....
WELL, I SEE THE SCARY LITTLE DEVIL GIRL IS FINALLY AWAKE.
MORNING!
WHAT THE @#$% WAS THAT FOR?!
OOOH... THAT?
THAT WAS JUST MY SUBTLE, LADY-LIKE WAY OF HINTING AT THE FACT THAT I TEND TO GET A BIT CRANKY....
...WHEN WOKEN UP AT STRANGE AND UNFAMILIAR HOURS OF THE DAY BY THE SOUND OF GUNFIRE.

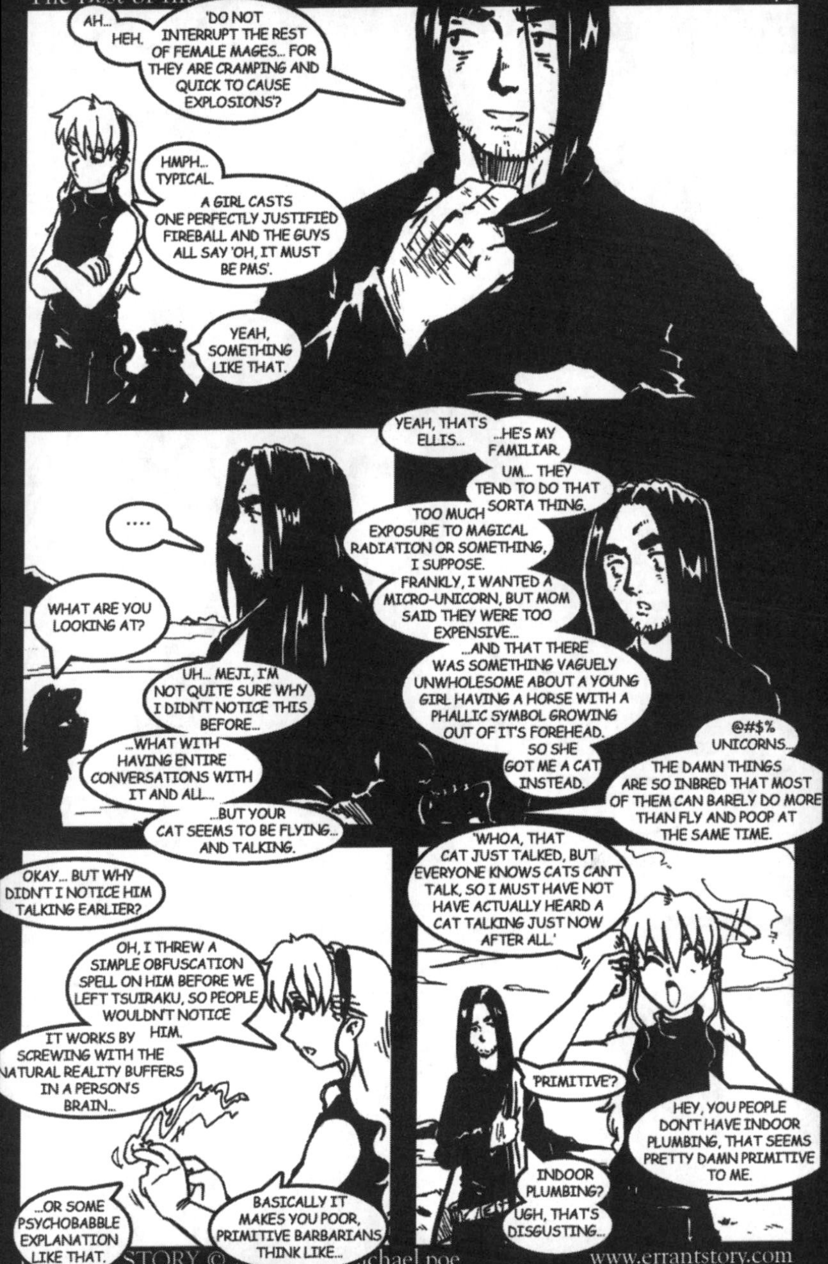
AH... HEH.
'DO NOT INTERRUPT THE REST OF FEMALE MAGES... FOR THEY ARE CRAMPING AND QUICK TO CAUSE EXPLOSIONS'?
HMPH... TYPICAL.
A GIRL CASTS ONE PERFECTLY JUSTIFIED FIREBALL AND THE GUYS ALL SAY 'OH, IT MUST BE PMS'.
YEAH, SOMETHING LIKE THAT.
....
WHAT ARE YOU LOOKING AT?
UH... MEJI, I'M NOT QUITE SURE WHY I DIDN'T NOTICE THIS BEFORE...
...WHAT WITH HAVING ENTIRE CONVERSATIONS WITH IT AND ALL...
...BUT YOUR CAT SEEMS TO BE FLYING... AND TALKING.
YEAH, THAT'S ELLIS...
...HE'S MY FAMILIAR.
UM... THEY TEND TO DO THAT SORTA THING.
TOO MUCH EXPOSURE TO MAGICAL RADIATION OR SOMETHING, I SUPPOSE.
FRANKLY, I WANTED A MICRO-UNICORN, BUT MOM SAID THEY WERE TOO EXPENSIVE...
...AND THAT THERE WAS SOMETHING VAGUELY UNWHOLESOME ABOUT A YOUNG GIRL HAVING A HORSE WITH A PHALLIC SYMBOL GROWING OUT OF IT'S FOREHEAD.
SO SHE GOT ME A CAT INSTEAD.
@#$% UNICORNS...
THE DAMN THINGS ARE SO INBRED THAT MOST OF THEM CAN BARELY DO MORE THAN FLY AND POOP AT THE SAME TIME.
OKAY... BUT WHY DIDN'T I NOTICE HIM TALKING EARLIER?
OH, I THREW A SIMPLE OBFUSCATION SPELL ON HIM BEFORE WE LEFT TSUIRAKU, SO PEOPLE WOULDN'T NOTICE HIM.
IT WORKS BY SCREWING WITH THE NATURAL REALITY BUFFERS IN A PERSON'S BRAIN...
...OR SOME PSYCHOBABBLE EXPLANATION LIKE THAT.
BASICALLY IT MAKES YOU POOR, PRIMITIVE BARBARIANS THINK LIKE...
'WHOA, THAT CAT JUST TALKED, BUT EVERYONE KNOWS CATS CAN'T TALK, SO I MUST HAVE NOT HAVE ACTUALLY HEARD A CAT TALKING JUST NOW AFTER ALL.'
'PRIMITIVE'?
HEY, YOU PEOPLE DON'T HAVE INDOOR PLUMBING, THAT SEEMS PRETTY DAMN PRIMITIVE TO ME.
INDOOR PLUMBING? UGH, THAT'S DISGUSTING...

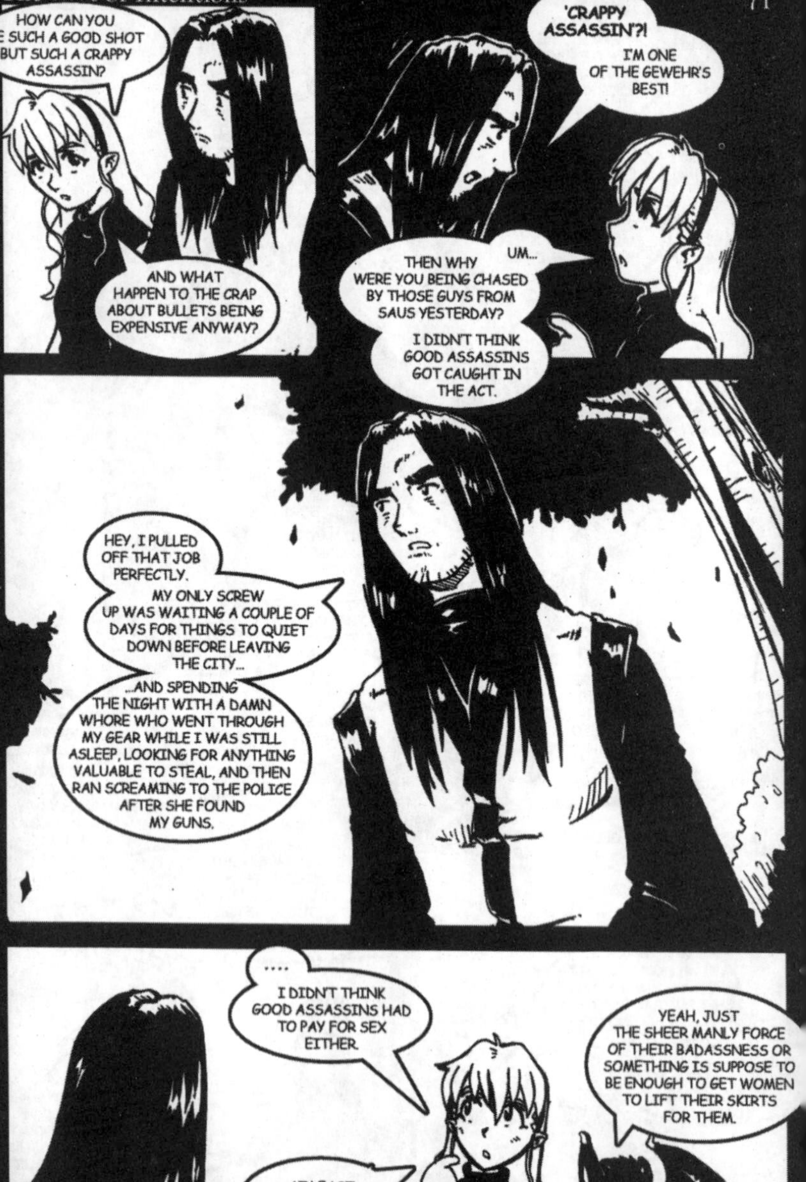
HOW CAN YOU BE SUCH A GOOD SHOT BUT SUCH A CRAPPY ASSASSIN?
AND WHAT HAPPEN TO THE CRAP ABOUT BULLETS BEING EXPENSIVE ANYWAY?
'CRAPPY ASSASSIN'?!
I'M ONE OF THE GEWEHR'S BEST!
UM...
THEN WHY WERE YOU BEING CHASED BY THOSE GUYS FROM SAUS YESTERDAY?
I DIDN'T THINK GOOD ASSASSINS GOT CAUGHT IN THE ACT.
HEY, I PULLED OFF THAT JOB PERFECTLY.
MY ONLY SCREW UP WAS WAITING A COUPLE OF DAYS FOR THINGS TO QUIET DOWN BEFORE LEAVING THE CITY...
...AND SPENDING THE NIGHT WITH A DAMN WHORE WHO WENT THROUGH MY GEAR WHILE I WAS STILL ASLEEP, LOOKING FOR ANYTHING VALUABLE TO STEAL, AND THEN RAN SCREAMING TO THE POLICE AFTER SHE FOUND MY GUNS.
....
I DIDN'T THINK GOOD ASSASSINS HAD TO PAY FOR SEX EITHER.
AT LEAST THAT'S HOW THEY ARE IN BOOKS.
YEAH, JUST THE SHEER MANLY FORCE OF THEIR BADASSNESS OR SOMETHING IS SUPPOSE TO BE ENOUGH TO GET WOMEN TO LIFT THEIR SKIRTS FOR THEM.

....
I DON'T BLOODY WELL CARE IF IT IS SUPPOSE TO BE THE TEARS OF LUMINOSITA WASHING AWAY OUR SINS OR NOT...
I STILL DON'T SEE WHY WE HAVE TO LET OURSELVES GET SOAKING WET INSTEAD OF USING MAGIC TO KEEP THE RAIN OFF US LIKE THE DAMN MAGES DO.
HRM... NASTY NIGHT TO BE WALKING ABOUT...
YES, IT SURLY IS, SIR.
CAN I HELP YOU, SON?
HMMM... YES, ACTUALLY I THINK YOU COULD.
TELL GOOD, SIR...
ABOUT HOW TALL ARE YOU?

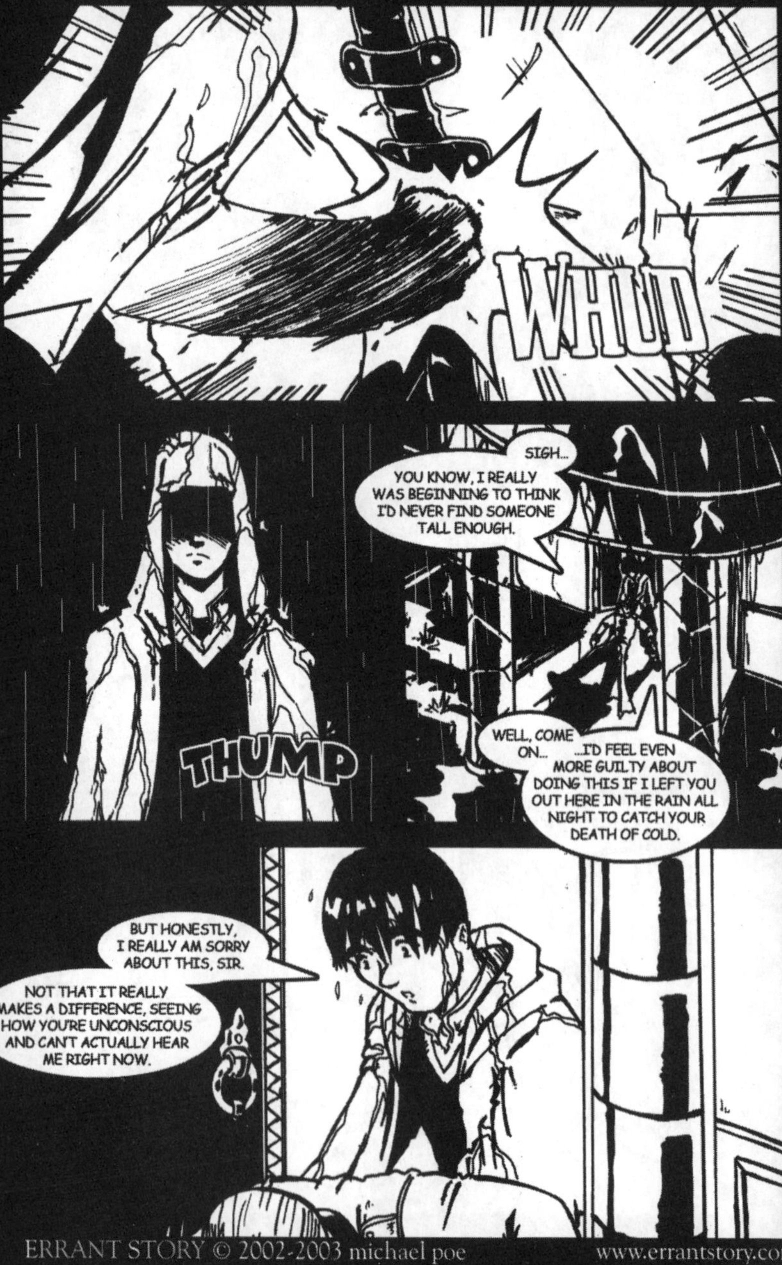
WHUD
THUMP
SIGH...
YOU KNOW, I REALLY WAS BEGINNING TO THINK I'D NEVER FIND SOMEONE TALL ENOUGH.
WELL, COME ON...
...I'D FEEL EVEN MORE GUILTY ABOUT DOING THIS IF I LEFT YOU OUT HERE IN THE RAIN ALL NIGHT TO CATCH YOUR DEATH OF COLD.
BUT HONESTLY, I REALLY AM SORRY ABOUT THIS, SIR.
NOT THAT IT REALLY MAKES A DIFFERENCE, SEEING HOW YOU'RE UNCONSCIOUS AND CAN'T ACTUALLY HEAR ME RIGHT NOW.

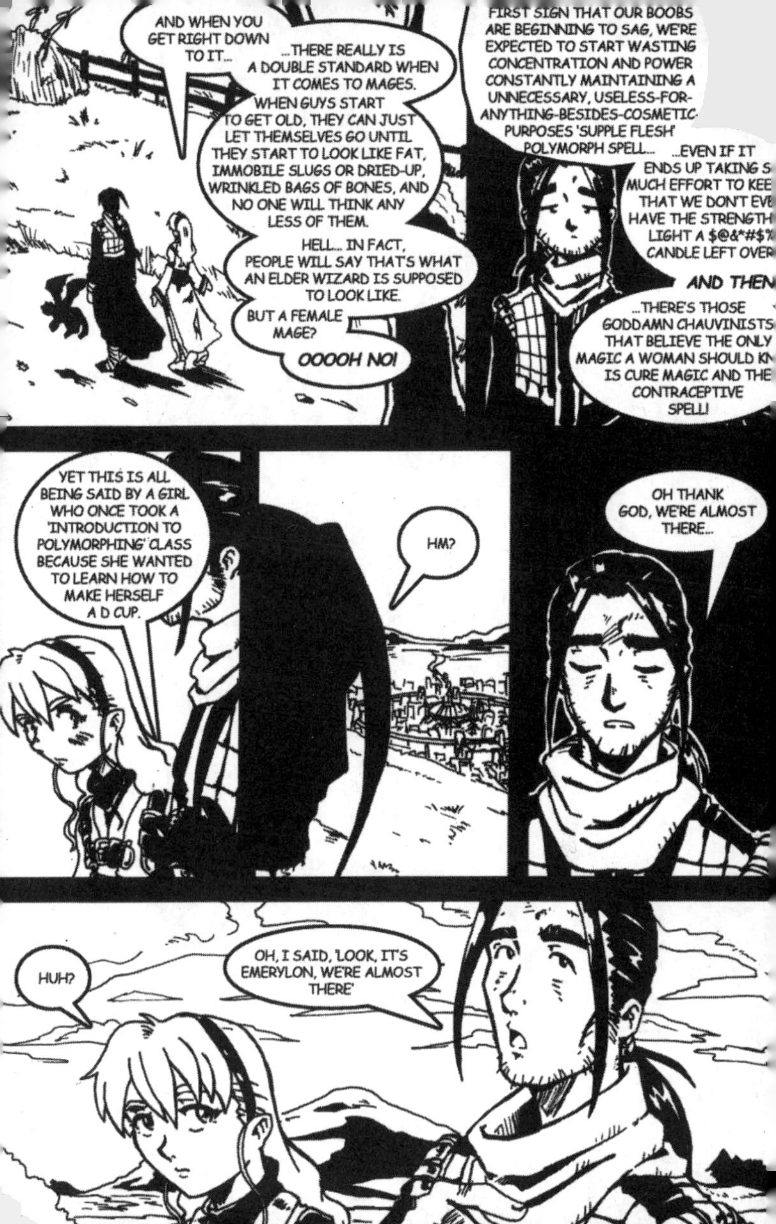
AND WHEN YOU GET RIGHT DOWN TO IT...
...THERE REALLY IS A DOUBLE STANDARD WHEN IT COMES TO MAGES.
WHEN GUYS START TO GET OLD, THEY CAN JUST LET THEMSELVES GO UNTIL THEY START TO LOOK LIKE FAT, IMMOBILE SLUGS OR DRIED-UP, WRINKLED BAGS OF BONES, AND NO ONE WILL THINK ANY LESS OF THEM.
HELL... IN FACT, PEOPLE WILL SAY THAT'S WHAT AN ELDER WIZARD IS SUPPOSED TO LOOK LIKE.
BUT A FEMALE MAGE?
OOOOH NO!
FIRST SIGN THAT OUR BOOBS ARE BEGINNING TO SAG, WE'RE EXPECTED TO START WASTING CONCENTRATION AND POWER CONSTANTLY MAINTAINING A UNNECESSARY, USELESS-FOR-ANYTHING-BESIDES-COSMETIC-PURPOSES 'SUPPLE FLESH' POLYMORPH SPELL...
...EVEN IF IT ENDS UP TAKING S MUCH EFFORT TO KEE THAT WE DON'T EVE HAVE THE STRENGTH LIGHT A $@&*#$ CANDLE LEFT OVER
AND THEN
...THERE'S THOSE GODDAMN CHAUVINISTS THAT BELIEVE THE ONLY MAGIC A WOMAN SHOULD K IS CURE MAGIC AND THE CONTRACEPTIVE SPELL!
YET THIS IS ALL BEING SAID BY A GIRL WHO ONCE TOOK A 'INTRODUCTION TO POLYMORPHING' CLASS BECAUSE SHE WANTED TO LEARN HOW TO MAKE HERSELF A D CUP.
HM?
OH THANK GOD, WE'RE ALMOST THERE...
HUH?
OH, I SAID, 'LOOK, IT'S EMERYLON, WE'RE ALMOST THERE'

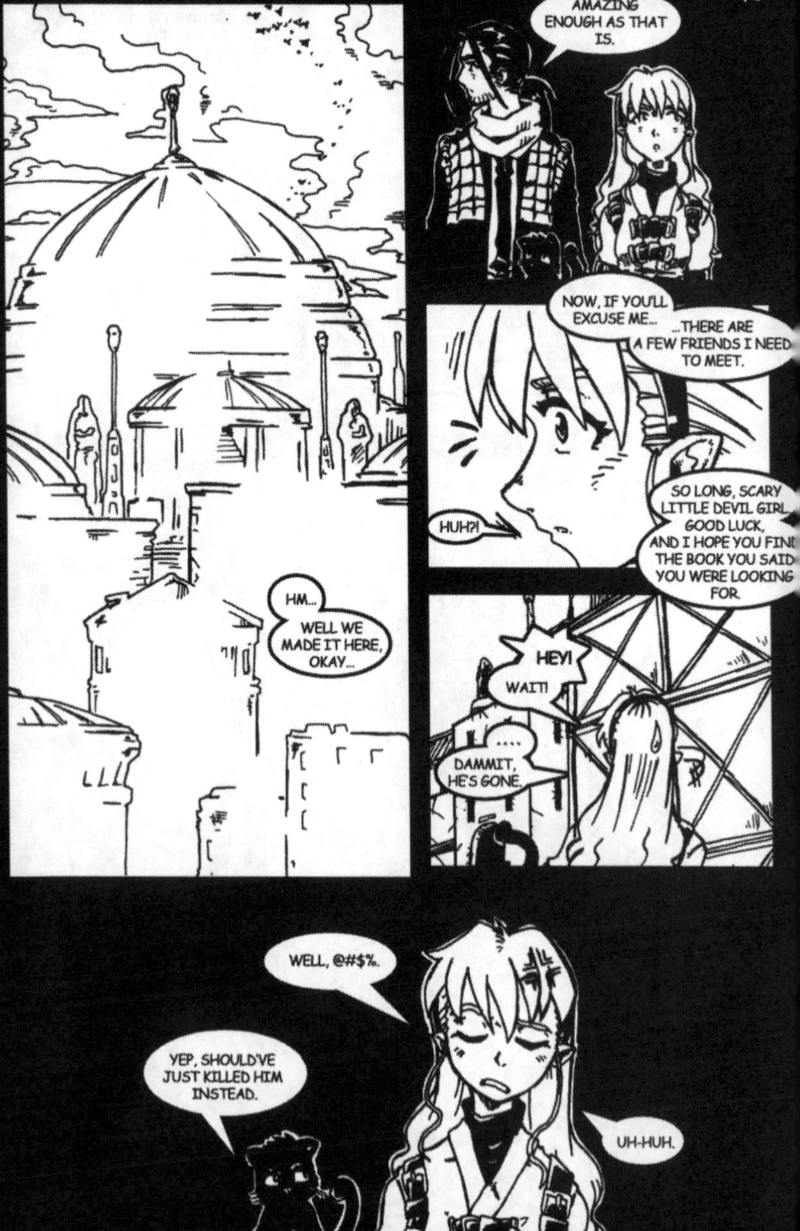
HM...
WELL WE MADE IT HERE, OKAY...
AMAZING ENOUGH AS THAT IS.
NOW, IF YOU'LL EXCUSE ME...
...THERE ARE A FEW FRIENDS I NEED TO MEET.
HUH?!
SO LONG, SCARY LITTLE DEVIL GIRL. GOOD LUCK, AND I HOPE YOU FIND THE BOOK YOU SAID YOU WERE LOOKING FOR.
HEY!
WAIT!
....
DAMMIT, HE'S GONE.
WELL, @#$%.
YEP, SHOULD'VE JUST KILLED HIM INSTEAD.
UH-HUH.

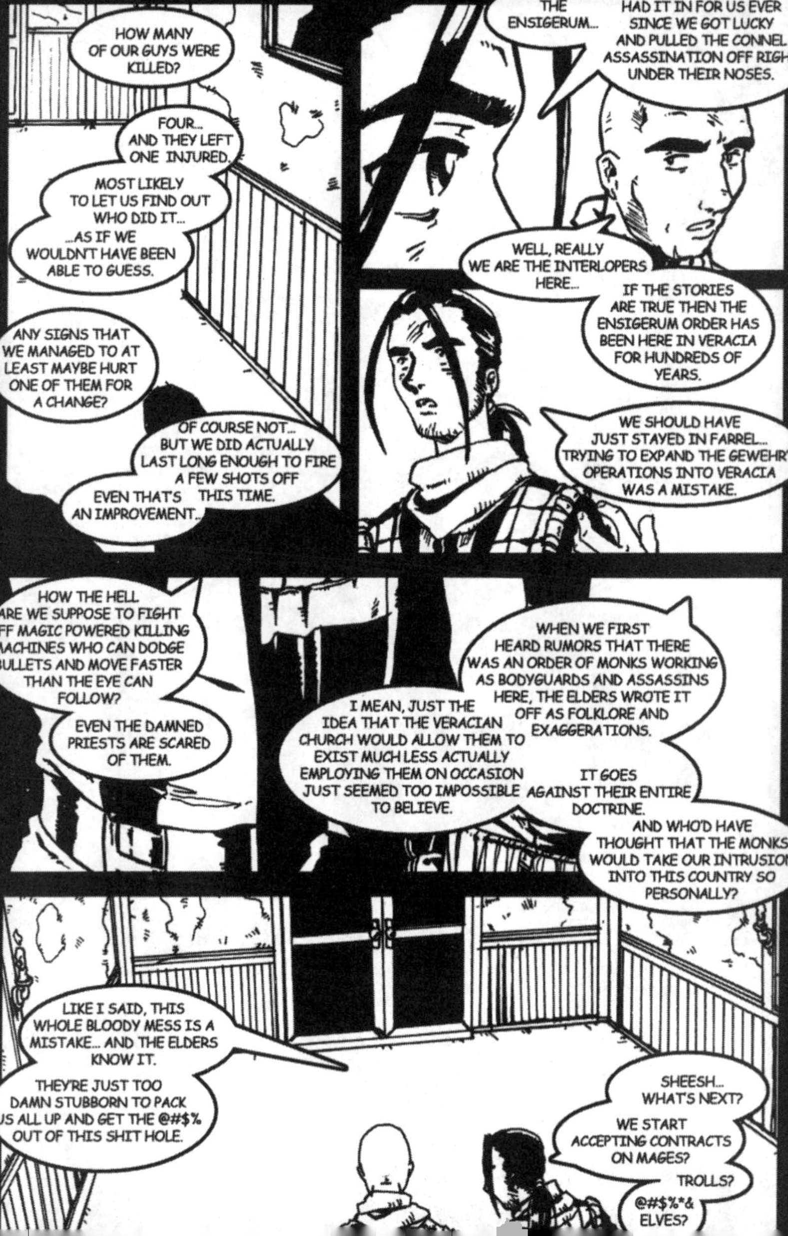
HOW MANY OF OUR GUYS WERE KILLED?
FOUR... AND THEY LEFT ONE INJURED.
MOST LIKELY TO LET US FIND OUT WHO DID IT...
...AS IF WE WOULDN'T HAVE BEEN ABLE TO GUESS.
ANY SIGNS THAT WE MANAGED TO AT LEAST MAYBE HURT ONE OF THEM FOR A CHANGE?
OF COURSE NOT... BUT WE DID ACTUALLY LAST LONG ENOUGH TO FIRE A FEW SHOTS OFF THIS TIME.
EVEN THAT'S AN IMPROVEMENT...
THE ENSIGERUM...
SIGH... THEY'VE HAD IT IN FOR US EVER SINCE WE GOT LUCKY AND PULLED THE CONNEL ASSASSINATION OFF RIGHT UNDER THEIR NOSES.
WELL, REALLY WE ARE THE INTERLOPERS HERE...
IF THE STORIES ARE TRUE THEN THE ENSIGERUM ORDER HAS BEEN HERE IN VERACIA FOR HUNDREDS OF YEARS.
WE SHOULD HAVE JUST STAYED IN FARREL... TRYING TO EXPAND THE GEWEHR'S OPERATIONS INTO VERACIA WAS A MISTAKE.
HOW THE HELL ARE WE SUPPOSE TO FIGHT OFF MAGIC POWERED KILLING MACHINES WHO CAN DODGE BULLETS AND MOVE FASTER THAN THE EYE CAN FOLLOW?
EVEN THE DAMNED PRIESTS ARE SCARED OF THEM.
WHEN WE FIRST HEARD RUMORS THAT THERE WAS AN ORDER OF MONKS WORKING AS BODYGUARDS AND ASSASSINS HERE, THE ELDERS WROTE IT OFF AS FOLKLORE AND EXAGGERATIONS.
I MEAN, JUST THE IDEA THAT THE VERACIAN CHURCH WOULD ALLOW THEM TO EXIST MUCH LESS ACTUALLY EMPLOYING THEM ON OCCASION JUST SEEMED TOO IMPOSSIBLE TO BELIEVE.
IT GOES AGAINST THEIR ENTIRE DOCTRINE.
AND WHO'D HAVE THOUGHT THAT THE MONKS WOULD TAKE OUR INTRUSION INTO THIS COUNTRY SO PERSONALLY?
LIKE I SAID, THIS WHOLE BLOODY MESS IS A MISTAKE... AND THE ELDERS KNOW IT.
THEY'RE JUST TOO DAMN STUBBORN TO PACK US ALL UP AND GET THE @#$% OUT OF THIS SHIT HOLE.
SHEESH... WHAT'S NEXT?
WE START ACCEPTING CONTRACTS ON MAGES?
TROLLS?
@#$%*& ELVES?

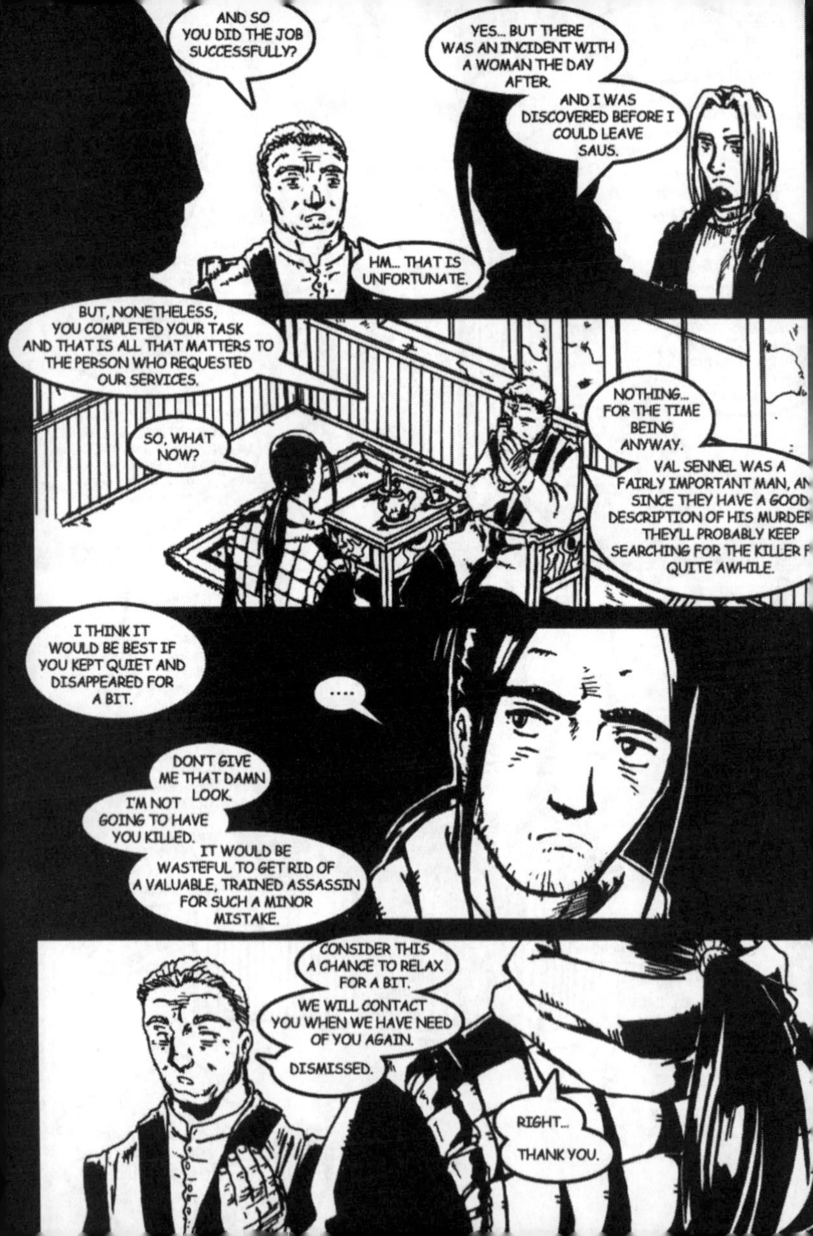
AND SO YOU DID THE JOB SUCCESSFULLY?
YES... BUT THERE WAS AN INCIDENT WITH A WOMAN THE DAY AFTER.
AND I WAS DISCOVERED BEFORE I COULD LEAVE SAUS.
HM... THAT IS UNFORTUNATE.
BUT, NONETHELESS, YOU COMPLETED YOUR TASK AND THAT IS ALL THAT MATTERS TO THE PERSON WHO REQUESTED OUR SERVICES.
SO, WHAT NOW?
NOTHING... FOR THE TIME BEING ANYWAY.
VAL SENNEL WAS A FAIRLY IMPORTANT MAN, AN SINCE THEY HAVE A GOOD DESCRIPTION OF HIS MURDER THEY'LL PROBABLY KEEP SEARCHING FOR THE KILLER F QUITE AWHILE.
I THINK IT WOULD BE BEST IF YOU KEPT QUIET AND DISAPPEARED FOR A BIT.
....
DON'T GIVE ME THAT DAMN LOOK.
I'M NOT GOING TO HAVE YOU KILLED.
IT WOULD BE WASTEFUL TO GET RID OF A VALUABLE, TRAINED ASSASSIN FOR SUCH A MINOR MISTAKE.
CONSIDER THIS A CHANCE TO RELAX FOR A BIT.
WE WILL CONTACT YOU WHEN WE HAVE NEED OF YOU AGAIN.
DISMISSED.
RIGHT...
THANK YOU.

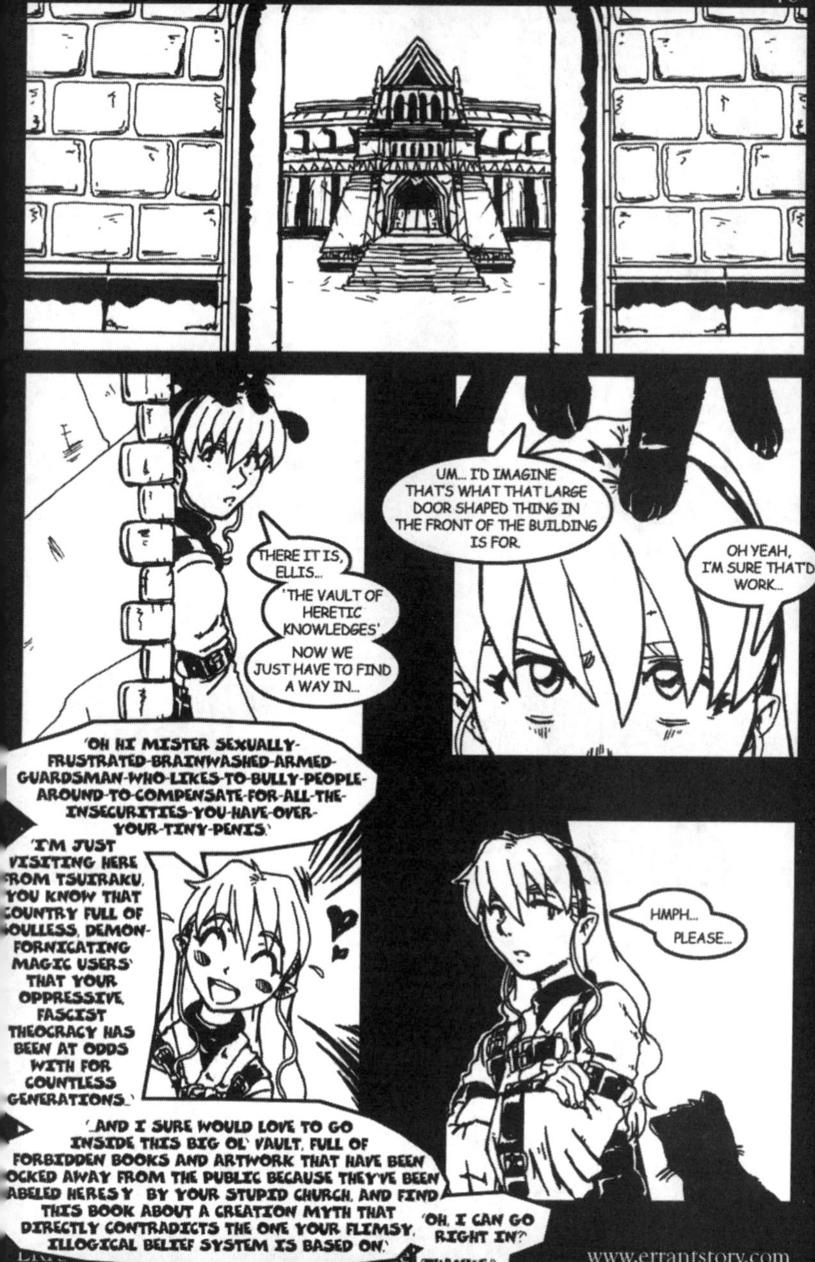
THERE IT IS, ELLIS...
'THE VAULT OF HERETIC KNOWLEDGES'
NOW WE JUST HAVE TO FIND A WAY IN...
UM... I'D IMAGINE THAT'S WHAT THAT LARGE DOOR SHAPED THING IN THE FRONT OF THE BUILDING IS FOR.
OH YEAH, I'M SURE THAT'D WORK...
'OH HI MISTER SEXUALLY-FRUSTRATED-BRAINWASHED-ARMED-GUARDSMAN-WHO-LIKES-TO-BULLY-PEOPLE-AROUND-TO-COMPENSATE-FOR-ALL-THE-INSECURITIES-YOU-HAVE-OVER-YOUR-TINY-PENIS.'
'I'M JUST VISITING HERE FROM TSUIRAKU, YOU KNOW THAT COUNTRY FULL OF OULLESS, DEMON-FORNICATING MAGIC USERS' THAT YOUR OPPRESSIVE, FASCIST THEOCRACY HAS BEEN AT ODDS WITH FOR COUNTLESS GENERATIONS.'
HMPH... PLEASE...
'...AND I SURE WOULD LOVE TO GO INSIDE THIS BIG OL' VAULT, FULL OF FORBIDDEN BOOKS AND ARTWORK THAT HAVE BEEN OCKED AWAY FROM THE PUBLIC BECAUSE THEY'VE BEEN ABELED HERESY BY YOUR STUPID CHURCH, AND FIND THIS BOOK ABOUT A CREATION MYTH THAT DIRECTLY CONTRADICTS THE ONE YOUR FLIMSY, ILLOGICAL BELIEF SYSTEM IS BASED ON.'
'OH, I CAN GO RIGHT IN?'
'THANKS!'

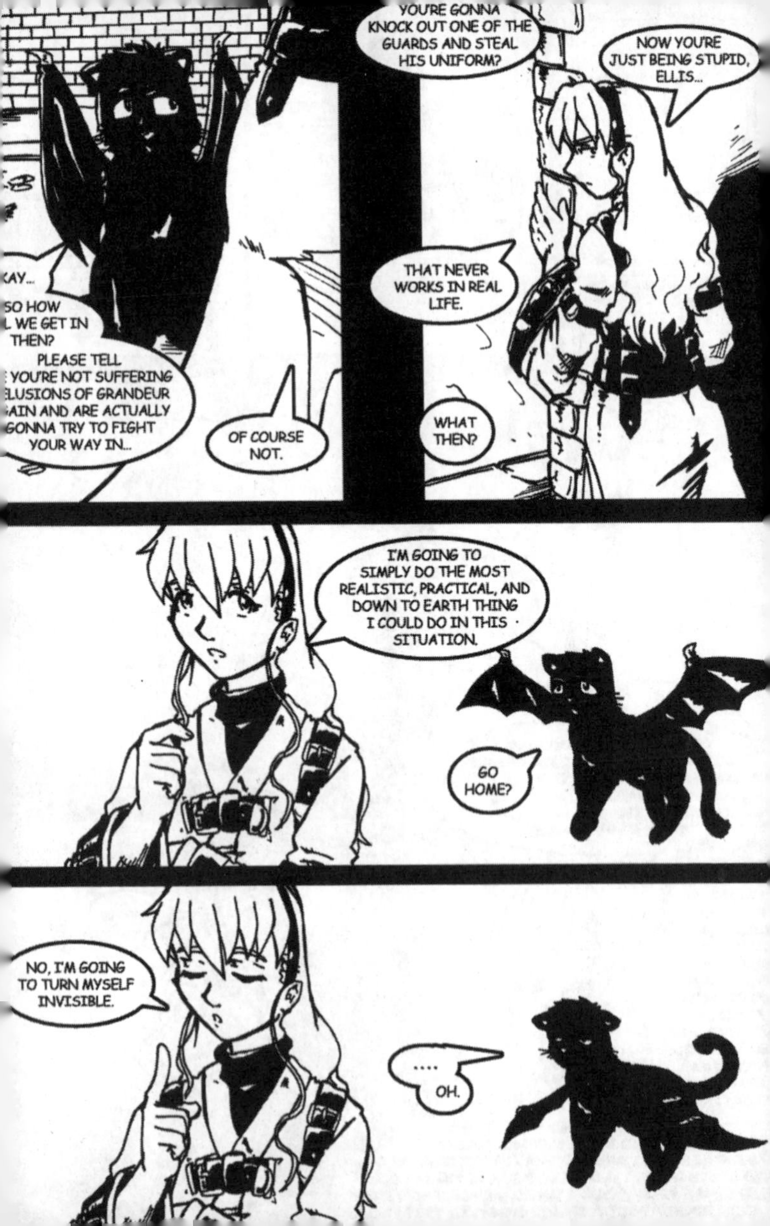

KAY...
SO HOW
L WE GET IN
THEN?
PLEASE TELL
E YOU'RE NOT SUFFERING
ELUSIONS OF GRANDEUR
GAIN AND ARE ACTUALLY
GONNA TRY TO FIGHT
YOUR WAY IN...
OF COURSE NOT.
YOU'RE GONNA KNOCK OUT ONE OF THE GUARDS AND STEAL HIS UNIFORM?
NOW YOU'RE JUST BEING STUPID, ELLIS...
THAT NEVER WORKS IN REAL LIFE.
WHAT THEN?
I'M GOING TO SIMPLY DO THE MOST REALISTIC, PRACTICAL, AND DOWN TO EARTH THING I COULD DO IN THIS SITUATION.
GO HOME?
NO, I'M GOING TO TURN MYSELF INVISIBLE.
....
OH.

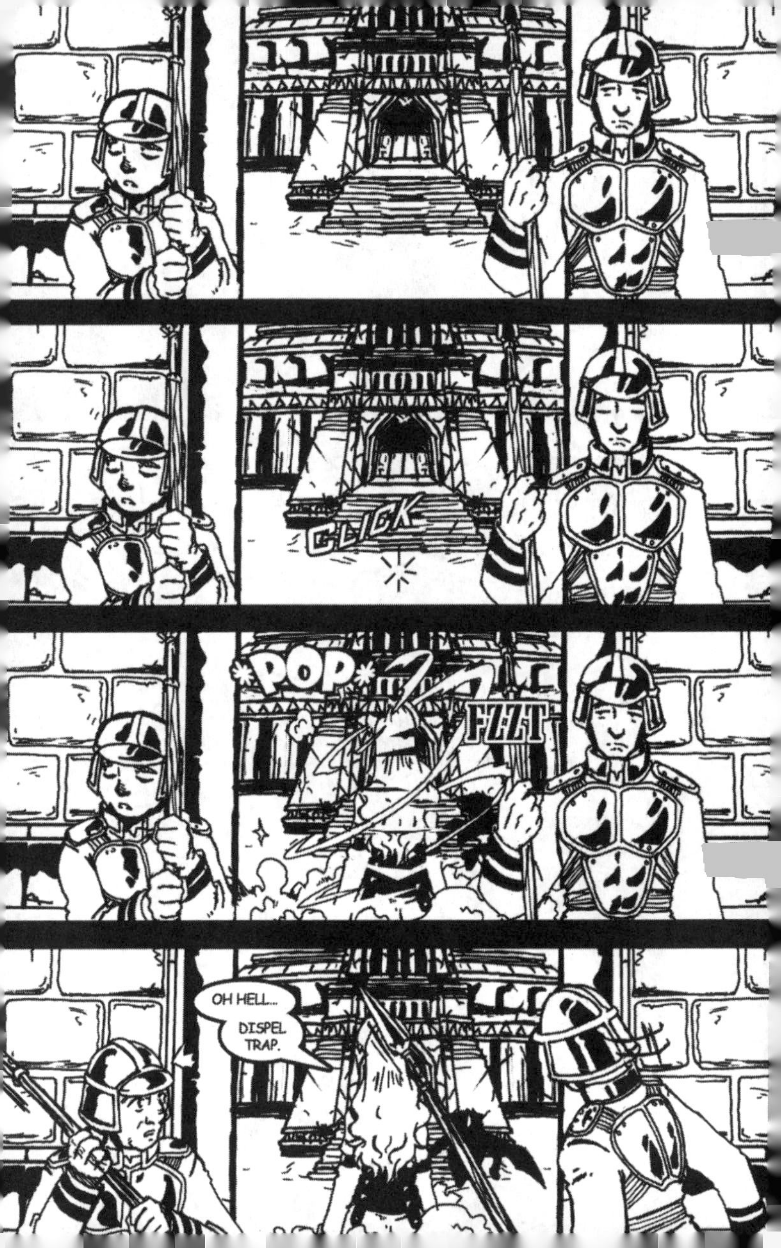
CLICK
POP
FZZT
OH HELL...
DISPEL TRAP.

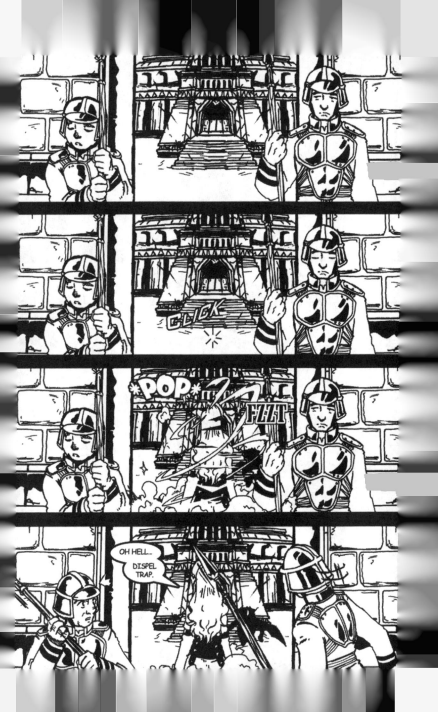

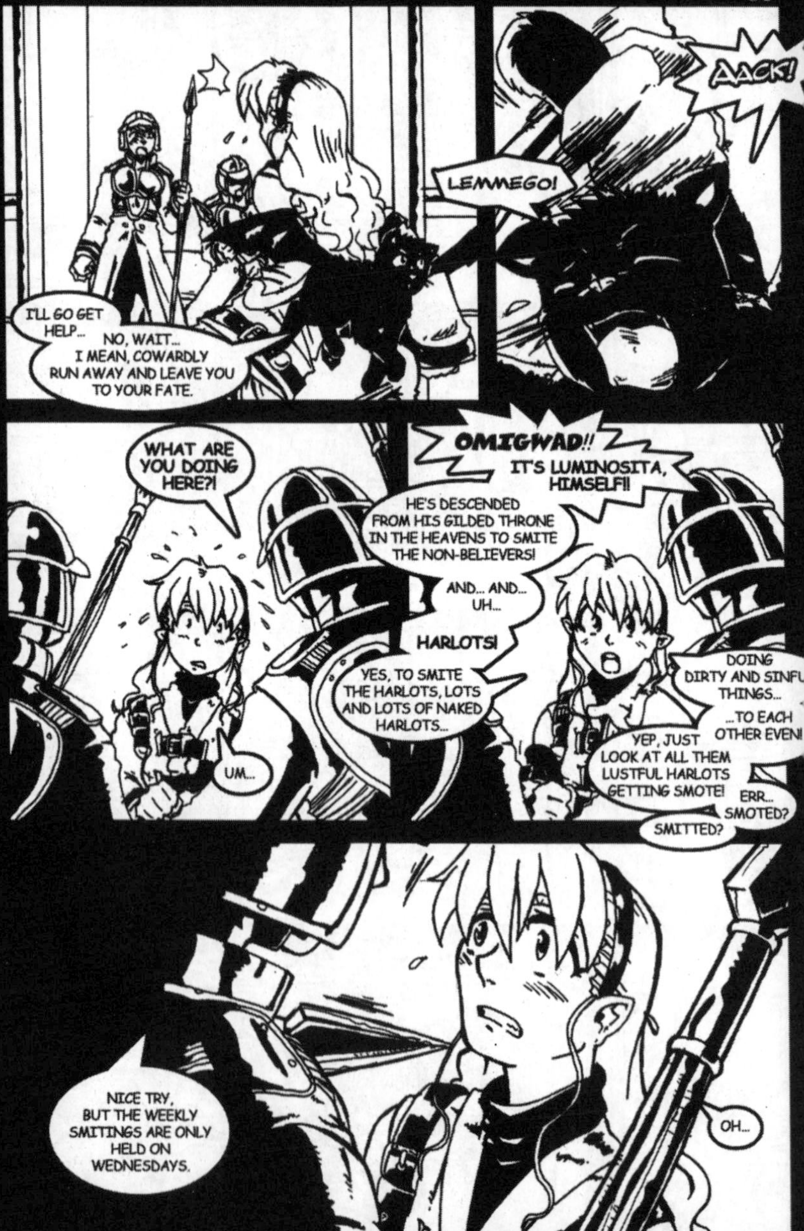
I'LL GO GET HELP...
NO, WAIT... I MEAN, COWARDLY RUN AWAY AND LEAVE YOU TO YOUR FATE.
AACK!
LEMMEGO!
WHAT ARE YOU DOING HERE?!
UM...
OMIGWAD!!
IT'S LUMINOSITA, HIMSELF!!
HE'S DESCENDED FROM HIS GILDED THRONE IN THE HEAVENS TO SMITE THE NON-BELIEVERS!
AND... AND... UH...
HARLOTS!
YES, TO SMITE THE HARLOTS, LOTS AND LOTS OF NAKED HARLOTS...
DOING DIRTY AND SINFU THINGS...
...TO EACH OTHER EVEN!
YEP, JUST LOOK AT ALL THEM LUSTFUL HARLOTS GETTING SMOTE!
ERR... SMOTED?
SMITTED?
NICE TRY, BUT THE WEEKLY SMITINGS ARE ONLY HELD ON WEDNESDAYS.
OH...

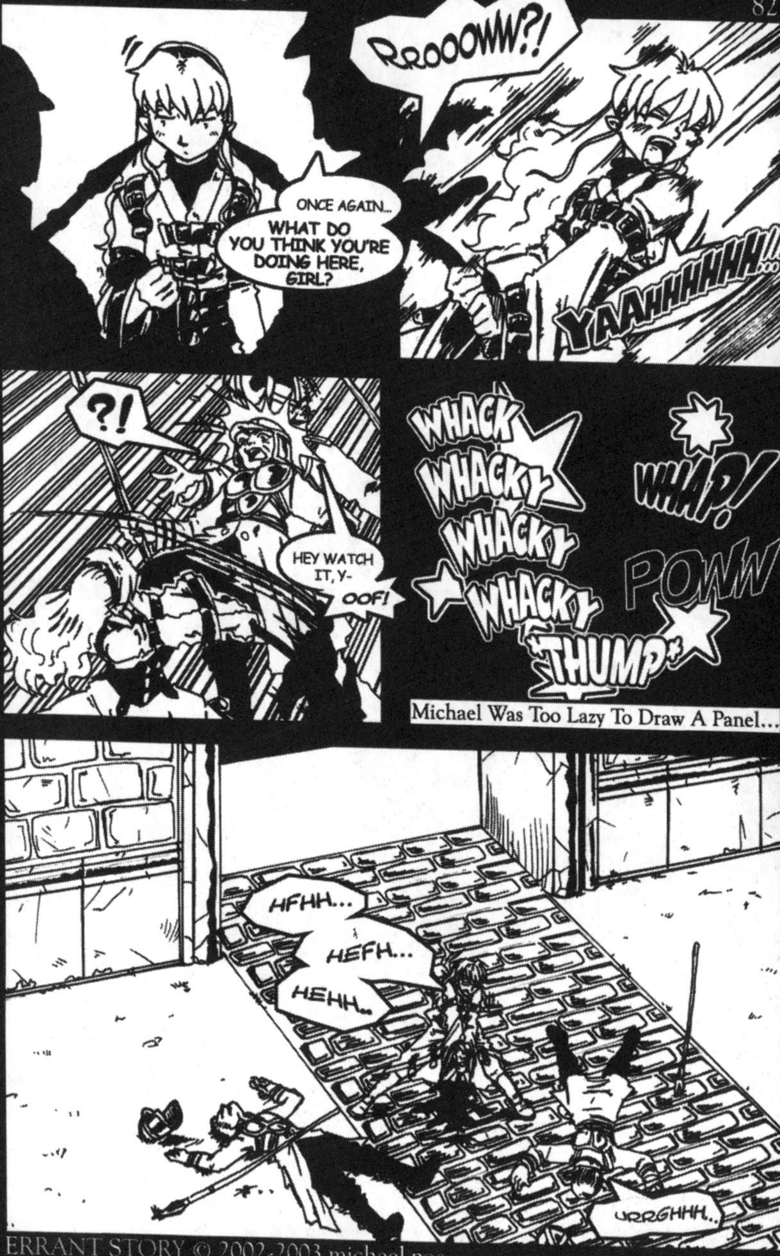
ONCE AGAIN...
WHAT DO YOU THINK YOU'RE DOING HERE, GIRL?
RROOOWW?!
YAAHHHHHH!!...
?!
HEY WATCH IT, Y-
OOF!
WHACK
WHACKY
WHACKY
WHACKY
THUMP
WHAP!
POWW
Michael Was Too Lazy To Draw A Panel...
HFHH...
HEFH...
HEHH..
URRGHHH..

WELL...
WHERE THE HELL IS IT?
WHERE'S WHAT?
A BOOK DIRECTORY...
YOU KNOW...
CRYSTAL BALL-LOOKING THINGY, DISPLAYS A LISTING OF ALL THE BOOKS AND THEIR LOCATION OR SOMETHING.
OH...
HEY, MAYBE THEY JUST WRITE THE NAME OF THE BOOK, AND WHAT SHELF IT'S ON, DOWN ON A LITTLE CARD AND STICK 'EM IN ONE OF THESE TINY DRAWERS WITH THE LETTERS ON THEM INSTEAD...
....
ELLIS...EVEN THESE PEOPLE AREN'T THAT ARCHAIC...

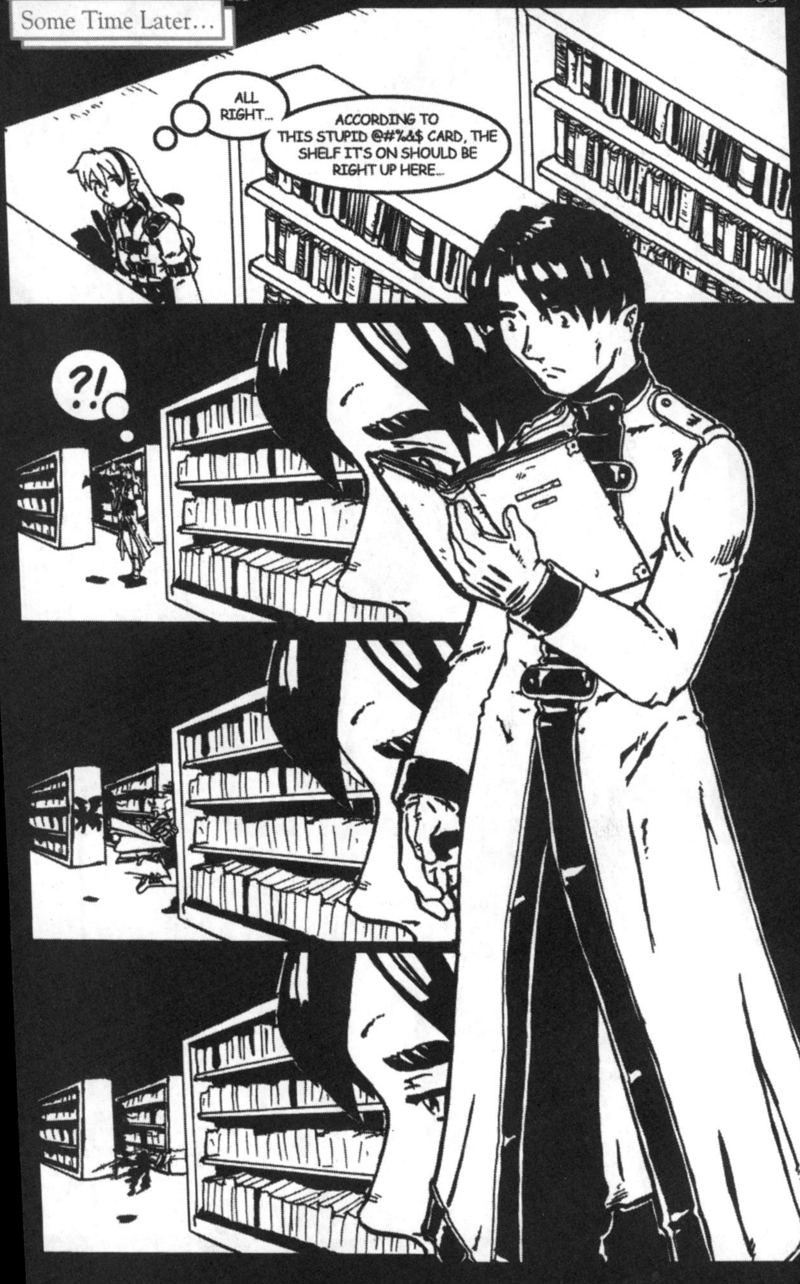
Some Time Later…
ALL RIGHT...
ACCORDING TO THIS STUPID @#%&$ CARD, THE SHELF IT'S ON SHOULD BE RIGHT UP HERE...
?!

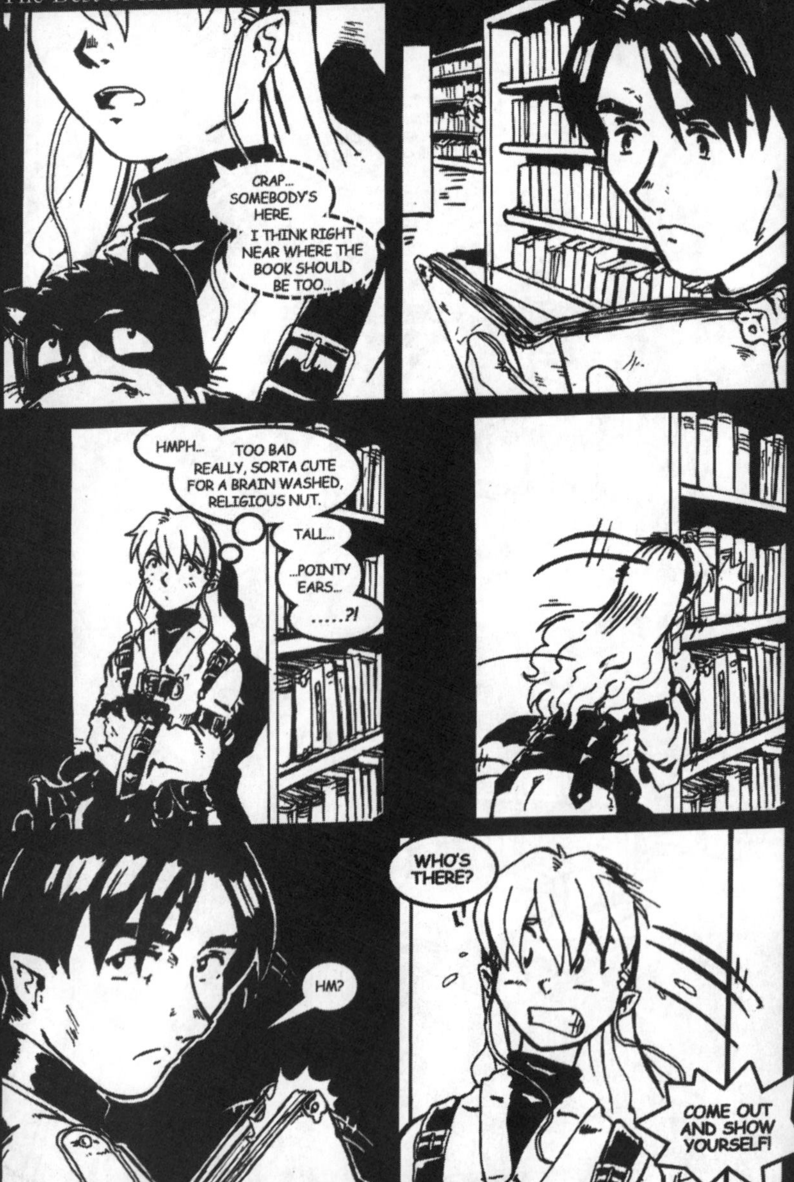
CRAP... SOMEBODY'S HERE.
I THINK RIGHT NEAR WHERE THE BOOK SHOULD BE TOO...
HMPH... TOO BAD REALLY, SORTA CUTE FOR A BRAIN WASHED, RELIGIOUS NUT.
TALL...
...POINTY EARS...
......?!
HM?
WHO'S THERE?
COME OUT AND SHOW YOURSELF!

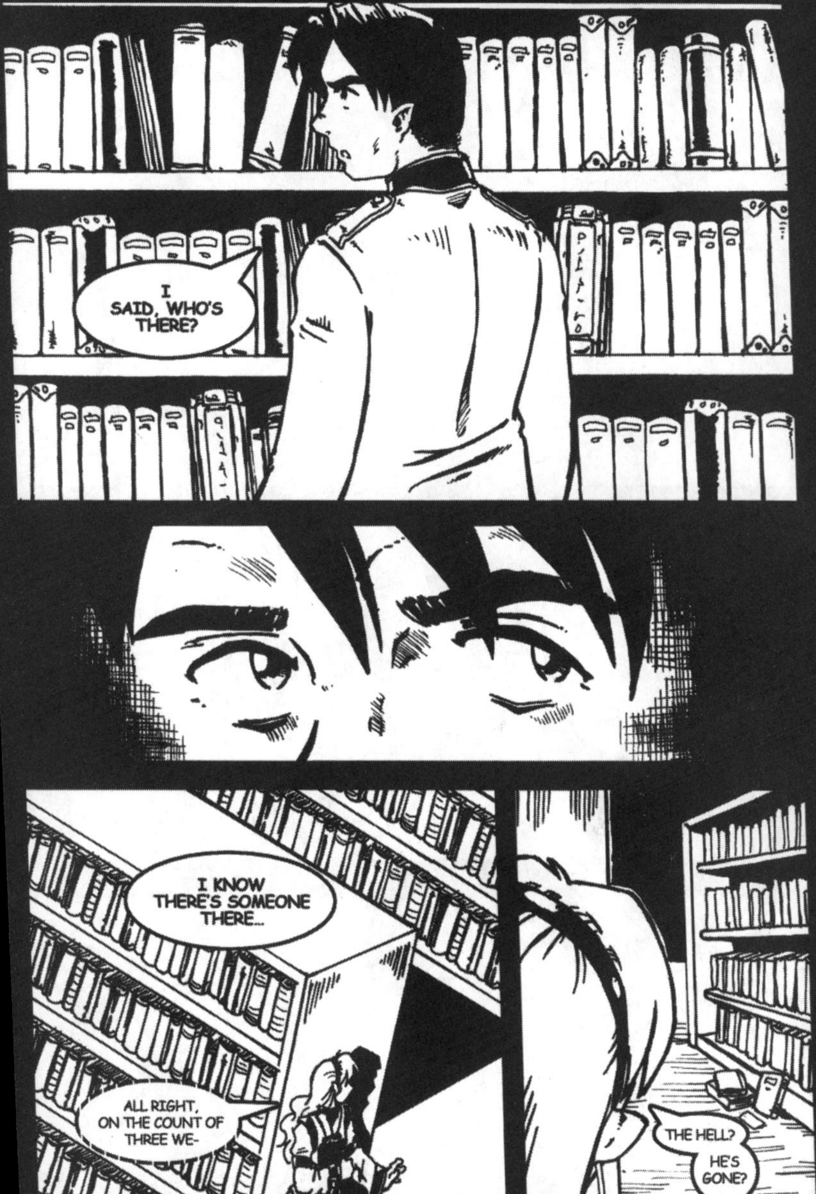
I SAID, WHO'S THERE?
I KNOW THERE'S SOMEONE THERE...
ALL RIGHT, ON THE COUNT OF THREE WE-
THE HELL?
HE'S GONE?

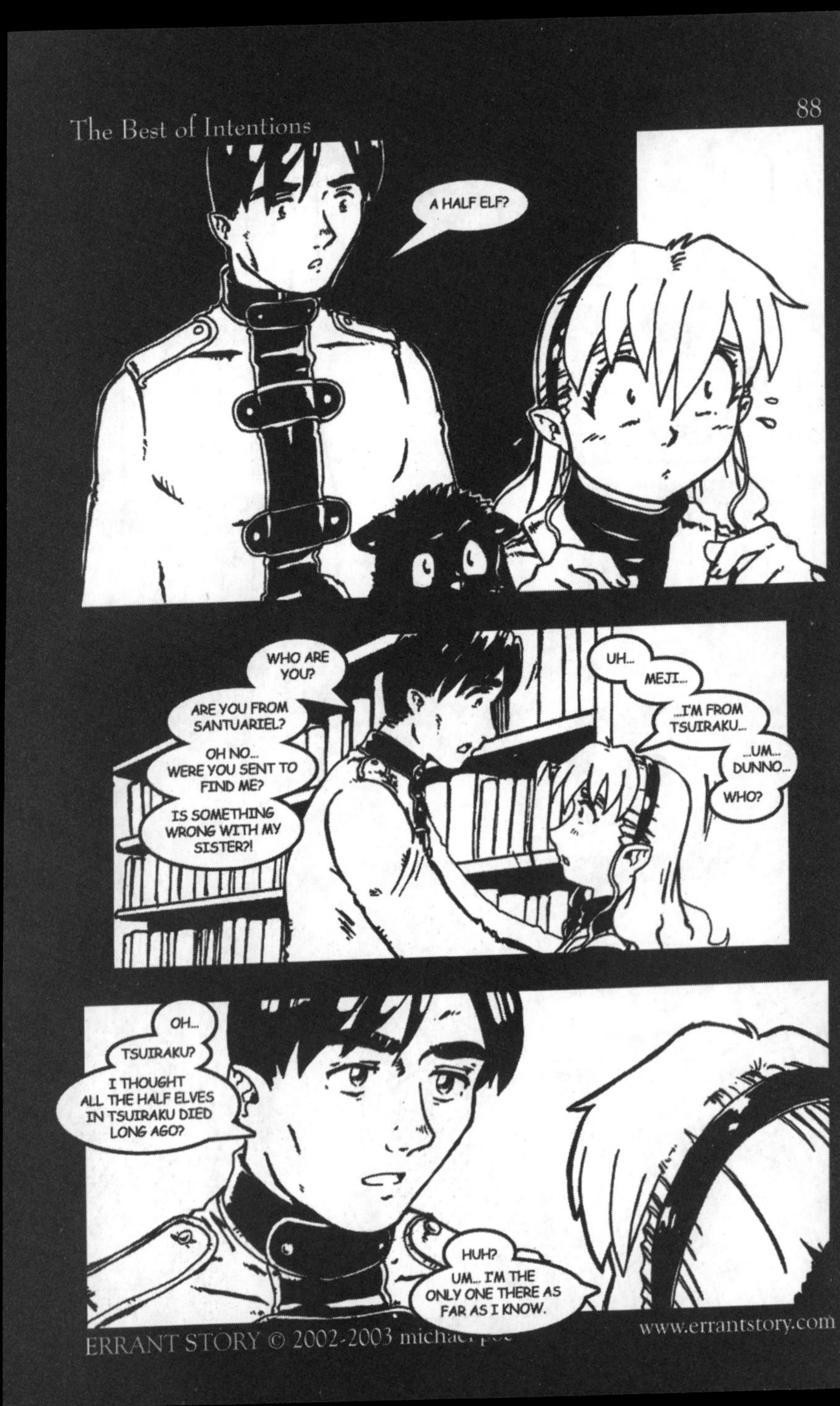
A HALF ELF?
WHO ARE YOU?
ARE YOU FROM SANTUARIEL?
OH NO... WERE YOU SENT TO FIND ME?
IS SOMETHING WRONG WITH MY SISTER?!
UH...
MEJI...
...I'M FROM TSUIRAKU...
...UM... DUNNO...
WHO?
OH...
TSUIRAKU?
I THOUGHT ALL THE HALF ELVES IN TSUIRAKU DIED LONG AGO?
HUH?
UM... I'M THE ONLY ONE THERE AS FAR AS I KNOW.

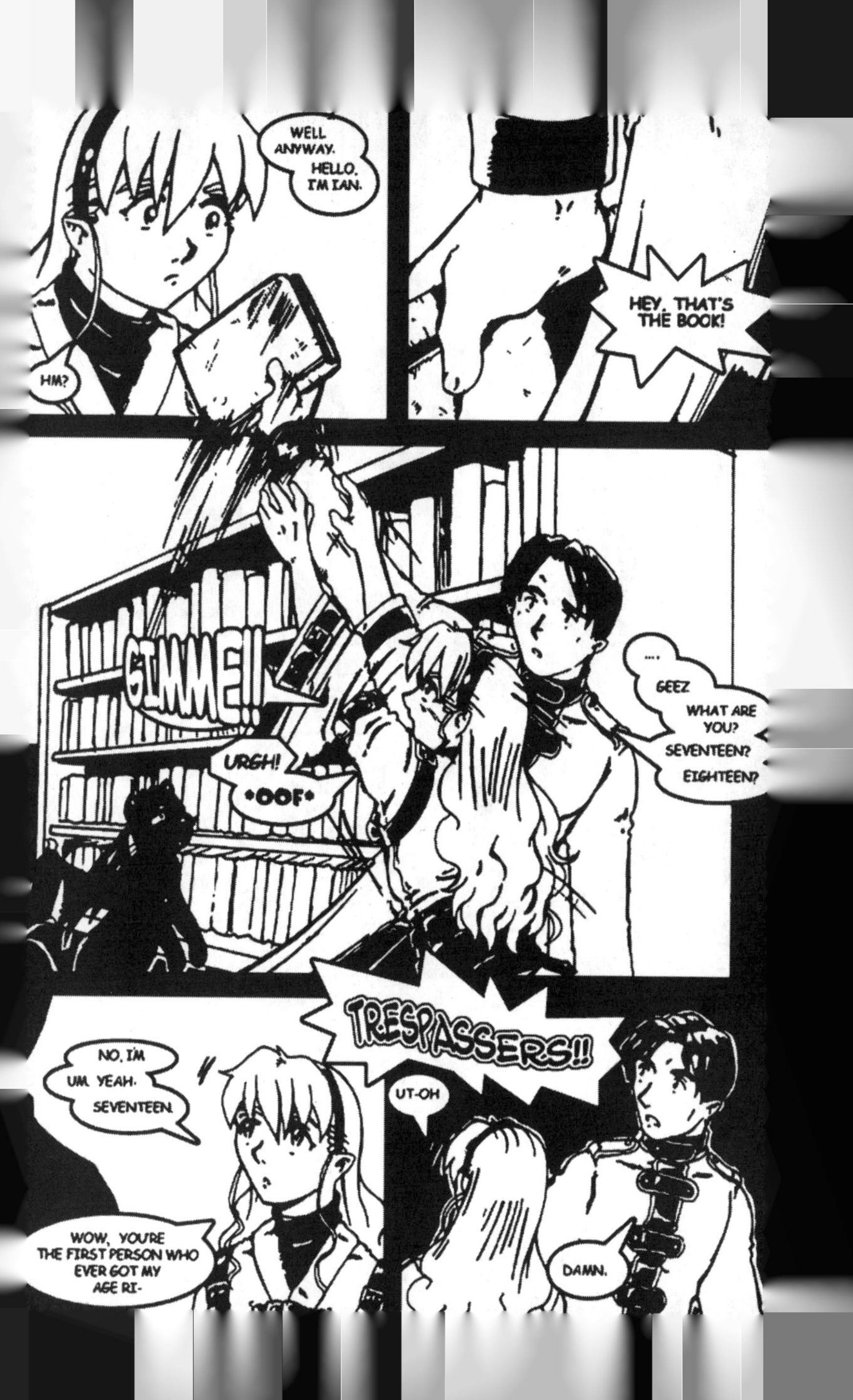
WELL ANYWAY. HELLO. I'M IAN.
HM?
HEY, THAT'S THE BOOK!
GIMME!!
URGH!
OOF
....
GEEZ WHAT ARE YOU? SEVENTEEN? EIGHTEEN?
NO, I'M UM YEAH. SEVENTEEN.
WOW, YOU'RE THE FIRST PERSON WHO EVER GOT MY AGE RI-
TRESPASSERS!!
UT-OH
DAMN.

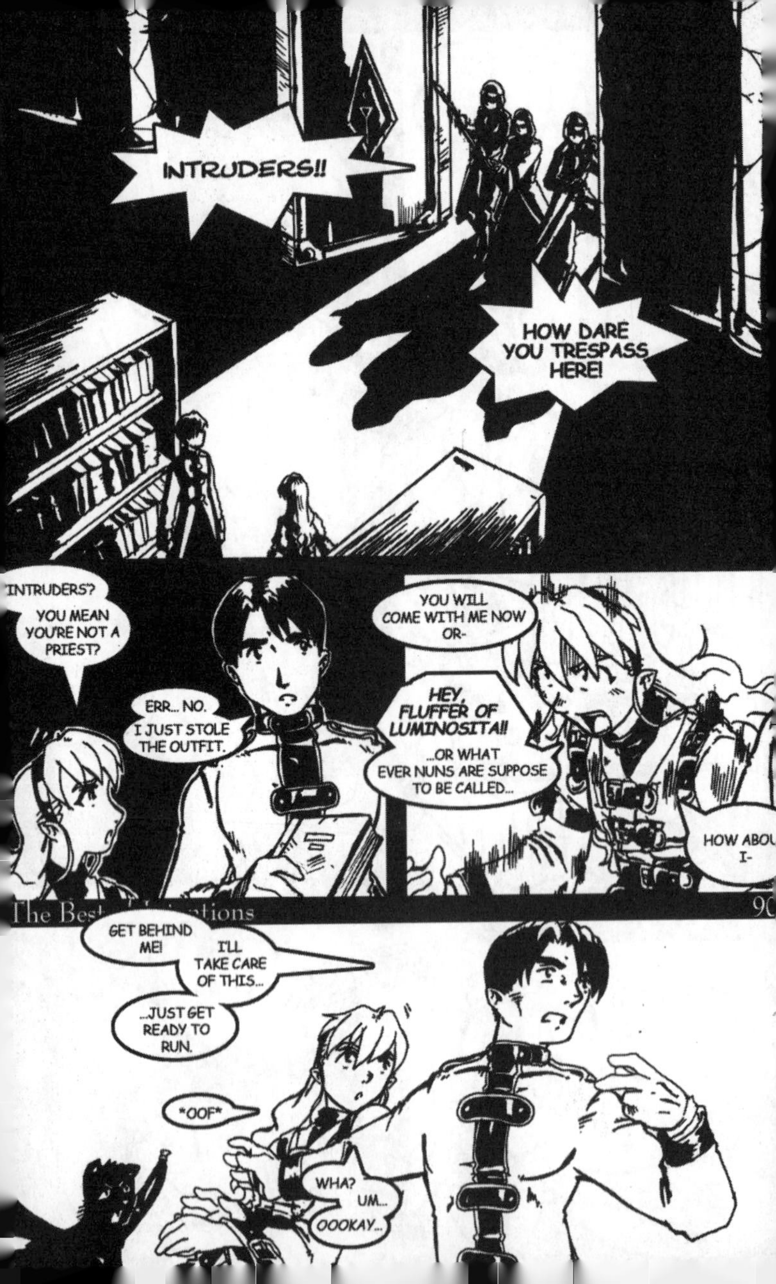
INTRUDERS!!
HOW DARE YOU TRESPASS HERE!
"INTRUDERS?
YOU MEAN YOU'RE NOT A PRIEST?
ERR... NO.
I JUST STOLE THE OUTFIT.
YOU WILL COME WITH ME NOW OR-
HEY, FLUFFER OF LUMINOSITA!!
...OR WHAT EVER NUNS ARE SUPPOSE TO BE CALLED...
HOW ABOU
I-
GET BEHIND ME!
I'LL TAKE CARE OF THIS...
...JUST GET READY TO RUN.
OOF
WHA?
UM...
OOOKAY...

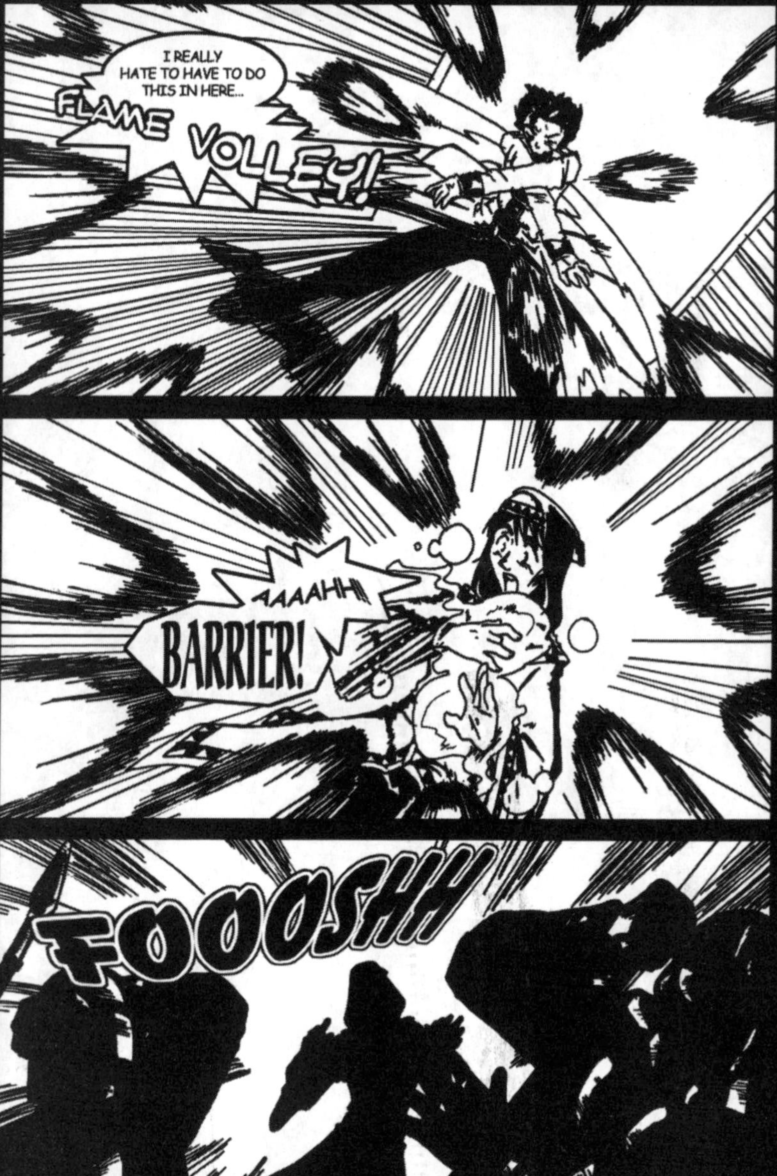
I REALLY HATE TO HAVE TO DO THIS IN HERE...
FLAME VOLLEY!
AAAAHH!
BARRIER!
FOOOSHH

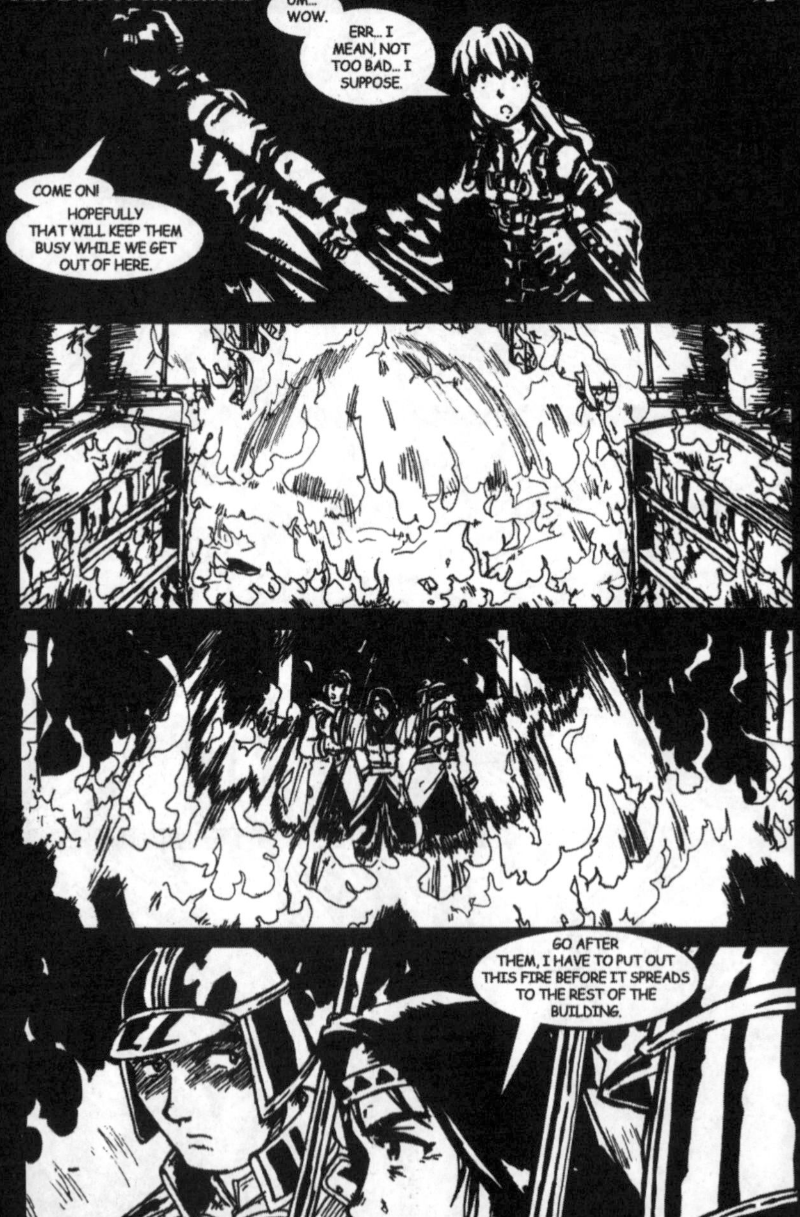
UM... WOW.
ERR... I MEAN, NOT TOO BAD... I SUPPOSE.
COME ON! HOPEFULLY THAT WILL KEEP THEM BUSY WHILE WE GET OUT OF HERE.
GO AFTER THEM, I HAVE TO PUT OUT THIS FIRE BEFORE IT SPREADS TO THE REST OF THE BUILDING.

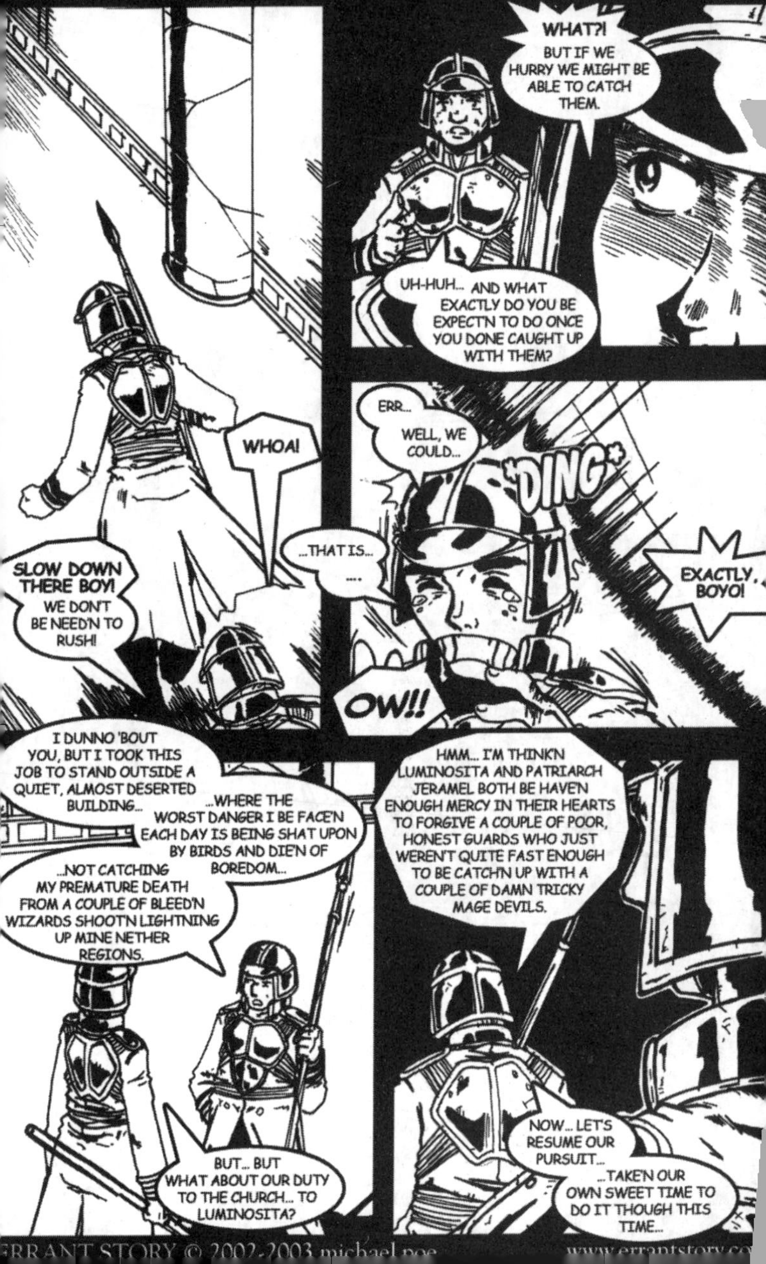
WHOA!
SLOW DOWN THERE BOY! WE DON'T BE NEED'N TO RUSH!
WHAT?! BUT IF WE HURRY WE MIGHT BE ABLE TO CATCH THEM.
UH-HUH... AND WHAT EXACTLY DO YOU BE EXPECT'N TO DO ONCE YOU DONE CAUGHT UP WITH THEM?
...THAT IS... ....
ERR... WELL, WE COULD...
DING
EXACTLY, BOYO!
OW!!
I DUNNO 'BOUT YOU, BUT I TOOK THIS JOB TO STAND OUTSIDE A QUIET, ALMOST DESERTED BUILDING...
...WHERE THE WORST DANGER I BE FACE'N EACH DAY IS BEING SHAT UPON BY BIRDS AND DIE'N OF BOREDOM...
...NOT CATCHING MY PREMATURE DEATH FROM A COUPLE OF BLEED'N WIZARDS SHOOT'N LIGHTNING UP MINE NETHER REGIONS.
BUT... BUT WHAT ABOUT OUR DUTY TO THE CHURCH... TO LUMINOSITA?
HMM... I'M THINK'N LUMINOSITA AND PATRIARCH JERAMEL BOTH BE HAVE'N ENOUGH MERCY IN THEIR HEARTS TO FORGIVE A COUPLE OF POOR, HONEST GUARDS WHO JUST WEREN'T QUITE FAST ENOUGH TO BE CATCH'N UP WITH A COUPLE OF DAMN TRICKY MAGE DEVILS.
NOW... LET'S RESUME OUR PURSUIT...
...TAKE'N OUR OWN SWEET TIME TO DO IT THOUGH THIS TIME...

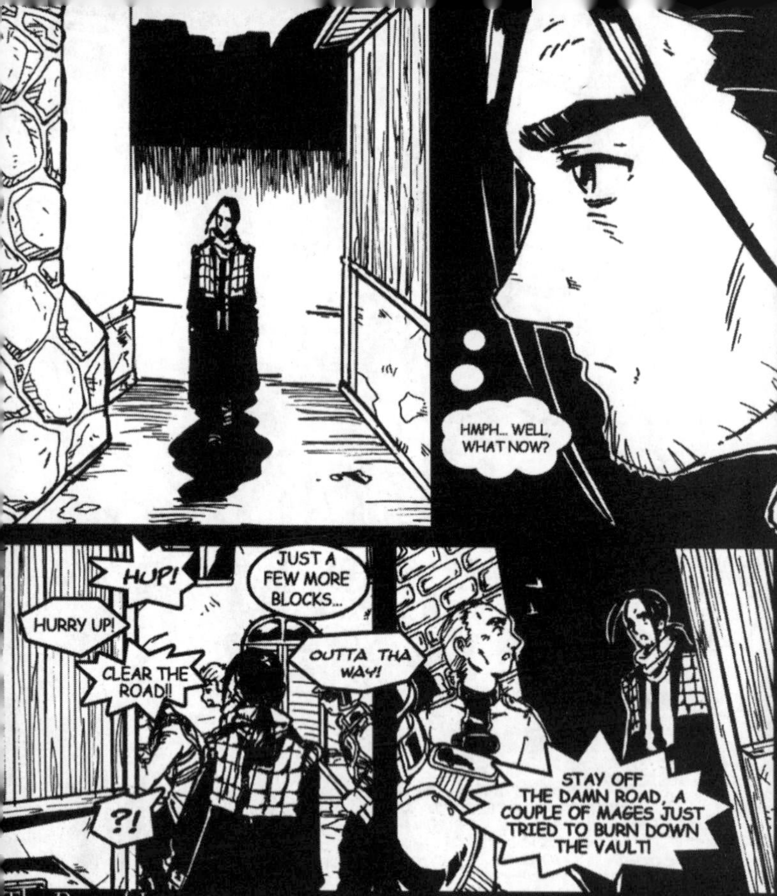
HMPH... WELL, WHAT NOW?
HUP!
JUST A FEW MORE BLOCKS...
HURRY UP!
CLEAR THE ROAD!!
OUTTA THA WAY!
?!
STAY OFF THE DAMN ROAD, A COUPLE OF MAGES JUST TRIED TO BURN DOWN THE VAULT!

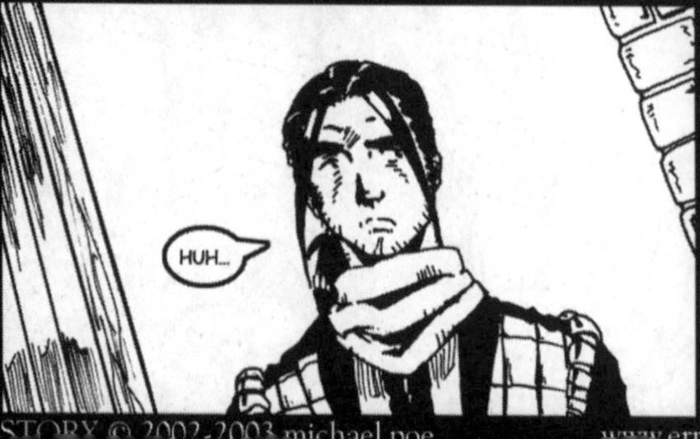
HUH...

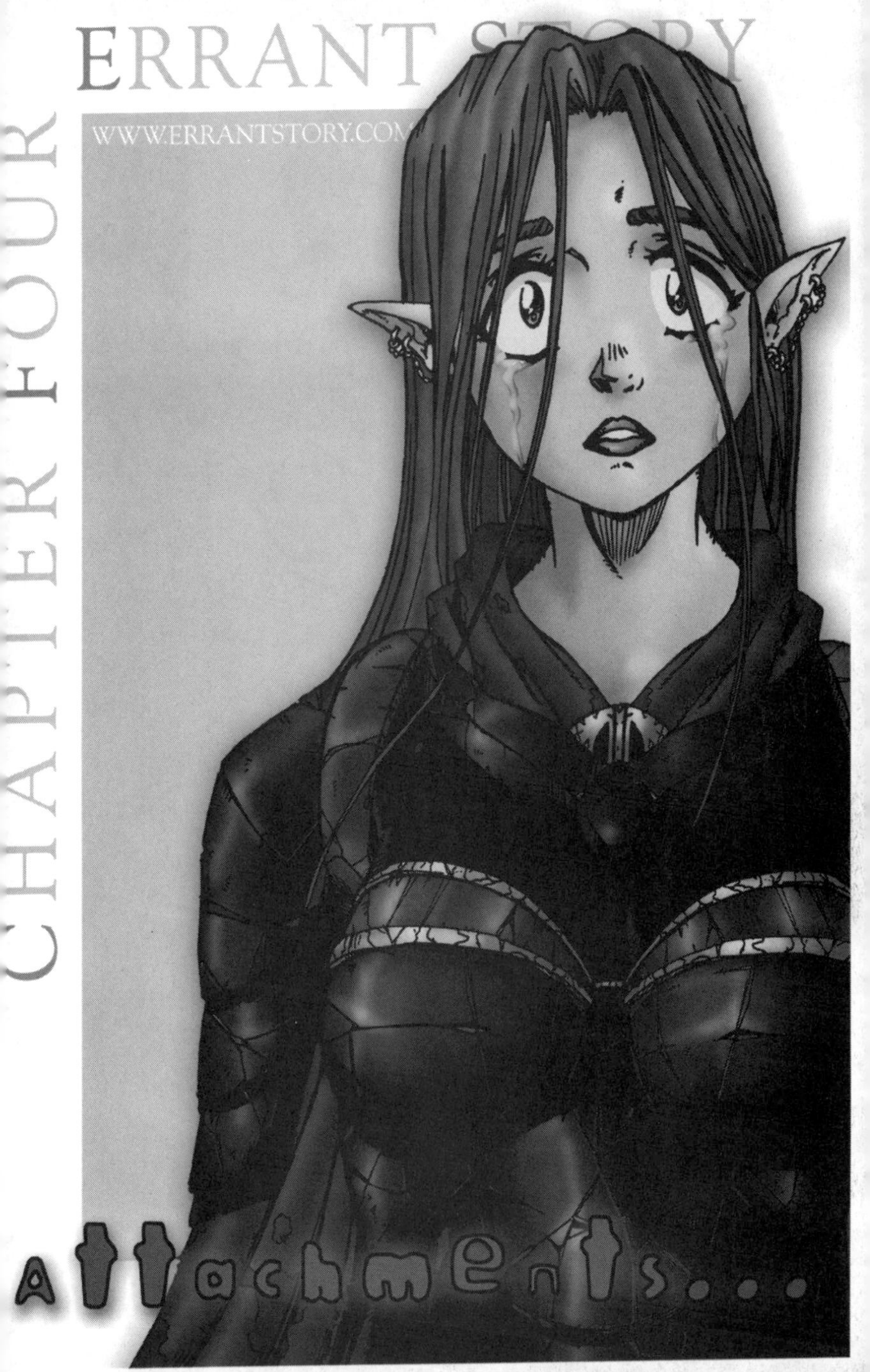
ERRANT STORY
WWW.ERRANTSTORY.COM
CHAPTER FOUR
Attachments...

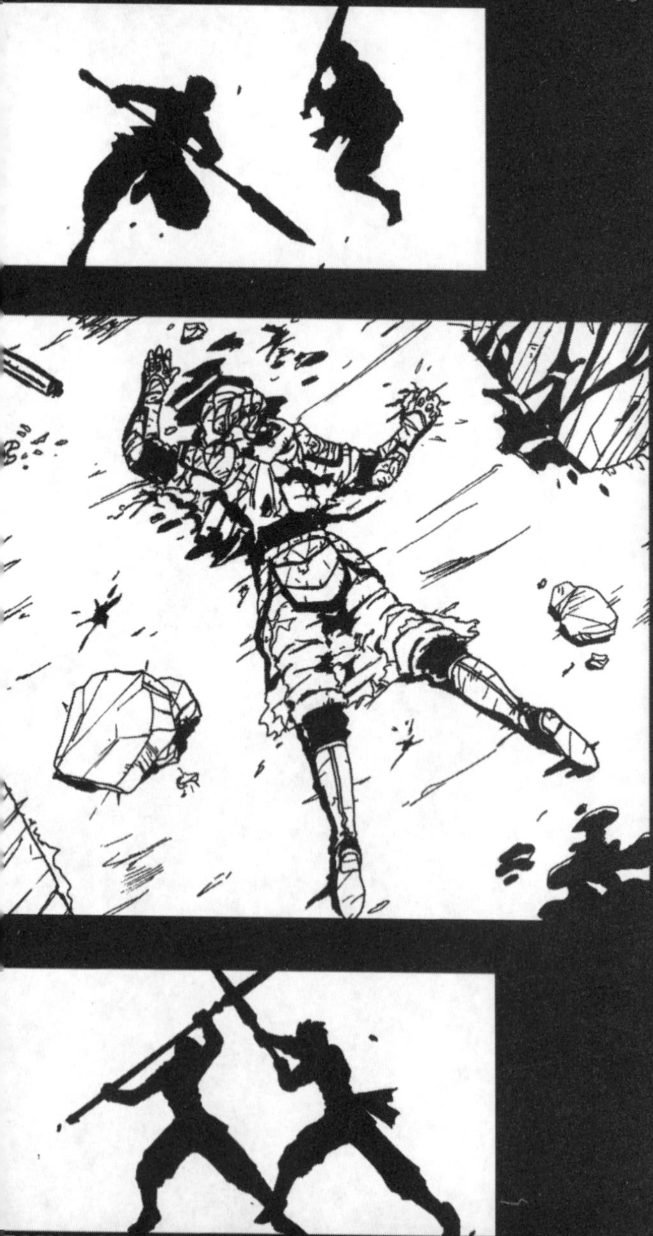

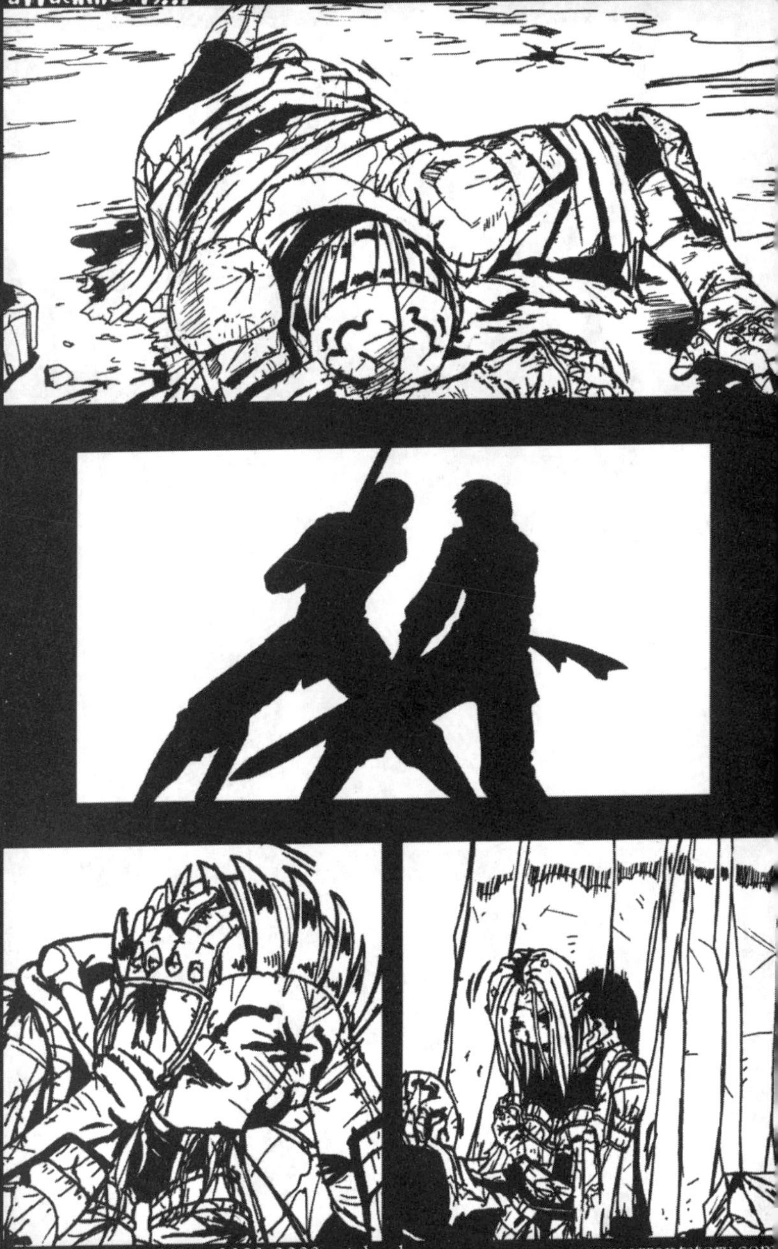

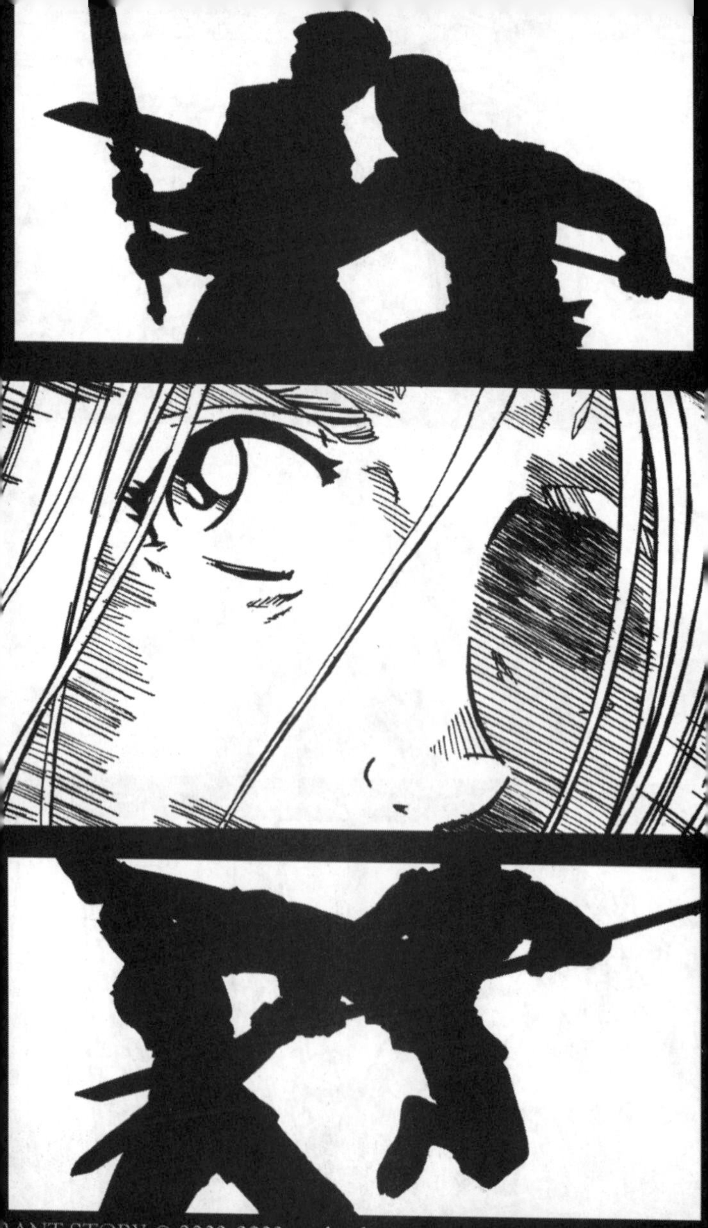

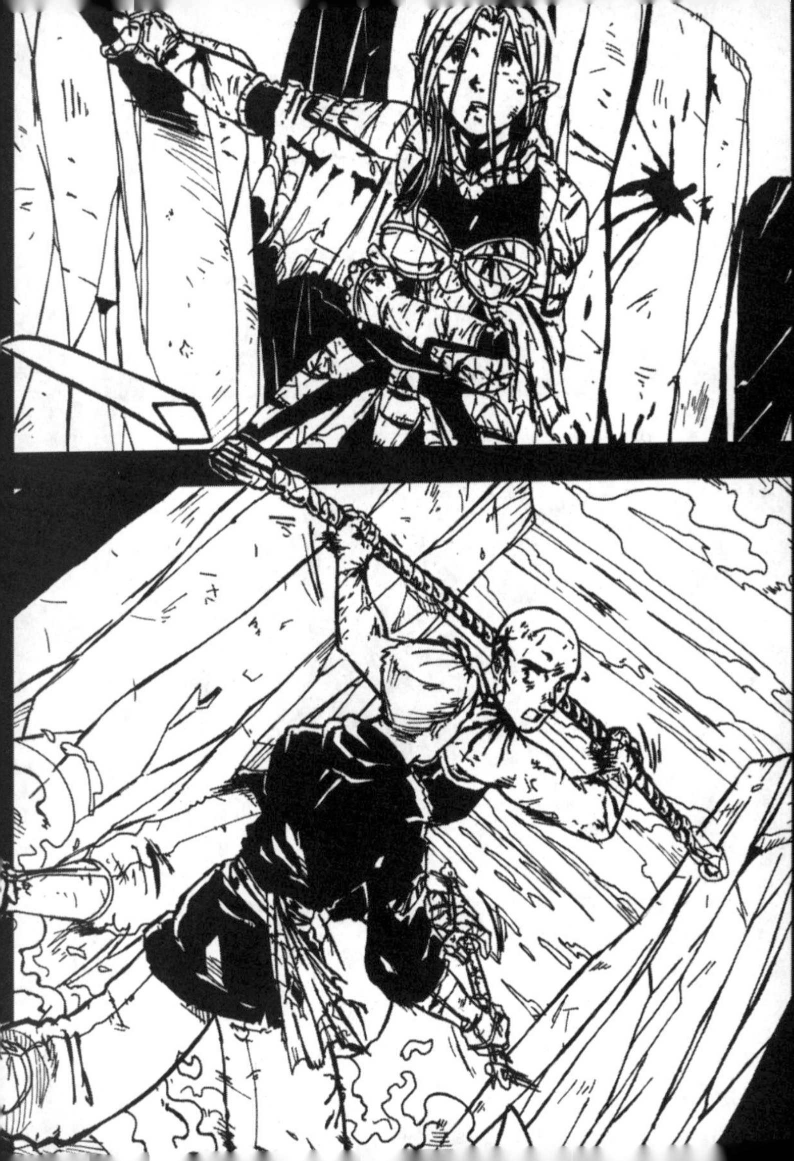

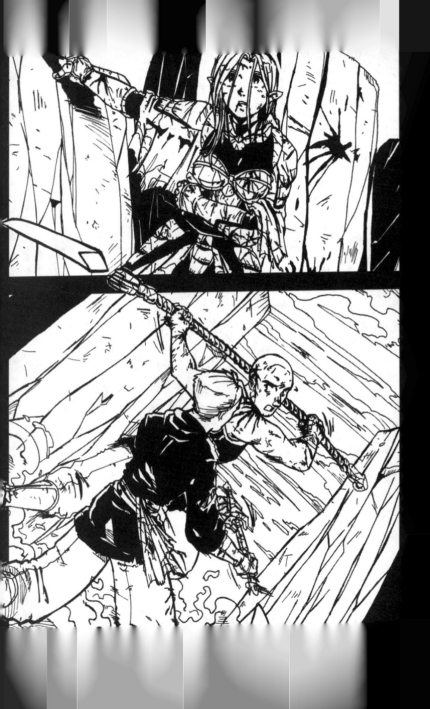

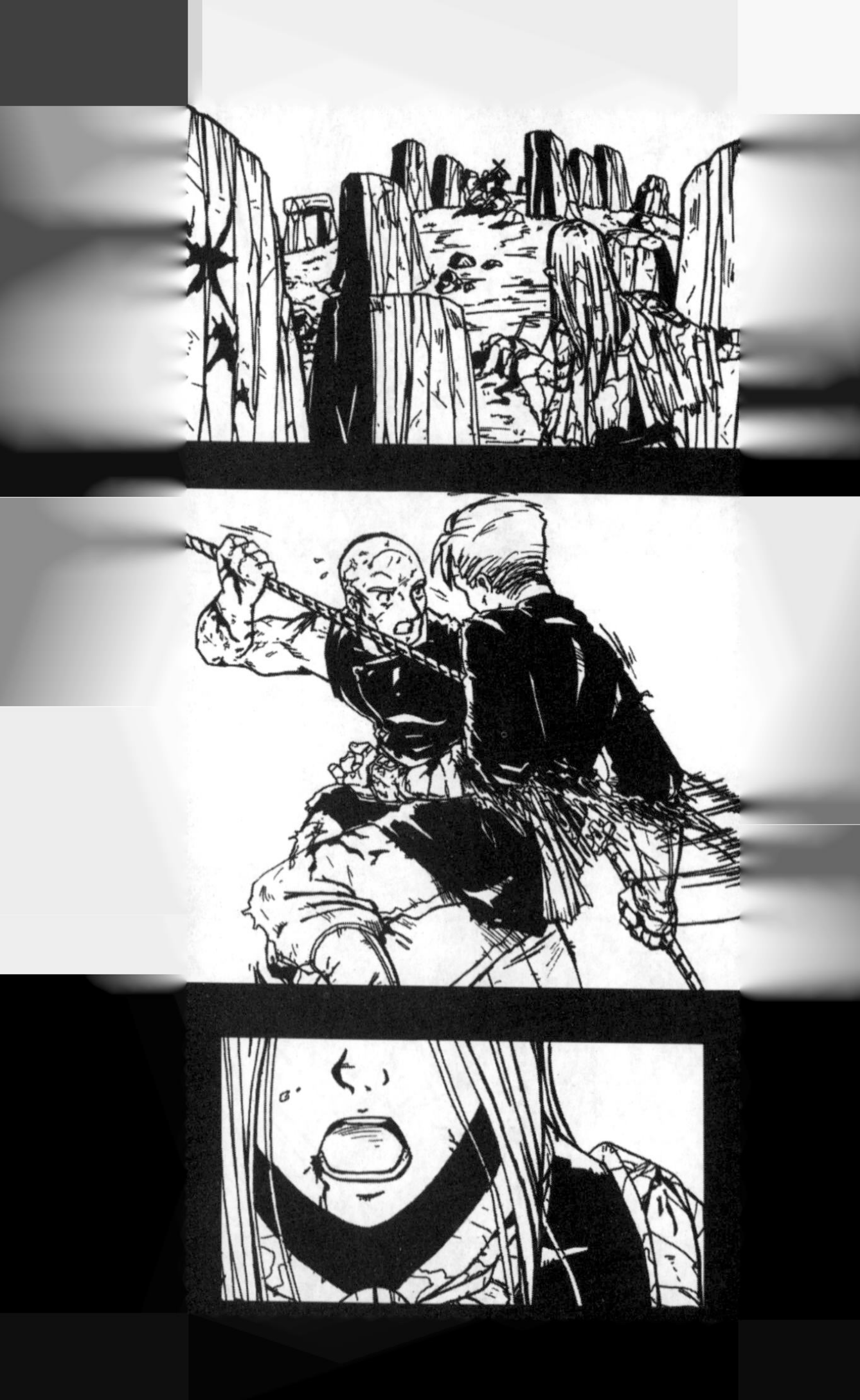

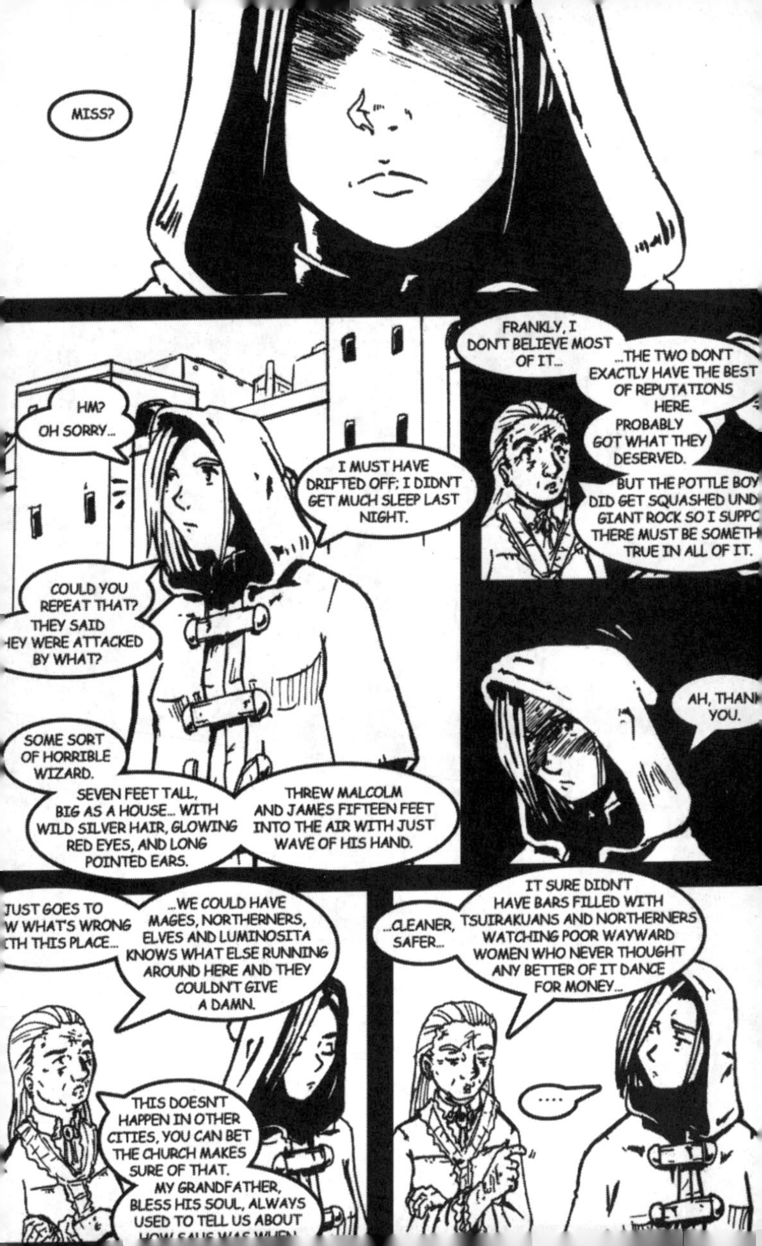
MISS?
HM? OH SORRY...
I MUST HAVE DRIFTED OFF; I DIDN'T GET MUCH SLEEP LAST NIGHT.
COULD YOU REPEAT THAT?
THEY SAID HEY WERE ATTACKED BY WHAT?
SOME SORT OF HORRIBLE WIZARD.
SEVEN FEET TALL, BIG AS A HOUSE... WITH WILD SILVER HAIR, GLOWING RED EYES, AND LONG POINTED EARS.
THREW MALCOLM AND JAMES FIFTEEN FEET INTO THE AIR WITH JUST WAVE OF HIS HAND.
FRANKLY, I DON'T BELIEVE MOST OF IT...
...THE TWO DON'T EXACTLY HAVE THE BEST OF REPUTATIONS HERE.
PROBABLY GOT WHAT THEY DESERVED.
BUT THE POTTLE BOY DID GET SQUASHED UND GIANT ROCK SO I SUPPO THERE MUST BE SOMETH TRUE IN ALL OF IT.
AH, THANK YOU.
JUST GOES TO W WHAT'S WRONG ITH THIS PLACE...
...WE COULD HAVE MAGES, NORTHERNERS, ELVES AND LUMINOSITA KNOWS WHAT ELSE RUNNING AROUND HERE AND THEY COULDN'T GIVE A DAMN.
THIS DOESN'T HAPPEN IN OTHER CITIES, YOU CAN BET THE CHURCH MAKES SURE OF THAT.
MY GRANDFATHER, BLESS HIS SOUL, ALWAYS USED TO TELL US ABOUT
...CLEANER, SAFER...
IT SURE DIDN'T HAVE BARS FILLED WITH TSUIRAKUANS AND NORTHERNERS WATCHING POOR WAYWARD WOMEN WHO NEVER THOUGHT ANY BETTER OF IT DANCE FOR MONEY...
....

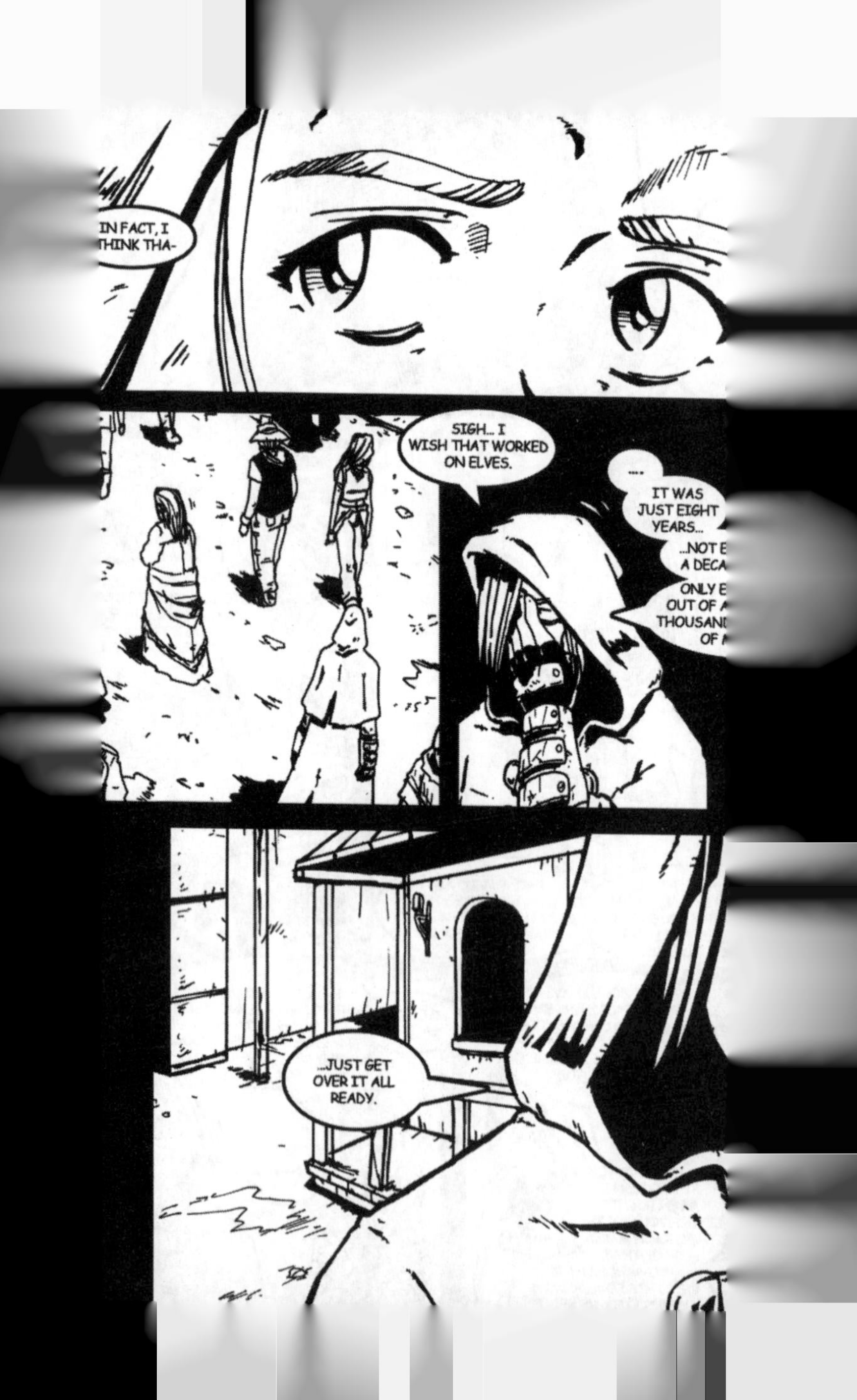

IN FACT, I THINK THA-
SIGH... I WISH THAT WORKED ON ELVES.
....
IT WAS JUST EIGHT YEARS...
...JUST GET OVER IT ALL READY.

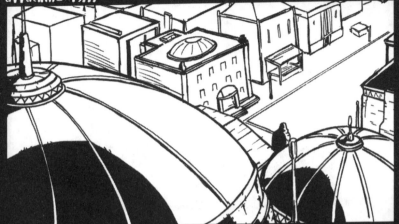

EXCUSE ME, MA'AM...

...OR MISS...

CAN I SEE SOME IDENTIFICATION?

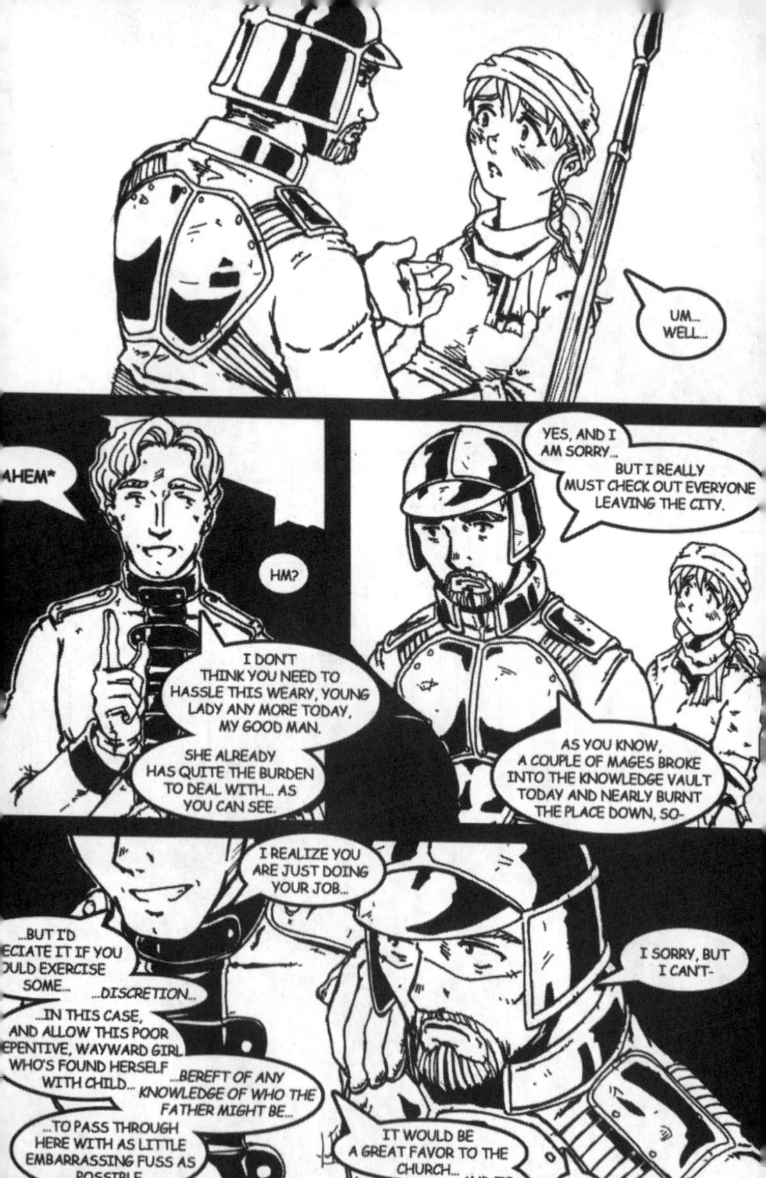

UM... WELL...
AHEM
HM?
I DON'T THINK YOU NEED TO HASSLE THIS WEARY, YOUNG LADY ANY MORE TODAY, MY GOOD MAN.
SHE ALREADY HAS QUITE THE BURDEN TO DEAL WITH... AS YOU CAN SEE.
YES, AND I AM SORRY...
BUT I REALLY MUST CHECK OUT EVERYONE LEAVING THE CITY.
AS YOU KNOW, A COUPLE OF MAGES BROKE INTO THE KNOWLEDGE VAULT TODAY AND NEARLY BURNT THE PLACE DOWN, SO-
I REALIZE YOU ARE JUST DOING YOUR JOB...
...BUT I'D ECIATE IT IF YOU OULD EXERCISE SOME...
...DISCRETION...
...IN THIS CASE, AND ALLOW THIS POOR EPENTIVE, WAYWARD GIRL WHO'S FOUND HERSELF WITH CHILD...
...BEREFT OF ANY KNOWLEDGE OF WHO THE FATHER MIGHT BE...
...TO PASS THROUGH HERE WITH AS LITTLE EMBARRASSING FUSS AS POSSIBLE.
I SORRY, BUT I CAN'T-
IT WOULD BE A GREAT FAVOR TO THE CHURCH...
...AND TO MYSELF.
....
...OH.

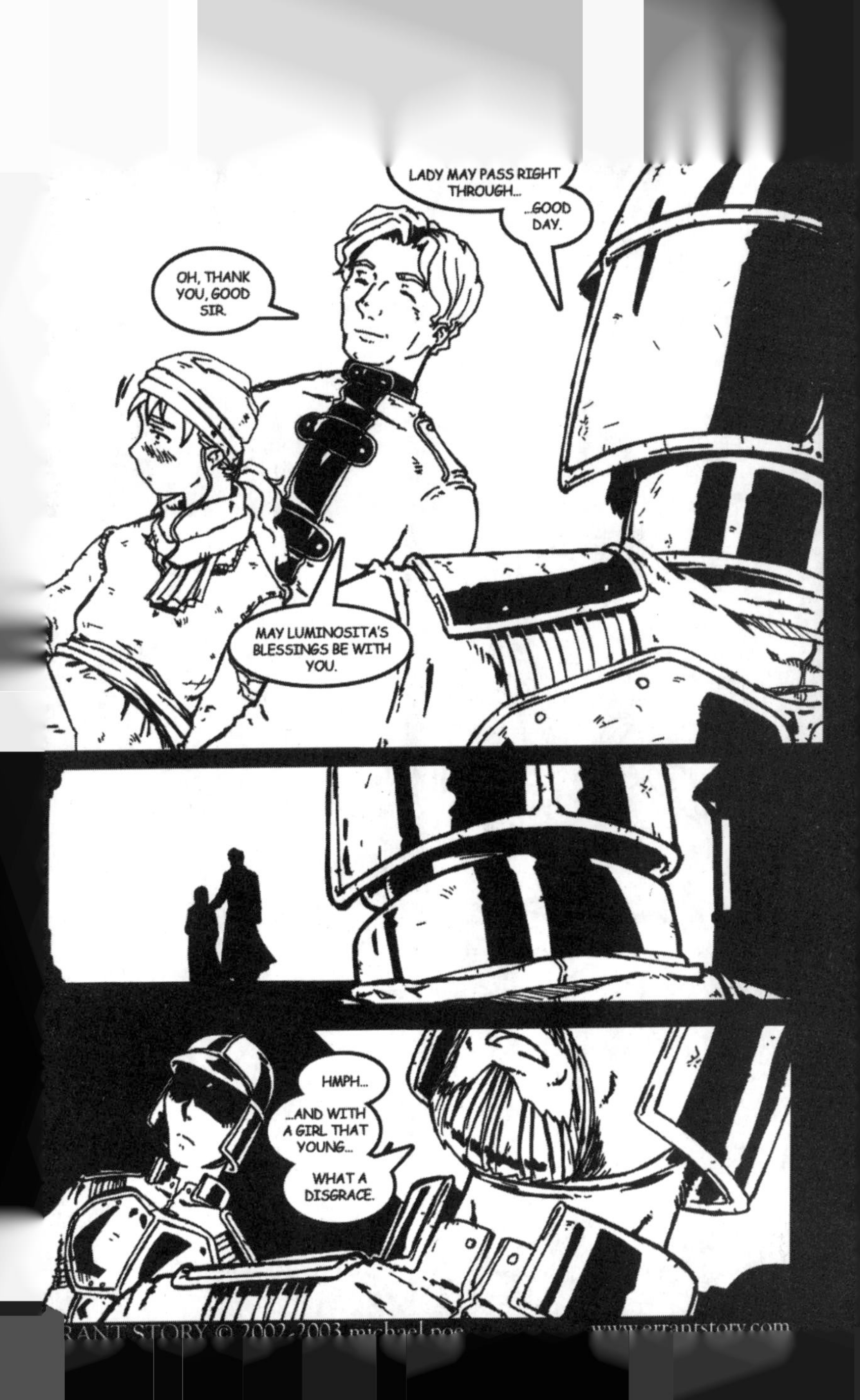
LADY MAY PASS RIGHT THROUGH...
...GOOD DAY.
OH, THANK YOU, GOOD SIR.
MAY LUMINOSITA'S BLESSINGS BE WITH YOU.
HMPH...
...AND WITH A GIRL THAT YOUNG...
WHAT A DISGRACE.

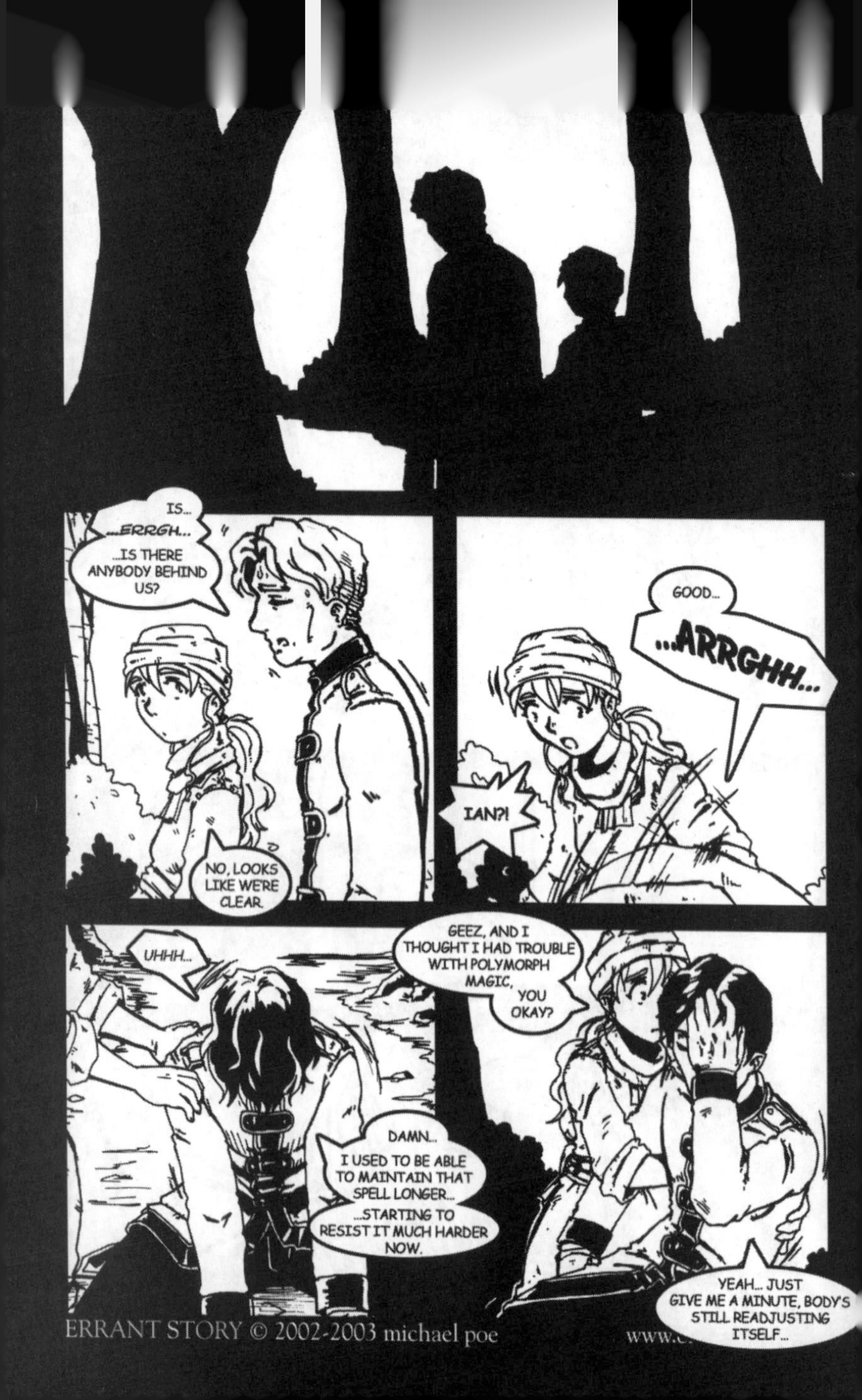
IS...
...ERRGH...
...IS THERE ANYBODY BEHIND US?
NO, LOOKS LIKE WE'RE CLEAR.
GOOD...
...ARRGHH...
IAN?!
UHHH...
DAMN... I USED TO BE ABLE TO MAINTAIN THAT SPELL LONGER... ...STARTING TO RESIST IT MUCH HARDER NOW.
GEEZ, AND I THOUGHT I HAD TROUBLE WITH POLYMORPH MAGIC,
YOU OKAY?
YEAH... JUST GIVE ME A MINUTE, BODY'S STILL READJUSTING ITSELF...

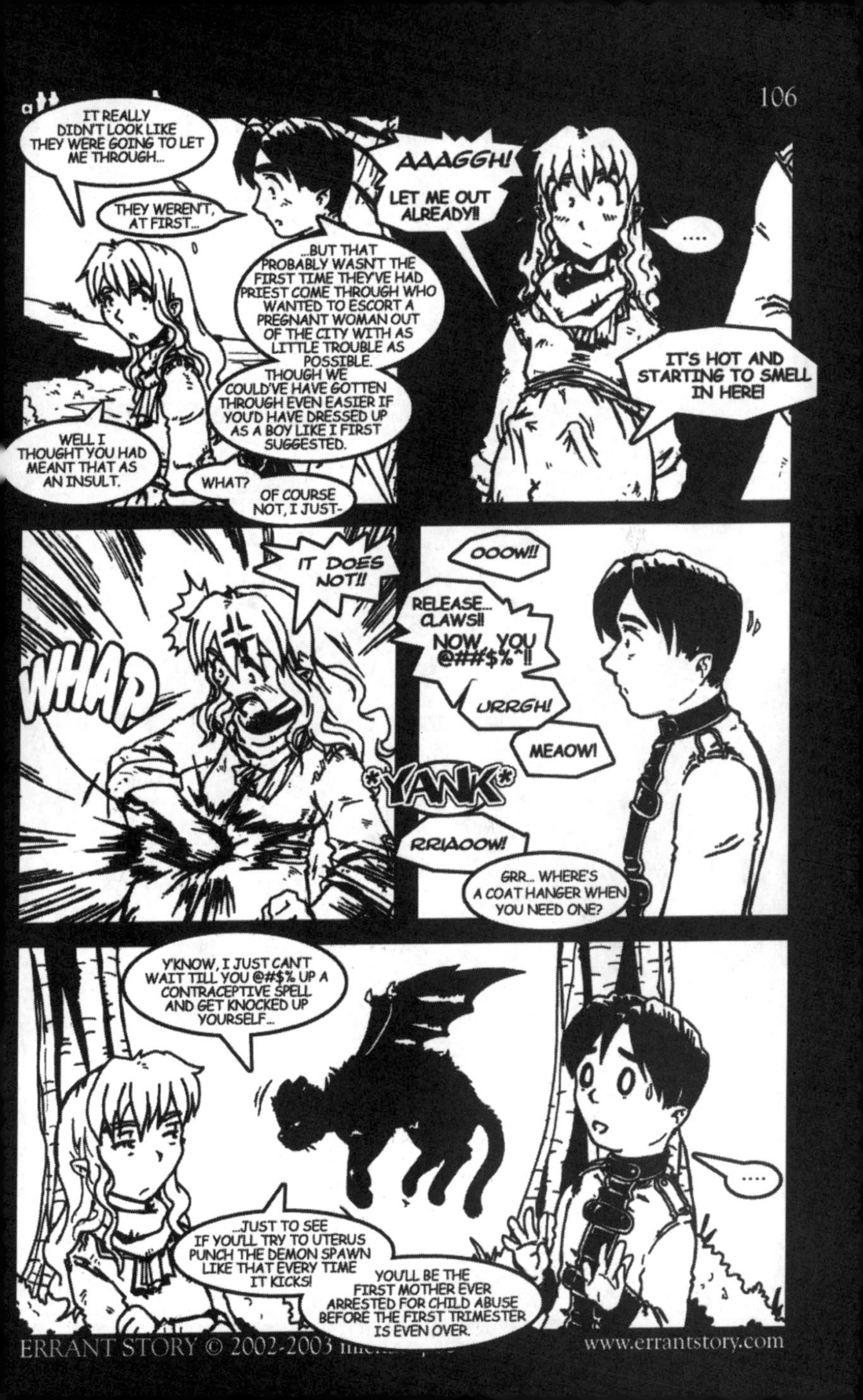
IT REALLY DIDN'T LOOK LIKE THEY WERE GOING TO LET ME THROUGH...
THEY WEREN'T, AT FIRST...
...BUT THAT PROBABLY WASN'T THE FIRST TIME THEY'VE HAD PRIEST COME THROUGH WHO WANTED TO ESCORT A PREGNANT WOMAN OUT OF THE CITY WITH AS LITTLE TROUBLE AS POSSIBLE.
THOUGH WE COULD'VE HAVE GOTTEN THROUGH EVEN EASIER IF YOU'D HAVE DRESSED UP AS A BOY LIKE I FIRST SUGGESTED.
WELL I THOUGHT YOU HAD MEANT THAT AS AN INSULT.
WHAT?
OF COURSE NOT, I JUST-
AAAGGH!
LET ME OUT ALREADY!!
....
IT'S HOT AND STARTING TO SMELL IN HERE!
WHAP
IT DOES NOT!!
YANK
OOOW!!
RELEASE... CLAWS!!
NOW, YOU @##$%^!!
URRGH!
MEAOW!
RRIAOOW!
GRR... WHERE'S A COAT HANGER WHEN YOU NEED ONE?
Y'KNOW, I JUST CAN'T WAIT TILL YOU @#$% UP A CONTRACEPTIVE SPELL AND GET KNOCKED UP YOURSELF...
...JUST TO SEE IF YOU'LL TRY TO UTERUS PUNCH THE DEMON SPAWN LIKE THAT EVERY TIME IT KICKS!
YOU'LL BE THE FIRST MOTHER EVER ARRESTED FOR CHILD ABUSE BEFORE THE FIRST TRIMESTER IS EVEN OVER.
....

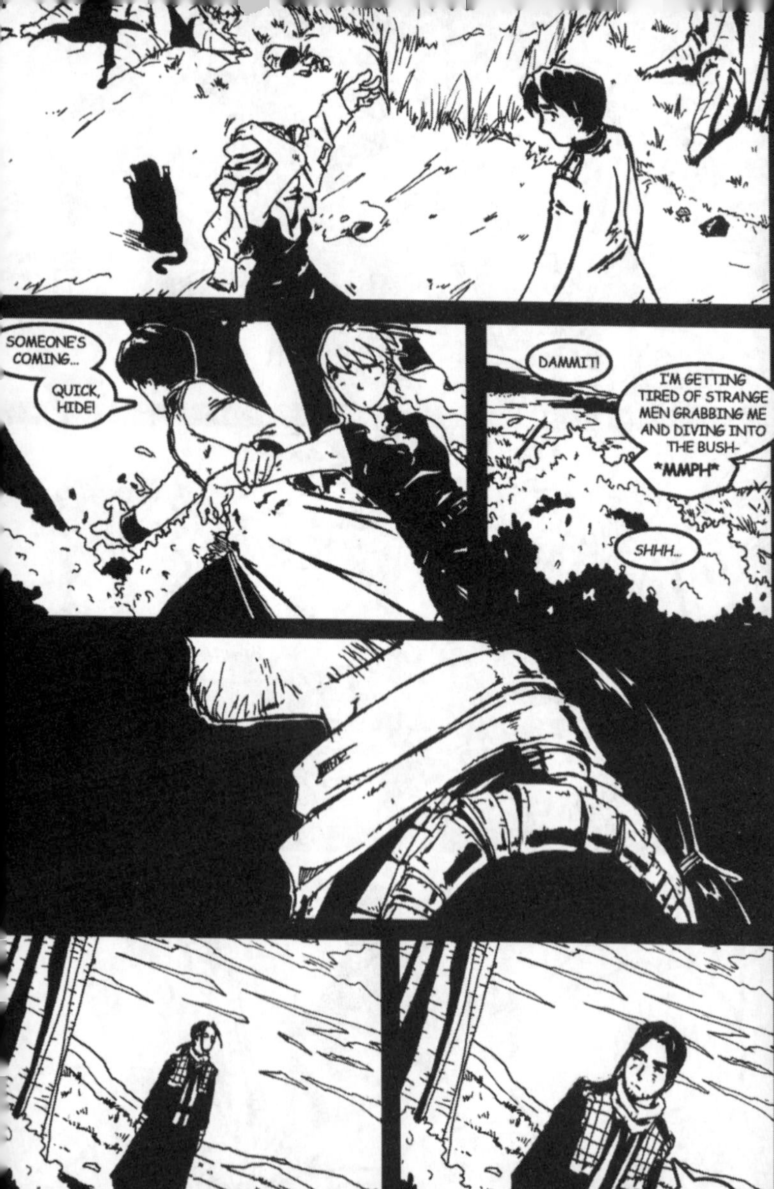
SOMEONE'S COMING...
QUICK, HIDE!
DAMMIT!
I'M GETTING TIRED OF STRANGE MEN GRABBING ME AND DIVING INTO THE BUSH-
MMPH
SHHH...
HMM...

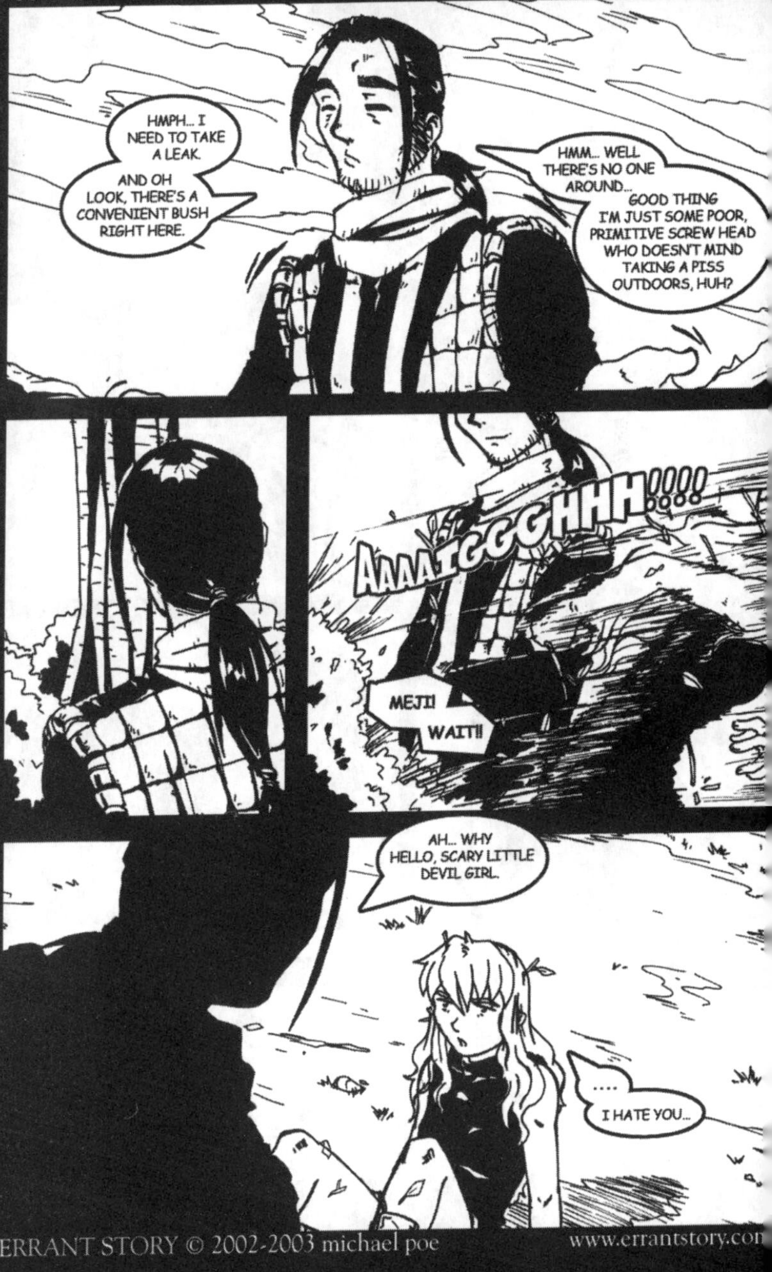
HMPH... I NEED TO TAKE A LEAK.
AND OH LOOK, THERE'S A CONVENIENT BUSH RIGHT HERE.
HMM... WELL THERE'S NO ONE AROUND...
GOOD THING I'M JUST SOME POOR, PRIMITIVE SCREW HEAD WHO DOESN'T MIND TAKING A PISS OUTDOORS, HUH?
AAAAIGGGGHHHH!!!!
MEJI!
WAIT!!
AH... WHY HELLO, SCARY LITTLE DEVIL GIRL.
....
I HATE YOU...

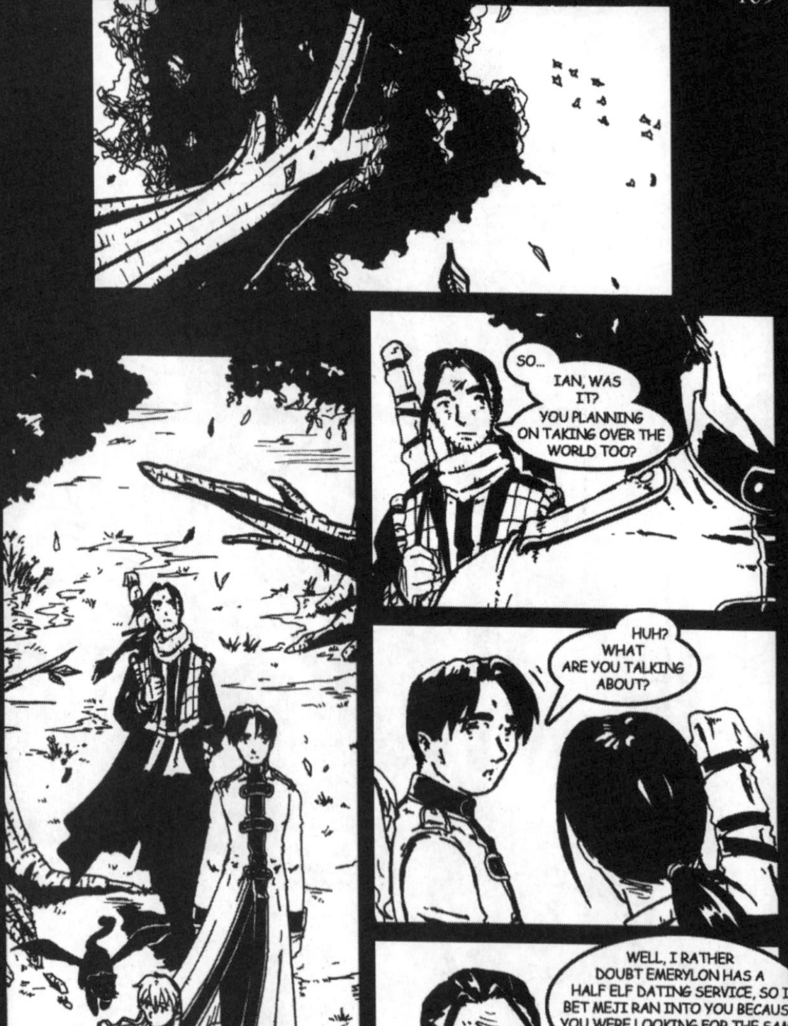
SO... IAN, WAS IT? YOU PLANNING ON TAKING OVER THE WORLD TOO?
HUH? WHAT ARE YOU TALKING ABOUT?
WELL, I RATHER DOUBT EMERYLON HAS A HALF ELF DATING SERVICE, SO I BET MEJI RAN INTO YOU BECAUS YOU WERE LOOKING FOR THE SAM BOOK SHE SAID SHE WAS AFTER, RIGHT?
DON'T TELL ME YOU'RE DOING A DAMN SCHOOL PROJECT TOO...

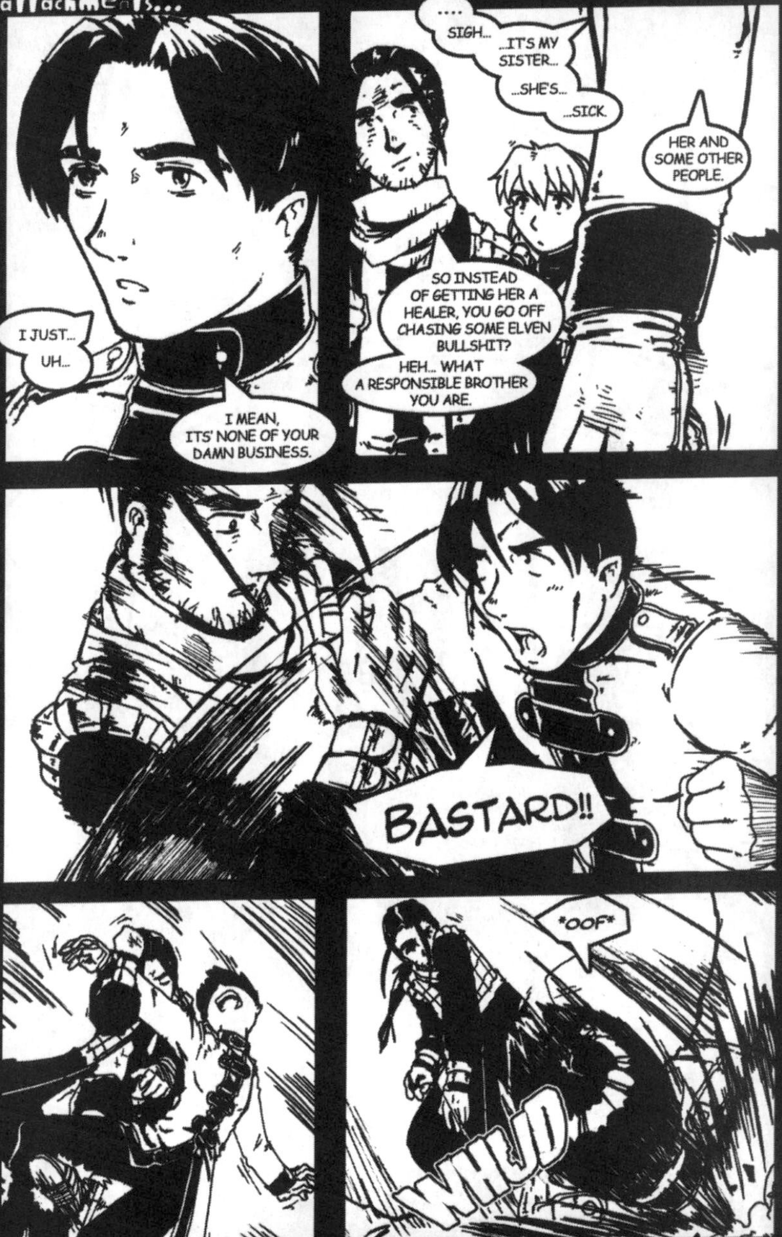
I JUST...
UH...
I MEAN, ITS' NONE OF YOUR DAMN BUSINESS.
.....
SIGH...
...IT'S MY SISTER...
...SHE'S...
...SICK.
HER AND SOME OTHER PEOPLE.
SO INSTEAD OF GETTING HER A HEALER, YOU GO OFF CHASING SOME ELVEN BULLSHIT?
HEH... WHAT A RESPONSIBLE BROTHER YOU ARE.
BASTARD!!
OOF
WHUD

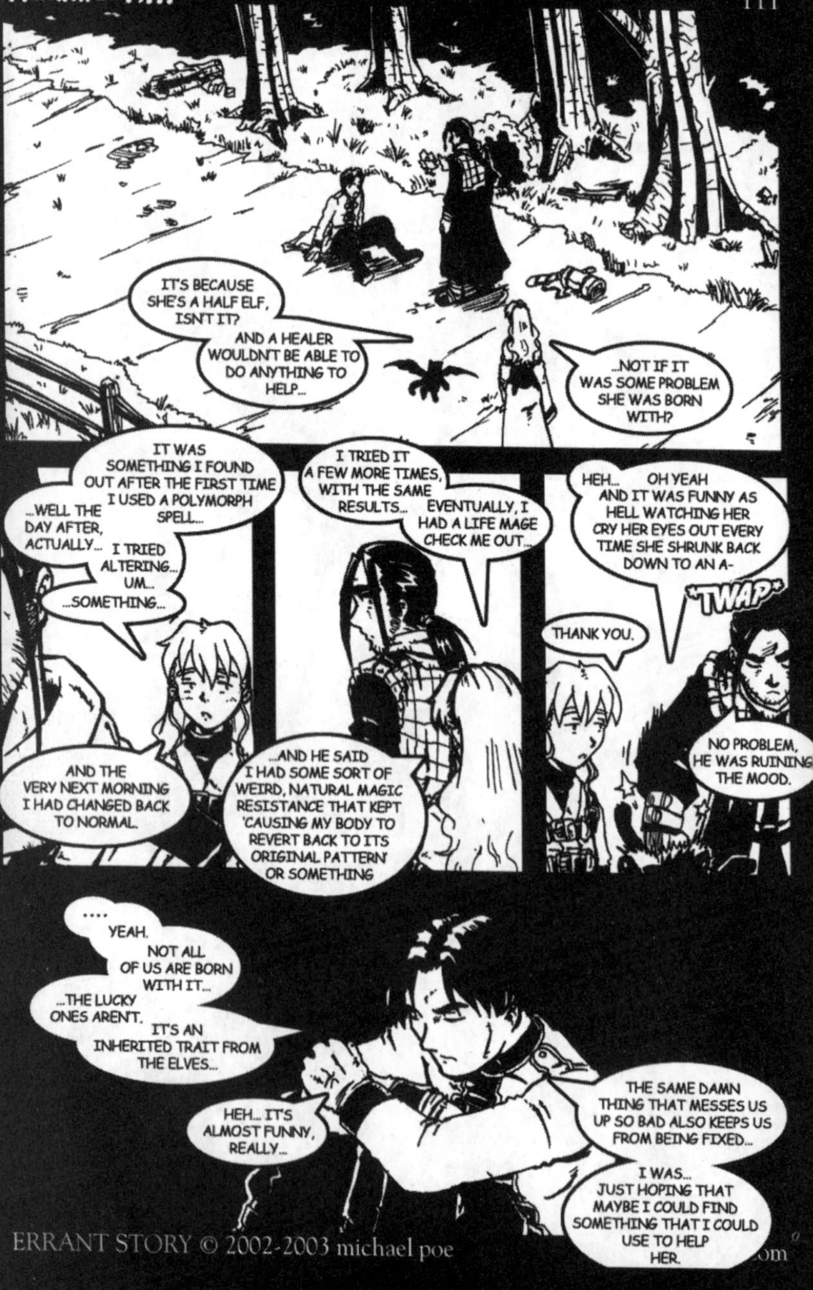
IT'S BECAUSE SHE'S A HALF ELF, ISN'T IT?
AND A HEALER WOULDN'T BE ABLE TO DO ANYTHING TO HELP...
...NOT IF IT WAS SOME PROBLEM SHE WAS BORN WITH?
IT WAS SOMETHING I FOUND OUT AFTER THE FIRST TIME I USED A POLYMORPH SPELL...
...WELL THE DAY AFTER, ACTUALLY...
I TRIED ALTERING... UM... ...SOMETHING...
AND THE VERY NEXT MORNING I HAD CHANGED BACK TO NORMAL.
I TRIED IT A FEW MORE TIMES, WITH THE SAME RESULTS...
EVENTUALLY, I HAD A LIFE MAGE CHECK ME OUT...
...AND HE SAID I HAD SOME SORT OF WEIRD, NATURAL MAGIC RESISTANCE THAT KEPT 'CAUSING MY BODY TO REVERT BACK TO ITS ORIGINAL PATTERN' OR SOMETHING
HEH... OH YEAH AND IT WAS FUNNY AS HELL WATCHING HER CRY HER EYES OUT EVERY TIME SHE SHRUNK BACK DOWN TO AN A-
TWAP
THANK YOU.
NO PROBLEM, HE WAS RUINING THE MOOD.
.... YEAH. NOT ALL OF US ARE BORN WITH IT... ...THE LUCKY ONES AREN'T. IT'S AN INHERITED TRAIT FROM THE ELVES...
HEH... IT'S ALMOST FUNNY, REALLY...
THE SAME DAMN THING THAT MESSES US UP SO BAD ALSO KEEPS US FROM BEING FIXED...
I WAS... JUST HOPING THAT MAYBE I COULD FIND SOMETHING THAT I COULD USE TO HELP HER.

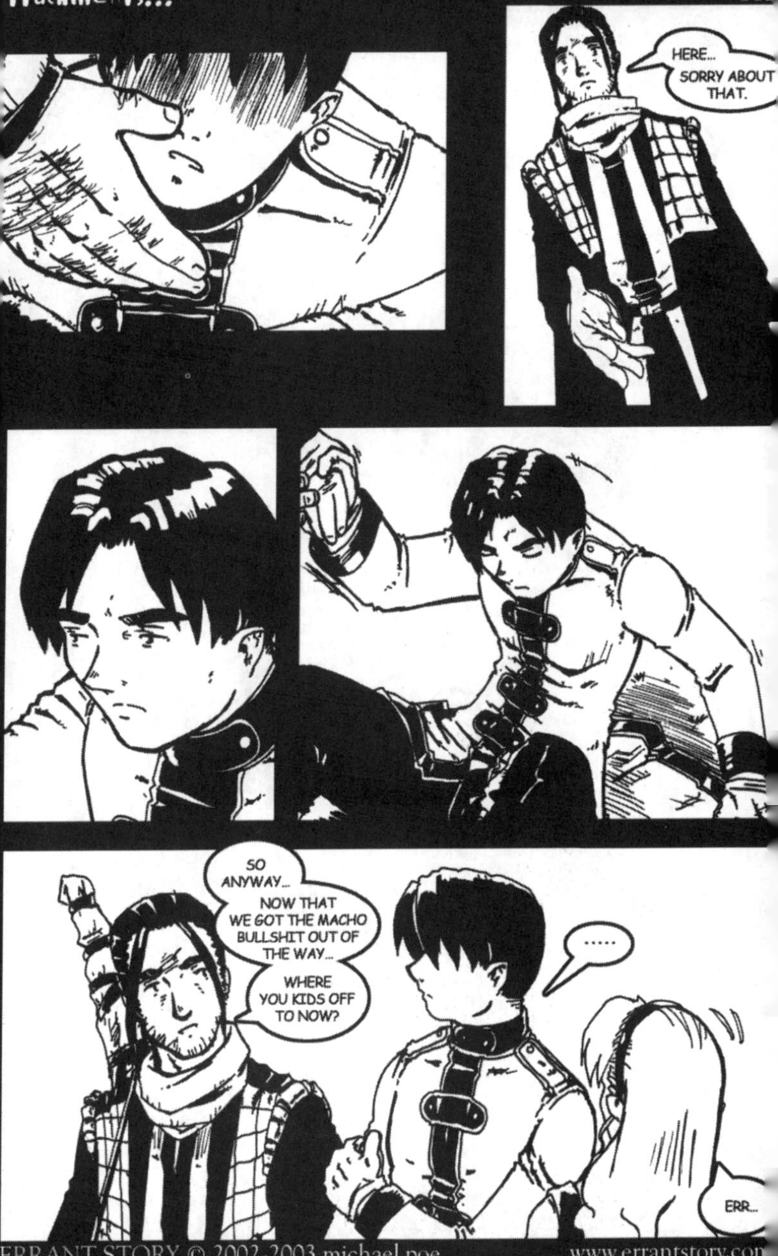
HERE... SORRY ABOUT THAT.
SO ANYWAY...
NOW THAT WE GOT THE MACHO BULLSHIT OUT OF THE WAY...
WHERE YOU KIDS OFF TO NOW?
......
ERR...

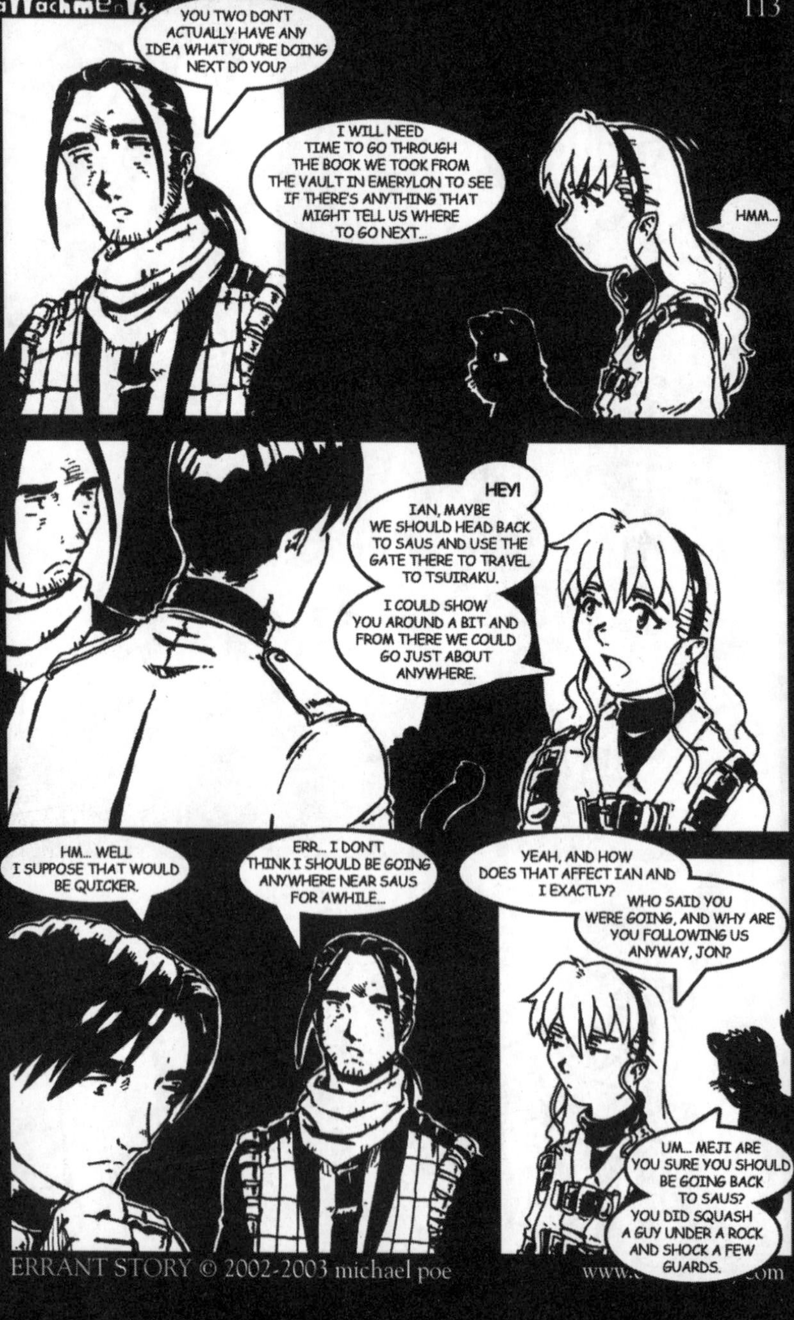
YOU TWO DON'T ACTUALLY HAVE ANY IDEA WHAT YOU'RE DOING NEXT DO YOU?
I WILL NEED TIME TO GO THROUGH THE BOOK WE TOOK FROM THE VAULT IN EMERYLON TO SEE IF THERE'S ANYTHING THAT MIGHT TELL US WHERE TO GO NEXT...
HMM...
HEY! IAN, MAYBE WE SHOULD HEAD BACK TO SAUS AND USE THE GATE THERE TO TRAVEL TO TSUIRAKU.
I COULD SHOW YOU AROUND A BIT AND FROM THERE WE COULD GO JUST ABOUT ANYWHERE.
HM... WELL I SUPPOSE THAT WOULD BE QUICKER.
ERR... I DON'T THINK I SHOULD BE GOING ANYWHERE NEAR SAUS FOR AWHILE...
YEAH, AND HOW DOES THAT AFFECT IAN AND I EXACTLY?
WHO SAID YOU WERE GOING, AND WHY ARE YOU FOLLOWING US ANYWAY, JON?
UM... MEJI ARE YOU SURE YOU SHOULD BE GOING BACK TO SAUS? YOU DID SQUASH A GUY UNDER A ROCK AND SHOCK A FEW GUARDS.

HEY!
MAYBE YOU SHOULD THANK...
...ERR, THANKING, WHATEVER THE HELL YOU PEOPLE THANK, THAT I'M EVEN OFFERING TO COME ALONG.
WHAT?!
YEAH, YOU HAVE ANY IDEA WHAT I'D CHARGE PEOPLE FOR THIS KIND OF THING NORMALLY?
NO, BUT I'M SURE IT'D BE WAY TOO DAMN MUCH!
....
ACTUALLY, MEJI...
...I THINK IT MIGHT BE A GOOD IDEA IF HE DID COME WITH US.
AH, FINALLY... SOMEONE SENSIBLE.
WHA? BUT- BUT- BUT... WE DON'T NEED HIS HELP...
....
...FINE...
BUT HOW ARE WE GOING TO GET INTO SAUS THEN WITH A DAMN WANTED CRIMINAL FOLLOWING US?
EH... DON'T WORRY ABOUT IT.
I'LL FIGURE OUT SOME WAY TO GET IN...
...SOMEHOW...
HEH, WOULDN'T BE MUCH OF AN ASSASSIN IF A LITTLE THING LIKE...
...EVERY BLOODY COP IN SAUS LOOKING FOR ME...
...WAS ENOUGH TO KEEP ME FROM GETTING IN SOMEPLACE.
...HEH...
GROAN...
EXACTLY WHY AM I SUBJECTING MYSELF TO THIS NOW?

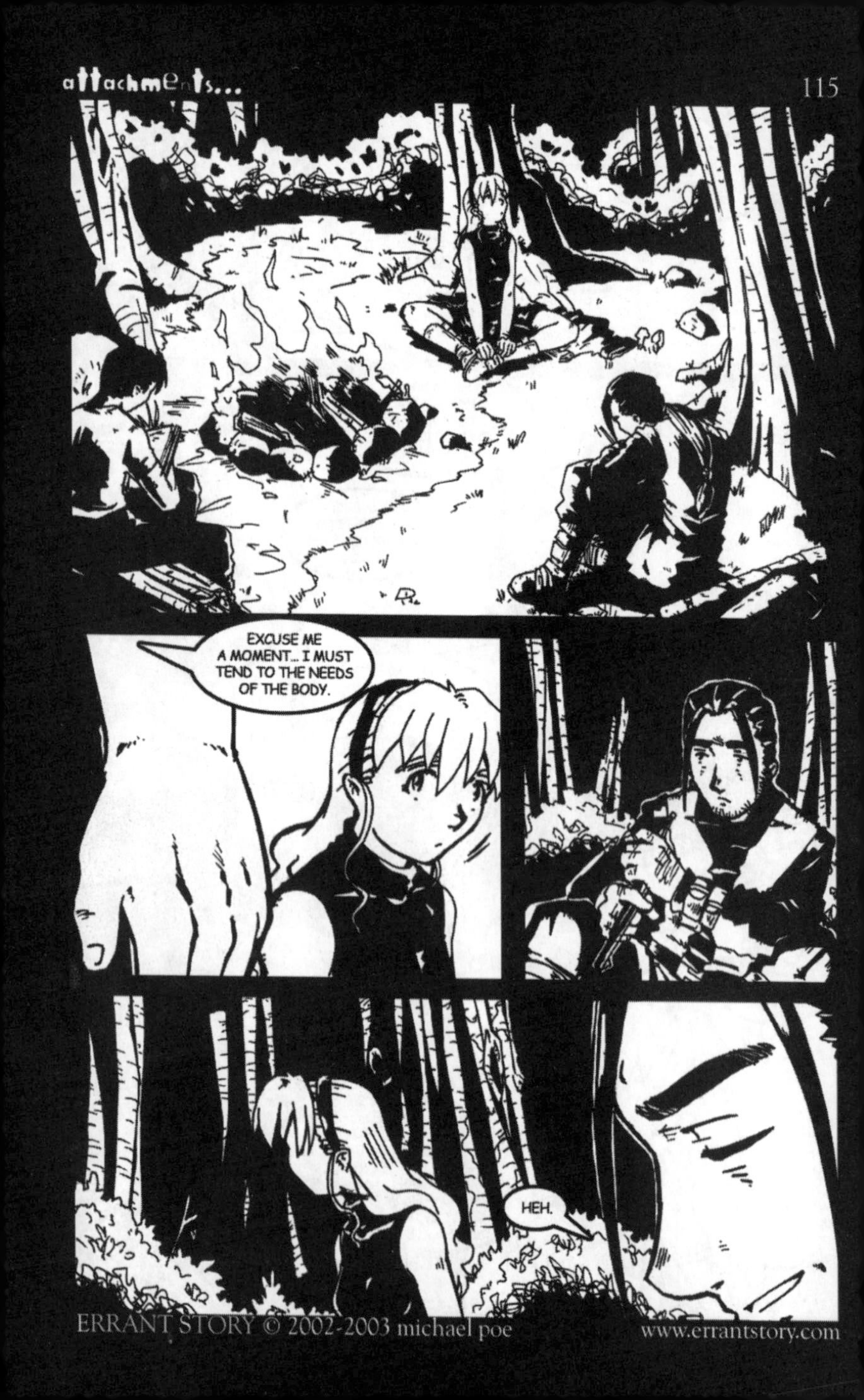
EXCUSE ME A MOMENT... I MUST TEND TO THE NEEDS OF THE BODY.
HEH.

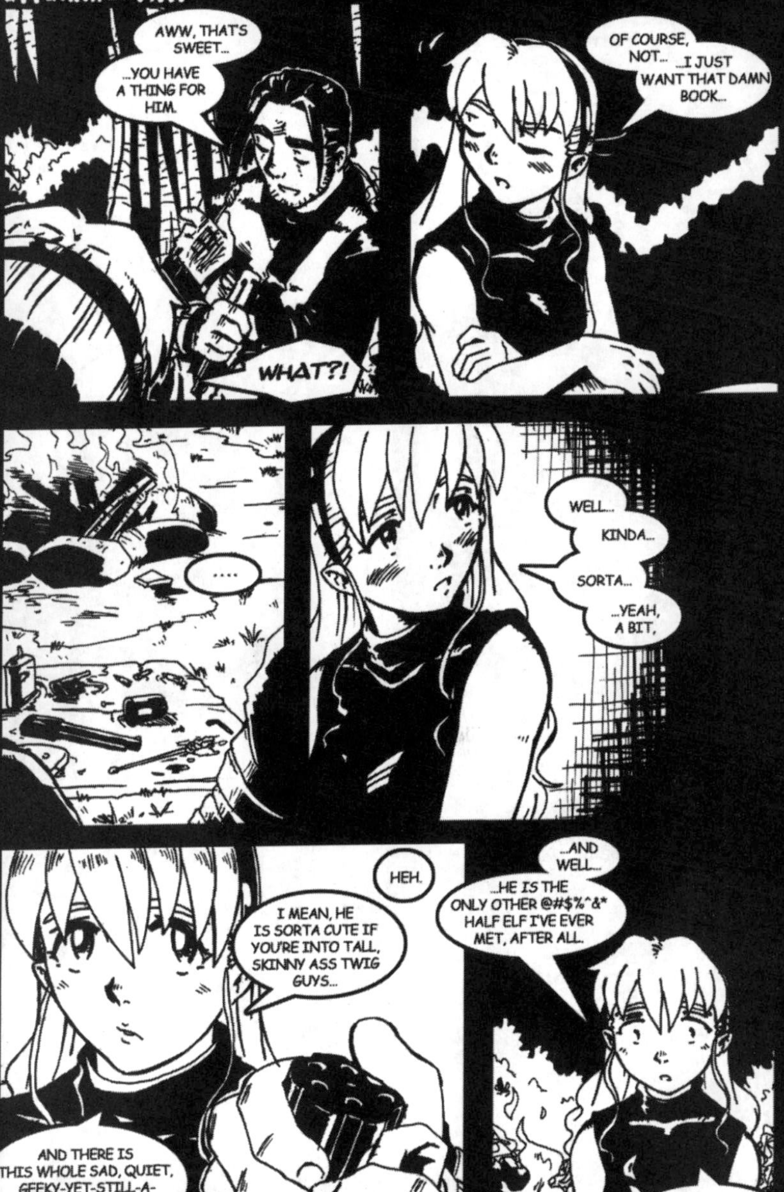
AWW, THAT'S SWEET...
...YOU HAVE A THING FOR HIM.
WHAT?!
OF COURSE, NOT...
...I JUST WANT THAT DAMN BOOK...
....
WELL...
KINDA...
SORTA...
...YEAH, A BIT,
I MEAN, HE IS SORTA CUTE IF YOU'RE INTO TALL, SKINNY ASS TWIG GUYS...
HEH.
AND THERE IS THIS WHOLE SAD, QUIET, GEEKY-YET-STILL-A-BADASS-THING ABOUT HIM...
...AND WELL...
...HE IS THE ONLY OTHER @#$%^&* HALF ELF I'VE EVER MET, AFTER ALL.
THAT SORTA COUNTS FOR A LOT.

WELL...
THERE AREN'T THAT MANY OF YOU GUYS AROUND, RIGHT?
MAYBE YOU TWO WERE JUST MEANT TO GET TOGETHER... ...OR NOT.
YOU THINK SO?
EHH... WHO KNOWS?
AND, OF COURSE, IT WOULD ALSO DEPEND ON HOW IAN FEELS ABOUT THE MATTER.
OH... HMM... RIGHT.
HEY, AREN'T YOU BREAKING YOUR SERIOUS, ENIGMATIC KILLER CHARACTER BY TALKING ABOUT THIS SORT OF THING?
HM? OH YEAH, YOUR RIGHT...
I MEAN...
'GRRR... I LIKE GUNS.'
'I HOPE WE FIND SOME RICH OLD LADIES SOON, SO I CAN KILL 'EM AND STEAL THEIR MONEY!'
THERE, THAT MORE LIKE IT?
HEH... MUCH BETTER.

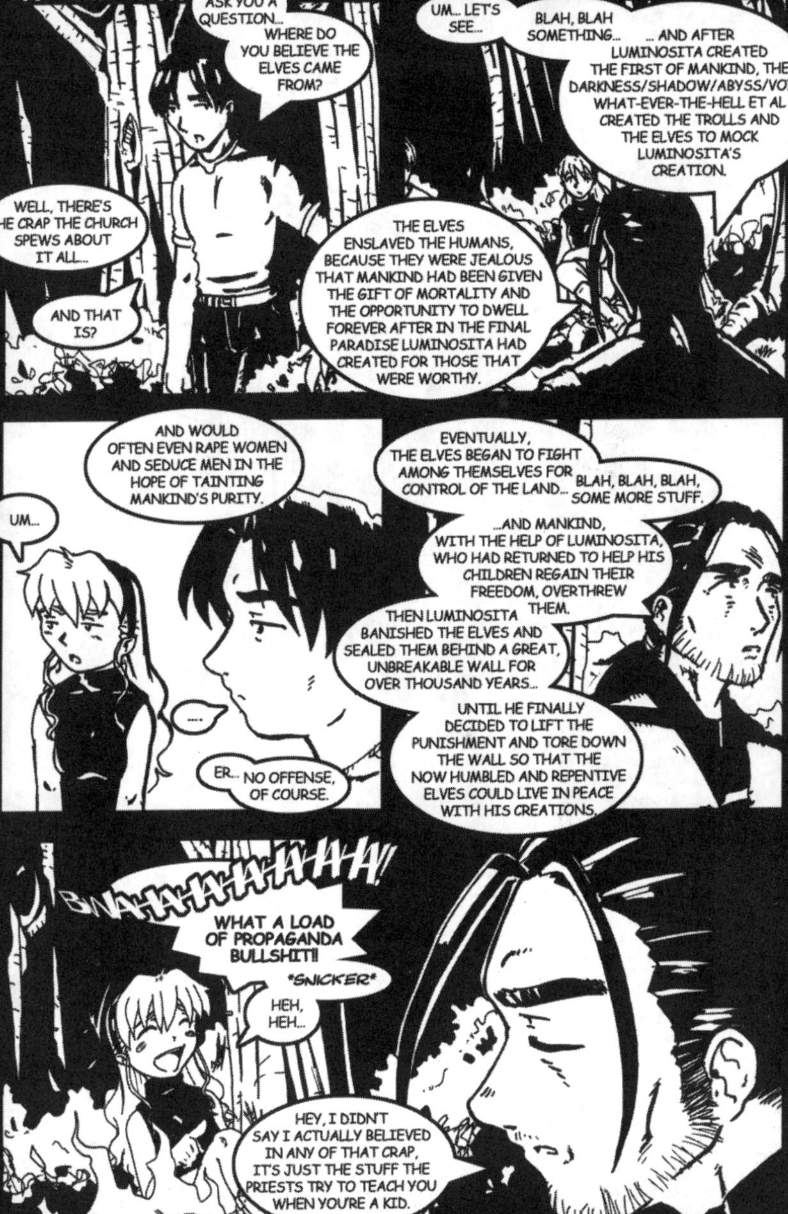
CAN I ASK YOU A QUESTION...
WHERE DO YOU BELIEVE THE ELVES CAME FROM?
WELL, THERE'S THE CRAP THE CHURCH SPEWS ABOUT IT ALL...
AND THAT IS?
UM... LET'S SEE...
BLAH, BLAH SOMETHING...
... AND AFTER LUMINOSITA CREATED THE FIRST OF MANKIND, THE DARKNESS/SHADOW/ABYSS/VOID/WHAT-EVER-THE-HELL ET AL CREATED THE TROLLS AND THE ELVES TO MOCK LUMINOSITA'S CREATION.
THE ELVES ENSLAVED THE HUMANS, BECAUSE THEY WERE JEALOUS THAT MANKIND HAD BEEN GIVEN THE GIFT OF MORTALITY AND THE OPPORTUNITY TO DWELL FOREVER AFTER IN THE FINAL PARADISE LUMINOSITA HAD CREATED FOR THOSE THAT WERE WORTHY.
AND WOULD OFTEN EVEN RAPE WOMEN AND SEDUCE MEN IN THE HOPE OF TAINTING MANKIND'S PURITY.
UM...
....
ER... NO OFFENSE, OF COURSE.
EVENTUALLY, THE ELVES BEGAN TO FIGHT AMONG THEMSELVES FOR CONTROL OF THE LAND...
BLAH, BLAH, BLAH, SOME MORE STUFF.
...AND MANKIND, WITH THE HELP OF LUMINOSITA, WHO HAD RETURNED TO HELP HIS CHILDREN REGAIN THEIR FREEDOM, OVERTHREW THEM.
THEN LUMINOSITA BANISHED THE ELVES AND SEALED THEM BEHIND A GREAT, UNBREAKABLE WALL FOR OVER THOUSAND YEARS...
UNTIL HE FINALLY DECIDED TO LIFT THE PUNISHMENT AND TORE DOWN THE WALL SO THAT THE NOW HUMBLED AND REPENTIVE ELVES COULD LIVE IN PEACE WITH HIS CREATIONS.
BWAHAHAHAHAHAHAHAH!
WHAT A LOAD OF PROPAGANDA BULLSHIT!!
SNICKER
HEH, HEH...
HEY, I DIDN'T SAY I ACTUALLY BELIEVED IN ANY OF THAT CRAP, IT'S JUST THE STUFF THE PRIESTS TRY TO TEACH YOU WHEN YOU'RE A KID.

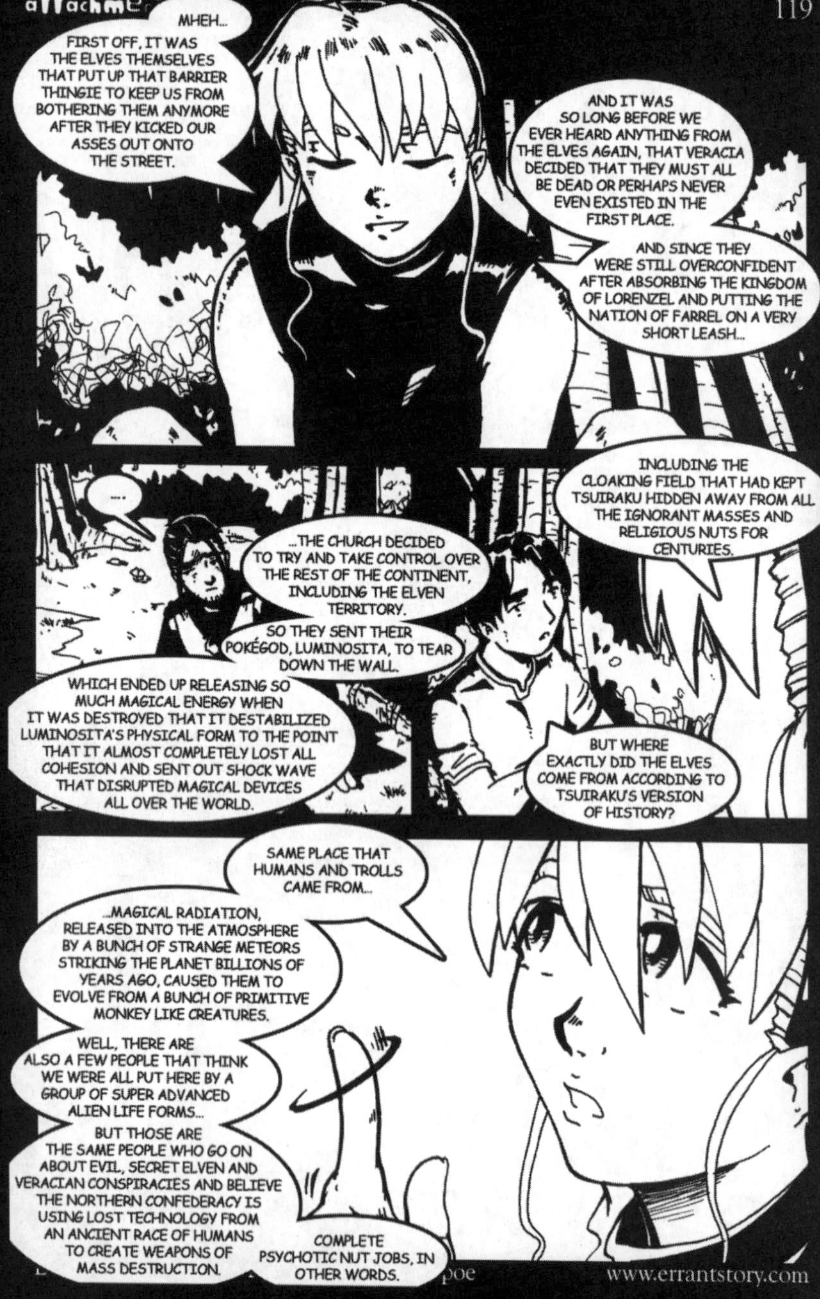
MHEH...
FIRST OFF, IT WAS THE ELVES THEMSELVES THAT PUT UP THAT BARRIER THINGIE TO KEEP US FROM BOTHERING THEM ANYMORE AFTER THEY KICKED OUR ASSES OUT ONTO THE STREET.
AND IT WAS SO LONG BEFORE WE EVER HEARD ANYTHING FROM THE ELVES AGAIN, THAT VERACIA DECIDED THAT THEY MUST ALL BE DEAD OR PERHAPS NEVER EVEN EXISTED IN THE FIRST PLACE.
AND SINCE THEY WERE STILL OVERCONFIDENT AFTER ABSORBING THE KINGDOM OF LORENZEL AND PUTTING THE NATION OF FARREL ON A VERY SHORT LEASH...
....
...THE CHURCH DECIDED TO TRY AND TAKE CONTROL OVER THE REST OF THE CONTINENT, INCLUDING THE ELVEN TERRITORY.
SO THEY SENT THEIR POKÉGOD, LUMINOSITA, TO TEAR DOWN THE WALL.
WHICH ENDED UP RELEASING SO MUCH MAGICAL ENERGY WHEN IT WAS DESTROYED THAT IT DESTABILIZED LUMINOSITA'S PHYSICAL FORM TO THE POINT THAT IT ALMOST COMPLETELY LOST ALL COHESION AND SENT OUT SHOCK WAVE THAT DISRUPTED MAGICAL DEVICES ALL OVER THE WORLD.
INCLUDING THE CLOAKING FIELD THAT HAD KEPT TSUIRAKU HIDDEN AWAY FROM ALL THE IGNORANT MASSES AND RELIGIOUS NUTS FOR CENTURIES.
BUT WHERE EXACTLY DID THE ELVES COME FROM ACCORDING TO TSUIRAKU'S VERSION OF HISTORY?
SAME PLACE THAT HUMANS AND TROLLS CAME FROM...
...MAGICAL RADIATION, RELEASED INTO THE ATMOSPHERE BY A BUNCH OF STRANGE METEORS STRIKING THE PLANET BILLIONS OF YEARS AGO, CAUSED THEM TO EVOLVE FROM A BUNCH OF PRIMITIVE MONKEY LIKE CREATURES.
WELL, THERE ARE ALSO A FEW PEOPLE THAT THINK WE WERE ALL PUT HERE BY A GROUP OF SUPER ADVANCED ALIEN LIFE FORMS...
BUT THOSE ARE THE SAME PEOPLE WHO GO ON ABOUT EVIL, SECRET ELVEN AND VERACIAN CONSPIRACIES AND BELIEVE THE NORTHERN CONFEDERACY IS USING LOST TECHNOLOGY FROM AN ANCIENT RACE OF HUMANS TO CREATE WEAPONS OF MASS DESTRUCTION.
COMPLETE PSYCHOTIC NUT JOBS, IN OTHER WORDS.

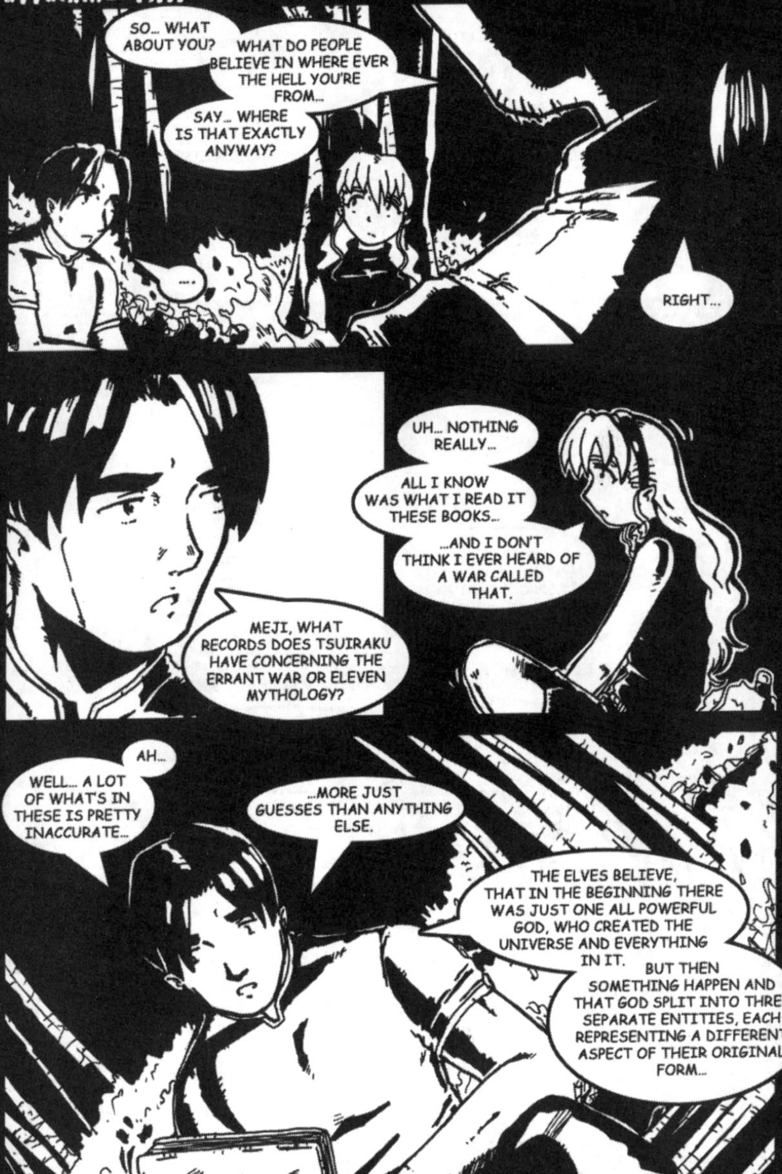
SO... WHAT ABOUT YOU?
WHAT DO PEOPLE BELIEVE IN WHERE EVER THE HELL YOU'RE FROM...
SAY... WHERE IS THAT EXACTLY ANYWAY?
....
RIGHT...
MEJI, WHAT RECORDS DOES TSUIRAKU HAVE CONCERNING THE ERRANT WAR OR ELEVEN MYTHOLOGY?
UH... NOTHING REALLY...
ALL I KNOW WAS WHAT I READ IT THESE BOOKS...
...AND I DON'T THINK I EVER HEARD OF A WAR CALLED THAT.
AH...
WELL... A LOT OF WHAT'S IN THESE IS PRETTY INACCURATE...
...MORE JUST GUESSES THAN ANYTHING ELSE.
THE ELVES BELIEVE, THAT IN THE BEGINNING THERE WAS JUST ONE ALL POWERFUL GOD, WHO CREATED THE UNIVERSE AND EVERYTHING IN IT.
BUT THEN SOMETHING HAPPEN AND THAT GOD SPLIT INTO THREE SEPARATE ENTITIES, EACH REPRESENTING A DIFFERENT ASPECT OF THEIR ORIGINAL FORM...

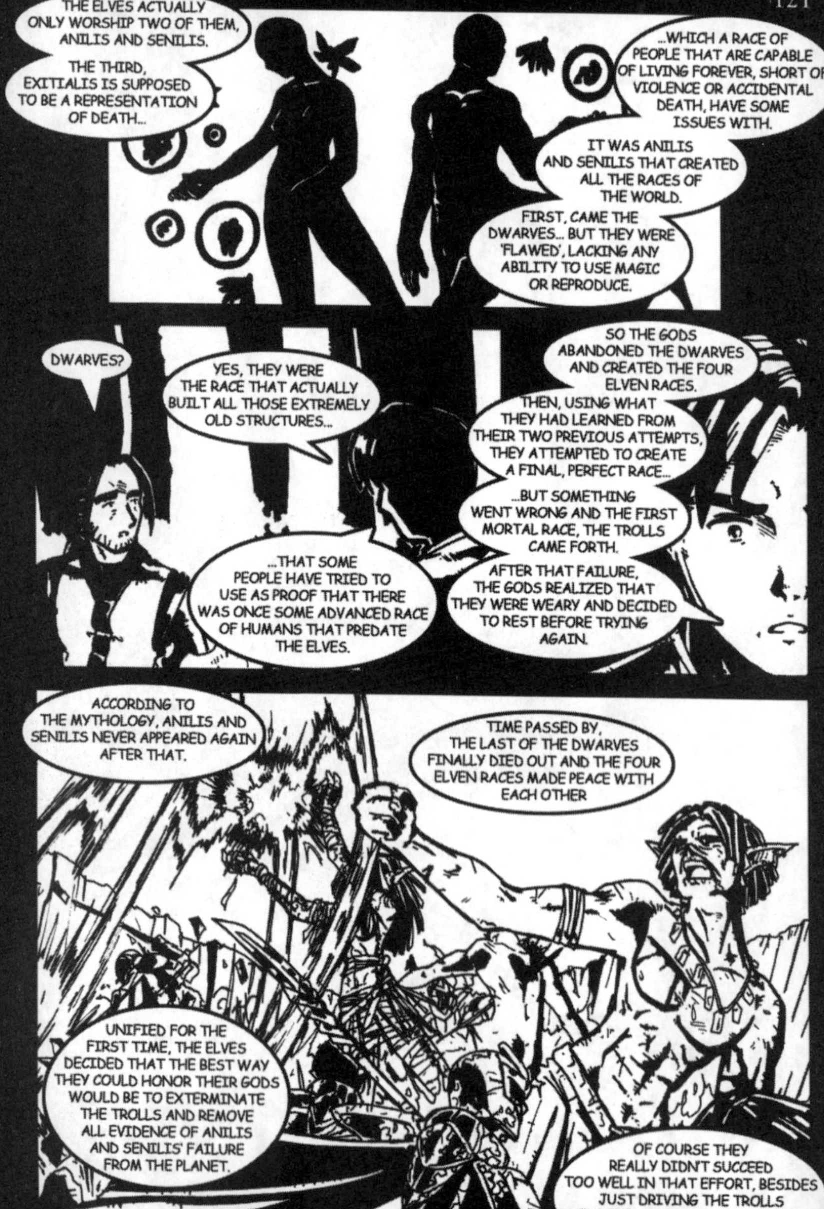
THE ELVES ACTUALLY ONLY WORSHIP TWO OF THEM, ANILIS AND SENILIS.
THE THIRD, EXITIALIS IS SUPPOSED TO BE A REPRESENTATION OF DEATH...
...WHICH A RACE OF PEOPLE THAT ARE CAPABLE OF LIVING FOREVER, SHORT OF VIOLENCE OR ACCIDENTAL DEATH, HAVE SOME ISSUES WITH.
IT WAS ANILIS AND SENILIS THAT CREATED ALL THE RACES OF THE WORLD.
FIRST, CAME THE DWARVES... BUT THEY WERE 'FLAWED', LACKING ANY ABILITY TO USE MAGIC OR REPRODUCE.
DWARVES?
YES, THEY WERE THE RACE THAT ACTUALLY BUILT ALL THOSE EXTREMELY OLD STRUCTURES...
...THAT SOME PEOPLE HAVE TRIED TO USE AS PROOF THAT THERE WAS ONCE SOME ADVANCED RACE OF HUMANS THAT PREDATE THE ELVES.
SO THE GODS ABANDONED THE DWARVES AND CREATED THE FOUR ELVEN RACES.
THEN, USING WHAT THEY HAD LEARNED FROM THEIR TWO PREVIOUS ATTEMPTS, THEY ATTEMPTED TO CREATE A FINAL, PERFECT RACE...
...BUT SOMETHING WENT WRONG AND THE FIRST MORTAL RACE, THE TROLLS CAME FORTH.
AFTER THAT FAILURE, THE GODS REALIZED THAT THEY WERE WEARY AND DECIDED TO REST BEFORE TRYING AGAIN.
ACCORDING TO THE MYTHOLOGY, ANILIS AND SENILIS NEVER APPEARED AGAIN AFTER THAT.
TIME PASSED BY, THE LAST OF THE DWARVES FINALLY DIED OUT AND THE FOUR ELVEN RACES MADE PEACE WITH EACH OTHER
UNIFIED FOR THE FIRST TIME, THE ELVES DECIDED THAT THE BEST WAY THEY COULD HONOR THEIR GODS WOULD BE TO EXTERMINATE THE TROLLS AND REMOVE ALL EVIDENCE OF ANILIS AND SENILIS' FAILURE FROM THE PLANET.
OF COURSE THEY REALLY DIDN'T SUCCEED TOO WELL IN THAT EFFORT, BESIDES JUST DRIVING THE TROLLS FURTHER UP NORTH INTO LANDS THAT ONCE BELONGED TO THE DWARVES.

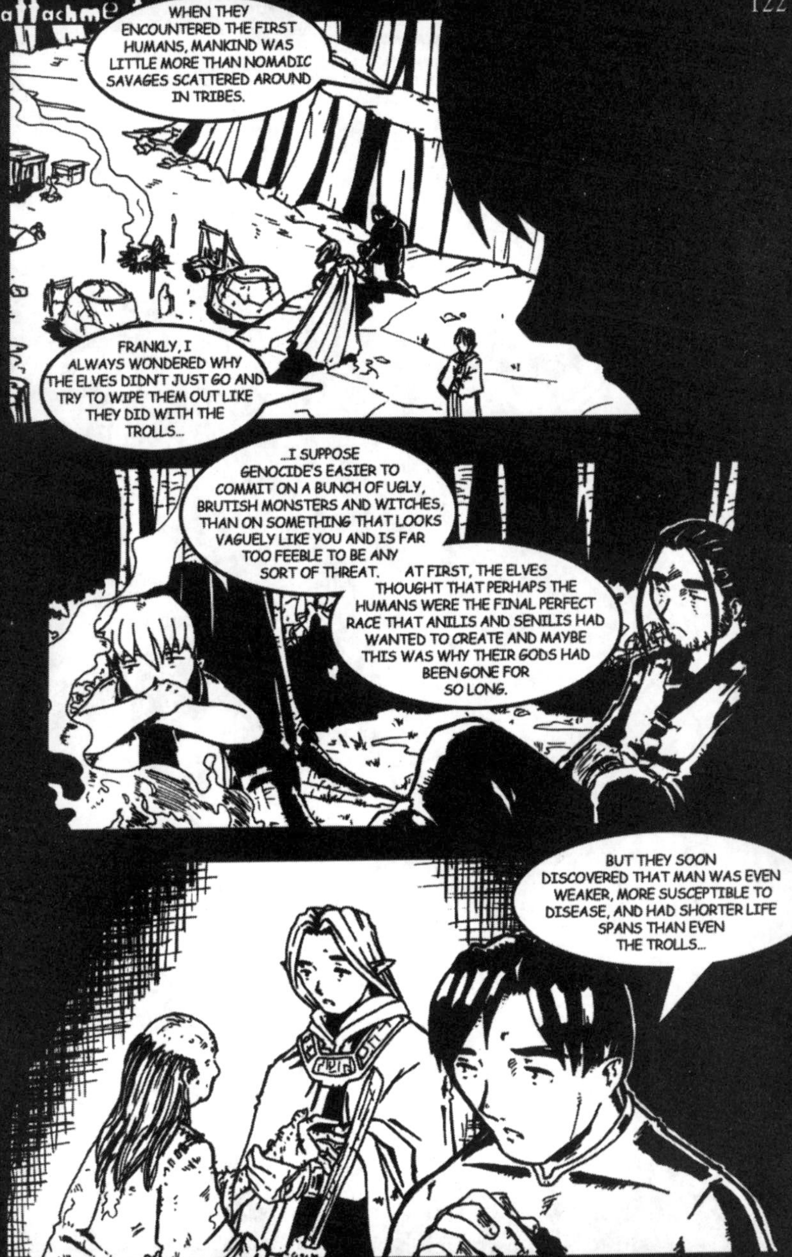
WHEN THEY ENCOUNTERED THE FIRST HUMANS, MANKIND WAS LITTLE MORE THAN NOMADIC SAVAGES SCATTERED AROUND IN TRIBES.
FRANKLY, I ALWAYS WONDERED WHY THE ELVES DIDN'T JUST GO AND TRY TO WIPE THEM OUT LIKE THEY DID WITH THE TROLLS...
...I SUPPOSE GENOCIDE'S EASIER TO COMMIT ON A BUNCH OF UGLY, BRUTISH MONSTERS AND WITCHES, THAN ON SOMETHING THAT LOOKS VAGUELY LIKE YOU AND IS FAR TOO FEEBLE TO BE ANY SORT OF THREAT.
AT FIRST, THE ELVES THOUGHT THAT PERHAPS THE HUMANS WERE THE FINAL PERFECT RACE THAT ANILIS AND SENILIS HAD WANTED TO CREATE AND MAYBE THIS WAS WHY THEIR GODS HAD BEEN GONE FOR SO LONG.
BUT THEY SOON DISCOVERED THAT MAN WAS EVEN WEAKER, MORE SUSCEPTIBLE TO DISEASE, AND HAD SHORTER LIFE SPANS THAN EVEN THE TROLLS...

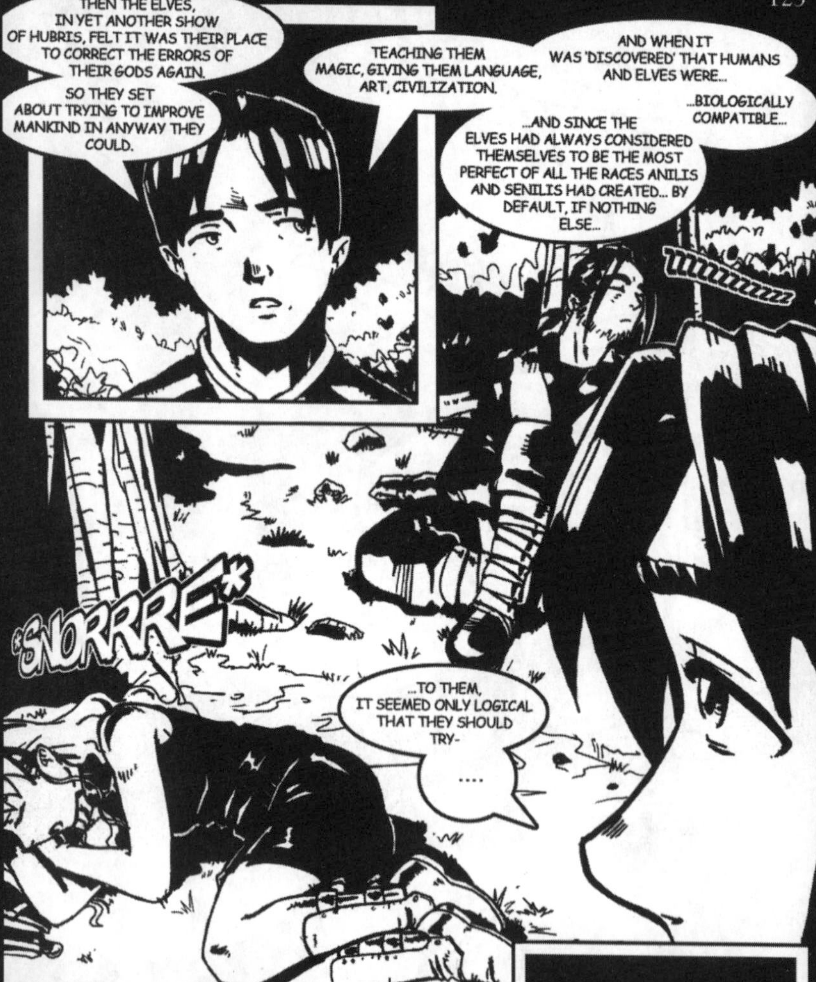
THEN THE ELVES, IN YET ANOTHER SHOW OF HUBRIS, FELT IT WAS THEIR PLACE TO CORRECT THE ERRORS OF THEIR GODS AGAIN.
SO THEY SET ABOUT TRYING TO IMPROVE MANKIND IN ANYWAY THEY COULD.
TEACHING THEM MAGIC, GIVING THEM LANGUAGE, ART, CIVILIZATION.
AND WHEN IT WAS 'DISCOVERED' THAT HUMANS AND ELVES WERE...
...BIOLOGICALLY COMPATIBLE...
...AND SINCE THE ELVES HAD ALWAYS CONSIDERED THEMSELVES TO BE THE MOST PERFECT OF ALL THE RACES ANILIS AND SENILIS HAD CREATED... BY DEFAULT, IF NOTHING ELSE...
zzzzzzzzzz
SNORRRE
...TO THEM, IT SEEMED ONLY LOGICAL THAT THEY SHOULD TRY-
....
UH...
I WAS FINALLY GETTING TO THE IMPORTANT STUFF...
...REALLY...

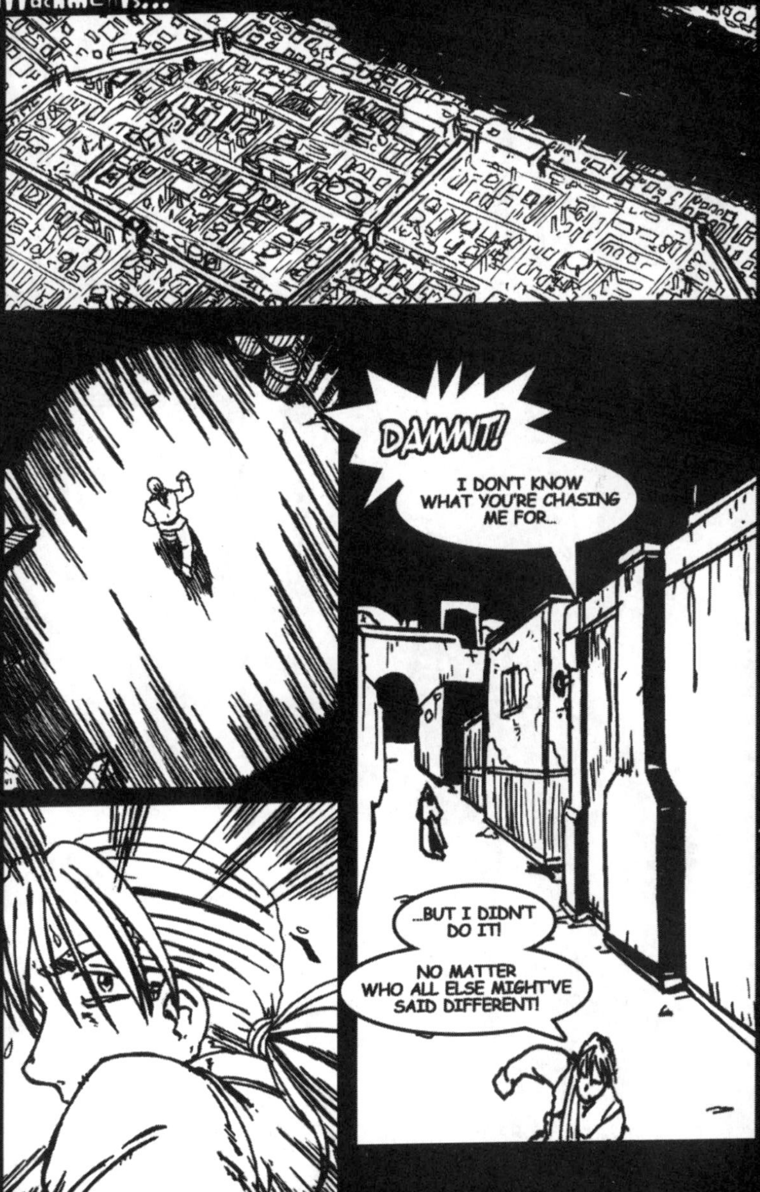
DAMMIT!
I DON'T KNOW WHAT YOU'RE CHASING ME FOR...
...BUT I DIDN'T DO IT!
NO MATTER WHO ALL ELSE MIGHT'VE SAID DIFFERENT!

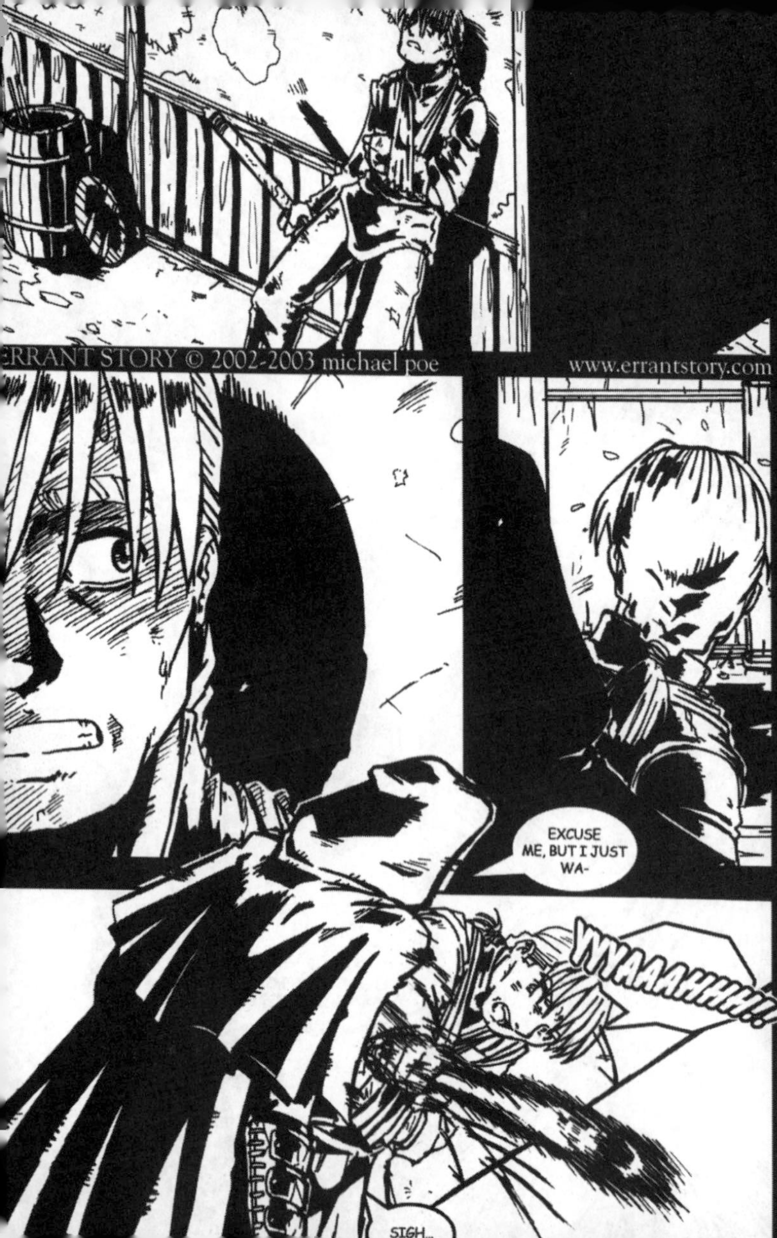
ERRANT STORY © 2002-2003 michael poe
www.errantstory.com
EXCUSE ME, BUT I JUST WA-
YYAAAAHHHH!!
SIGH...

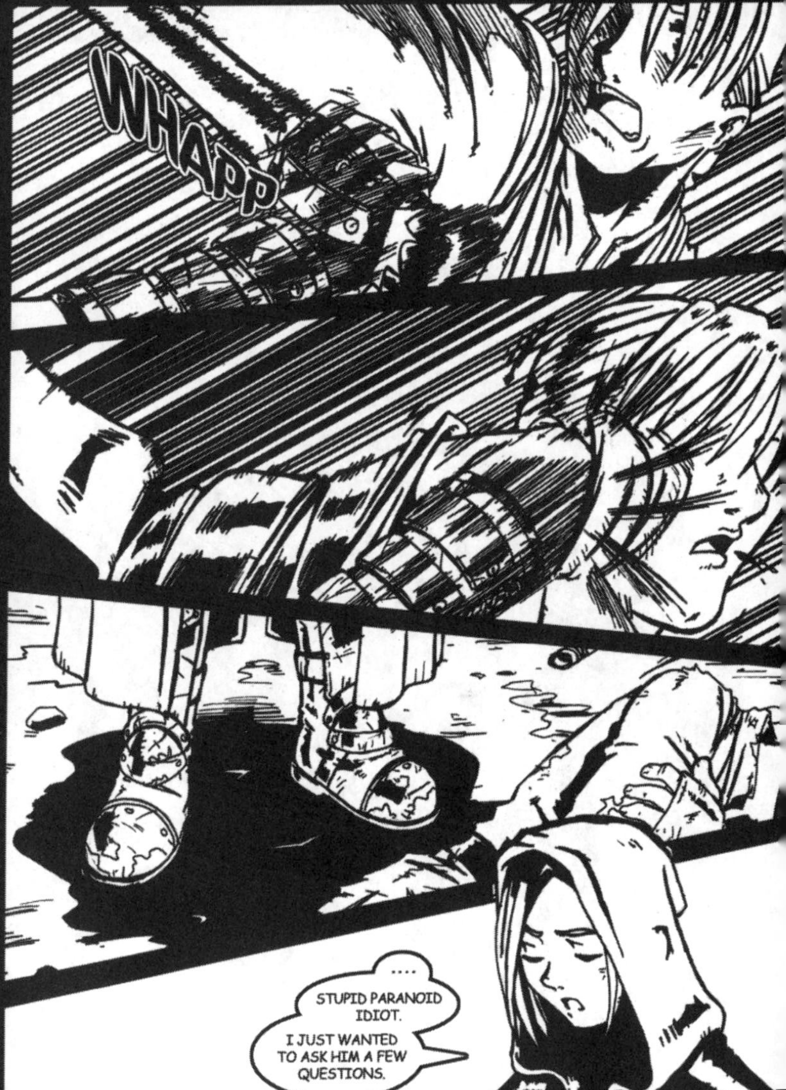
WHAPP
....
STUPID PARANOID IDIOT.
I JUST WANTED TO ASK HIM A FEW QUESTIONS.

[OTHER BOOKS BY MICHAEL POE]

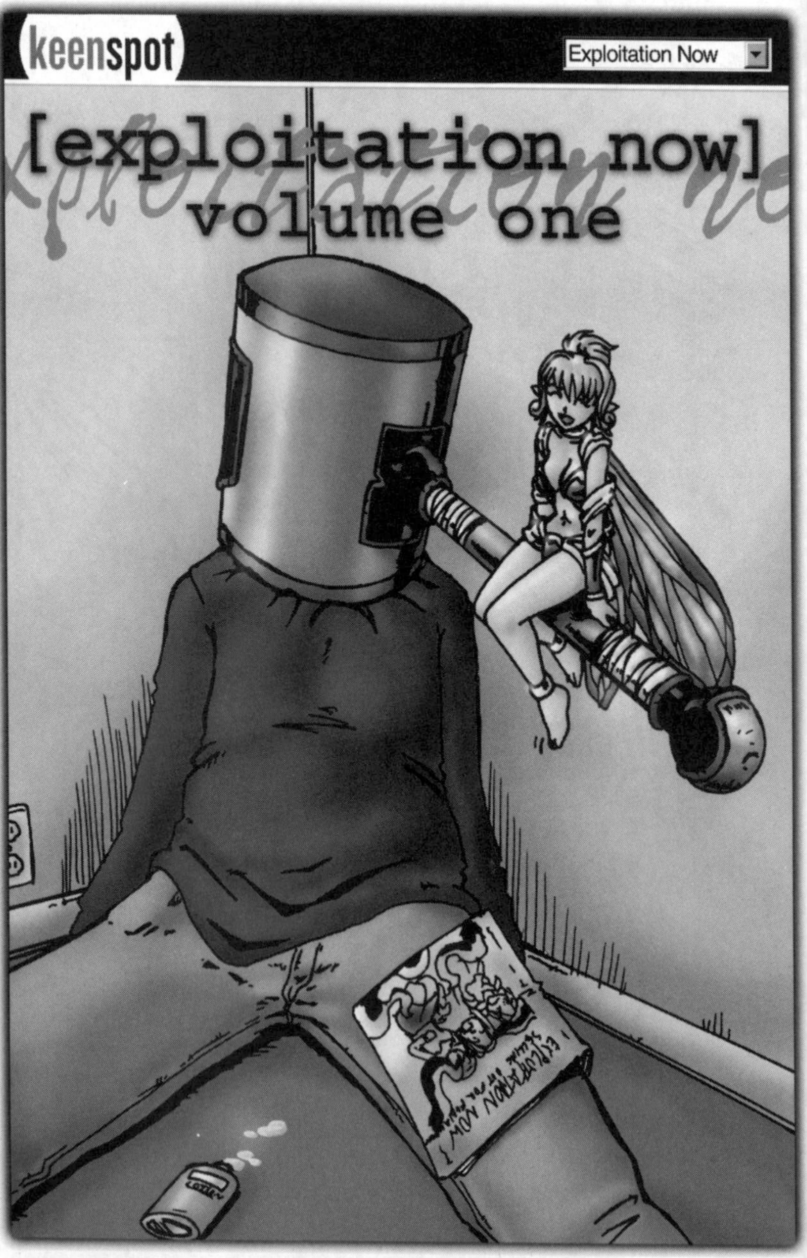
keenspot
Exploitation Now
[exploitation now]
volume one

ISBN 0-972235-06-X

[OTHER BOOKS BY MICHAEL POE]

ISBN 1-932775-02-1

File Edit View Favorites
Address http://www.keenspot.com/
Google
webcomics books & swag forums premium quickkeen services
keenspot
errant story
by Michael Poe
er·rant adj. 1. Roving, especially in search of adventure: knights errant., 2. Straying from the proper course or standards: errant youngsters.
Anyway, this is an RPGesque fantasy story about those things.
adventure
Antihero For Hire
Basil Flint
Everything Jake
Lost and Found
Skirting Danger
Wandering Ones
gaming/technology
ADVENTURERS!
Gaming Guardians
General Protection Fault
Help Desk
RPG World
Sore Thumbs
sci fi
College Roomies From Hell
It's Walky!
Limited Space
Melonpool
Nukees
Schlock Mercenary
Zortic
surreal
BoxJam's Doodle
Checkerboard Nightmare
Chopping Block
Framed
just another Vice
Krazy Larry
Men in Hats
Road Waffles
Superosity
life
Avalon
Friendly Hostility
Gene Catlow
girly
Hound's Home
Queen of Wands
Sinfest
Striptease
The Suburban Jungle
Wapsi Square
You Damn Kid
funny
Alice!
Boy Meets Boy
Funny Farm
Greystone Inn
LWIBH!
Newshounds
SSDD
Soap on a Rope
fantasy
Alien Dice
Bruno the Bandit
Clan of the Cats
Dominic Deegan
El Goonish Shive
Elf Life
Errant Story
Melpomene*
Zebra Girl
archives
take a look at Keenspot's vault.
Keenspot is the largest publisher of exclusive webcomics! Founded in February 2000, we are now the home to over 50 comics, and the list keeps growing. Select one of our titles above for a wild journey into the world of Keenspot.
news spot
Clippy Clippy!
YOU DAMN KID VOL. 1 is now available for order.
posted by Chris Crosby on 4/15/2004 01:55:27 AM
Comixpedia Interviews Keenspot Co-CEOs
Check out this interview with me and Darren in Comixpedia.
posted by Chris Crosby on 4/5/2004 08:23:58 AM
NO JOKE! Krazy Larry Returns.
Done
Internet

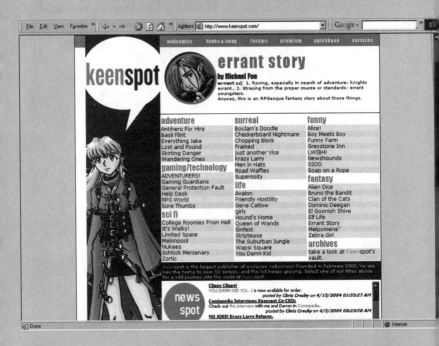